GARGOYLE GUARDIAN CHRONICLES

BOOKS 1 – 3

REBECCA CHASTAIN

This book is a work of fiction. Names, characters, dialogue, places, and incidents either are drawn from the author's imagination or are used fictitiously. Any resemblance to actual persons, living or dead, business establishments, locales, or events is entirely coincidental.

Mind Your Muse Books
PO Box 374
Rocklin, CA 95677

ISBN: 978-0-9992385-0-9

ALSO BY REBECCA CHASTAIN

THE MADISON FOX ADVENTURES

A Fistful of Evil

A Fistful of Fire

A Fistful of Flirtation

A Fistful of Frost

Madison Fox Novella Box Set

NEVER MISS ANY NOVEL NEWS: Join Rebecca's newsletter today!

Visit RebeccaChastain.com

To Cody, who makes every day magical

ACKNOWLEDGMENTS

This trilogy would not have been possible without you—thank you for reading my novels! It means the world to me!

Noel, thank you for sharing your geology expertise and letting me pick your brain about rocks and minerals. Thanks to you, Mika doesn't sound like a Wikipedia version of an earth elemental.

For the amazing covers, thank you, Clarissa!

I owe a lot of gratitude to my beta readers, Cathy, Christina, Deb, Debbie, Karl, Kimberly, Maghon, Rebecca, Sara, and Scott, whose sound advice helped shape this series in small and major ways.

Thank you to my stellar editing team, Carrie and Amanda! Carrie, you're everything I could want in a copyeditor, and I appreciate the extra input you provide in your edits—including not letting me get away with superfluous phrases. Amanda, you've saved me from sounding like an idiot too many times to count, and I'm indebted to you!

Thank you, Mom, for encouraging my love of reading as a child and continuing to champion all my stories. Your word today is *alula*, used in *Curse of the Gargoyles* just for you.

As always, I couldn't have done this without my incredible husband. Cody, I cherish your love, support, good counsel, and amazing Photoshop skills. Thank you for backing my dreams!

CONSTRUCTIVE ELEMENTS

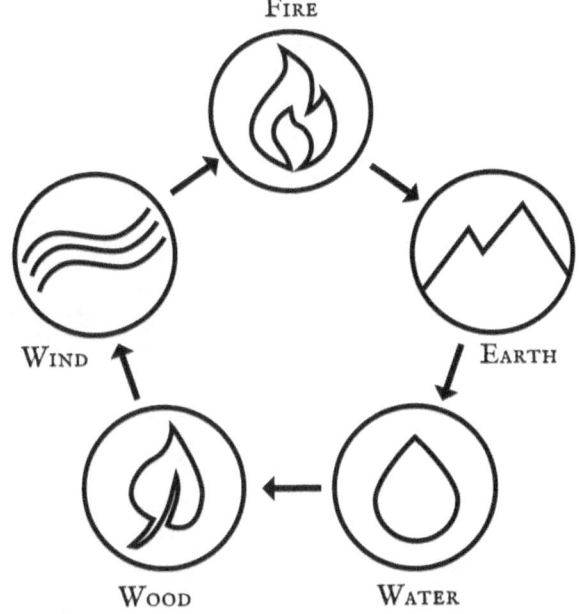

DESTRUCTIVE ELEMENTS

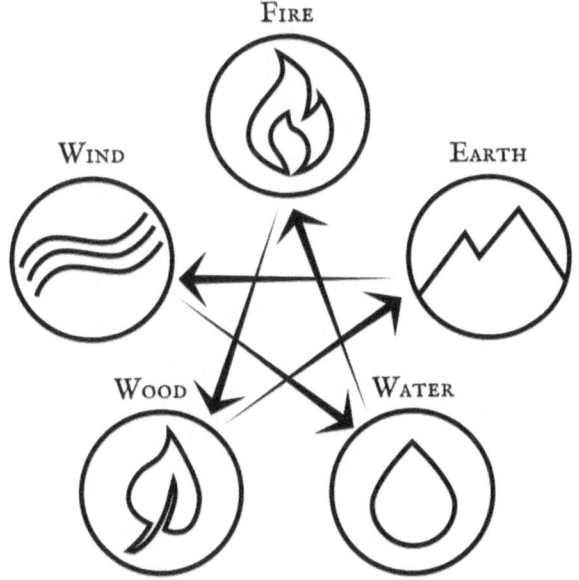

TABLE OF CONTENTS

MAGIC OF THE GARGOYLES

GARGOYLE GUARDIAN CHRONICLES
BOOK 1

ABOUT MAGIC OF THE GARGOYLES

To help a baby gargoyle, Mika will risk everything...

Mika Stillwater is a midlevel earth elemental with ambitions of becoming a quartz artisan, and her hard work is starting to get noticed. But when a panicked baby gargoyle bursts into her studio, insisting Mika is the only person she'll trust with her desperate mission, Mika's carefully constructed five-year plan is shattered.

Swept into the gritty criminal underworld of Terra Haven, Mika must jeopardize everything she's worked so hard for to save the baby gargoyle from the machinations of a monster—and to stay alive...

1

With one last twist of a filament of earth magic, I fused together the delicate seams of the quartz tube. Slumping forward, I braced my elbows on the table and rested my cheekbones on my palms, cupping my weary eyes in darkness. Six down, six finicky tubes to go. The specifications of this project taxed my substantial skills with quartz magic, which was the point. This project would launch my business and prove that even though I was only a midlevel earth elemental, my quartz skills were equal to or better than more powerful full-spectrum elementals. These fussy tubes would fund the down payment on the lease for the shop I coveted in the Pinnacle Pentagon Center. I could finally quit my demeaning job at Jones and Sons Quarry, be my own boss, and begin a career creating one-of-a-kind quartz masterpieces I could take pride in.

My entire future rested on these fragile vials, and they were due tomorrow at four.

Dull pain pounded my back muscles. Night had crept over the city while I worked, and my jerky movements as I stood and stretched were reflected in the semicircle of bay windows in front of my work-table. Purple smears of exhaustion beneath my eyes were exaggerated in the dark windows, and my pale face floated above a dirt-smeared navy shirt. I checked the clock: almost midnight. Sixteen hours until my deadline, and eight of those would be taken up by my Jones and Sons workday. There was no time for a break. If anything, I needed to work faster.

Groaning, I redid my ponytail, tucking shorter wisps of my hair behind my ears before giving my hard wooden chair the stink eye. Mentally chanting, *Pinnacle Pentagon*, to motivate myself, I reached for another seed crystal.

Frantic tapping shook the glass in the balcony door. I pulled the door open, knowing it was Kylie, my best friend and the tenant who shared my second-floor apartment balcony. "I really can't talk. I need to finish—"

"Help! Help! They've got—"

Something small and hard slammed into my stomach. I staggered backward into my chair and crashed to the floor. A small boulder skipped across the wooden floor and smashed into the wall.

"You're a human!"

I shrieked. The voice came from inside my room. I twisted, scrambling onto my bed.

Against the wall, the rock moved.

Beautiful blue dumortierite quartz veined with green aventurine twisted into a winged panther no bigger than a house cat. A pissed-off, solid-stone, magical, winged house cat. A gargoyle—no, a baby gargoyle. A hatchling.

Her eyes glowed feverishly. Long polished blue claws gouged into the floor when she launched into the air. Her agile stone wings unfolded with a soft gritty sound.

I lurched backward across the bed until I was pressed against the wall. The mattress shook when the hatchling pounced on the space I'd just vacated. Sharp claws bunched in my yellow bedspread. She raised her muzzle, mouth open, and sniffed the air.

I eased toward the foot of the bed, readying my escape into the hallway.

"It's you! Your magic smells so good. I thought—"

My magic has a smell?

The gargoyle's eyes darted to the open door, then back to me. She arched her stone back and hissed at me, the sound dying to a hair-raising growl. The tip of her stone tail slashed back and forth, gouging my wooden headboard.

"I need help."

"My help?" Gargoyles—even baby gargoyles—didn't interact with midlevel elementals like me, and they certainly didn't ask for our help. "There's a full-spectrum elemental just—" I started to point up the street but froze when she snarled at me.

"No other humans! Before it's too late." The gargoyle's words were smooth coming out of her rock throat, with just a hint of a lisp from her tongue working around enormous teeth.

I stared into her glowing blue eyes, seeing past the bared fangs and agitated movements, reading her fear for the first time. I reached for her, then pulled my hand back when she shied from me.

"Too late for what?"

"You can save him. Hurry!"

"Save him? Save who? If someone is hurt, I can send for a healer." Where were this gargoyle's parents?

"No. I need you." Large blue eyes implored me. "Please!"

A thousand reasons why I should find someone else to help the gargoyle crowded my mind, but the hatchling's urgency was contagious. Someone was injured. I didn't want to waste time arguing with her, but was I really the best choice? I could work earth, but healing usually took someone talented with all five elements.

"Are you sure you don't want me to get—" *someone stronger?* I started to ask, but she cut me off with another sharp, "Please!"

Gargoyles were creatures without guile, and this baby was obviously terrified for someone's life. If she thought I could help, I had to try. I took a deep breath. "Okay. Let's go."

The gargoyle whirled and launched for the open doorway, moving with the silent fluidity of a flesh-and-blood panther.

"I'll take the stairs," I said. I snatched up my shoes and coat and raced to the door.

My studio apartment was one of four on the upper floor of a converted Victorian house. At midnight, everyone else in the house was asleep, just the way my landlady Ms. Josephine Zuberrie liked it.

As I sprinted down the stairs as quietly as possible, shoes in hand, I reviewed everything I knew about gargoyles. It wasn't much. Gargoyles favored those strongest in magic. When they chose, they could enhance a person's magic, but I'd only heard of them doing so during large-scale rituals conducted by a five linked full spectrums. Despite being creatures of earth, they were not partial to any particular elemental magic; instead, they were attracted to a person's strength of earth, wood, air, water, or fire magic.

Which is why, as a midlevel earth elemental, this was the first time I'd spoken with a gargoyle.

I eased the front door shut and dropped my shoes to the porch, wiggled my feet into them, and yanked the laces tight. When I spun around, the gargoyle dropped from the roof to the porch railing, almost clipping my head with a heavy rock wing. I swallowed a startled scream.

"Hurry," she trilled. With a squeal of protesting wood, followed by the crack of stone smashing into stone, the gargoyle leapt from the balcony to the sidewalk ten feet below. Wincing, I raced down the porch steps after her, praying to be out of sight before Ms. Zuberrie investigated the racket.

By the time I reached the sidewalk, the gargoyle had almost a block lead on me, moving unexpectedly fast for such a small creature made of stone. In wing-assisted leaps, she bounded into the darkness. I sprinted headlong down the center of the deserted street, chasing the sporadic glimpses of panther-shaped dumortierite in the puddles of lamplight. The baby gargoyle kept me in sight, but only just. My lungs and legs burned after the first five blocks. My vision tunneled to the broken asphalt and gargoyle in front of me. I didn't notice when the lamps ended, only that the dark blue gargoyle was harder to see, and by the time I did take in my surroundings, we were deep in the blight and I was lost.

2

The blight was the oldest part of the city, long since abandoned by the wealthy and middle class, left to crumble and rot, along with its impoverished residents. It was a seedbed for crime and a haven for the immoral. Doorways glowed with protection spells and menacing traps. Unseen eyes tracked me from the shadows.

Alarm skittered through my body, giving me fresh energy. Ms. Zuberrie's neighborhood was on the fringes of the blight—holding it at bay, according to my landlady—and her endless repertoire of blight tales gave me nightmares. To be here, at night, alone, was sheer insanity.

A high-pitched sound, like an animal being gutted alive, echoed through the hulking shadows of old warehouse buildings, setting my neck hair on end. I slowed, having lost sight of the gargoyle. Menacing shapes loomed in the darkness to either side of the desolate road. I identified each item as I jogged past—*empty trailer, rubble from a collapsed wall, enormous splintered wooden ward*—trying to reassure myself.

Someone rounded the far corner of the warehouse at a sprint, coming right for me. There wasn't time to hide. I crouched, heart in throat. Before I could gather my magic, a wide-eyed, scrawny boy tore past me. He glanced once over his shoulder, but it wasn't at me. I watched until the darkness swallowed him, then turned with new dread back in the direction he had come—and the direction the gargoyle had disappeared.

Voices bounced off the warehouse walls, footsteps following. I sprinted for a pile of rusty barrels and crouched behind their bulk. Seconds later, a horse-size fireball blazed down the street, scorching the pavement and casting sinister light on the graffiti-crusted buildings. I tucked into a tight ball, shielding my face from the heat and my body from visibility.

The fire hit a stone wall at the end of the street and burned out. Blinded, I blinked to clear the flaming after-image. Whooping and shouting reverberated off the metal walls.

"Enough! Save it for the splinter-heads."

I peeked between the barrels. Five guys rounded the corner, a dozen fist-size glowballs darting chaotically around their heads. Three men followed. No, more. A whole gang. They milled together less than ten feet from where I hid, body-slamming each other and loosing war cries, all caught up in the same high. In the dizzying, erratic light, I could make out two important details: Every single one of them was dressed in bright orange Fire Eater gang colors, and all of them were linked with a potent amplification spell.

Easing back on my heels, I curled into the tightest ball possible. Fire Eaters ruled half of the blight, and updates of the city guard's ongoing attempts to contain their violent acts were featured prominently in the headlines of the *Terra Haven Chronicle*. From the size of that fireball and the amount of magic resonating among the men, I could predict tomorrow's feature story.

I didn't even think about touching my magic, fearing they would sense it. I didn't breathe. I maintained my cramped huddle until the men rounded the far bend in the street. Only then did I let out my breath and suck in a new one. I waited until I could no longer hear even an echo of their voices before I uncurled.

"Hurry!"

I jumped and clutched my heart. The gargoyle leapt from the rooftop above me and raced around the warehouse wall where the Fire Eaters had emerged. *I shouldn't be here,* I told myself. *This is a horrible, horrible mistake.* But I'd promised the baby gargoyle I'd help. I couldn't turn back now.

I rounded the corner and froze.

Moonlight bathed the expansive loading dock, illuminating an elaborate chalk pentagram the likes of which I'd never seen before. Someone had drawn five pentagrams, one atop the other, each skewed a few degrees so that every angle had five points. In the center was a small lump of rock. The dock was empty of people. The tiny gargoyle paced the edge of the mutated pentagram's circle.

I edged forward, squinting at the lump in the center of the pentagram. My toes kicked something small, sending it clanging into the warehouse's collapsed metal roof. I spun, checking my surroundings. I was still alone. I scanned the shadowed ground. Focus talismans—candles, rocks, glass, wooden carvings, crude fans—were scattered in every direction. There were enough for fifteen people, not the traditional five. If I hadn't just seen a mob of Fire Eaters with the power of linked full spectrums, I wouldn't have believed this mutated pentagram was anything other than graffiti.

I wove a standard five-element test sphere. It popped into existence in front of me, then flattened to a pentagram the size of my palm, each side glowing with the magic of its specific element. If any harmful magic remained, especially a trap, it would alert me before I blundered into it.

I floated the glowing pentagram safely across the chalk twice before I let the small star dissipate. I crept toward the lump. In the moonlight, it was impossible to make out its form. Kneeling, I grabbed fire, forming a ball of light. A small sun burst into existence above my head. I gawked.

Light was the most basic fire spell, one I used every day. My glow-balls were never larger than my cupped hands—any bigger and they were too weak to produce light. Yet the sun above me was larger than my head, and I could see molten flames arc within it, twisting and turning hypnotically. It was like I'd jumped from midlevel to full spectrum.

"Impossible," I breathed. The chalk pentagram was bathed in daylight. Was this strange design the reason for my enhanced powers? Had the Fire Eaters' spell left charged fire elemental magic I couldn't detect within the circle?

The lump of rock moved. I stumbled backward, tripping and landing on my butt. The sun cast sharp shadows across the rock, the flickering fire within it making the rock look like it quivered. Slowing my breathing, I extinguished the sun and replaced it with a manageable ball of soft light, keeping an eye on the rock. When I realized what I was seeing, I scrambled forward again.

The rock opened its toucan-shaped mouth and released a high-pitched cry that wrenched my heart. The baby gargoyle didn't look to have the strength to lift its thick neck, and its long, spindly tail lay lifeless.

"Can you save him?"

I jumped, having forgotten all about the gargoyle panther. She pawed at the chalk circle, careful not to cross it.

My caution morphed to horror when I realized the significance of the hatchling's placement. Using a magical creature as a pentagram focus drained the creature of its own magic and its life. Rumors said the average magical creature doubled a person's power when used as a focus, but gargoyles were natural elemental enhancers when they chose; a scumbag who used a gargoyle as a focus would get a far greater boost. The idea was repulsive in theory, enraging in reality. It was black magic, punishable by nullification.

I examined the injured gargoyle closer. Unlike the panther-shaped hatchling, this one's body was mostly rose quartz, with sporadic coils of blue dumortierite. Jagged patches marred his otherwise smooth sides, and his entire stomach looked like raw, unpolished crystal. Acting on instinct, I reached for earth energy, refined it to resonate with quartz, and probed the baby gargoyle as if I planned to work the quartz. The sensation was like trying to capture an echo. The gargoyle was quartz, but he was also so much more: He was alive.

I twined fire around the earth magic and trickled wood, air, and water into the mix until I had the right magical resonance. I pressed the mixture into the hatchling. A backlash of pain and fear ricocheted through the magic—not from my actions, but from the horror the gargoyle had already endured. The gargoyle's feet and wings ended in acid-eaten, eroded lumps. Gasping for breath, I eased my magic out of the hatchling. My stomach heaved, but there was nothing to vomit.

When I glanced up, I met the healthy gargoyle's eyes, seeing her anguish and anger. "I don't know what to do," I said, swiping at wet cheeks.

"You have to help him."

"I don't know how." Helplessly, I stared at the suffering gargoyle. His movements were weak. He was dying, drained of magic and in so much pain.

3

I wasn't lying: I had no idea what to do. But I couldn't do nothing. I slid magic into the gargoyle, gritting my teeth against the avalanche of pain transmitted back to me. Closing my eyes, I sank into the quartz as I would into a normal project, feeling the pattern of the rock. The hatchling was vastly more complex than any quartz I'd touched before, containing thousands of intertwining striations hosting the intricate patterns of life. Quartz was a hardy mineral in all forms, yet this gargoyle felt like he would shatter in a gust of wind. Too much of his magic—his life—had been siphoned from him. More continued to leak from the raw wounds of his missing limbs. If I had any chance of saving the gargoyle's life, the wounds had to be sealed. Closing them wouldn't be good enough, though. Not if he was to have a future. His limbs needed to be regrown.

"I can't do this alone," I said, looking into the eyes of the stone panther. "I'm not strong enough." But maybe I would be if I used the magic leaking from the injured hatchling. I balked at the thought, then realized that even if I was okay with stealing the injured gargoyle's magic, I'd be depleting the very resource I was trying to replenish.

The panther hissed and snapped her tail in rhythmic pops. "Bring

Herbert out here first," she finally said, keeping just outside the pentagram's circle.

I reached for the injured hatchling—Herbert—and he twitched, squealing, trying to escape me without any limbs or energy to use.

"Shh. It's okay. We're here to help." Herbert's rock body was too light, and my fear for the hatchling's fading life sent fresh tears dripping down my cheeks. Working quickly, I scuffed five of the chalk lines leading to the earth anchor; then I broke the outer circle.

The panther growled when I set Herbert down several paces from the abomination that had nearly killed him. She sniffed him, then me. I knelt and touched Herbert's toucan beak. His eyes were closed now, and I reached out with magic, fearing the worst.

"He's alive. Barely. We need to work fast."

"Sit," she ordered.

I sat, and the panther curled her bulk into my lap, claws flexed against my crossed calves.

A wellspring of gargoyle-enhanced magic dropped inside me. My stomach lurched at the free-fall sensation before I tapped into my magic and effortlessly pulled three times my usual amount. This is what it was like to be a full spectrum.

The hatchling was quartz. Even without enhancement, and despite being only a midlevel earth elemental, my quartz specialty was near full-spectrum level. With gargoyle enhancement, I could do anything, even heal a gargoyle.

Using a delicate pulse of woven magic, I coaxed the jagged hatchling's side to grow.

The flame within Herbert flickered, and the beast went limp. Frantic, I pumped more fire into him, then traces of the other elements, and waited until he stabilized. The baby didn't have enough body or life left to grow new appendages, even with my influx of magic.

I sat back, trying to be analytical rather than emotional. This was a common problem with quartz. There was only so much manipulation a piece could take without the infusion of additional quartz. I prayed the same would apply to the gargoyle and thanked the gods that I was rarely without seed crystals. I placed a pearl-shaped clear crystal on the gargoyle's still side where his wing should have been and dove back in.

Coaxing the seed to grow was as easy as breathing, but integrating the gargoyle's complex internal networks to the lifeless seed and matching the seed crystal's growth patterns with the gargoyle's required all my skill and concentration. Just when I got the hang of it, having stretched almost an inch out of the seed crystal, the connecting fibers from the gargoyle stagnated.

Puzzled, I squinted at the half-wing lump. Rose quartz ran through clear quartz like veins, ending in a jagged edge. However, where the fibers refused to grow was smooth like the gargoyle's body. I hadn't done that. The stone panther hadn't, either. Her magic was a passive boost to mine, providing no input. Somehow, even while unconscious, Herbert was guiding the design, defining the shape of his wing as I regrew it. In awe, I refocused on the weave of magic. As I guessed, once I switched growth directions to flow toward the jagged edges, the hatchling's body responded to my manipulations again. Now that I knew what to feel for, I worked faster and finished the wing in minutes.

One healed appendage out of six made a meager impact on the gargoyle's suffering. Working diligently, I used seed crystals to grow stubby legs that ended in oversize paws. Then, easing the gargoyle over, I regrew the other wing. With each healed limb, the gargoyle's pain receded. The life seeping from him ebbed until he was whole—weak, but no longer dying.

A hollowness opened within me when the panther cut off her magic amplification. I released my magic and swayed against the backwash of exhaustion. The panther pushed from my lap to nuzzle the unconscious gargoyle. I watched the two hatchlings, realizing from their magical patterns that they were siblings, despite their radically different appearances.

A concussive boom rocked the ground, passing through me with a physical pulse. To the east, a giant fireball erupted against the pale horizon. Screams echoed through the block, too close for comfort.

Lightning cut the night sky, followed by the shudder of an earthquake. Magic crackled in the air. Whoever the Fire Eaters had been after, they'd found them.

"We need to get out of here," I said.

The tiny stone panther's eyes glowed with fear. She seemed torn between fleeing and staying crouched over her brother.

"Come with me. I'll keep you both safe." Anywhere was safer than staying here. Getting outside the blight and back to Ms. Zuberrie's sounded like a good start. After that, we could work on a long-term plan.

Rapid-fire concussions rattled the loading dock, collapsing another section of roof in an earsplitting crash. Dust billowed over us. The sour copper taste of rust caught in my throat. I coughed and staggered to my feet after two trembling attempts. Healing Herbert had strained the bounds of my energy levels, physically and magically. But even if I'd been at full strength, I wouldn't have stuck around in warring gang territory.

The panther watched me, still looking undecided.

"Do you know the way back to my home?"

Finally, she nodded. I released a pent-up breath. I lifted Herbert, now asleep and healing, to my chest. It was like cradling a small boulder. My arms trembled.

The stone panther loped toward the dock's northern exit. Rubbing grit out of my eyes, I stumbled after her.

I tried to remain alert to my surroundings, but exhaustion deteriorated my focus. Keeping the panther in sight and staying on my feet were the best I could muster. Herbert gained weight with each step. After a few blocks, the sound of fighting faded and I paused long enough to stuff the hatchling under my shirt, tucking the cloth back in and cradling my arm under the cotton-covered bulk. With my shirt distributing the hatchling's weight, he felt a little lighter, and with Herbert hidden from view, I felt a little safer.

I wasn't the only person concerned with safety: Costly whole-house wards shimmered over most homes, and the number of blatant traps had doubled in the last half hour. The turf battle rocking the blight had everyone cowering in their safety zones.

Twice I heard city guards, once on flying platforms and once marching double time on foot. Both times, the panther took us through side alleys so our paths didn't cross. I had enough where-withal to be thankful we were avoiding questioning, but mainly I lamented the extra steps the detours demanded of my drained body.

An eon later, the panther stopped, and I stared numbly at Ms. Zuberrie's house. The hatchling flapped up to my studio balcony, her flight path erratic and heavy. For the first time, it occurred to me that healing Herbert had drained her, too.

Grabbing the banister railing for support, I pulled myself up the stairs. I set Herbert at the foot of my bed, then fell face-first onto my comforter and into blackness.

4

"Wake up, girl. There's a baby gargoyle on the balcony," Kylie whispered against my ear. I jolted awake. Sunlight streamed through the bay windows, sparkling on the half dozen finished tubes on my worktable. Only six, when there needed to be twelve as of . . . a few hours from now. Impossible. I groaned and sat up. My head pounded. I rolled my shoulders to work out my neck's kink. Maybe if I got right to work, I could finish most of them before—

"Crap! Work!" I lurched from the bed. I was hours late. Without an explanation or notification. Silvia Jones had a zero-tolerance policy for tardiness. This was the only excuse she'd need to fire me. Unfortunately, I needed my job awhile longer while I built up my clientele. My gaze fell on the unfinished project again. If I didn't finish the vials, I wasn't going to have a business. I needed the referrals this project would bring.

"Did you hear me, Mika?" Kylie asked. She plopped onto the bed, her blue eyes tracking my frantic movements.

"Yes. Gargoyle. She's still here." I scribbled a note: *Battling deadly illness; refusing to go into the light.* Maybe Silvia would take pity on me.

"She? You know about the gargoyle? What are you writing? Wait.

You expect Ms. Be-Sick-on-Your-Own-Time Jones to believe that? Let me do it." Kylie formed a bubble of air magic and recited a compelling plea on my behalf, wrapped it in tight bands of air, and sent it rocketing off to Silvia's message box. I stared enviously after it. Kylie was a strong air elemental—almost a full spectrum. I wouldn't have been able to create a message bubble that large, and it would have traveled no faster than walking speed once released. "Did you like my emphasis on how contagious you are?" Kylie grinned. "Now, spill. What's with the gargoyle?"

Recounting the previous night's adventure made it feel surreal. While I spoke, I watched the panther hatchling, who was perched on the balcony railing, tight against the house and all but hidden in the eave's shadow. She sat still as stone, unblinking, unbreathing. Unnerving. Kylie's mouth was hanging open by the time I finished.

"Wow, Mika. That was . . ." Her blue eyes grew round. "Do you think the abused hatchling was connected to the Fire Eater attack last night? The *Chronicle* said they took out four blocks. The casualties are in the double digits."

"I know it was," I said. "Where's Herbert? Did you see him outside?"

Kylie shook her head. I could see her mind working over everything I'd told her. When I noticed the lump under the covers at her hip, I grinned. Flipping back the covers, I revealed the sleeping form of Herbert. Kylie leapt to her feet.

"Oh my goodness! I almost sat on him."

Herbert's long stone toucan beak stretched wide in a yawn and his eyes blinked open. When he saw us, he shrieked and leapt into the air. Heavy rose-veined crystal wings buffeted us, and we dove for cover in opposite directions.

"Open the door!" I yelled.

Kylie lurched for the balcony door and threw it open. The winged panther woke and spun. One moment she was a statue, the next she was sailing into the room. The panther caught Herbert in her paws and dropped him to the ground, pinning him in place. Kylie and I watched, wide-eyed, as the baby gargoyles snarled at each other. It took several minutes for the panther to calm Herbert, and when she finally let him up, Kylie and I both took a step back.

"She's okay," the panther said, pointing at me with a wing. "She saved you."

Seeing Herbert calm down, I eased to the floor and Kylie mirrored me. "I'm Mika. This is my best friend, Kylie. She's okay, too."

Kylie nodded enthusiastically. "I want to help, if you need it."

The panther shook her head. "Herbert and I are the last of our nest."

"No, Anya. They live." Herbert's voice was higher pitched than his sister's.

"I only sense you," Anya said. She lifted her cat face, scenting the air.

"They're shielded by the bad man. The one who took us."

My heart sank.

With Kylie doing most of the questioning, we learned that Herbert was one of four hatchlings taken from their wilderness nest and caged. Only Anya, who had been away from the nest when it was ambushed, had been spared.

"He sold me. For money!" Herbert said. "Humans are evil."

"Not all of them. Mika healed you. I helped."

I thought Anya sounded proud, and I couldn't tell if it was of herself or me.

"Why did you choose Mika last night for help? Why not a full-spectrum elemental?" Kylie asked.

It was a reasonable question, and I tried not to be offended. I also recognized that tone. Kylie had gone into reporter mode. She may work at the local coffee shop, but Kylie's ambition was to be a famous journalist, and she was well versed in the requisite story-sniffing rudeness.

"I don't know what a full spectrum is," Anya said. She sat on her haunches, and her wings rustled. In a normal cat, I would have said she was embarrassed. "I thought Mika was a gargoyle."

"You what?" I asked.

"The magic you were doing. It smelled like a gargoyle. If I'd known you were human . . . I don't like humans. I don't trust them."

With good reason. From what I could tell, Anya and Herbert were only a few weeks old, and their only inter-actions with humans, other than with me and Kylie, had been horrific.

"Where are the others?" Kylie asked.

"In cages." Herbert's long tail lashed back and forth, bunching the area rug beneath him. "The bad man is going to sell them like he did me." The hatchling's tail stilled and he trembled in place. Anya leaned into him, and a gravelly purr rumbled in her throat.

"A black market," Kylie breathed. Her bright blue eyes lit up, and I didn't need telepathy to know she was seeing her byline beneath the front-page headline. "You can count on us to rescue your siblings," she announced.

"We can tell the authorities. They'll know where to look."

"We can do more than that." Forming complex bubbles of air magic, Kylie spoke into them, whispering, "Gargoyle hatchlings, gargoyles for sale," and a dozen other phrases, one per bubble. When she finished, each collapsed into a boomerang shape and whirled out into the city, fading from sight almost immediately. Even for Kylie, the rumor scouts formed and moved fast. She gave me wide eyes, and I examined the hatchlings. In his fear, Herbert had leaked a thin current of magic, and Kylie's rumor scouts had soaked it up.

"As soon as those return, we'll know where they're kept," Kylie said, recovering from her surprise.

Information would be good, but I wasn't going to delay notifying the people who actually knew what to do if they encountered a black magic wielder. So as Kylie got ready for work, I rushed to the nearest guard office.

Hours later, I dragged myself back to Ms. Zuberrie's. The excursion had been a waste of time and energy. The guards took one look at me and my midlevel elemental skills and dismissed my recounting of healing Herbert as attention-seeking lies, especially when I told them I'd been in the blight just blocks away from the huge Fire Eater battle. I hadn't thought to bring the only two individuals who could substantiate my story—Herbert and Anya.

Despite their refusal to offer assistance, the guards had insisted on following protocol, which required filing a report about my "wild and foolish" claims. After making me wait over an hour, they passed me off to a trainee hardly old enough to be assigned a desk. He spent forty-five minutes trying to trick me into confessing to taking hallucinogens before ushering me to the door with a final, "We'll keep your report on file." It had sounded like a threat, as if the guards were now monitoring my sanity.

"Stupid bigoted guards." I stomped up the porch stairs. I was no closer to finding the kidnapped hatchlings *and* I'd lost precious work hours. I opened the front door to Ms. Zuberrie's and came face-to-face with my deadline in the form of a stout dark-haired woman with an upturned nose and sour expression: Althea Stoneward, healer apprentice for the prestigious Blackwell-Zakrzewska Clinic and my contact for the unfinished project upstairs. My stomach sank even as I plastered on a smile.

5

"I have been waiting," Althea announced.

"I'm so sorry. I need a little more time—"

"More time? We have been more than generous with our deadline. Are you breaking your contract?"

"No! Of course not." I eased into the foyer, shut the front door, and cast a furtive glance into the living room and then the dining room, relieved to see we were alone. "I have six finished and—"

"The order was for twelve."

"I ran into . . . time constraints." After my experience at the guard station, I was reluctant to attempt the truth with Althea. If she thought I was claiming to be a gargoyle healer, she would cancel my contract and see my reputation ruined beyond repair. "Let me get you the six I finished."

Before she could protest, I darted upstairs. When I returned with the six vials wrapped in cloth, her face was red with irritation and her arms were crossed. I grabbed a vial and thrust it into her hands. She glared, then turned her attention to the quartz. Lifting it to the light, she examined it in silence, looking for flaws I knew she wouldn't find. Wordlessly, she scrutinized the rest.

"I need just one more day," I said, fingers crossed behind my back.

She rewrapped the vials and scowled down her upturned nose at me. "One day, Mika Stillwater. You'll deduct twenty percent from your fee for the delay, too." She slammed the door behind her.

I collapsed against the nearby wall, thanking the gods for small favors. Then I trudged up the stairs to get to work on my new impossible deadline. There was still a chance I could salvage my dreams. Twenty percent loss of pay would leave me with enough money for a down payment on the Pinnacle Pentagon shop and apartment—I'd just have to keep my day job a little longer to make ends meet. *A temporary setback,* I promised my heavy heart.

After taking a quick shower and inhaling a handful of blueberries, I settled at my desk and selected a seed crystal from my stash. On second thought, I dropped a handful of seed crystals into my pockets, just in case. *In case an injured gargoyle waltzes by?*

I squelched a wave of guilt. I'd done what I could to help find Anya and Herbert's siblings. I was a midlevel earth elemental, not a full-spectrum air elemental. Aside from alerting the guards, I had no other way of locating stolen property of any kind, let alone kidnapped magical creatures. I could only hope that Kylie's rumor scouts produced information that would make the guards believe me. I'd be sure to take Anya and Herbert along then, too. In the meantime, fretting wasn't going to produce any leads, and at least this way I wasn't neglecting my responsibilities.

I cleared my thoughts to focus on the crystal in front of me. Pulling strands of earth element and fine-tuning it to resonate with quartz, I fed it to the seed crystal. With astonishing ease, the seed grew and reshaped.

A faint hum cocooned my magic. Far from annoying, it soothed my restlessness and resonated with my magic, amplifying it. I recognized it as gargoyle influence, but I was surprised when I could follow the sensation to the source, locating Anya by only the feel of her magic. For reasons I wasn't going to question, Anya was generously boosting my magic from where she huddled in the shadows on the balcony railing with Herbert.

The vial shattered. In my distraction, I had stretched the crystal too thin. Grimacing, I pulled my thoughts back to my work. Gargoyle enhancement was helpful only if I focused.

The next vial broke when Kylie burst into my room, startling me into dropping it. I gritted my teeth and used a quick sweep of air to pull the shards into a pile before turning to my friend. Kylie was already talking.

"It's tonight! I've got the location and the time and everything. I can't believe it. Those rumor scouts returned so complete! Normally I get a snippet or a line or two, but these were whole conversations. I bet you I'd recognize the voices of the people if I heard them again."

"Whoa. Slow down. What's tonight?" I asked.

"The hatchling auction. I know how to get in, too, but we've got to hurry."

My stomach clenched with dread. "We? Don't you mean the guards?"

"So they believed you?"

"No."

"Okay." Kylie didn't pause, and I realized she'd never expected the guards to believe my incredulous rescue tale. "They're doing a demonstration first. That's what the auction guy, Walter, said. I mean, I think he's the auctioneer. He gave the first order; the rest just repeated it to the others. He said he'd provide a demonstration first... to showcase the hatchlings' usefulness." I could see Kylie absorb the horror of her words, and her excitement deflated.

"When?"

She glanced out the windows at the evening light. "At dusk."

"Where?"

"New Hope, in the south temple."

Of course. On the west side of Lincoln River, the suburb of New Hope was isolated from the city of Terra Haven and preferred it that way. New Hope was what the blight wanted to be when it grew up, populated with profitable, if questionable, establishments. The dilapidated south temple was the perfect cover for a clandestine black market.

"They have all three of the hatchlings," Kylie said. "If we don't rescue them before they're sold, they're all going to die."

"We can't just mosey in and demand they hand over the hatchlings."

"That's exactly what we'll do. Well, not *exactly*. We'll buy our way in. It's an auction, after all. The door fee is only ten thousand—"

"*Only ten thousand!* Where would we get that much money?"

"You've got some savings, right?"

A little over six thousand, and that was slated for the lease on my ideal showroom at the Pinnacle Pentagon Center. I'd been saving for three years, sacrificing and scrimping to make my dream of independence a reality. Endless nights, I had worked on painstaking projects like these vials to build a reputation in an oversaturated market, and people were starting to take notice. I was on the precipice of success, but it all depended on opening my shop and going into business for myself full-time. If I was forced to keep my day job to make ends meet, I was going to lose this hard-won momentum, and potential clients would look elsewhere for their needs.

Anya dropped to the wooden deck with a thud and prowled into my studio. "Did you find them?" she asked.

"Yes, but they're still being held by the bad man," Kylie said.

Woken by Anya's movement, Herbert followed on heavy wings, his flight path as haphazard as a falling leaf.

I remembered the lump of rock I'd mistaken him for last night and his wails of pain. Someone had sold him to people who burned him, devoured his life for their magical gain, and left him to die a slow, painful death. That same monster was planning to do it again to three more hatchlings.

It shamed me to realize it was taking serious consideration to decide between delaying my dreams and saving the hatchlings' lives. The decision should have been immediate and required no thought.

"I've only got a little over six thousand," I said.

"I've got some, too." Kylie darted toward the door.

"Wait. Can we both get in for ten thousand?"

Kylie slowed and turned back to me. "No. Only one of us."

"It should be me," I was flabbergasted to hear myself say. Kylie only nodded. "But then what? It's not like we can buy the hatchlings and I don't have the power to take them by force. I can't stop . . . I'm not trained . . . I'm . . ." *I'm only a midlevel earth elemental,* I finished silently.

"You have to stall the auction. Get us more time." Kylie turned to address Anya. "You and your brother can help me. If you talked with the guards—"

"Guards! No! I won't go back." Herbert curled into a tight ball, rose quartz–veined crystal wings wrapping around his quivering body.

6

"Back?" I echoed.

"To him," Herbert said.

I shared a look with Kylie. "You were taken by a Terra Haven guard?"

"How do you know?" Kylie asked gently.

"Because he said so." Herbert's answer was muffled and garbled by the chattering of his jaw.

"Anyone could say—"

"Was he in uniform? Did his shirt have any symbols?" I asked, interrupting Kylie.

Herbert's head jerked in a nod. "A circle with a zigzag line, a leaf, a drop, some squiggles, and a flame."

Having spent the day staring at this exact logo on the shirts of the guards at the station, I recognized Herbert's description of the icons for the constructive cycle that formed the Terra Haven guard badge. Kylie and I shared a look.

"This bad Walter guy isn't a guard, no matter what he wore," Kylie said. "Guards protect."

"I swear, the guards will help us," I said.

"*You* can save them," Anya said, her pleading gaze fixed on me. "You saved Herbert. You can save the others."

Kylie glanced at the clock on the wall. "We've got to try, Mika. You delay them. I'll bring the *good* guys. Now that we have the auction location, they can't ignore us."

If we believed that, I wouldn't be going to the auction at all.

Kylie must have read my doubts. "You just have to get us a little time."

"You really believe you can convince them?"

"I won't let you down, Mika." Kylie dashed to her room to fetch her money.

I watched Herbert shiver in his traumatized huddle. Anya stared at me with a faith I didn't deserve.

I grabbed my life savings, hesitating with the weight of the money in my hands before stuffing it into a nondescript satchel, feeling like I was plunging my hopes and dreams into the dark enclosure with it.

———

I TOOK A PUBLIC AIR BUS ACROSS TOWN, PACING IN THE AISLE THE WHOLE way. There were faster modes of travel—flying platforms, personal air taxis, gryphons—but none within my skill or price range. The sun had dipped behind the ragged skyline by the time I disembarked, and while my instincts insisted I approach the temple cautiously, time was running out. I forced myself to sprint through the darkening streets.

The last time I'd visited the south temple, I was five. In sixteen years, even the temple's illusions of its former glory had deteriorated. Exterior walls were cracked, and in several places, giant gaps exposed the interior to the elements. The scrap of park remaining around the temple was musty with decay. Hardy vines strangled eroding statues and sucked the life from the withered trees looming over the entrance. Not a single lamp was lit.

Dead leaves crackled underfoot as I raced across the grounds to the entrance, praying this foolish stunt wouldn't get me killed. This wasn't going to be like last night. I wasn't rushing in after the fact. I would be in the midst of black magic wielders, rubbing elbows with powerful criminals and trying to thwart a corrupt guard.

I'd wracked my brain for an alternate plan the entire bus ride and drawn a blank. All my hopes rested on Kylie being more convincing with the guards than I had been.

Copper chains rattled in the shadowy depths of the vestibule. It was a distinctive sound, one that, once heard, was never forgotten. Kludde. I froze, ice running through my veins. My heart hammered against my rib cage as it approached. Fleeing would do no good. A kludde could match me at any speed. I gathered fire in my thoughts, ready to throw pure magic at the beast if it charged. If I was lucky, setting its face on fire might slow it a little.

I saw the copper chain links first, each as thick as my wrist. Then the kludde's eyes, over a foot higher than mine, caught a glimmer of fading light. I shrank back, careful to not move my feet, trying not to behave like prey even as my gibbering instincts insisted I was. Looking part Great Dane, part wolf, and part madness, the kludde towered over me, standing on its hind legs. Its coarse coat consisted of layers of the darkest shadows. Sinister yellow eyes pierced me, intelligent and malevolent. Enormous crow's wings rustled against its backside. My throat constricted, cutting off air. *Please don't let it open its wings.* Open wings meant it was hunting, and I was the only victim in sight.

The heavy chain snapped, and the kludde growled, tossing a glare over its shoulder. Behind the beast loomed a person, though in the darkness I couldn't be sure he was human. He was tall enough to be a troll, with expansive shoulders to match. His face looked human. His dark eyes terrified me more than the kludde's.

"It's a f-fi-fine night for a p-picnic," I stammered, repeating the code words from Kylie's rumor scouts.

"It would be better under a full moon." The man's voice was a pitch above a growl. Drool dripped from the kludde's open mouth as it tracked me.

"The darkness suits my mood," I said. These lines had sounded more ridiculous in Kylie's bright apartment.

The kludde snarled, hackles raised, when the man yanked it back, leaving space for me to squeeze inside the maw of the temple. I stepped forward on trembling legs, only to be stopped by a beefy arm thrown across my path.

"Money," he growled.

The kludde's hot breath parted my hair. I was pinned between the man and kludde, trapped. Either of them could kill me before I could so much as scream. I jammed a hand into my satchel and pulled the money out. The man snorted at the fluttering bills before snatching them from my shaking hand and counting them. I waited for his grunt of assent, then fled into the temple's dark confines.

There was just enough light to avoid the majority of rubble, and I didn't slow until I escaped the kludde's sight. A few twists beyond the main entrance, I heard muffled voices and remembered my purpose. Another turn, and the floor dropped away to shadowy basement stairs. I hesitated on the landing, heartbeat thundering in my ears. I could still turn back. No one but the door guard—and the kludde—had seen me. I could leave safely.

And have lost your savings on top of abandoning three hatchlings to be tortured and killed. I clutched the seed crystals in my pocket and forced my feet down the stairs.

7

I didn't know what to expect, but it wasn't the brightly lit chamber I found. At one time, the room had functioned as a place for private ceremonies, with an enormous pentagram etched into the floor, circled by a groove of colored stones to represent each element. The room could hold at least fifty comfortably. It felt cavernous with only five people in it.

Everyone turned to stare at me, and I paused on the threshold. A man and woman wore matching masks that concealed the top half of their faces, and the perpetually shifting layers of the woman's dress disguised her body even better. For that movement, an air spell worth twice tonight's door fee had to be woven into the fabric. A third person wore a simple cloth hood that covered all but his eyes, but his abnormal height—easily equal to that of the kludde—and wide shoulders marked him as male. Beside him stood a man in a university professor's uniform of tweed and corduroy. However, a faint shimmer at the periphery of his face revealed a poorly connected seam in his illusion spell; the benevolent grandfather's face was a fake. Standing apart from the main group was a dark-haired tattooed man who would have looked at home in the blight. *Mercenary,* I thought. Though no weapons were visible on him, I was sure that he could have given the guard upstairs a good fight. He wore no camouflage, illusion or otherwise.

I hadn't considered a disguise, and now I cursed my lack of foresight. In jeans, a pale blue T-shirt, and my black canvas button-up jacket, with a student's leather satchel draped diagonally across my chest, I looked as out of place as I felt. I slipped into the room and skirted to the left.

I fidgeted while we waited, staying well clear of the room's other occupants. With no distractions, my doubts overwhelmed all other thoughts. What if I couldn't stall the auction? What if Walter didn't bring the hatchlings here? Even if Kylie convinced the guards to arrest everyone, we might never find them.

No, we'd find at least one. The demonstration hatchling. The thought wasn't reassuring.

In a few minutes, a dozen new people filtered into the room, restricting my movement. Most, again, were disguised, and the few who weren't radiated strong I'd-like-to-kill-you vibes. Still, I received the most curious stares. Everyone could see I didn't belong there.

"Welcome." The disembodied male voice turned everyone's head. A seamless illusion dropped, opening the round room over three feet in every direction. I wasn't the only one to gasp at the power display.

Walter stepped forward from where he'd been observing us behind the illusion. There was nothing about the man's appearance that identified him as evil incarnate. He was slight, barely taller than my five-nine, with sandy brown hair and green eyes. He had a boyish smile. If I'd seen him in a café, I might have found him handsome; with a wounded gargoyle in his grip, however, he was repulsive.

The mutilated hatchling was hardly larger than my cupped hands, half the size of Anya. He trembled in a magic trap in Walter's palm, his variegated citrine body glistening in the bright spell lights attached to the ceiling. The tips of his feet and wings had been burned away, and they twitched spasmodically. His little lion face— complete with expressive eyebrows never found on a real lion—was pinched with pain. Enormous golden eyes scanned the room, glossy and unfocused. Every so often, he lifted his head, mouth stretched open, but no sound made it past the muzzle of air woven to dampen his cries.

Rage flooded my body until I shook with it instead of fear.

"Tonight you have the unprecedented opportunity to elevate yourself to a full spectrum, with limitless power and limitless possibilities." Walter's voice carried through the still room. "There is untapped potential in each gargoyle, even one so small as this." He hoisted the mutilated hatchling into the air. I looked away from his pitiful, soundless cries in time to see the double doors to the exit swing soundlessly closed and an illusion cover it. I rubbed my sweaty palms on my pants and willed a platoon of guards to burst through the illusion.

"The power is there for the taking—for the right price." Walter's smile turned hard. "But first, a small demonstration for the skeptics."

Walter stepped into the center of the pentagram, hatchling in hand, and everyone crowded to the walls, several people running to clear the pentagram's circle. Walter's eyes slid closed, and he breathed deep. On a long exhale, his eyes opened to half-mast and a small, self-satisfied smile curled his lips. A wall of raw magic raced through the star's lines, then rushed to fill the circle containing the pentagram. The magic pulled from the baby gargoyle's wounded limbs, and a fine dust drifted toward Walter's feet as the magic ate away the hatchling's stone flesh.

Around the room, people gasped and murmured at the display of power most hadn't seen outside of a full temple ceremony hosted by five linked full spectrums. The vultures surged forward, jostling one another until they ringed Walter and the pentagram. I held back, sickened by the sight of the magic leeching from the struggling hatchling.

"Some of you might have heard of my first customer and the tiny explosion they unleashed on the blight last night." Walter winked. The Fire Eaters' battle had been splashed across every news feed today. No one could have missed it. "What would you do with that amount of power?"

From across the room, I felt his magic build as he wove together the five elements. A sphere popped into existence around him, hesitated, then expanded in all directions at once. There wasn't time to flee, and there was nowhere to go. The wall of magic slammed into the crowd, and the bidders swayed like a human ripple in a pond. Then it squeezed over me, a solid slimy sheet of magic stretching against my skin as if I were naked. I fought to stay on my feet. My magic swelled, uncalled and ineffectual. Then Walter's bubble snapped together behind me and raced outward, leaving a greasy film behind. I staggered forward, but my senses tracked the magic out and up, where it mushroomed to encase the entire temple. A ward. A monstrously powerful ward. One that would keep out anyone attempting to pass. One at least seven times larger than a single full spectrum could create. I pictured a wall of guards pitting themselves ineffectually against the ward. A chill of fear made me shiver.

The excitement in the room ratcheted higher. I caught a glimpse of the hatchling and wanted to cry. His head lolled limp, but I knew he wasn't dead. Magic still leeched from his open wounds, feeding directly to Walter.

Hang in there, little guy.

Someone slid behind me, and I spun to see what they were doing, trusting no one in this room at my back. It was the professor. He wasn't paying any attention to me or to Walter's performance at the center of the pentagram. He was examining the walls. I watched him pause in front of a section of plaster and squint. He leaned back and forth, then touched the wall, pulling back with a jerk.

I hadn't realized I'd stepped closer to him until he reached inside his professor's coat and pulled out a long, slender knife. I backpedaled, far too slow. He seized my bicep, and the steel point of the knife pricked my neck.

"Don't be scared, girl." His hot breath whispered against my ear, and I shuddered.

"What—"

"Shh."

A few people near us noticed the professor's knife against my throat and sidled away. There'd be no help from these lowlifes.

"Reach out and touch the wall. Right there. Let's see what happens."

Walter's voice droned in the background, but his words didn't make sense in my acute panic. I could feel the swell of his magic. In my mind, I saw the gargoyle's limbs crumble away with the surge of magic siphoned from him.

The knife jabbed my neck and I hissed at the sting. Where was Kylie? How had this ever seemed like a good plan? If it hadn't been obvious that I was way out of my element before, it was painfully clear now. I had no fighting skills, no defense training. I'd never had to think about it before. And right now, all I could think was that I didn't want to die.

"Now, girl!" the professor hissed. The stench of sweat and garlic oozed from him, coiling in my throat.

I stretched my fingers toward the wall. The faint tell-tale glimmer of yet another illusion masked this section of the wall. Just how strong was Walter? And how much longer could the hatchling survive?

Move away. Look away. Don't touch. I pulled my hand back.

"Push through it," the professor said, emphasizing his words with the pressure of his knife.

I reached forward again, and again I felt a compulsion to retreat. An illusion combined with a subtle ward, one designed for people to not even notice it was there.

I gritted my teeth and shoved my fingertips into the ward. Flames licked my flesh. With a yelp, I jerked free and examined my skin. My fingertips were red, pulsing with the pain of a burn.

"Hurts, don't it? Let's see what happens if you get closer." The professor shoved me with a strength that belied his guise of age.

"No!" I fell against the warded illusion and my cry strangled on a scream of agony. The ward ensnared me. Fire engulfed my body. I convulsed, every twist and flail winding me tighter in the trap, ratcheting the pain. I screamed again as my skin melted. I scrabbled for water magic and doused the ward, and the ward soaked it up. I couldn't break free!

I wrenched my head back toward the professor. A sea of faces watched me writhe, not a single one looking concerned. *Help me!* I begged, but I couldn't form the words between screams.

8

My vision blackened, and I lashed out with magic again, desperate. Without control, my raw magic reverted to the strongest, most familiar form: quartz earth energy. I stabbed at the ward, and it split, a tiny fracture tearing like wet cloth under my weight. I fell. I couldn't find my hands to brace myself, and I slammed into the rock floor behind the ward.

Residual panic launched me to my knees, then kept me conscious when the pain washed over me. My entire body felt raw from skin down to bone.

"There's one in every crowd," Walter said, tsking. "If anyone else would like to test me, you're welcome to die, too. Now, bidding starts at fifty thousand."

Walter's words registered. That had been a death spell, not just a ward! I jerked toward the ceremony room. It was like looking through murky water. No one looked my way, not even the professor. Somehow I had survived, and Walter couldn't tell that his murderous ward had failed.

Now would be a really good time to show up, Kylie. There was no way I was making it back through that ward. I was trapped until the auction was over and Walter's spells dropped. If he found me alive after that, I had no delusion I'd remain breathing for long. Stuck on this side of the ward, it would be impossible to delay the auction, too.

I dropped my head to rest on the floor, taking shallow breaths until the pain receded enough to think. I wasn't going to wait here to be discovered.

My eyes slowly adjusted to the gloomy light coming through the wall illusion, and I examined the small, dark alcove. I was in a storage room of some sort. The walls were smooth and wrapped back around the circular ceremonial room where the auction was currently under way. I felt along the wall, taking baby steps deeper into the darkness, until my foot crunched into something hard.

I reached blindly for the object. It gave with a tingle beneath my tender fingertips, like a cloth of magic. A ward. I jerked back. I'd had more than enough of Walter's wards.

I glanced back toward the death ward. It was out of sight around the bend. I could either blunder along into another ward that might kill me, or I could chance creating a little light.

Drawing a trickle of fire magic, I set a small pea-size flame in the air in front of me.

Two tiny sets of terror-filled baby gargoyle eyes glowed in the faint light. I dropped to my knees in front of them, feeling hope for the first time.

The hatchlings' mouths moved in panicked cries caught behind soundproofed traps, and they struggled futilely against magical bonds.

"It's okay. I'm here to help. Anya sent me," I whispered. They quivered and swiveled heads on weak necks, looking for an escape that didn't exist.

When I reached toward the first one, he keened wildly, thrashing as much as the bonds permitted. He looked like a baby Chinese dragon, with a wide, square head and feathery rock tufts behind his ears. The net around him glowed red, the magic matching his blood-orange carnelian body getting brighter the more he struggled. His right side was perfect and whole. His left, though . . . Magic sucked into the net from the ragged wounds on the bottom of his two left feet and the tip of his left wing. Even without the trap holding him, there was no way the injured baby dragon could escape.

Cautious of both Walter's magic and the hatchling, I hovered my hand above the trap. The energy pattern was almost familiar—weaves of earth and fire with swirls of wind and a whirlpool of water. The earth energy resonated with quartz, a pattern I was intimately tune to. Seed crystals fused to the floor acted as anchors, holding the net—and the hatchling—in place. A subtle band of magic stretched from the net to the death ward around the corner, sustaining it. Since Walter had created the ward, any excess magic drained from the hatchling would feed into him. It was a brilliant design—from Walter's perspective.

I had no idea how to proceed. I had no experience with negating black magic traps. However, I couldn't predict how much longer the auction would last or how long it would take Kylie to convince the guards. I had to improvise, and freeing the hatchlings was a good start. I wasn't going to get a better opportunity. Gathering my resolve, I grabbed a seed crystal anchor.

It wouldn't budge, no matter how much I strained. I couldn't force a finger through a hole in the net, either. A clean slice of solid, five-elements magic only made the hatchling spasm in pain. Balancing my elemental magic to match Walter's and feeding it into the crystal made the trap hum and the hatchling convulse. I jerked back and swiped sweat from my forehead. Working *with* the net wasn't the answer. I needed to counter it.

Fire burns wood, wood breaks up earth, earth stops air, air dries water, water extinguishes fire. It was the destructive element cycle every child learned by the time they could talk, and I chanted it now to focus my thoughts.

With surgical precision honed from long hours of delicate work, I sliced the earth magic channeled through the quartz with an equal level of wood magic. Earth collapsed and fire burned bright, feeding off the new wood energy. The hatchling tried to bite me, but he hit the bonds of magic and flopped back, exhausted.

"I'm sorry, little guy," I whispered. I added a trace of fire to expunge all wood, then doused the trap with water, pouring my magic over the fire faster and faster until it was extinguished. The net morphed in a blink, spinning the deluge of water magic into whirlpools. The gargoyle's magic sucked from his wounds in a gush and he passed out.

Panicked, I threw air into the net, drying the water with a concentrated blast. It took more effort than extinguishing the fire, my elemental contributions strengthening the net even as I fought it. I was panting by the time the last drop of water magic evaporated. Only air whipped through the net now, but it dried up the hatchling's life with maniacal vigor. Grabbing earth magic, I dammed the air at each seed crystal. The first three were the hardest, the air pummeling the blockades of earth, disrupting my concentration as I created the next, but by the time I'd dammed five of the seven seed crystals, the air energy had fizzled down to a gentle breeze. I plugged the last two crystals, and the net dissipated. Magic leeched from the unconscious hatchling, but it was no longer actively siphoned.

I lifted my shirt hem with a trembling hand and wiped the sweat from my face. One down, one to go. I crawled toward the other gargoyle, this one a mutilated cygnet, though it took a long stare to make sense of the bulbous body and slender neck. With only one identifying wing tight against her body, the hatchling was a gross mimicry of a Thanksgiving dinner platter. Her rock feathers were a spectrum of purple, pink, and orange agate, as was the cage sucking away her life. Her body was almost the size of my head, making her the largest of all the hatchlings. She snaked her beak at me, eyes wild with pain.

I already felt like I'd worked a full shift at Jones and Sons, drained physically and magically from destroying the first net. But I'd succeeded in weakening Walter at least a little. I was congratulating myself as I rested until I realized that without the dragon hatchling's extra power feeding Walter through the ward, Walter was pulling more magic from the remaining two hatchlings.

The thought made me pause. If I removed the net from the cygnet, all the drain would be on the hatchling Walter held for demonstration. The lion had already looked close to death. Would my rescue of these hatchlings kill him?

Did I have a choice? Once Walter finished the bidding, he would collect these hatchlings. If I didn't act now, my hesitation would take away the one advantage I had: surprise.

Grimly, I bent to work on the cygnet's net. I knew what to expect this time, and while I countered the surges of each element faster, it was no less draining on my energy reserves. At least when I finished, the cygnet was still cognizant.

I collapsed against the wall. Urgency warred with weariness. The light illuminating the bend of the wall was brighter. Without the reinforcing magic from the hatchlings' nets, the illusion and ward covering the entrance had weakened. Similarly, the sounds of the auction room were no longer muted. I could hear Walter's voice and those of the bidders. The bidding had escalated to astronomical amounts, but it also sounded like it was winding down. So far, everyone was still focused on Walter at the center of the magic-filled pentagram, but I knew it wouldn't be long before someone noticed the flimsy illusion. Especially Walter. At my side, the cygnet was wisely silent.

"Triage time," I whispered. Plucking seed crystals from my pocket, I surged quartz-tuned earth element magic, equal parts fire and a balance of wood, air, and water through it and into the unconscious stone dragon, starting with his front foot, clamping my teeth against the agonizing backlash.

Just as with Herbert, the dragon guided the growth of the seed crystals, defining the shape of his limbs even as I wove and stretched the complicated amalgam of elements. I looked up after the dragon's front leg was whole to find the other hatchling watching with intent, glowing eyes.

"I told you, I'm here to help," I whispered. The world went fuzzy when I swung my head back to the dragon. Exhaustion was catching up with me fast, but there wasn't time to rest. I could only be grateful that the hatchlings weren't as injured as Herbert had been. Without

Anya's assistance, regrowing the minor damage to the hatchling's limbs taxed my magical limits.

The dragon regained consciousness when I finished growing his back leg. He leapt to his new red-veined crystal feet, threw his head back, and loosed a shriek. I grabbed his muzzle and clamped his jaw shut. The dragon yanked from my hold, whipping his head to stare at the cygnet, then down at his feet, then finally up at me.

Voices swelled, and I knew my luck had just run out.

9

I cast through my repertoire of skills for something resembling a weapon. There was nothing I could create that another slightly stronger elemental couldn't destroy. A string of candle flames—the largest fire I could build without something flammable to burn—wouldn't hold off a house cat, let alone the greedy masses and psychopathic black magic practitioners in the next room. Not even my stronger quartz skills would help me here. I couldn't form a quartz wall strong enough to stop someone. The only ward I knew how to create on a large scale was a tint to block the sun for mornings I wanted to sleep in.

Anything's better than nothing. I grabbed earth element, tinting it the deepest onyx of smoky quartz, so dark it was almost black, then formed a sheet of air and bound them together across the storage room opening, patching the illusion. If anyone looked into the nook, they'd see nothing but a dark shadow. The only problem with my solution—okay, *one* of the many problems with my solution—was it cut off my light, too. I fed a little fire into the pinprick of flame I had created earlier, stretching it to about an inch long, and placed it on the far side of the hatchlings.

In the flickering light, two pairs of glowing eyes watched me. The dragon shifted on his new crystal legs, whined softly, and rested his head on my knee as if in apology. I gave him a pat with hands numb with fear and got back to work. Fortunately, the dragon's wings were tiny, smaller than Herbert's despite the dragon being bigger, and it took only a few moments to regrow the mutilated appendage. The instant the hatchling was whole, a gush of energy surged into me, pushing exhaustion aside.

"Thank you," I whispered.

A shuffle of footsteps drew closer, audible over the growing murmurs in the crowd.

"You're flirting with death touching that ward," Walter barked.

"I can see through it, and I don't see the dead girl," a woman said from a few feet away. There was more shuffling and several curses and yelps of pain.

"Stand clear," Walter ordered, sounding like he was right behind me.

We were out of time. I threw open the top flap of my satchel and snatched the cygnet around the middle, stuffing her inside, head up, just in case gargoyles needed to breathe. I did my best not to touch her open wounds, but it was a tight fit in the bag, and the leather scraped the swan's sides. She whimpered but didn't protest. There was no space left for the dragon.

Grunting, I tugged thirty pounds of solid rock to the wall, then laid the flap across the cygnet's head, leaving it gapped at either end for air. I scooped the dragon up and showed him the space between the bag and the wall.

"Hide," I urged. Trusting eyes blinked once at me; then the hatchling wriggled his sinuous body into the small gap, curling his stone tail tight to the leather satchel. I wove another tinting ward over the bag, pulling color from the plaster wall and stone floor into the ward. It was illusion on a scale normally unachievable for me, but with the dragon gargoyle's enhancement, it was almost easy.

A backlash of magic slapped my body, and the oily pressure of Walter's gigantic ward disappeared with the sting. Exclamations echoed through the nook.

"I thought you said nothing could get through that ward," someone accused.

I rubbed my arms. Did that mean the lion hatchling was dead?

"Wait—" Walter cried.

The room erupted in noise. In rapid succession, I heard the unmistakable sounds of flesh hitting flesh, the ring of steel being drawn, and then the deafening crack of thrown lightning. Screams pierced the ringing in my ears.

Should I grab the hatchlings and make a run for it? No. Rushing through a crowd of panicked felons with the hatchlings they coveted was suicidal. Plus, I had no idea where the little lion was. Or even if he still lived.

Against every instinct, I remained crouched in the storage room.

"Halt! Terra Haven guards! Show me your hands!"

The authoritative voices echoed through the main chamber, and I collapsed on my butt with relief. Kylie had succeeded. Everything was going to be okay. I took my first full breath since I'd agreed to this crazy rescue plan.

A slice of nullifying wood and earth cut through my ward as if it were a child's creation. The backlash rattled my brain in my skull.

"Bloody kludde and their useless handlers!" Walter cursed. He raced around the corner of the nook and skidded to a stop. "You!" The limp hatchling flopped in Walter's left hand, and it was impossible to tell if he lived. In Walter's right was a glossy black crossbow that pointed unerringly at my chest. My head went light on my shoulders, the tip of the arrow filling my vision.

Walter scanned the ground. "Where are the hatchlings?"

"I . . . I don't know—" I stopped speaking on a squeak when Walter slid his finger to the trigger. Too late, I thought to shout for help. Not that anyone would hear me. I couldn't see the ceremony room from my position, but it sounded like the fighting had doubled despite the guards' arrival. Or because of it. Even if the guards could have heard me, they couldn't react faster than an arrow.

"Where are they?" Walter barked.

Not waiting for my answer, he formed a complicated spike of

woven magic. When he released it, the tip flipped left and pierced my ward, disintegrating it. Walter's smile was cold. He flicked a sphere of light into the space near my satchel. With the crossbow never wavering from my chest, he dropped the limp hatchling to the stone floor, bent, and flipped open the top of the satchel. The cygnet snapped at him, and he jerked back, flipping the top closed again.

Helplessly, I watched him grasp the handle, fury and fear pounding in my bloodstream. He turned, hefting the satchel, and centered me in the crossbow's sights.

"Nice try, thief," he said.

My insides coated with ice. "Please—"

From behind the satchel, the dragon hatchling launched. He bit down on Walter's wrist, crushing bone in his rock jaws. Walter screamed and jerked. The crossbow fired. Plaster shards splintered into my face, the arrow missing me by less than a foot. I lurched into Walter. He slammed against the wall, bag and bow falling when he tried to catch himself. Recovering, he swung his left arm at me. The attached hatchling came with it. I ducked too late, and the dragon smashed into my raised forearm and head, knocking me back into the opposite wall. The hatchling dropped to the ground, stunned.

Walter and I stared at the healed hatchling.

"Drop your weapon!" a voice shouted from the mouth of the alcove, still out of sight but loud enough to penetrate my deafened eardrums.

Walter's gaze darted from the healed hatchling to his bow to the satchel.

"No," I cried, pushing from the wall. I tackled him, and we both went down. Walter kicked my thigh, and it went numb. I landed a punch to his gut; then his elbow glanced off my temple. The world skittered, and when it righted, he was on his feet. Walter tore away yet another illusion, this one from the far end of the storage room. Behind it was a smooth wall, but when Walter hit a disguised switch, a hidden panel slid open.

Walter spun to retrieve the hatchlings. Scrambling forward, I wrapped my body around the satchel and limp lion gargoyle.

"Halt! Terra Haven guard!" Footsteps pounded closer.

With a curse and a final kick to my side, Walter fled, empty-handed.

Two guards rounded the corner, glowballs and trap-springer spells preceding them. There were no weapons in their hands—none were necessary; they were trained in defensive and offensive magic, the kind that could stop an arrow or drop an attacker from across the room.

"Hands where I can see them," the woman said.

My skin tightened as a shield sliced between me and my magic. I stretched my hands up beside my head.

"He ran that way." I pointed with a finger.

The male guard approached with null bands—handcuffs that did the work of the spell currently cloaking me.

Something small and heavy landed on my side, hissing.

"What *is* that?" The guard paused. I raised my head to look down my body. The dragon hatchling snaked up my side to perch on my hip. His tiny mismatched wings were flared and his large square head gaped to show bloodred teeth and tongue. Magic rushed back to me at his touch.

"A gargoyle hatchling," I said. I eased a hand to the satchel and flipped the top open. The cygnet squirmed and hissed at the guards. "Hurry. Walter's escaping."

It took long, agonizing minutes to convince the guards I had nothing to do with the harm inflicted on the cygnet and for them to send guards after Walter. I had little hope they'd catch him after his head start. When I was finally allowed to sit up, I moved immediately for the limp demonstration hatchling they hadn't noticed in the curve of my body. The tiny lion weighed less than Herbert had after being used by the Fire Eaters.

"Whoa, there. What're you doing?" demanded the guard who had been called to the nook while the other two chased Walter.

"Helping him."

"I've got orders to round everyone up. You're coming with me."

I ignored him, gathering the familiar blend of quartz earth and fire, with trace levels of the other three elements, and eased it into the hatchling. A tiny spark within him responded. Tears sprang to my eyes. "I'm so sorry I wasn't faster," I whispered to him, feeding him more energy.

"None of that now," the guard said. He grabbed my elbow and pulled me to my feet. The dragon circled my ankles, tail lashing, but he didn't interfere. The guard picked up my bag, bunching the flap so the hissing mutilated baby swan couldn't bite him, and marched me back to the main room. The dragon followed in a strange bunching lope.

Light blazed from a dozen magical sources. I blinked against the brightness. Guards swarmed the room, collecting evidence, but my gaze was drawn to the still bodies near the door. Two men, one stabbed through the chest, blood soaking his shirt and pooling on the stones, the other decapitated. I glanced away, my stomach churning. There were six prisoners in the room. Each was confined by magic and metal and separated by space, wards, and guards. All six sets of eyes tracked our progress across the room.

The only way out was past the bodies.

10

The guard's guiding grip shifted to support me when the world went light and fuzzy as we approached the decapitated body.

"Don't look down," he urged.

I locked eyes on the stairwell and let him direct me, floating detached from my own feet. The bitter copper smell of blood yanked me back to my body. Another step and the putrid stench of loosed bowels and raw flesh clogged my nostrils. I gagged.

"Not here!" The guard rushed me forward, and we made it to the stairwell before I threw up. He waited until I finished, then half dragged me up the stairs.

Fresh air hit my face and cleared my head, and I remembered the dying hatchling clutched to my chest for the first time since seeing the bodies. I jerked free of the guard and stopped.

"Keep going," he ordered.

"No. Let me heal it first."

"My orders—"

"Stuff your orders." I was bruised and battered, exhausted and nauseous; I was in no mood to be bullied.

"Don't make me cuff you."

I ignored the guard and knelt. The dragon hatchling loped toward us. His stubby legs hadn't been able to keep up. I felt a twinge of guilt for having forgotten him, too, but mostly gratitude as my weariness faded with his magical boost. I tumbled a handful of seed crystals from my pocket and focused on the lion hatchling and the magic still leeching from his burned-off limbs.

The cub absorbed seed crystal after seed crystal, devouring my magic. Like Herbert, the cub's four legs and wings had been burned away. Even with the dragon hatchling amplifying my power, my magic was clumsy by the time I got to the lion's fourth leg. The elemental strands quivered with fatigue when I painstakingly finished the final wing. The lion hatchling remained unconscious, but he was resting, not dying.

As I worked, I was vaguely aware of the guard kneeling beside me, watching with rapt curiosity. When I leaned back, I went into freefall; then I was in the guard's arms, supported against his broad chest. The dragon hatchling curled up against my sprawled leg, tucked his nose under his tail, and went to sleep. His magical amplification dropped away, and with it my consciousness. The guard shook me, and I fought against the darkness. *Not yet.*

I reached for the satchel and the final hatchling, but my arm wasn't working right. It felt so good to relax against the man's warm chest. My eyes drifted closed again.

"This looks cozy," a woman said from above me.

"Captain!" The guard shifted and I dropped toward the floor, only to be caught before impact. "Uh, sir. I was just . . . She fainted and I . . . The gargoyle, sir, she healed it," the guard stammered.

There was a commotion behind us; then Kylie was at my elbow. She grinned at me. "I knew you could do it, Mika."

At her heels were two huge gargoyles, one a pony-size onyx and amethyst gryphon, the other a cross between an enormous goat and a winged pit bull, with a body made of spotted green jasper. The temple floor trembled beneath the gargoyles' steps. Their eyes glowed with rage.

The guard's grip on me tightened, and I thought I probably would have been afraid if I hadn't been so tired. The goat-headed pit bull sniffed the air, then bounded on huge rock dog paws down the stairs to the ceremony room. A handful of guards rushed after her.

The gryphon stopped at my feet and thrust her face in mine. Under the scrutiny of those fierce eagle eyes, I found it hard to breathe. Then her attention shifted, first to the unconscious lion in my lap, then to the dragon curled at my leg. When she spotted the scared cygnet, still injured and wrapped in my leather bag, she sat back on her haunches. A small blue-green winged panther slid from under the protection of her wings and landed at her feet, scurrying under the gryphon's belly to peer through her thick legs.

Anya.

"May I assist you?" the gryphon asked. Her voice was soft, completely at odds with her enormous stone body.

It took a moment for my brain to catch up. "Please."

I tried to sit up on my own. The guard lifted me.

A trickle of gargoyle-enhanced magic strengthened my exhausted mind and body. It was different from the feel of the hatchlings' power boosts. This was controlled and refined. With the gryphon's strength guiding my magic, healing the cygnet went quickly. When I finished, the cygnet twined her long stony neck against my arm, then fell asleep draped across my lap.

When I looked up, a pair of healers were kneeling beside me, their body language saying they'd been waiting, and watching, for some time. The gryphon remained rooted at my side while the healers stuffed dry energy cakes down my throat, followed by a pitcher of water. The tender lumps on my head were prodded and my arm was wrapped in a coil of mending wood magic. When the medics gave the okay, the captain walked me through the last two days, starting with Anya finding me in my studio up until I healed the baby lion. Then she made me go through it all again.

She questioned Anya, too, but the baby gargoyle's accounting of the events from the time her siblings were kidnapped was convoluted at best. From what I heard, the captain didn't learn anything useful about Walter. After a few minutes, Anya flew onto the gryphon's back and hid beneath her wings, and I was reminded of how young she was. A few weeks old, and she'd already seen the worst of humanity. It was a wonder she had trusted Kylie and me to help her.

The captain released me a little after dawn, and the gryphon accompanied Kylie, me, and the hatchlings home. Since the rescued hatchlings were all still sleeping, Kylie volunteered to carry the dragon, I cradled the lion, and the gryphon carried the cygnet on her back, holding it in place with her wings. Anya rode with her swan sister.

The trip home was a blur. I had a vague impression of Ms. Zuberrie demanding an explanation for our arrival by guard transport and peppering us with questions about the gargoyles, but Kylie intercepted her. The last thing I remembered was opening the door to the balcony for the gargoyles to use as they desired, then collapsing onto my bed, the lion nestled against my stomach.

11

The sun was setting when I woke. My hand went immediately to the bed in front of me, and finding myself alone, I sat up. My entire body protested. I groaned, stretching cramped arms and fingers. Dirt lay in flakes on my bedspread and sifted to the floor from my pants. My pillowcase was grubby. I grimaced, and not for the first time I wished I could afford self-cleaning sheets and clothes, ones with water and air magic woven into the fibers.

My grumbles were cut short when I noticed the lion perched on my slender bookcase. He was squeezed between a battered copy of *Five Steps to Financial Independence* and a dusty misshapen crystal globe, one of my earliest quartz projects. The cub looked like solid, carved citrine with crystal limbs. He didn't move, and his eyes were flat rock, not glowing.

I was across the room in three strides, pressing my hands to his sides and probing him with the gargoyle magic pattern. Life blazed under my fingertips. The lion woke, thin rock eyelids lifting.

"Oh, I'm sorry," I said, panic receding. He wasn't dead, just sleeping. I should have guessed that; a dead hatchling couldn't move himself from my bed to the bookcase. He yawned, his rock jaw almost unhinging, then shifted to lie down, chin resting on his clear paws. His eyelids slid closed and he stilled. Already I could see veins of gold spreading through his tiny wings and oversize paws. The strength and adaptability of gargoyles were marvels.

Wonder could overshadow my crustiness for only so long. I peeled off my gritty clothes, tossed them in the hamper, and melted under the stream of hot water in my shower. It was dark outside when I finally dressed and thought to check my message bowl. There were two air-pocket messages, both pulsing red with urgency. I touched the edge of the bowl and activated the first message with a nudge of air and earth.

"Mika Stillwater." My boss's voice swelled from the bubble, each word crisply enunciated. Silvia Jones was a strong earth talent, with only a child's grasp of air element. Crafting any message was a sure-fire way to irritate her, but she sounded more peeved than normal. My stomach sank. I'd missed a second day of work and hadn't sent a message this time.

"I do not run a charity. You are well aware of the rules. Two days' absence requires a doctor's note and advance notice." I scoffed. *Advance notice for being sick?* "I expect you to bring a doctor's note tomorrow. If this is *inconvenient*, your contract with Jones and Sons will be terminated." The bubble crackled in the air before fizzling out.

I slumped in my worktable chair. If everything had gone according to plan, the freelance medicinal vials would be finished, my handsome paycheck collected, my savings holding a lease at Pinnacle Pentagon, and I'd be delivering my resignation at the month's end. My gaze slid to the gilded box still open atop the coffee table. The red velvet insides that had housed my life savings were bare. Glumly, I reached for the message bowl and activated the other bubble.

"When you sign a contract saying you'll complete a project by a deadline, that is when it's due," Althea's voice snapped through the room. "Your avoidance tactics are juvenile and unprofessional. This is the first and last project you'll do for Blackwell-Zakrzewska. Unless you want a formal mark against you, in reputation and filed with the Terra Haven Business Bureau, you will have the remainder of the vials ready for me by seven tomorrow morning. Do not attempt to stall again."

I slumped farther in the chair. Not only was I going to have to grovel to Silvia, but I'd also just lost my most important client. Even without a formal complaint, there would be no stopping rumors.

"That woman should be begging for your services," Kylie said. She stood in my open balcony doorway, hands on hips, glaring at the message bowl. Her wispy blond hair lifted on the night breeze, and Kylie caught it up with a frustrated gesture and trapped it in a hair tie. "Are her precious vials more important than lives? I think not. Which is exactly what I told her."

"You saw her? Today?"

"Yes. She prissed in here, looking down her nose at me and Ms. Zuberrie, demanding we wake you—"

I groaned. "You should have! Now she's going to slander my name." I covered my face in my hands and braced my elbows on my knees, seeing my dreams crumble behind my eyelids.

"She's the one who deserves to have her reputation blackened. A healer apprentice who puts more importance on some stupid project than life. Absurd!"

"You still should have woken me."

"Why? So you could tell her yourself that you're not done? You're not, right?"

I shook my head.

"Besides, I don't think I *could* have woken you. You slept through our shouting match right outside your door. Now guess what."

I dropped my hands from my face and sat up. I wasn't in the mood for guessing games. Fortunately, Kylie wasn't patient enough to wait.

"You're looking at the *Terra Haven Chronicle*'s evening-edition front-page author!"

"You sold a story?" I asked, stuffing aside my misery for the moment. This was Kylie's dream. Just because mine was shattered didn't mean I would rob her of her moment.

"Not *a* story. Your story! And the hatchlings'. I hope you don't mind that I quoted you a few times. You're a city hero, Mika! When I told the editor at the *Chronicle* what I had, she bought the exclusive and contracted two follow-up stories. Can you believe it?!"

"Of course I can," I said, privately squirming at the mention of *my* story. "Congratulations, Kylie!"

"Oh! Here—" She ran across the balcony and returned with the *Chronicle*. There I was on the front page, bent over the cygnet, repairing her wing.

"Who took the picture?" I asked, not remembering any photographers.

"You should see your face." She laughed. "You didn't think I would show up empty-handed, did you?"

"You didn't. You brought the guards."

"Nope. I brought the gargoyles."

"How?" I'd been too tired last night to ask how Kylie had convinced the guards.

"I figured that if Anya didn't trust people, she would trust gargoyles. So we found the two you saw. After Anya talked to them, they went to the guards with me. They couldn't dismiss me then. And once the guards saw that huge ward, they stopped dragging their feet and called in backup."

"Just in time, too," I said. "You're the real hero, Kylie. I'd be dead without you. All I did was—"

"Hold that thought," Kylie said. She whipped together threads of air and water, weaving a giant sphere and dropping it over both our heads. At my quizzical look, she said, "Better than memory. It'll catch everything we say. What did you think my follow-up story was going to be, Mika? I've been dying to hear what happened all day, and I know my readers feel the same."

"*Your* readers?"

Kylie winked. "Spill."

I spilled, telling her everything that happened from the moment I'd come face-to-face with the kludde to collapsing in the guard's arms after healing the lion. She bombarded me with questions, drawing out details I'd happily have forgotten. I made sure to empha-size that I hadn't been heroic. I knew how Kylie's imagination worked, and I didn't want her getting carried away.

Kylie waved my words aside. "You saved the hatchlings' lives. *That's* heroic."

"That was nothing more than any earth elemental would have done."

"But—"

"Kylie, I was terrified every step of the way. I shook in my boots when confronted with the kludde. I *froze* when Walter had the crossbow on me. The little dragon has more courage than me."

"Modesty is good, but being blinded by it? Stupid. Mika, you might have been scared out of your wits, but you still went through with the rescue. *You saved the hatchlings' lives.*"

"You would have done the same."

Kylie touched her hands to the edges of the sphere and it contracted to a globe that fit in her hand. With a flick, she sent the spell winging toward her room.

"I couldn't have done the same, Mika," Kylie said. "I don't know anyone else who could, not even another earth elemental. Mika, your specialty is so much more than quartz. Do you hear what I'm saying? Your specialty is healing a magical creature. That's . . . that's down-right rare."

"But it's mainly just quartz and fire," I protested.

"You're being obtuse," Kylie said. "Now read my first front-page piece."

Kylie thrust the paper into my hands. I blushed at her opening paragraph: *Last night, a lone woman bravely infiltrated a megalomaniac's lair to rescue three tortured gargoyle hatchlings. Mika Stillwater, an earth elemental and quarry project manager, acted at the behest of two orphan gargoyles, stepping into the role of hero as if she were born to it.*

"Really? This is . . ."

"True," Kylie said.

"Embarrassing. I told you—"

"Oh, hush. Read."

Kylie filled in the backstory, highlighting Herbert's rescue and the atrocities he'd endured. There was a good deal about the guards' actions—the unit who broke Walter's ward, their strategic capture of the kludde and its handler, the raid on the temple—but no mention that they hadn't believed me or Kylie without the backing of two adult gargoyles.

Eight people were arrested for attending the illegal auction. The police are tracking down leads on a dozen others. Walter Pratt remains at large, the article concluded.

"They didn't catch him," I said.

Kylie shook her head. "In the confusion, most people got away, though I obviously didn't say that. That wouldn't earn me any favors and it might alarm the public. I went by the station today to see if there was an update. They think Walter's gone to ground. My rumor scouts confirm it. There hasn't been a useful peep about him."

"He really liked having the power," I said, remembering Walter's expression of triumphant superiority when he created the enormous ward that rocked us all. "He's not going to stop."

"I don't think so, either. Look at how many people showed up for the auction. He was going to make a fortune."

"Speaking of money . . . Any word on getting my—our—money back from what the police confiscated from the kludde handler?"

"I think that's the last thing on their mind," Kylie said. She patted my arm; I didn't feel consoled. My final hope to salvage my career imploded.

Her gaze went to the lion on my bookcase. "How's he doing?"

"Good. Sleeping." I wanted to curl up on my bed and savor the oncoming depression, but that would be uncharitable. Not to mention counterproductive. I still needed to finish Althea's project before I headed off to work tomorrow. But first: "Are the two adult gargoyles still here?"

"They went home this morning."

"Oh." I hadn't had a chance to thank them or to explain that I hadn't been trying to overstep my abilities by being the one to heal the hatchlings rather than searching for someone stronger. "Did the other hatchlings go with them?"

"Nope. They're all still here." Kylie grinned and bounced on her toes. "Four gargoyles, even if they are very small, lined up on a house full of nobodies has created quite a stir in the neighborhood. Ms. Zuberrie acts put out by all the visitors we've had today—it's been nonstop, Mika; everyone found an excuse to drop in—but you can tell she's never been happier."

I grinned back. Holding court must have thrilled Ms. Zuberrie to her toes.

Kylie followed me out to the balcony. The hatchlings were outlined against the twilit sky, all four in a tight clump close to the balcony edge. Four pair of glowing eyes watched us. Everyone looked okay. I felt an unexpected swell of pride.

The dragon spread his crimson-veined crystal wings and launched straight at me. I caught him and staggered back against the wall, my arms straining under twenty pounds of wriggling rock. Bracing his front paws on my chest, hind paws on my palms, he put his square, stone-bearded face in mine and, very precisely, enunciated, "Thank you."

His voice carried an undercurrent of chimes.

"You're welcome," I said. A flash popped, blinding me. The gargoyle jerked from my arms and flapped to the balcony railing, growling at Kylie.

"That'll look great with the next article," she said, unapologetic.

I wasn't sure what would happen next. I didn't have any experience with baby gargoyles, or gargoyles of any kind. "Um. You guys are welcome to stay here as long as you want," I told the hatchlings. "Or to go, if that's what you want..."

The dragon flew to the bookcase, landing on the shelf beside the lion and knocking several books and knickknacks to the floor. The cub opened an eye, saw the dragon, and closed it. Herbert flew to my worktable. The cygnet stretched her wings, then folded her head under one and went to sleep. Anya closed her eyes, too.

I glanced at Kylie, and she shrugged.

"I guess they're staying. I need to get writing," she said. "I've got an article due tomorrow." She danced in place, then left, singing.

"And I need to finish the vials," I told the room at large, settling into my work chair.

Herbert picked up a seed crystal, tossed it to the back of his mouth, and swallowed it. His eyes bulged. He hunched forward, and with a loud, wet hacking sound, threw up. The crystal landed in a slimy puddle and rolled across my worktable.

12

After the last few days' excitement, it was unfair to rise with dawn, dress in dull work attire, and trudge down to breakfast, only to be intercepted by Althea in the foyer. Stifling a sigh, I summoned a smile.

"I see your friend's description of your 'condition' was an exaggeration," she said.

"Have you been waiting long?" I asked, wondering how I'd missed the bell chime.

"Three days too long, Mika Stillwater."

I winced. I'd walked right into that one.

"Let me just—"

"Your lack of professionalism is appalling. I am a forgiving person—"

I gaped at the lie.

"—otherwise I'd see you never worked in this city again. It's not as if your services are unique," Althea said. "There are a hundred other earth elementals in the city who can do what you do."

My spine snapped straight. "If that were so, you would have contracted through someone else," I said, shocked by my boldness even as I spoke.

Althea's face pinched tighter. "Quality is of no use to me if it is to the detriment of punctuality."

How long had she been waiting to use that line? "If you'll just wait—"

"I am through waiting!"

"—here," I continued, speaking over her. "I will return with your vials, Althea Stoneward."

She clamped her mouth shut, affronted I'd used her full name as if she were an apprentice under my authority. I turned away before she could see me smile. Feeling a little more perky, I trotted back upstairs. I would be delighted to see the last of Althea.

I was three steps into my room before a prickling sensation on my neck registered. I glanced around. Adrenaline spurted through me. The lion and dragon were imprisoned on my bookcase in cages of crackling destructive magic. The dragon twisted in panic, but the lion stared behind me, wide eyes affixed.

Dread loosened my body, and I spun toward my bed. Lying, hands clasped behind his head, muddy boots crossed at the ankle atop my pillow, was Walter Pratt.

"Hello, Hero Stillwater," Walter said, rolling to his feet.

"How did you find—" No, I knew the answer to that question. The article in the paper. "How did you get in here?"

"I see you've restored the hatchlings. Very useful," he said. "Opens up a world of possibilities."

He was only a fraction taller than me and similar in build. There should have been nothing terrifying about him, with his sandy-haired, boy-next-door looks. But up close, I could see madness in his green eyes. The open door was just three steps away, the balcony a little farther. A shout would echo downstairs and also reach Kylie's room, if she was there.

Walter flicked a hand, and a blast of air closed the door. I jumped, eyes darting to the balcony, but Walter shifted to block that escape. He tossed a handful of objects at me. I flinched and ducked, instinct restoring movement to limbs I'd forgotten existed. I grabbed for air, fashioning a deflective shield even as the items clattered around my feet. I glanced down. Over a dozen seed crystals rolled chaotically before snapping into a perfect circle around me. Walter engaged the crystals.

A blanket of magic smothered me, bearing down as if to flatten me. My neck strained, my spine compressed. I collapsed to my hands and knees. The pressure eased, allowing me to twist to look up at Walter.

"Much better, Mika." His smile chased ice through my veins, jolting me from my stupor. I grabbed for magic. It trickled to me, warped and weak from the swirl of wood, fire, and air that trapped me. I was no match for Walter's power, and we both knew it.

"You and I will make a great team," Walter said.

I screamed, finding my voice at last. "Help! Kylie! Help!"

Walter cocked his head to the side and cupped his ear; bruises circled his left wrist from the dragon's bite. "What's that, Mika? Did you say something?"

My stomach sank. I screamed again, wordless frustration and fear unleashed into a sound-consuming void. Walter was one step ahead of me, again.

"Tsk-tsk, Mika. Don't interrupt. I'm annoyed with you. Do you know how long it took to set up last night's auction? And then you ruined it all. I could happily kill you for that."

I kicked a crystal with a booted foot. Pain convulsed up my heel, through my ankle, my knee, my hip, vibrating through every joint and muscle of my body. When it receded, I was lying on my side, knees curled to my chest. Walter's feet were in my line of sight. He was standing at my worktable.

"You have some skill," he said, holding out one of the vials I had finished last night. "Such delicate work." He dropped it. The vial shattered against the floor in a musical tinkling of paper-thin crystal. "Each one as perfect as the last," he mused, selecting another and dropping it. Shards sparkled across the hardwood floor.

"Stop," I said. It came out soft, pathetic, breathless. I rolled to my knees. The cage had constricted, but I squished under it, refusing to remain vulnerable on my side. "Stop!" I shouted. I couldn't lift my head to see above Walter's thighs. Another vial fragmented against the floor. "Stop it, you sick bastard!"

I stared at the shards of my labor and welcomed the surge of anger. It helped me think. Walter had trapped me in a net just as he had trapped the gargoyles. I'd removed the nets at the temple; I could remove this one. I wasn't a helpless hatchling. I was an earth practitioner. No one was going to bind me with quartz.

I probed the seed crystal in front of me. A whirlwind of wood and fire and air suffocated the trickle of magic I held in a feeble grasp. Doing my best to ignore Walter while simultaneously appearing to be doing nothing more than hanging on his every word, I relaxed into the chaotic energy, searching for a pattern. Four times, it knocked me out of its weave, my dribble of magic buffeted by the raw power of Walter's creation. On the fifth try, I found a weak link at a seed crystal where the magic funneled through narrow bands.

"Your death, however satisfying that might be," Walter continued, "is a shortsighted goal at best." A vial crashed to the floor. "Your abilities are too valuable. With you, there is no limit. I can sell the hatchlings a hundred times, and when they're returned, useless, you will repair them. It's a beautiful cycle, Mika."

Bile washed up my throat. Walter didn't respect the lives of the magical creatures, and he certainly didn't value my life. He viewed the hatchlings and me only in terms of his monetary and magical gain. But I wasn't going to be a victim and neither were the hatchlings.

I cut the flow of power from the first seed crystal. It rolled an inch toward me, unfettered by the binds of the spell. I prayed Walter wasn't paying attention and focused on the next crystal. It took three more severed links before I felt a difference in the level of magic I could pull. I worked even faster, snapping the locks on my cage with increased efficiency.

"Full spectrums will look *average* compared to me. Full-five companies will beg for my services." Walter laughed.

Eight of the fifteen seed crystals were disconnected, and the prison holding me cracked into a semicircle of wild magic. Walter whirled from the table in shock.

I scrambled away from the snapping current of power. Walter shoved the freed crystals toward me with a blast of air. I was ready this time. I opened myself wide to raw power. Hundreds of hours working with quartz made it easy to resonate my magic with the seed crystals hurtling through the air. I thrust my power through each crystal, claiming and stacking them in a line across the floor at my feet, forming a half-inch wall between Walter and myself. At the last second, I felt the seed crystals at my back lift and spin in my direction, dragging the deadly, uncontrolled magic with them.

13

I sidestepped, crashing into my coffee table. Dividing my focus, I held the clean crystals at my feet and pressed destructive elements into the hazardous seeds still in Walter's control. I worked faster than ever before, breaking the links between Walter's erratic net and each crystal while it was still in the air. Walter's unfettered magic flared out of control, scorching a flat line in the bathroom wall before extinguishing. The empty crystals clattered to the floor and scattered.

"You can't win this fight," Walter said. "You're hardly a medium spectrum, and I'm so much more."

It was true. That didn't mean I had to give up, though.

"Kylie! Guards!" I yelled. As I predicted, Walter launched an air net to catch the sound, and that gained me precious seconds. I jammed earth magic through the scattered crystals, aligning them with the seven in my control. With a shove of blunt earth element, I grew them together in a single rod. Just as fast, I severed the crystal in four places, making five bars of quartz, each as long as my palm. With a blast of air, I knocked them toward Walter. If I could get them around him, it would make a far stronger cage than the string of seed crystals—

Walter threw up a wall of air, blocking the crystal. "Ah, ah, ah," he said, shaking a finger at me. He increased the push of air, and I strained to hold the quartz bars in place. The brilliance of my spontaneous plan betrayed me as Walter turned it against me.

Walter grinned and added an ounce more of air, toying with me. The crystal bars inched closer. In a head-to-head challenge, Walter's magic eclipsed mine, and I'd lost my advantage of surprise.

At Walter's feet, a handful of crystal shards shifted in our elemental battle. I almost dropped my weave of air when I *felt* those shards move. In straining to force the quartz bars around Walter, I'd left myself wide open to all quartz, and even broken, the residue of my magic in the shattered, fragile quartz responded. The beginning of a crazy plan formed.

I pulled a trickle of magic from the wall of air holding the crystal bars at bay. They jumped three inches toward me before I slowed them to a slide again. Walter barked a laugh.

"Give up now, Mika, and come with me. You know it's inevitable."

In two feet, the crystal bars would trap me, and Walter was eroding that distance with alarming speed. Panicking seemed like a good option, but I smothered the urge.

Only my extensive work with quartz enabled me to quest with a feeler of earth magic through the shards while most of my attention remained on the air struggle between us. I directed magic through the brittle scraps beneath and around Walter's booted feet, connecting each fragment into a complex web. As the crystal bars slid another hand span toward me, I expanded the linked network of earth magic, at first as large as Walter's feet, then as wide as his shoulders.

Sweat slid down my spine and beaded on my forehead. Walter's magic shifted, earth twining into the crystal bars. He was setting the net again, and I knew, ironically, I wouldn't escape from the anchors I'd created. With a cry, I shifted my push on air to a pull, and the crystal bars shot past me. I slammed my full strength into the web of earth beneath Walter.

Wood, air, and fire spiraled and snapped in a containment field

Walter had taught me. Only, instead of forming a circular cage of power, individual lines of binding magic arced from each shard, forming a bundle of ropes. Each rope unfurled and snaked to Walter, knotting around his legs.

Walter countered, slicing at the bonds with destructive magic faster than I'd cut his anchors. I didn't stop him. Instead, I spread the net wider and wider, through the fragments on the table and under the table, and scattered a yard in every direction. We were working with quartz, my specialty; even though Walter had more strength, he couldn't match my speed or dexterity. He severed a dozen anchors while I grew thirty more. Cables of magic climbed his body, grappling his wrists, his torso, his neck, his ears, thumbs, and belt loops. Each strand cut through Walter's magic, weakening him until he was unable to sever the smallest of my anchors. I didn't stop, though. I wove the net through every shard and fragment until Walter was ensnared in a woven cocoon of magic, immobilized except for his eyes. Not even his mouth could open with the snarl of magic wrapping his jaw shut.

The trap was erratic at best, since the shards were scattered haphazardly around the room. If I let my hold slacken even a fraction, I knew Walter would find a way to wiggle free.

Casting about the room, I saw the crystal bars. One was at my feet, and I belatedly felt the sting of where it had slammed into my shin. The other four were against the bathroom wall. Not daring to pull a drop of magic from the net, I gathered the bars with my hands and placed them evenly around Walter and the shards, squeezing behind my worktable and pushing aside my coffee table until I had an approximation of a circle. It took extreme dexterity to weave the frayed ends of the modified trap into the crystal bars while maintaining magic through hundreds of irregular fragments. I didn't stop until all the shards were tied off and each crystal bar reinforced. I looked for weak links like I'd exploited in Walter's trap, finding none. With numb pride, I stepped back and examined my work.

It was . . . beautiful. Every line of magic glimmered with broken refractions of light from its shard of origin, giving Walter the illusion of being swathed in spun crystal.

A muffled whimper made me turn. The hatchlings! I stumbled to the bookcase and demolished the cages holding them. With all my practice and Walter's magic weakened by my trap, it was easy. I threw open the balcony door and darted outside. On the railing, Anya, Herbert, and the cygnet were ensnared together. I disbursed Walter's sinister magic cage and rushed back into my room to check on my prisoner.

"Mika! Are you okay?" Kylie gripped the balcony railing, eyes darting from me to Walter.

At the sight of her, my adrenaline crashed, and the world blackened, swirled with excessive color. I dropped to the floor, my legs collapsing beneath me.

"Mika!"

Kylie was at my side, supporting me against her body. "Is that Walter?" she asked.

I nodded, the movement taxing my exhausted body.

"I'm through waiting, Mika Stillwa—" Althea burst into the room and stopped in her tracks. "Wha-what is . . . Who is . . . Mika?"

The kernel of compassion that had called Althea to Blackwell-Zakrzewska kicked in, and the apprentice healer crossed the room to press her hands to my temple. A cool wash of magic slid across my skin, giving me a measure of strength.

"What is going on here?" she demanded.

Feet pounded on the stairs, and we all turned toward the commotion in the doorway.

14

"I run a proper house," Ms. Zuberrie protested. "Who do you think holds the blight at bay on this block? Where were you last year when those heathens were burning the tops off all the trees on this street? I could have used a squad then."

Three guards, linked and magic primed, stacked up at the door. Two more fell in line behind them. Althea shrieked and cowered behind me. Kylie clutched my hand. Behind the guards, I could just see Ms. Zuberrie's white-blond head craning to peer over the guards' backs.

The guards scanned the room with eyes that missed nothing and showed no surprise at Walter's frozen form. Each wore head to toe gray, their uniforms bearing only a single elemental marking on their stiff collars, and I realized these weren't ordinary guards. These were Federal Pentagon Defense agents, elite individuals trained to work as a unit against extreme threats.

With practiced efficiency, Terra Haven's five most deadly FPD warriors swarmed through my studio—not pausing at the sight of the traumatized hatchling gargoyles clinging to the railing. Two crossed the balcony and disappeared into Kylie's room. The wood elemental remained at the door, his tall frame blocking Ms. Zuberrie. Moments later, they reconvened, magic relaxed and link dissipated. The water and earth elementals—a slender woman with copper hair and a tall woman I'd mistaken for a man at first—moved to the far side of my worktable, studying Walter. The fire and air elementals, two men cut from the same broad, unyielding cloth, stood between my bed and the coffee table, looming over where Kylie, Althea, and I crouched. The giant wood elemental managed to make the two burly guards look diminutive when he stepped fully into the room.

"See, I told you nothing was wrong," Ms. Zuberrie said. "Mika's a good girl. She wouldn't . . ." Ms. Zuberrie clutched the door frame, her eyes riveted on Walter. But my landlady was nothing if not resilient, and she recovered with remarkable speed. "Mika, just what is going on here?" she demanded, marching into my room. She made it two steps; there simply wasn't any more space in my studio apartment.

"Ma'am, we'll take it from here," the air elemental said in a deep voice.

"That's good to know," Ms. Zuberrie said, "but I'll not be going anywhere. This is my establishment." She gave the guard her sternest glare, which he ignored.

"I . . . I have nothing to do with"—Althea flapped a hand toward the network of magic squeezing Walter—"with *that*." She stood, puffing her chest and looking down her nose at me. "Mika, consider our—"

"Ma'am, please go with Officer Marciano. We'll need your statement," the air guard said, cutting off Althea's haughty speech.

"I really don't have time—"

"We appreciate your cooperation," the wood giant Marciano said, his quiet, authoritative voice ending Althea's protests. He guided the healer apprentice from the room with one large hand on her back, sweeping Ms. Zuberrie along with them. The loss of three people made my apartment almost breathable again.

Kylie and I scrambled to our feet. Standing didn't lessen my growing claustrophobia. The dragon leapt from the bookcase to my chest, and Kylie braced my back while he clambered to my shoulders, getting tangled in my long hair. Wincing, I gathered my hair and planted my feet to balance the extra twenty pounds of rock wrapped around my neck.

"Who can explain what happened here?" the fire elemental demanded. He had dark blue eyes, a five o'clock shadow at eight in the morning, and a jaw that could bench press twice my body weight.

"Ah, that's Walter Pratt," I said.

"And you are?" asked the air elemental. His brown eyes were bracketed with crow's-feet, and some silver lightened his brown hair. I found it much easier to talk to him than the fire elemental.

"I'm Mika Stillwater."

"Kylie Grayson," Kylie said, holding out her hand. The air elemental smiled a fraction and shook her hand. "I'm so pleased with how quickly you responded. Can you tell me who tipped you off to Walter's intentions?"

"She sounds like a reporter," the fire elemental growled.

"Do you know who Walter Pratt is, Guard . . . ?" Kylie let the question trail off.

"It's Captain Monaghan," the air elemental said. "And, yes, we're well aware of Mr. Pratt. I'd like to know who bound Pratt."

I could feel Kylie gather herself to speak, so I cut in. "I did, sir."

"Just you?" the fire elemental demanded.

"Yes, sir."

The squad members exchanged glances. Kylie couldn't let the silence rest.

"Captain Monaghan, can you explain how you learned of Pratt's presence in Mika's room?"

"Velasquez, please escort Ms. Grayson to her rooms and take her statement," the captain said.

"Ms. Grayson." The fire elemental motioned for Kylie to precede him from the room.

"Winnigan, check the rest of the house and yard, then assist Marciano," Captain Monaghan said, addressing the redhead water elemental. He turned to the earth elemental. "Seradon, what do you—"

"Sir, I think I should stay." Kylie faced the captain, ignoring Velasquez's outstretched hand.

"Ma'am, it would be best if you returned to your rooms—"

"Let me put it this way, Captain," Kylie interrupted. "I'm not leaving Mika's side unless I'm carried out."

Velasquez twitched in Kylie's direction, then crossed his arms and settled back on his heels at a gesture from the captain. I felt a wash of gratitude for Kylie's loyalty and support, even if she was partially motivated by her quest for a story.

"Very well, Ms. Grayson. But"—he held up a hand when Kylie opened her mouth—"you must remain silent."

Kylie crossed her arms and pinched her lips in an unconscious mimicry of Velasquez's posture. It wasn't nearly as intimidating on Kylie's slender frame.

The guards shuffled aside for Winnigan, the water elemental, to squeeze past and exit the apartment. With six people—one frozen and two men whose presence took up twice as much room as their extra-large bodies—my apartment felt short on air.

"Walk me through what happened here," Monaghan said.

Kylie wove a quick sphere of air, preparing to record my words as if they were a message. Monaghan's expression tightened, but he didn't say anything and Velasquez only growled once.

I started with Kylie's article in the paper, then stammered my way through the explanation of Walter's attack. Monaghan listened without interrupting. I did my best to ignore Velasquez, who did a phenomenal impression of a grumpy gargoyle. Seradon, the earth elemental, continued to examine Walter as I talked, but she cast frequent glances at the hatchlings.

"Pratt is a stronger elemental than you," Monaghan said when I finished. "At best, you're a medium spectrum. He's nearly a full spectrum. How is it that you were able to overpower him?"

I stared at Walter's cocooned body. "I didn't. I mean, I couldn't overpower him, but I was faster. I have a knack for quartz."

"I'll say," Seradon muttered.

"You said you learned how to do this"—the captain tipped his head toward Walter—"from Pratt, but this isn't his MO. I've never seen anything like it."

"I modified Walter's trap."

"Spur of the moment, in the middle of your struggle with Pratt." Captain Monaghan made it sound like an accusation.

"Through jagged quartz," Seradon added.

I nodded.

"Mika's got more skill with quartz in her pinkie than most full-spectrum earth elementals have in their entire body," Kylie said.

The squad members let that ride.

"Is it true that you healed the hatchlings?" Seradon asked. She moved closer to peer at the dragon, but she never put her back to Walter.

"Mika's a gargoyle healer," Kylie confirmed.

"I just used quartz to heal their burned-off limbs," I said, uncomfortable with accepting the label of *healer* when I didn't know what I was doing.

"No. I could just heal limbs," Seradon said, holding the dragon's paw. He nuzzled her hand. "You regrew and . . . knit them back together." The dragon trilled. Seradon stepped back and refocused on me. "I've never met a healer who wasn't full-spectrum before. Of course, I've never met a midlevel earth elemental who could work such complex magic."

"I can't. I mean, it's only with quartz. It's my specialty."

"A full-spectrum-strength specialty," Seradon mused. "That's a new one, too, but I don't have another explanation."

Captain Monaghan wasn't convinced and made me demonstrate the net I'd used to ensnare Walter on a free shard. By the time I finished, Winnigan had returned to crowd the room.

The captain finally turned to Kylie, who was bouncing on her toes to restrain her questions.

"You asked me how we knew to come," he said. "We've been tracking Pratt for two weeks, and the night of the auction, we were able to identify his magical signature. When he started throwing his magic around here, we mobilized."

Kylie blurted out several more questions, but I didn't listen. I kept replaying FPD Seradon's compliments and confirmation that I was a gargoyle healer. When the captain addressed me again, he had to repeat himself before I noticed.

"Can you undo it? I think we've let Walter stew long enough, Ms. Stillwater."

"Uh." I eyed the tangled mess of earth and wood and fire. I was tempted to say no and let Seradon unravel it, but when Kylie gave me an encouraging nod, I knew I had to at least try.

I stepped away from Kylie and closer to Walter. Seradon circled around the far side of the table to stand behind Walter. Velasquez, the fire elemental, shifted to stand behind me, forcing Kylie to move back near the door. Winnigan and Monaghan moved to ring Walter. I felt the readiness in the squad—to apprehend Walter, but just as likely to control any backlash of magic that got away from me.

There was a flurry at the balcony door. Anya, Herbert, and the cygnet careened into the room. Anya dropped to the captain's feet, Herbert landed on a clean edge of my worktable, and the cygnet alighted on Velasquez's shoulder, buffeting his head with her crystalline wings. The fire elemental cursed and steadied the hatchling, then glared at me. I looked away before he caught my smile.

All mirth died when I stared at Walter. He was facing me, hate burning in his eyes. Taking a deep breath, I reached for my magic. It came in a gargoyle-enhanced rush. Working on what I'd learned when I'd destroyed Walter's traps, I unraveled the larger strands of magic from the crystal bars, feeding the destructive magic into each shard at the source. The anchors released like unsnapped buttons, quick and efficient. This wasn't Walter's magic; it was my own, and it responded with gratifying alacrity. Still, even after the bars were removed, there were hundreds more anchors, and it was at least ten minutes before I felt the weave holding Walter weaken.

Suddenly Velasquez lifted me and deposited me behind him. I yelped and dropped my magic. The squad ignored me. As a unit, they converged on Walter, who was fighting free of the remaining bonds. For a second, Walter's magic flared, hot and bright, and then the squad snapped null cuffs to his wrists and plucked the bow from his waist.

"It was all her!" Walter shouted. "She primed the auction. She stole the hatchlings. I had nothing to do with it. She was holding me captive. Arrest her! She's—"

The cygnet launched from Velasquez's shoulder, her clawed lion's feet slashing toward Walter's face. He screamed in terror.

Velasquez plucked the hatchling from the air, opened a window, and gently tossed her out. She squeaked and flapped around the bay windows to the balcony door, angling for Walter again, only to be brought up short by Anya's hiss. Squawking her disappointment, the cygnet landed on the captain's head, purple-veined crystal feathers ruffled. Even Velasquez smiled at the sight.

15

"Check it out," Kylie said, slapping down the *Terra Haven Chronicle* onto my desk.

I rolled the final vial into a cloth and slid it into the pouch with the others. When I glanced up, I groaned.

"Gargoyle Healer Mika Stillwater Instrumental in Capturing Felon" was typed in boulder-size letters across the top of the page. Below it was a picture of Walter being dragged down Ms. Zuberrie's front steps by the full-five squad, with me framed in the doorway, the dragon hatchling standing on two legs on my shoulder.

"Did you see the byline?"

"Kylie, I saw you race ahead of the squad to take the picture," I said. She planted her fists on her hips and pouted. "Congratulations on getting another front-page story. But really? *Instrumental*?" I wasn't sure how I felt about the bold letters proclaiming me to be a gargoyle healer, either. I had the potential, but I still had a lot to learn. I would have said "fledgling healer" or "healer in training." Or better yet, I wouldn't have mentioned me at all.

"Don't be modest, Mika. It's no fun. Now read!"

She spread the paper open and moved the bag of vials to the coffee table. Herbert cracked an eye at us, then curled up tighter on the edge of my table in the sunbeam. His limbs were still mostly translucent crystal, but the veins of rose quartz and blue dumortierite were longer, reaching nearly to the tips of his wings and down to his toes. The other hatchlings were healing, too, and none seemed slowed by their crystal limbs in the meantime. Even the lion was outside today, perched on the eaves.

"You're not reading," Kylie said.

I read. I squirmed through the parts that mentioned me, feeling that Kylie exaggerated my actions in the events, but her depiction of the full-five squad was dead-on. Reading about Walter's imprisonment filled me with a sense of triumph all over again.

"The managing editor has already hired me to cover Walter's trial. Depending on how that goes, I could be taken on as staff. Isn't that great?"

"You'll be running that paper in a year," I said, believing it.

Kylie glowed. "What about you? What are you going to do?"

"Not work for Silvia Jones," I said.

"You quit! Good for you."

"Actually, she fired me."

"What!"

"She sent a message this morning. Said she didn't need someone with my 'reputation' in her office and how Jones and Sons did not employ people who 'fraternize with criminals.' She also accused me of having a second job that was, and again I quote, 'interfering with my performance and attendance at Jones and Sons and a direct violation of my employment contract.' At least she'll be sending my final check today."

"That woman has no business sense. She would be lucky to get someone with your reputation in her office. Good riddance!"

I smiled. I should have been overjoyed to never return to Jones and Sons, to never have to suffer another lecture from Silvia or be condescended to by her sons again, but I was really going to miss the steady paychecks. Without my savings, even with Althea's reduced payment for the remaining vials, I barely had enough to buy groceries after this month's rent.

"Now you can concentrate on running your business," Kylie said.

"My savings are gone, Kylie. I can't run a business while I have no money."

"Throw away that five-year plan, Mika, and just leap in. Work for yourself full-time."

"In the meantime, Ms. Zuberrie will evict me."

Kylie snorted. "Evict the city hero? Hardly. She's loving all the attention of having you here. Plus, if you leave, so will the gargoyles, and she's not giving that up. Her cleaning spells have double their usual strength. You should see the kitchen: the tan floor tiles are white now."

"My shop at the Pinnacle Pentagon has already been leased. I can't work from here—"

"What have you been doing for the last three years?" Kylie asked.

"That was different. Maybe if I took another quarry job..." I trailed off as Kylie crouched and peered under my bed. "What are you doing?"

"Looking for Mika."

"What?"

"My friend doesn't just give up, so I know you're an impostor."

"I'm not giving up! I'm being prac—"

"If you say you're being practical, I'm going to hurt you."

"What would you have me do? Live paycheck to paycheck?"

"Why not? It won't be forever."

I glared at Kylie. It was easy for her to be optimistic. She was riding high from landing her dream job, and she had paychecks coming her way. I had nothing: no clients, no job, no money, no prospects. In three days, my dreams had plummeted from attainable to impossible.

My gaze fell on Herbert. *If I could do it all over again, would I do anything differently?* The answer was immediate: of course not.

I took a deep breath and pushed aside self-pity. "At least we'll still be neighbors," I said, meeting Kylie's blue eyes.

"And you won't turn into a snob living in that hoity-toity neighborhood," Kylie agreed.

"And my apartment has more gargoyles than the Pinnacle does."

Kylie grinned. "You could charge more, too, as a gargoyle-enhanced practitioner."

I grinned back. This was starting to sound like it might work. "And who knows what sort of business your article will generate for me."

"I bet you have people lined up at the door."

As if in response, the front doorbell chimed.

"That'll be Althea," I said. I grabbed the swaddled bundle of vials and headed for the stairs, Kylie trailing behind me.

Althea waited in the foyer, lips pursed, nose in the air, though her shifting eyes and startled jerks at every sound coming from the kitchen spoiled her aloof airs. I wondered if she was looking for gargoyles or criminals or maybe the full-five squad to come barreling out of the dining room. Nervous or not, she inspected each vial before handing over my payment. She was just turning to leave when the door sprang open and a harried woman rushed in. Her silk clothes were rumpled and her hair had fallen from its chignon, but there was no mistaking the full-spectrum status in her bearing. Two boys trotted in behind her, both in their teens.

"Ms. Gideon!" Althea said, clearly shocked to see the powerful lady on my doorstep.

"Althea Stoneward? I wouldn't think you'd need a gargoyle healer," the woman said, her gaze darting between me and the healer apprentice.

"I am here on business for Blackwell-Zakrzewska—" Althea's eyes widened and she clamped her mouth shut. I smiled. In her attempt to make herself seem more important, Althea had just endorsed my skills to a full spectrum.

"If you or Blackwell-Zakrzewska have any further need of someone skilled with quartz, Althea, please keep me in mind," I said, making the most of the situation. Althea scowled at me before bidding the full spectrum good-bye. When the door slammed behind her, Ms. Gideon's words sank in.

"Are you Mika Stillwater?" Ms. Gideon asked.

I nodded, my tongue stuck to the roof of my mouth.

"Good. We need your help." She gestured, and her oldest son stepped forward, a small gargoyle in his arms. The upper half of her body was a dog's head, torso, and front legs; the lower half was the tail end of a sea horse, including a sea horse's delicate fin-wings. Her entire body was composed of intricate swirls of black, gray, and red agate. The gargoyle's gray eyes were dull and her face pinched.

"Um, I'm not really—" *trained for this,* I was going to finish, but Kylie cut me off.

"Right this way," she said, gesturing toward the living room. The boy thrust the gargoyle into my arms and everyone marched expectantly after Kylie. I staggered behind them, excuses forming in my head. The gargoyle weighed at least forty pounds, and I sank to the floor before I dropped her. Large puppy eyes blinked at me, and then the gargoyle relaxed in my arms, completely trusting. I met Kylie's gaze, then Ms. Gideon's.

"I'm willing to pay whatever it takes," Ms. Gideon said.

"Oh, that's not—"

"I'd be happy to discuss Mika's fees while she works," Kylie said. Kylie drew Ms. Gideon to the side of the room, away from me. The lady's oldest son followed, but the younger one knelt across from me.

"Can you help Aretha?" he asked, his voice cracking over the words.

I looked away from his hopeful expression and into the soulful eyes of the gargoyle.

I'd spent a lifetime honing my quartz skills to prove I was better than average, to prove that I was good enough to compete with full spectrums and worthy of others' respect. I'd never dreamed that those skills would translate into something far more important: saving lives. I felt a rush of pride at the thought; I was a gargoyle healer.

"Yes. I can help."

CURSE OF THE GARGOYLES

GARGOYLE GUARDIAN CHRONICLES
BOOK 2

ABOUT CURSE OF THE GARGOYLES

Mika was trying to save a gargoyle, not doom the world...

Mika Stillwater isn't known for her skills with combat magic. As a gargoyle healer, she spends her days mending broken appendages and curing illnesses in the living-quartz bodies of Terra Haven's gargoyles. But when a squad of the city's elite Federal Pentagon Defense warriors requests her assistance in freeing a gargoyle ensnared in a vicious invention, Mika jumps into the fray.

No one could have predicted that her involvement would ignite a chain reaction set to destroy the city, the world, and magic itself.

1

"How's Oliver doing, Mika?" Kylie asked.

I jerked and glanced up from the journal open across my lap. We sat outside at a bustling café, soaking in the afternoon sun, and while I'd started out focused on double-checking my notes about my latest patient, a prasiolite and onyx gargoyle who had ingested moldy quartz loam, I'd long since stopped seeing the words. Instead, I'd been idly spinning a pentagram of the five elements above the pages, tuning them to perfect harmony with Oliver.

"Should I get another coffee?" Kylie asked, indicating her empty cup.

"Let me check." We'd been here a little over an hour. It was probably long enough.

I nudged the pentagram into flight, lifting it above the heads of people in the busy city pentagon before zeroing in on Oliver. The half-grown gargoyle crouched two buildings over and three stories up on his favorite perch on the peak of the library's marble facade, craning his long neck to peer over the edge to watch people come and go. Several government buildings and a few restaurants, including the café, ringed the pentagon, but Oliver preferred the magic of library users. I'd chosen the table where Kylie and I sat partially because it afforded me a view of Oliver at all times, but mostly because it was an outdoor seat close enough for me to reach him with my magic.

The pentagram kissed Oliver's side and dipped into his body. In the past five months, I'd perfected the elemental blend of my gargoyle companion: carnelian quartz earth, with a strong band of fire and smaller portions of wood, water, and air. I tried to be discreet and not disturb him, but he lifted his head to find me even as my magic told me he was feeling balanced and healthy.

"He's better now," I told Kylie. "Between an hour or two a week here and a couple hours at the market, he's stabilizing."

I let the weave dissolve and shut the journal. It'd been a gift from Kylie, and she'd had *Mika Stillwater, Gargoyle Healer* embossed in gold on the leather cover. After all these months, I still got the same nervous thrill at seeing my name and title together. Most of the time I still considered myself a midlevel earth elemental with a specialty in quartz—a specialty that happened to make me uniquely suited to work with the living quartz bodies of gargoyles. I loved my new career as a healer, but I kept expecting someone more powerful and knowledgeable to come along and replace me.

Standing, I hefted my bag filled with twenty-five pounds of seed crystals that I'd purchased earlier and wedged the journal on top before tightening the drawstring. Kylie deftly wove a basket out of air and levitated the cumbersome bag to knee height. I admired her skill. I could have created the same elemental lift, but I would have needed a boost of extra magic from Oliver to help me. I grabbed the over-the-shoulder straps and used them like a leash to keep the bag close to us as Kylie collected her research books and we exited the café.

"Do you think Oliver will stay behind this time?" Kylie asked.

"I doubt it." *He might if I encouraged him to.* I ignored the thought. "He's not like other gargoyles. He likes to wander."

"I think he just likes to be near you," Kylie said.

"Which is the problem." Gargoyles had a symbiotic relationship with humans. They could enhance our magic, making them coveted additions to any building or home. In turn, while they bolstered a person's magic, they also fed off it. Despite being made of stone, gargoyles required a balance of the elemental energies to be healthy. I suspected it was why most gravitated toward busy public buildings and the households of full spectrums, where the inhabitants all possessed powerful control over all five elements. Living with me, Oliver consumed mostly earth, and it threw his system out of whack, making him lethargic and potentially stunting his growth. As soon as I'd realized the problem, we'd started making frequent trips to public places where he could supplement his diet.

"It's not a problem," Kylie said. "You've figured out how to keep him healthy, and when he's with you, he's happy. Besides, look at it from his perspective. He's assisting Terra Haven's one and only gargoyle healer. I bet the other gargoyles are jealous."

"Ugh. That makes me sound disgustingly self-important."

Oliver released a trill loud enough to turn every head in the busy pentagon, and the sound lifted my heart. He launched from the roof, startling a flock of pigeons when he unfurled enormous stone eagle's wings from his sinuous Chinese dragon body. Oliver was a glossy orange red of almost pure carnelian, from his square muzzle and stone beard to the feathery rock tufts at the tip of his long tail. With the sun shining through his rock feathers, he looked like he was suspended on wings of fire as he dove toward us. The graceful roll of his long body through the air made it easy to forget he weighed over a hundred pounds—until he landed too hard and his stone feet clapped against the cobblestones loud enough to echo through the surrounding buildings.

"Where are we going now?" Oliver asked. His voice had deepened as he'd grown, but it still carried the undercurrent of chimes and in no way sounded like it came from a stone throat.

Here was the moment to encourage Oliver to stay. With the variety of elementals who frequented the library, it would be a good, healthy home for him. But the words stacked up in my throat, and I swallowed them.

Oliver and his four siblings had been my first gargoyle healer case, and after I'd saved them, they'd stuck around to roost on the Victorian where Kylie and I both rented rooms. However, over the last few months, the other four had begun to explore various rooftops around the city, looking for more permanent homes. I kept waiting for Oliver to follow suit, all while hoping he'd stick around a little longer. Life without him was going to be lonely.

"To the gallery and then home. Unless you have somewhere else to go, Kylie," I said. I'd been pointedly avoiding looking at Kylie so she wouldn't see my guilt, but I glanced her way when she didn't respond.

Kylie had stopped a few feet behind us, eyes riveted on a whirl of tangled air hurtling through a gap in the buildings and heading straight toward her. Though it moved fast enough to blur, I recognized her signature elemental twist on the bubble of captured sound: One of Kylie's rumor scouts had found something.

She pulled her white-blond hair aside as the air cupped her ear, feeding the message privately to her. Her blue eyes lit up and a flush brightened her pale cheeks.

"Well?" I asked. "What's the story?" If anything put that glow on my journalist friend's face, it was the possibility of a front-page piece of news.

"I don't know. Maybe nothing. I've got to go."

The weave dropped from beneath my bag and it crashed to the cobblestones, jerking my shoulder with it.

"Oh, sorry. Here." Kylie thrust her books into my arms. "I'll send word if I'll be done by dinner. Bye!" She spun and sprinted toward the nearest alley, shoulder-length hair streaming behind her as she disappeared around the corner.

"Okay, then. It's just you and me, Oliver." I crouched to add Kylie's books to my bag. This wasn't the first time Kylie had literally raced away, chasing a story. If it panned out, I'd find out about it tonight or tomorrow. In the meantime, I had errands to finish and work of my own. "Unless you want to stay," I forced myself to say.

"I want to see what sold," he said.

The tightness in my chest eased as I shared a smile with the little gargoyle.

I swung one strap of the bag over my shoulder and rested the awkward, poky bulk against my left hip, leaning to the right to compensate. After two steps, I switched sides with Oliver. His long body and four stubby legs gave him a bunching, loping gate, and his back kept bumping the bottom of the bag. Perhaps *little* wasn't the right term for him anymore. He was almost three feet long and half as tall with his wings closed. When he'd first come to live with me, he'd been small enough to hold. If I didn't stunt him and he kept growing at a normal rate, he'd reach over six feet long.

"Want to make any predictions?" I asked.

"The gargoyle pendants will be sold out, of course," he said. "Especially the ones of me."

"That goes without saying." My lifelong dream of becoming Terra Haven's preeminent quartz artisan had veered off course when I'd discovered I could heal gargoyles. Now, I wouldn't change a thing, but I still enjoyed working with inert quartz, and since being a gargoyle healer provided sporadic income, I made jewelry and sold the items through a local gallery to supplement my earnings.

"Maybe the wind current earrings, too," Oliver said, eyeing the earrings I wore. I wriggled my head to set the earrings in motion, and the gargoyle's bright eyes tracked the movement.

Like all my pieces, the earrings were made out of quartz. These were carnelian—at Oliver's request—and I'd reshaped the sturdy rock to slender, twisting ribbons so light the breeze fluttered them against my neck. Maintaining the structural integrity of the quartz while stretching it so thin took a level of skill that had taken me almost a decade to master. I owed my abilities as a gargoyle healer to those years of dedication, too. I'd worn my hair up so the sun could shine through the slivers of orange rock and catch people's eyes. Since I was the only person in the city escorted everywhere by a gargoyle, I tended to attract attention, and I wasn't above trading on the free advertising.

Oliver wriggled the ruff of rock fur behind his ears, as if he were trying to mimic the movement of my earrings. Laughing at his antics, I completely missed seeing the bundle of elemental energy barreling toward me. The outer air layer hit me like a pillow upside the head, then bounced back and expanded into an oval sheet of fire held together with traces of air and water. Heat radiated from it, and I retreated a step when the golden and red flames reshaped into the perfect likeness of a man's face. He scowled, his bright eyes blazing straight into mine.

"Mika Stillwater," he snapped. "Your services are required on an urgent matter. Come at once."

Seeing the fiery face move was disconcerting enough; hearing the burning mouth bark my name chased a thrill of alarm down my spine. I clutched the handle of my bag tighter and shifted another step back. The disembodied flaming head followed.

I'd seen long-distance projections sent with such precision before, but only as invitations to special events. Given the tension in the man's face, he wasn't summoning me to a social gathering.

I opened my mouth to respond, but he looked to the side at something only he could see, then back at me. This time his gaze rested beyond my shoulder, and I realized it was a captured message, not a projection. I also realized I knew him.

"Your specialty is needed," he growled. The sphere collapsed into an arrow of pure flame. It darted away from me, then spun and pointed left down a side street. It held that position, quivering in place.

"Wasn't that—"

"Full-spectrum guard Velasquez," I said, finishing Oliver's question. *The most powerful fire elemental I'd ever met,* I added silently. You didn't make it into the ranks of the Federal Pentagon Defense, the country's most elite law enforcement organization, unless you were a full spectrum or nearly so. I'd had the good fortune to meet the local FPD full-five squad when I'd rescued Oliver and his siblings, but I hadn't expected to encounter the specialized team again, let alone receive a personal summons from the burly fire elemental.

Velasquez's words sank past my surprise. The only reason he would need me was if a gargoyle was in trouble.

"We need to hurry," I said, yanking my backpack's straps securely over both arms.

"Someone needs us!" Oliver shouted gleefully.

The moment I lurched into motion, the flaming arrow moved. As if attached to me by a stiff tether, it kept exactly the same distance between us even as I picked up my pace to a run. Oliver loped like an enormous inchworm ahead of me, his back arching and straightening with each stride, and he unfurled his wings for short glides to increase his speed.

Watching his increasingly long leaps, I was struck by a feeling of déjà vu. It'd been a race through the streets after a baby gargoyle that had altered the course of my life. Until that moment, I'd been a rather typical earth elemental, with a stable job and a life spent mostly behind a worktable. These days, I did a lot more rushing about, usually racing toward injured gargoyles, and I didn't think I'd ever get used to this nauseating jolt of adrenaline.

Between Oliver's stone feet pounding on the cobblestones, my heavy steps, and the clatter of seed crystals knocking together in my bag, we made enough racket to sound like a rampaging minotaur. People scurried out of our way and gawked from the edges of the road. Several waved and pointed, calling out encouragement. A few actually knew my name.

Our guiding arrow took us through downtown, winding along the least crowded roads. We pounded down wide sidewalks and through narrow alleys, and every time the arrow darted out of sight, I prayed it had stopped just around the corner so I could rest. My lungs and legs burned, and the heavy sack pummeled bruises into my lower back.

I zigzagged past a tavern and a haberdashery, before the narrow street opened into Focal Park. Or it should have. I stumbled to a halt. A massive blue-green ward twice as tall as the nearest building cordoned off the mile-long public park. As far as I could see up and down the street, emergency personnel held focal points of the shimmering ward at regular intervals. I braced my hands on my knees, sucking in oxygen. I'd never seen a ward that huge. It looked like it was designed to keep out an invading army.

And Velasquez's fiery arrow pointed straight at it.

———

A CROWD OF PEOPLE LOITERED OUTSIDE THE PARK'S EARTH ENTRANCE, where guards blockaded the pathway to a tunnel hidden behind the ward. Most of the people must have been herded from the park, judging by the number of blankets, picnic baskets, and various sports equipment they held. Questions rumbled through the displaced citizens, but I didn't hear any answers.

Together Oliver and I wormed through the crowd, and as people noticed Oliver, they cleared a path.

"Is there a sick gargoyle in the park?" someone shouted.

"I've heard gargoyles go berserk. Is that what happened?" another person asked.

I shook my head at the absurd question, but I couldn't take my eyes from the towering ward. What was Velasquez involving me in?

A woman burst through the crowd and grabbed my arm, and I yelped before recognizing Kylie.

"What's that?" she asked, pointing to the burning arrow hovering just this side of the ward. It'd received some nervous looks from the crowd and a few from the guards, too.

"Don't scare me like that," I said. "It's a summons from Velasquez." Kylie knew who the fire elemental was without me needing to remind her. She'd been there when the full-five squad had carted away the man who'd kidnapped Oliver and his siblings. Since then, she'd followed the squad more than once for a story. In fact . . . "Was your rumor scout about the captain?"

Flushing, Kylie crossed her arms defensively. "Yes."

My stomach sank. Kylie had a standing rumor scout patrolling for mention of Captain Grant Monaghan, the air elemental in charge of Velasquez's squad. If the captain was here, the whole squad probably was, which meant the danger level was far greater than a sick gargoyle. The ward more than confirmed it.

"What did he say?" Kylie asked.

"He needs me."

Kylie's eyebrows shot upward. "That's what Mr. Gruffy-Pants himself said?"

"Basically." My footsteps had slowed while I talked, and Oliver butted my palm with a soft whine. The same urgency hummed in my veins, but I couldn't have Kylie following us into danger.

"Wait here," I told Kylie. "I'll tell you everything later. It'll be an exclusive." I winked, then spun toward the tunnel entrance.

"Really? You thought that'd work?" Kylie fell into step on the other side of Oliver. "The people have a right to know what's going on in there, and if Grant is in there, I need to make sure he—ah, that the squad—is okay and . . . acting in the best interest of the citizens. A government that keeps secrets from the people is a corrupt government."

Her slipup was more telling than her ongoing protests about democracy and the balancing power of the press.

"Fine," I hissed as we approached the guards posted at the park entrance. The burning arrow hadn't moved from where it pressed an inch away from the ward, crushing my meager hope that Velasquez stood on this side of the ward.

"The park is closed," a tall woman in uniform said.

"I see that," I said, and Kylie snorted, then turned the sound into a cough. The guard scowled at us both. "I was summoned by FPD Fire Elemental Velasquez." I pointed to the arrow. "I'm a gargoyle healer, and he said I'm needed." I added a point toward Oliver, in case she'd missed the presence of the excited stone dragon who pranced between Kylie and me.

"And I'm her assistant," Kylie said. I wanted to protest, but I knew how much her career meant to her, and there was obviously a story on the other side of this magical curtain. Plus I was beginning to suspect her crush on Captain Monaghan might have developed into something more, so I kept my mouth shut and tried not to fidget.

The guard looped a bubble of air around the burning arrow and yanked it to us. She probed the elemental strands, and the message unfurled again. Velasquez's hard expression glared at the guard this time as he called me to his side without a single *please* or an ounce of deference in his tone.

When the message reverted to an arrow of flame, the guard released it and gestured for her companions to let us pass. Oliver trundled ahead with Kylie close beside him, but my footsteps lagged. As long as I remained on this side of the ward, I was safe.

But a gargoyle wasn't.

I hurried to catch up with Kylie and Oliver.

2

Kylie stepped through the ward first, and I jumped to the side, startled, when threads of air anchored to her ears unraveled and slid down the smooth blue-green sheet of the ward, followed by a shimmer of fire and water from her linen shirt. The elements dissipated once they came untethered from her body and clothing.

"Hey!" Kylie protested, out of sight on the other side of the ward.

I pushed through the ward, and my scalp tingled, but otherwise I felt nothing more than a slight pressure.

"It took me ten minutes to perfect that antiwrinkle weave," Kylie complained, glaring at the ward with her hands on her hips. This close, the shimmery blue-green wall seemed to stretch all the way to the puffy white clouds. "No wonder I couldn't pick up any sounds from the park. This is criminal. The government keeping secrets from the public is reprehensible."

I patted my head. When I'd pulled my hair back in a ponytail, I'd wrapped my head in a twist of air to keep flyaways from escaping into a frizzy mess. The ward had sluiced the infinitesimal magic from me, which meant it was a two-way barrier. It was the kind of ward I'd expect in a holding cell at a guard station, not encasing the enormous public park.

I turned my back to the ward. A steep rocky bank rose in front of us with only a sliver of sky visible between the tunnel entrance and the ward. The long tunnel carved through the hill normally had plenty of ambient light reflected from both ends along a series of strategically placed mirrors, but with the ward blocking the sunlight on our side, the mouth of the tunnel gaped black and foreboding.

Oliver loped into the darkness, the echoes of his footsteps creating a dozen phantom gargoyles.

I grabbed fire energy, formed a small glowball, and followed him. Kylie trotted to catch up, sending three small glowballs ahead of us. When no monsters jumped out of the darkness, I stepped up my pace to a jog. Seed crystals and books battered my back.

"What was all that around your ear?" I asked Kylie.

"Trade secrets."

"They looked an awful lot like modified rumor scouts. How many ways do you have to spy on people?"

"Shh." Kylie glanced over her shoulder. The acoustics of the tunnel might have carried our voices to the guards on the other side of the ward if not for the cacophony Oliver created. Kylie must have come to the same conclusion, because she said, "Being a journalist is as much about finding a story as it is about writing it. How am I supposed to know where the stories are if I haven't got feelers in the field?"

"Feelers? Are you stalking more than Captain Monaghan?"

"I don't stalk anyone."

"Right. You're my assistant."

"Exactly." She beamed.

"In that case, help me out." I ducked out of the straps of my bag and thrust it toward Kylie. Since she had insisted on coming along, I didn't feel bad letting her take the burden. Not that it was a burden to her. With speed I envied, Kylie layered a net of air and settled the bag on top of it. Air was her element, and the bag floated obediently at her side without her having to hold the straps.

Oliver waited at the tunnel's exit, and I released my glowball when I caught up with him, squinting against the bright sunlight as I scanned the grounds. Somewhere ahead of us lay a danger great enough to ward off the park and call in the FPD. I didn't want to rush in blindly.

Oliver had no such caution and launched into the sky. I ducked aside to avoid the back draft from his wings and gathered a wad of raw magic. I had no idea what I'd do with it, but I felt better holding it.

A soft breeze fluttered my ponytail, pulling the coolness of the tunnel across the back of my neck. On any other warm, sunny day, the large granite boulders and tall rock plateaus dotting the sloped hill in front of us would have been crowded with sunbathers of every species.

"This is creepy," Kylie whispered.

I agreed. I scanned the horizon from our vantage at the top of the earth section, visually tracing the massive ward that could have wrapped thirty city blocks with room to spare. They'd even run the ward through Lincoln River to our left, where it edged the water section of the pentagon-shaped park. Birds flitted through the canopy of a cluster of oaks nearby, chattering to themselves. A few squirrels scurried across the short grass. If it weren't for the lack of people and the daunting ward, I would have said nothing was wrong. No bolts of lightning pierced the sky. No horrors leapt from the rocks above us.

"What now?" I asked, stepping clear of the tunnel to check on Oliver.

A fiery arrow blossomed in the air a foot in front of me. I skittered backward and lashed out wildly with raw water and earth to counter the flames. My spastic defense missed the arrow by several feet and collapsed ineffectively on itself. The arrow floated down the hill, then froze in place, pointing the way.

A flush crept up my cheeks. We weren't under attack, and if we had been, my high-strung reaction would have been worthless.

"I guess we follow that," Kylie said, graciously not commenting on my bungled magic.

"Right." Not making eye contact, I jogged toward the arrow, unsurprised when it moved ahead of me on an invisible tether. I dodged tall pillars of rocks and leapt across the smaller gaps between the wide, smooth boulders. Without the burden of my heavy bag, I'd gotten my second wind and I practically flew down the slope. Kylie followed close on my heels, having no problem maintaining her air basket while running.

I scanned the park as I ran. The loudest sounds came from the right, where heavy reed wind chimes were scattered throughout the sculptures in the air section. The coal beds and shallow fire pits between the rock slope and air section were empty and quiet. Across the park, the botanical gardens twined up a slope above long grass sports fields. A small army could have hidden among the dense foliage and groves of trees, but only if they moved soundlessly.

The whole park naturally sloped to the left toward the streams and rowing ponds of the water section that fed into Lincoln River, but the arrow cut right, following a sand pathway that looped around the tiered rock gardens at the bottom of the earth section.

"I see them," Oliver shouted, diving haphazardly toward us. He flared his wings to cut his dive a few seconds too late and plowed furrows into the earth with all four feet. "They're in the center of the park. Hurry."

I pushed into a sprint. It'd taken us almost twenty minutes to reach the park. A lot could happen in that amount of time, especially to a sick gargoyle. Yet despite craning my neck to peer in every direction, I didn't see a cause for alarm, not even when I pounded up the slope to the heart of the park over a half mile from the tunnel and found the entire full-five squad.

The center of the park mirrored the outer boundaries in a smaller pentagon, this one marble, with a pentagram etched into it and the deep grooves coated with smooth glass. Centered on a ten-foot-tall plateau and ringed in sycamore trees and pillars of granite, the pentagram was used in elaborate and powerful spells, and I expected to find the captain and his squad arrayed at their respective focal points, deep in some massive weave of magic, fighting a colossal and scary enemy. Instead, they clustered to the side around a gargoyle standing in the shade of a sycamore.

Clutching a cramp in my side, I trotted across the pentagram toward the gargoyle. He stood frozen, elemental magic swirling around him, and a flashback to finding Oliver and his siblings paralyzed in life-draining traps jolted fresh alarm through me. A complex shield swirled around the trap, but someone blocked my line of sight before I could see more. Blinking, I took in the whole scene.

I didn't know anyone's first name but Captain Monaghan's—thanks to Kylie's obsession with him—but I remembered all their faces. Marciano loomed a head taller than everyone else, close to seven feet tall, as if his body had grown to mimic the trees of his element. He stood next to a slender redhead, the water elemental Winnigan, and they maintained the shield I'd caught a glimpse of. The captain had shifted closer to Seradon to study something she pointed to, and it was his broad chest and shoulders blocking my view. The man was intimidatingly large, which I supposed was useful in his profession, if aggravating right now. I might have mistaken the sturdy earth elemental beside him for a man, with her short brown hair and tall, muscled body, but next to the captain, Seradon almost looked petite.

"We're going to have to do this without her," the captain said. "We can't wait any longer."

"She's here." Velasquez stood a little apart, arms crossed over his thick chest. Everyone in the squad was in prime physical condition, but he looked like he could pick up the full-grown gargoyle in front of them and not break a sweat. His dark blue eyes shifted to track Oliver, who had veered wide around the pentagram and then rushed to the shielded gargoyle. Velasquez stepped in front of the charging stone dragon, and Oliver scrambled to stop without crashing into him, flapping his wings to counter his forward momentum.

I didn't hear what Velasquez said to Oliver because the captain and Seradon had turned to face me, and the weight of their combined gazes slowed my steps.

"Perfect timing," Seradon said with a friendly smile.

Velasquez's guiding arrow dove toward the shielded gargoyle. It flared wide and bubbled into a solid ball of flame, expanding in a flash. Seradon ducked to avoid being engulfed. Velasquez grabbed the wildly pulsing magic and slashed it apart. The arrow winked out of existence with a puff of smoke.

"Yep, not a moment too soon," Seradon said.

I stared. That wasn't how magic worked. A weave didn't morph into something else, and it didn't expand without added fuel.

"What's going on?" I asked.

"See for yourself," Seradon said, gesturing for me to examine the gargoyle.

I checked his face first, and his lifeless eyes ratcheted my tension.

That's just how gargoyles' eyes look when they're unconscious, I reminded myself, taking no comfort from the thought.

He had the body of an earthy brown jasper marmot, though far larger than the mammal counterpart ever grew. Standing on his back feet, he nearly looked me in the eye, and the reindeer antlers arching from behind his little ears stretched two feet above my head. Enormous wings draped his back, falling to curve against the earth behind his feet. Blue dumortierite tipped his feathers and antlers.

I paced around him, checking his body visually when all I wanted to do was get my magic into him. At one time, he'd been beautiful, but now pockmarks and erosion marred his hide, a sign of poor nutrition. Terra Haven had no shortage of the quartz loam all gargoyles needed in addition to a steady diet of magic, but something had prevented this gargoyle from getting a good meal.

I suspected it was the massive contraption encasing him. The shield warped the view, but I could make out oblong loops of wicker, metal, glass, alabaster—and feathers?—evenly spaced around the gargoyle and pressed so tightly to the length of his body that they bent and met above his head. Elements twisted along the loops and filled the empty space, but the ward distorted the details.

"Who let *you* in here?" Captain Monaghan barked, and I jumped. The imposing air elemental wasn't looking at me, though.

Kylie planted her hands on her hips and lifted her chin. She stood a head shorter than the captain, but she made it seem like they looked eye to eye. "The constitution."

Grant snorted. "You're stalking me."

"Wow. Carting around that massive ego must be a burden."

"How did you know where to find me?"

"Must have been the flaming arrow."

Grant narrowed his dark brown eyes, his face a thundercloud. I'd have taken a step back, but Kylie dismissed him, turning to face the gargoyle.

"How long's this . . . thing been on the gargoyle?" She leaned close to the shield, squinting at the magic flowing inside.

Grant grabbed her by her elbows, lifted her off her feet, and deposited her several paces behind us next to a slouched woman I hadn't noticed. "Stay here. Don't interrupt," he ordered.

Kylie's eyes bulged and she opened her mouth, but Grant had already turned away. She settled for crossing her arms and glaring at his back for all of a second before crouching beside the woman. The stranger slouched with her elbows on her bent knees and her head in her hands, rocking herself. Long black hair hid her face, and she flinched when Kylie touched her arm.

"I still say Mika shouldn't be here," Marciano said, his deep voice a gentle rumble. He didn't look away from the shield when he spoke. "She's going to get hurt."

"This is going to require a delicate touch, especially for the gargoyle," Seradon said. She watched the captain instead of the wood elemental. "Mika's a gargoyle healer and she has incredible strength in her specialty with quartz. You've seen her work. She can do things I can't. We need her."

In desperation, I'd once created a trap spun like a web through hundreds of pieces of quartz. My life and the lives of five gargoyles had depended on making the trap hold until the FPD arrived, so I'd put everything I had into it. Seradon had been impressed with my use of quartz—more so than I realized.

"That was a one-time thing," I said. "I haven't done anything that complex since."

"Well, you're about to. That damn contraption is fused to the gargoyle."

Fused? I bent to get a better view. There, on the gargoyle's neck, a rod of quartz had been grafted into the jasper fur, and both ends of the metal loop fed into the quartz. I watched, horrified, as a surge of raw elemental magic speared into the gargoyle, then retracted twice as strong, flowing through the quartz implant and circling the metal loop.

No wonder the gargoyle looked so terrible: The bizarre contraption was sucking out his life!

I pushed closer, only to be brought up short by Velasquez. He'd grabbed my bicep in an iron fist, preventing me from smacking into the squad's shield.

"Careful," he said.

"What are you waiting for?" When Velasquez didn't answer me, I spun to face the captain, breaking the fire elemental's grip on my arm. "We need to get that . . . that *thing* off the gargoyle."

"You need to understand what we're working against," Seradon said. "Elsa calls it a 'purifier.'"

"Elsa?"

Seradon glanced at the dark-haired woman on the ground. She'd stopped rocking and was talking quietly with Kylie. "It's supposed to separate the elements into their purest forms," Seradon continued. "It's her grand plan to manually create the magical enhancement of a gargoyle."

"That's impossible." Gargoyles were unique in their ability to enhance magic in others. With a boost from a gargoyle, a person could more than double the amount of magic they could wield. No artificial source or man-made contraption could replicate it. "Even if it were possible, what's it doing *feeding* off this gargoyle?"

"It turns out that to mimic a gargoyle's enhancement, she needed a gargoyle as a power source."

Before I could ask why Elsa wasn't in null bands and on her way to the nearest guard station, Seradon continued.

"If that wasn't bad enough, her idea of 'purifying' the elements is to rip them apart—polarize them into segregated sections—to make each stronger."

"What do you mean?" No matter the strength, the elements always coexisted.

"Look here. And here." Velasquez gestured around the gargoyle. "The *purifier*"—he spat the word—"isn't letting the elements touch inside the loops."

I stared at the end of the wicker loop as it sucked a pulse of magic from the gargoyle, draining its life one surge at a time. My fists clenched. Dragging my gaze from the horrific implant, I squinted at the space between the wicker and feather loops. Now that I knew what to look for beneath the elements in the ward, it didn't take me long to make out the raw wood energy eddying in complete isolation. I checked the space between the feather and glass loops. A funnel of air whipped through the tight space and buffeted the inside of Marciano and Winnigan's shield.

The polarized magic, as Seradon had labeled it, shouldn't have remained confined in between the segregated sections. The looping objects hooked into the gargoyle weren't solid; they were fragile-looking bands. Yet the magic reacted to them as if they were impenetrable walls. The only logic the two sections of the contraption followed was the most basic one: wood fed air. Every time a fresh surge of magic siphoned from the gargoyle to feed the wood section, the pocket of pure air also grew stronger, proving some interaction occurred between the two sections.

I moved with Velasquez, circling the gargoyle. Oliver paced at my heels, a low rumbling sound close to a growl vibrating in his throat. The pattern repeated all the way around the trapped gargoyle. The polarized elements each fed the next in a constructive cycle: wood strengthening air, air strengthening fire, fire strengthening earth, earth strengthening water, and water strengthening wood. The diabolical design ensured that the magic bled from the gargoyle perpetually strengthened the purifier.

As if having his life stolen in torturous increments wasn't enough, being bombarded by the divided magic had to be wrecking the gargoyle's internal systems. No wonder he was unconscious.

"How long has the gargoyle been trapped?" I asked. Judging by the pockmarks along his body, I'd have guessed months, but someone would have noticed the purifier at work long before now if that were the case. If it could do this much damage in a few minutes or hours, we were wasting precious seconds.

With a choked cry, Kylie stumbled back from Elsa and caught herself against a granite column. "She's got no magic," she blurted out. "I think Elsa is fried."

"Probably for life," Velasquez agreed. No sympathy registered in his tone.

A chill ran down my arms. Being able to see the elements and not touch them, to never again be able to use magic—I'd rather be dead than burned out.

"From what we can tell, she did it to herself when she hammered the last quartz nail into the gargoyle and activated it," Seradon said, her voice as flat as Velasquez's. "We were contacted when a concerned citizen saw the magic backlash."

Crap. This purifier was more dangerous than it looked, and it looked plenty sinister. "What are you waiting for? Free the gargoyle so I can get to work."

"That's the problem," Seradon said. "I can't remove the purifier without killing the gargoyle. I need you to do it."

"Me?" I squeaked. The last person who had worked on this contraption had been nullified. *Probably for life.* What made Seradon think I could succeed where she couldn't? She was an FPD squad member and a full spectrum, strong in earth *and* the other four elements. I was a gargoyle healer, a midlevel earth elemental at best. "I can heal the gargoyle once he's free"—I hoped—"but destroy this? I couldn't."

Oliver whined and brushed his cool, glass-smooth head against my palm. I swallowed hard.

"Next to Seradon, you're the person with the best chance," Velasquez said.

Startled, I met his gaze. I hadn't expected encouragement, however paltry, from the stoic fire elemental.

"You wouldn't be dismantling it all on your own, either, only the parts connected to the gargoyle," Seradon said.

What else was there? Once the purifier wasn't feeding on the gargoyle, it should collapse. If it were only a matter of removing the quartz from the gargoyle, I wouldn't hesitate. But I didn't need to see the weave around the loops to know it was far more complex than anything I'd encountered before.

"If she doesn't feel like she can do it, she shouldn't," the captain said. "One trick doesn't make her a quartz savant. The last thing this quake-storm needs is a rookie with limited pentacle potential and questionable linking skills."

"Hey!" Kylie protested. "Mika can do this." She marched into Grant's personal space, as if she could convince him through intimidation—as if she could intimidate him at all. "She's a *gargoyle healer*. It's in her blood."

The captain's shot at my limited elemental abilities stung my pride. I'd spent a lifetime perfecting my skills with quartz to prove I could compete with full spectrums in my field, and I'd done it. I could manipulate and refine quartz into creations so delicate they looked like spun sugar. I could heal the complex living quartz systems of gargoyles.

But spinning quartz or patching a gargoyle was a long way from practicing combat magic against a powerful weave that had nullified its creator, especially with a gargoyle's life on the line.

Seradon ignored Kylie's outburst and spoke to me. "This monstrosity is dangerous and getting more so—"

"Definitely getting more so," Winnigan said, her voice strained.

"Dormant or not, the gargoyle can't withstand much more of this," Seradon continued. "I'll back you up, but you should lead the magic. You're the healer."

"She said no," Grant said, turning away from Kylie's glare.

"She's scared," Velasquez said.

I broke my stare with the gargoyle's dead eyes to look at him. He held my gaze while continuing to speak as if I couldn't hear him. "Give her a second to warm up her courage."

He winked.

I blinked and looked away. Fear clogged my throat. *Nullified.* No healer had ever cured nullification. If I tried and failed, my ability to use magic could be permanently amputated.

"Captain, I need to be free to help with the shield," Seradon said. "If this thing unravels—"

"No. No," Elsa moaned, rocking faster. Kylie took a step toward her but stopped when Elsa looked up. Tears streaked the inventor's face, and her eyes darted wildly and unfocused.

"You're wrong! You're all wrong." Elsa burst to her feet and rushed the captain. He thrust Kylie behind him before catching the wild-eyed inventor and holding her at arm's length.

I touched Kylie's arm and pulled her farther to safety.

"If I could just..." Elsa wiggled her fingers, then clenched them into fists when nothing happened. Contempt twisted her features. "You're useless. You're all *useless*! Full spectrums don't deserve the power they have. They don't deserve to be the only people gargoyles favor. Power should be distributed by intelligence, not birth and not based on the decision of an *animal* with a rock for a brain. My purifier was going to fix it all and you'd have nothing to be so sparking *arrogant* about." Elsa included me in her scathing look, lumping me in with the FPD squad. "Can't you idiots see? You're wasting time. You can't contain it. You have to crush it. Now, before it kills us all. I tried. But I . . . but I . . ." Elsa wiggled her fingers again and a laugh more sob than mirth crumpled her.

The captain released her, his face a study of neutrality. "Someone needs to get her out of here."

"You can do this, Mika," Kylie whispered. "This gargoyle needs you."

Doubt ate at my stomach lining even as I longed to help the stone-still gargoyle. He had to be under enormous strain, and the longer we talked, the worse he faired.

"If we suppress the magic while that invention is embedded in the gargoyle, he'll die," Seradon said, shaking her head. "We can't—"

"You can. *You have to.*" Elsa clutched the front of Grant's uniform, her eyes feverish. She might have tried to shake him, but he didn't budge. "It's ripping the elements apart—it'll rip apart the city—and the gargoyle is the problem. I wouldn't be . . . be . . . I would be whole if the gargoyle wasn't broken. It's not moderating its boost. You have to snuff out the gargoyle to break the purifier or we'll all die."

Broken. Not *sick.* Not *injured.* Broken. Like the gargoyle was a tool, not a living creature.

Fury bubbled through my blood. I didn't know how Elsa had convinced or trapped the gargoyle into her horrifying machine, but it was clear she saw him only as a means to an end. It was the curse of gargoyles: Their giving nature made them the targets of greedy people who had no qualms about using and abusing them for a nonconsensual magic boost. That Elsa had tortured the gargoyle in her quest to mimic his ability to enhance magic only made it worse. She wanted to steal one of the facets of his very nature, and she thought nothing of killing him in the process.

Grant pried Elsa's fingers from his shirt and I shoved in between them, pushing Elsa back with my wrath.

"You created this disaster. You drilled your experiment into the *flesh* of a living creature, and you're blaming the *gargoyle*? You deserve to be nullified."

I spat my final words at the cowering woman and listened to them fade in the ensuing silence.

"They're gone. They're all gone," Elsa moaned. Her tears morphed into full-body sobs and she crumpled to the ground. I turned away.

Oliver reared up on his hind legs, flaring his wings and hissing at Elsa. I patted his head.

"We're not letting this gargoyle die because she's afraid." *Or because I am.*

Anger helped counter some of my fear. The gargoyles needed someone they could depend on to help them. I'd been passing myself off as a gargoyle healer; I couldn't turn aside now when things got dangerous. If Seradon thought I had a better chance of saving the marmot's life than she did, I had to try.

I looked up, expecting censure. Grant, Seradon, and Velasquez watched me approvingly. Kylie had her "I told you so" expression firmly in place when she met Grant's eyes.

"See? She got her courage all warmed up," Velasquez said.

3

"Okay. We'll let Mika give it a try," Grant said.

"Excellent idea, sir," Seradon said, earning a flat look from the captain.

I fisted the hem of my shirt in my shaking fingers to hide them. This was the right decision. I might not be the strongest elemental, but I was strong where it mattered. I was a gargoyle healer.

For now. If I get burned out, I won't be healing anyone, my traitorous subconscious whispered.

"Get up," the captain said, half lifting Elsa to her feet. He bound her hands behind her back with tight null bands. The spell in the ropes was redundant, but they still functioned as strong restraints. Elsa slumped forward, her long dark hair hanging in curtains on either side of her face. "Kylie Grayson, you will escort Elsa to the ward. I want her in the custody of the city guards."

"But—"

"And you *will* stay on the other side of the ward," Grant said, the full command of an FPD captain in his tone. "I'm not taking the chance of you distracting Mika."

Kylie's spine snapped straight, but rather than argue, she looked to me. I read the question in her expression: If I wanted her to, she'd go against Grant's orders and remain. I shook my head. As wonderful as it'd be to have her supportive presence, she wouldn't be able to do anything. I'd breathe easier knowing she was safe on the other side of the massive ward.

"Fine. Good luck, Mika." Kylie gave Oliver a quick pat and whispered something to him, then reached for Elsa.

"You're letting me go?" Elsa asked, bewildered.

"You're under arrest, but you can't stay here."

"Thank the gods." She fled. With her arms imprisoned behind her back, Elsa couldn't balance well, but that didn't slow her down. Kylie scrambled to catch up.

A fresh wave of icy trepidation slid down my body.

"Don't even think about spying," Grant called after Kylie. "No listening weaves are going to penetrate that ward."

"You know, this *is* kind of scary," Velasquez said to me. He peered at the divided magic inside the shield. "She was right. If the purifier gets loose, it'll rearrange the very laws of magic itself."

I glanced at his expression. His tone was matter-of-fact, without a hint of the terror his words evoked in me. Like the others in the squad, he looked focused, as if this level of danger was an everyday challenge. Maybe for them it was.

"You'll need to link with us—to get through our shield and for your safety," Seradon said.

Velasquez shifted to my left and Grant took a position to Seradon's right. Marciano and Winnigan moved so the squad was evenly spaced around the shield and gargoyle. Oliver launched into the air, flapping heavily to the rock pillar behind Grant where he could oversee everything. I glanced back the way Kylie had departed. She and Elsa were out of sight. In the enormous park, it was just the full-five squad, one half-grown gargoyle, a trapped gargoyle, and a very out-of-place midlevel earth elemental.

"Have you ever linked with five full spectrums before?" Seradon asked.

"No." Powerful people didn't tend to include midlevel people like me in their group spells.

"There's nothing special to it." Seradon squared off in front of me and I had to look up to meet her brown eyes. She smiled encouragingly, but I didn't try to smile back—fear had frozen my features. "Just like any other link, open yourself to equal parts of every element, then feed it to me. I'll pull you into the link and help you stabilize yourself."

"Okay." It sounded simple. I gathered earth, air, fire, wood, and water in equal amounts. My ability to manipulate air and water was limited, not even midlevel, which meant I barely held any wood, earth, and fire when I matched up their levels. I eased this thimble of power into Seradon, fidgeting with embarrassment. Seradon's stream of elemental energy merged into mine, linking us with a subtle hook.

"Good. Smooth," Seradon murmured.

The world dropped open inside me as magic flooded into me. I'd expected the link to feel like a gargoyle's enhancement. Their natural boost increased my own elemental strengths, giving me access to more magic, but this was so much more.

Five magical signatures pressed against the periphery of my awareness, but I couldn't pinpoint an individual. The link also had shape and intent. Elemental layers wrapped and wove through each other to create the shield, and I could see every strand and how it had been assembled. The purifier beat against the underside of the shield, and in noticing the tension in the shield, I became aware of the strain in the link. Holding the shield taxed the squad—or some of them. I couldn't tell if it was only Winnigan and Marciano becoming fatigued or all of them.

Magic blossomed anew inside me, and I recognized it this time. Oliver had joined us, enhancing the magic in our link. Awed by the amount of power available to me, it wasn't until Seradon gripped my elbow that I remembered I had a body. Oliver trilled, and I rediscovered my hearing. The young gargoyle's carnelian eyes glowed like small suns, and with his wings flared and his posture flexed with his intent focus, he looked majestic. Through the link, he cycled more magic than he'd access if he spent a week atop the library. If he hadn't been balanced earlier, he would be after this.

"It's disorienting the first time," Seradon said. I pivoted to look at her, and the park blurred in my vision. Inside the link, someone poured water into the cracks in the shield, shoring up weak points. Magic moved through me—pulled through me—without me using it, and the sensation spiraled my focus inward.

"I'd like to give you more time to get adjusted, but we need to work fast."

I nodded to show I understood, then closed my eyes when the horizon moved with my head.

"I'm going to pull you through the shield," the earth elemental continued. She'd taken my hand at some point, and her fingers tightened on mine. I squeezed back.

Somehow, Seradon collected *me* from the linked energy. With a feeling like she tugged the elements through me, she gathered my contribution and dipped it through the shield.

"I'll use the purifier's pathway to get us to the gargoyle," Seradon said. "Then it's up to you once we reach the quartz."

I opened my eyes. I could feel myself—or rather, my magic—resting on the underside of the shield, buffeted by the pounding pressure of the polarized water element, but the sensation was distant. Seradon was buffering me.

She had aligned us with a thin metal strip defining the line between the polarized water and earth elements, and I got my first good look at the complexity of the purifier. A tangle of helixes so dense they looked braided spiraled around the metal, each made of one strand of earth and one strand of water. Hundreds of tiny fingers of earth connected each helix, all of them feeding magic from the polarized earth section into the strands of water, strengthening them. In turn, the water strands spun pure water into the polarized section on the left.

I'd never seen anything like it, especially not the way the helixes cascaded down the empty center of the metal loop, maintaining a perfect wall between the two polarized elements. On the left, the spinning water strands kept the water from flowing back into the earth section. On the right, the earth strands absorbed energy from the polarized earth section and fed it through the helixes into the water.

Seradon used a scissor of air and wood to sever the helixes atop the metal and provide a clear path for us. Raw water element battered her weaves from one side, earth on the other, but they couldn't counter her destructive magic, not on the scale she wielded through the link. Faster than I would have thought possible, she tore apart the magic surrounding the thin metal and unplugged it from quartz.

Success! If we could break through all the loops and the magic that wrapped them as easily, we could take the power out of this contraption in no time.

It almost seemed like the marmot was helping or fighting back, too. A thin inner bubble of normal, coexisting elements rested between the gargoyle's pockmarked skin and the polarized energy.

Behind us, the helixes divided and duplicated, reweaving a tangled braid along the metal. Before today, I would have said with complete conviction that the elements required a person or creature to shape them into a pattern. Destroyed weaves dissipated; they didn't reconstruct a previous pattern—only this one just had.

"How is that possible?"

"Elsa might be able to explain it," Seradon said. "All I need to know is it rebuilds itself and it's faster than the five of us could counter, thanks to the fuel source of the gargoyle. That's partly why we need to disconnect it."

Of course. If it had been easy, the squad would have taken care of the problem already.

"Your turn," she said. "Cut off the purifier from the gargoyle, and we'll deal with the rest."

She made it sound almost easy.

I gathered a balance of elements, and magic swamped me, feeding from five incredibly powerful people and enhanced by Oliver. Flailing, I fought for control.

"Relax," Seradon said. "Let it go and try again."

With a gasp, I released the elements. Instantly, I was back to being a part of the link, not drowning in it. I took a deep breath, then teased a minuscule balance of elements from the link. A rush of magic responded, nearly as much as I could wield when enhanced by a gargoyle but still a manageable amount.

I probed the quartz implant. Elsa had drilled the ragged, two-inch hole with a blade of elemental wood, then wedged a sharp quartz crystal into the wound, fusing the rock to the gargoyle's muscles and flesh with crude bridges of earth. She hadn't even tuned the earth element to quartz, let alone to the specific resonance of the gargoyle's jasper body. She had anchored her doomed purifier to the gargoyle the way a person might pound stakes of a tent into the ground, as if the gargoyle had no more feeling than the soil. I gritted my teeth. Being nullified was too good a fate for Elsa.

I tuned my elemental bundle to resonate with the gargoyle by rote, narrowed the amount I held to a gentle stream, and slid a feeler into the marmot.

Ice-hard water blocked me, and my magic cut into the gargoyle when it should have penetrated painlessly. Grabbing more water, I matched my feeler to the unbalanced energies in the marmot. Pulses of pain, steady as a heartbeat, pounded into my brain through my connection to the gargoyle. I didn't have to open my eyes to know the pain strobed in rhythm with the purifier's energy as it drove polarized elements into the gargoyle and sucked out raw, enhancing magic.

I slid deeper into the gargoyle, then scrambled to reconfigure the elements I held to balance with the marmot, pulling in more wood and letting go of a lot of earth. This wasn't natural. A gargoyle should be the same resonance throughout. When I realized what it meant, my eyes popped open.

"He's polarizing on the inside," I said.

Seradon's sympathetic brown eyes slid from the gargoyle to me. "I know."

"I don't feel him fighting back. I thought he was because he's kept the magic near his skin normal, but inside it's like he's . . ." *Dead.* I didn't want to say it out loud, not within the marmot's hearing.

"While he's dormant, I don't think he can fight."

"How did Elsa do this to him?"

"Greed makes people do horrible things."

That wasn't what I meant. I wanted to know how she'd made the gargoyle "dormant" in the first place, but now wasn't the time for a drawn-out conversation. The gargoyle felt fragile. The divided energy was eroding his innards, and if he took much more abuse, he'd be torn apart from the inside out in a cruel and agonizingly slow death.

Taking a deep breath, I closed my eyes and retracted my elemental feeler from the gargoyle back to the quartz implant. It was time to prove myself worthy of my title.

I couldn't disconnect the thick bands of earth element welding the quartz to the gargoyle without hurting him, so I opted for quick slices of wood.

Magic oozed from the fresh cuts, and tendrils of helixes stretched toward the fresh wounds like magical leeches. I hacked them away and layered patches across the cuts, tuning my magic to the marmot's current balance on the inside and to strong jasper quartz on the outside, effectively sealing the cuts.

I would have preferred to use the crystal to pack the wound, reshaping it as I might a seed crystal into quartz the marmot's body could eventually absorb, but the impurities in the crystal made that impossible. If I'd been able to reach it, I would have extracted the foreign quartz with my fingers, but since the shield and purifier wouldn't let me physically close to the gargoyle, I had to remove it using the elements. I considered a burst of air to push it from the open wound, but I didn't want to cause the gargoyle additional pain from the backlash of pressure. I also didn't have time for any finesse. I grabbed the quartz crystal where it was attached to the metal loop of the purifier and reshaped the rock into a blunt knob too large to fit back into the gargoyle's wound.

I was admiring my handiwork when the purifier's weave reknit around the quartz and arced from the knob into the hole drilled into the gargoyle's neck. Raw magic pulsed out of the gargoyle through quartz embedded on the other side of his neck.

"No!" I sliced through the purifier's weave, tearing it apart all the way around the metal loop. The moment I stopped, the weave started to regrow. I switched strategies and attacked the wall of helixes suspended inside the loop. My blades of air and wood sliced a path from the top of the metal circle to the bottom, severing a thousand complex looping strands between the polarized water and earth sections.

The weave should have dissolved. The influx of earth flowing into water through the gap I'd created should have shattered the rest of the elemental wall. Instead, the barrier grew back together into the same pattern as before, and watching the magic rebuild itself made my skin crawl.

"You're making it worse. Concentrate on the gargoyle, Healer," Seradon said.

I jerked my attention back to the gargoyle, heart sinking to find him weaker. I severed the purifier's connection with the gargoyle again and grabbed the quartz knob, flattening it against the metal. It wasn't enough; the pathway was established, making the quartz redundant, and the purifier's weave jumped the gap again. I needed a blockade.

Hoping I could count on the purifier to behave like normal elemental magic, I formed a destructive pentagram, layering the elements to counter each other. I wedged the pentagram into the reshaped quartz and bound it in place with ties of quartz-tuned earth. When the purifier's weave hit the quartz this time, it burrowed into the pentagram, shredding it. Without the presence of all five elements to balance the pentagram, it couldn't withstand the influx of earth and water. I reshaped it, stronger this time in wood and air to counter the disproportional elements; then I grabbed the center of the pentagram and inverted the elements. I'd never tried such a complex maneuver before, yet with the strength of the squad behind my weaves, it was almost easy.

The purifier's energy fell through the center of the pentagram, then curved back to spin through the destructive elements embedded in the quartz. The affluence of energy reinforced the barricade, cycling through the pentagram in a nonstop five-pronged loop that prevented it from jumping the hairbreadth of space between the metal rod and the gargoyle's punctured neck.

"Good thinking. I wouldn't have considered using the quartz like that."

Seradon's voice floated across my consciousness but didn't fully register as I raced for the next quartz implant. With righteous fury, I severed the purifier's weave—this time wood and water from a wicker loop—then sliced through the clumsy earth bars grafting the quartz to the gargoyle. In seconds, I'd flattened the quartz onto the wicker, pulling it from the gargoyle's side in the process. I layered the five elements in a destructive pentagram, embedded it in the quartz, and inverted it, all before the purifier reknit the weave down the length of the wicker. Coating the open wound of the drilled hole with gargoyle-tuned patches took a little longer, as I had to compensate for the variations within the marmot. It wasn't my best work, but it'd hold until the squad could destroy the purifier.

I shifted to the next quartz, only to be brought up short as the magic I'd been using pulled away from me, taking bits and pieces of me with it. I scrabbled with metaphysical fingers to regain control.

"Easy. Hang on," Seradon said, squeezing my fingers until the bones ground together.

My eyes snapped open. The polarized magic fluctuated and dimmed as one of the squad siphoned a chunk of elemental wood through the shield and released it harmlessly into the air. The pressure of the purifier slackened, but the maneuver had weakened the shield's structure, and the squad strained to hold it together, using every scrap of our combined magic.

"I'm going to pull you out for a second."

I gasped as my part of the link flew up the wicker of the purifier, scattering tatters of the self-replicating helixes, then shot into the shield. The pressure of the polarized elements burst through my senses. The separation Seradon had maintained slipped, jerking my awareness to the bombarded shield. Magic dragged from me as someone—Winnigan? Grant?—wove increasingly complex patches, manipulating the elements faster than I would have been able to follow if I hadn't been part of the link. I watched in awe as more than thirty strands around the shield shifted and knotted into discrete patterns—at once. And I'd been impressed with being able to invert a tiny pentagram!

Inside the shield, the elements swirled more volatile than before. The sections I'd capped pulsed with new intensity, vibrating against the shield with increased strength.

"Oh no," I whispered. In protecting the gargoyle, I'd forced the magic to switch directions, and it hammered the shield with heightened ferocity.

"What happens if it breaks the shield?" I asked.

"We don't want to find out. Hold on; we're going back in."

Hold on? To what? I tried to find myself in the vast collective of energy, but it was like trying to find particles of my breath once it mingled with the air. Seradon fortunately had no problem. She scooped me out of the connection and together we slid through the shield, then plowed down a loop of expensive woven phoenix feathers, battering through the purifier's weave of wood and air.

The gargoyle's insides were worse than before, not better. I'd removed the purifier's water and wood anchors, but now magic pulsed uneven bursts into and out of the air, fire, and earth anchors, destabilizing the gargoyle's body with increased speed. The feedback of pain was muted, as distant as the gargoyle's life itself. We were losing him.

I prepared to slice through the earth element, fusing the third quartz crystal to the marmot's neck, only to be abandoned in limbo when the squad pulled magic through me to reinforce the shield again.

"This is bad," Marciano said.

My body floated far away, and having magic drawn from me doubled the sensation. Seradon held us in place this time, but her grip felt tenuous, and if I lost my focus on the quartz, I was afraid I'd be blown apart and trapped in the purifier's mutant weave.

"Can you slow down, Mika?" Grant asked.

"No." Not without sacrificing the gargoyle. "I need to go faster. The gargoyle is being torn apart."

"Do you have to make the purifier stronger?" Velasquez asked, his deep voice strained.

"The blockades are the only way to stop it from feeding off the gargoyle," Seradon said. "She's doing the right thing."

"Then we'll hold it," the captain said.

I didn't want to voice my doubts. They were a full-five squad. They knew far better than me what they were capable of, but it seemed like they could barely maintain the shield on the purifier now. When I blocked the last three links, the strain on them would be enormous, but I wasn't going to waste time arguing.

I delved into the quartz. Power leapt to my bidding again, and in seconds, I disconnected the crude implant, reshaped the quartz, and created and inverted a destructive pentagram, blocking the purifier's third link with the gargoyle. Applying the finishing patches took less tweaking this time; I was getting good at predicting the marmot's imbalance.

The magic available to me through the link squeezed down to a trickle.

"Captain?" Velasquez asked.

I didn't wait for Grant to respond. I dove for the next quartz. The purifier pulsed fire into the gargoyle, and vats of magic shot out of the gargoyle through the only other remaining link. If I cut away one quartz connection, the other would continue to feed polarized magic into the gargoyle. Without an outlet, it would fill the helpless marmot and shred his insides.

"Spin the shield," the captain said, his voice distant. "Set it on a counterpattern."

The shield bounced into a riotous, distracting pattern. I scrambled to reorient on the quartz, the gargoyle, anything to define my individuality. I latched on to the marmot, sinking an elemental balance into him, then jumping to correct the levels of my magic to match the internal structure of the abused gargoyle.

"Give it a destructive layer," Grant said.

"I'm going to break the last two at once," I said, talking over the others. I didn't have the ability to maintain my individuality, divide magic across the gargoyle to the two separate quartz bolts, *and* keep up with their conversation. "I think . . . I think that will cause the purifier to break up."

"That'd be lucky," Velasquez said, his voice close.

I readied the destructive pentagrams, holding them next to the gargoyle where the elemental magic remained in its natural state. The pentagrams slowly grew when they should have remained static, and I realized with fresh horror that the gargoyle was passively feeding its magic to me, to all of us, despite the copious amounts being drained from him by the purifier. I'd been wrong. He wasn't doing anything to fight back or protect himself.

"Now." I pulled on the magic of the link. It responded like taffy, but I demanded more. "I need to do this now." I yanked, and for a second I felt Seradon, then the others beyond her. I think the captain said something, but whether it was encouragement or protest, I didn't hear.

I slammed the pentagrams in place at the same time as I cut the quartz from the gargoyle. With separate strands, I reshaped the quartz into flat barriers and simultaneously shoved wads of jasper-tuned patches into the wounds before pulling the pentagrams through the quartz and inverting them.

The barriers snapped into place, and the world exploded.

4

The concussion tossed me into the air, and I landed on my back, half on top of a boulder. My head snapped against something marginally softer than granite. Blackness swooped through my vision; then my collapsed lungs inflated, and I sucked in a harsh breath. I stared at the sky and listened to my ears ring, the world as fuzzy as the fluffy clouds high above me. Twists of earth and fire canopied above me in a protective dome of magic—one I wasn't holding.

Raw panic jolted through me, and I snatched at the elements, terrified the blast had burned through me and left me nullified, able to see the elements but never work them again. Fire and a smaller amount of air, earth, wood, and water trickled into me along misaligned pathways. I sagged with relief. It wasn't the full amount I could usually draw, but I would heal. I was still a heal—

Oliver!

I jackknifed up—or tried to. The ground shifted beneath my butt and a steel band pinned my torso. I twisted, trying to see what trapped me. Seradon lay beside me, though slightly lower. She blinked groggily at the sky, blood trickling from her nose. I squirmed to try to reach her.

"Easy now," Velasquez said, his deep voice startlingly close. More surprising, I'd felt the rumble of his words against my back. I was lying on top of the fire elemental! How had that happened?

The steel band lifted, and my brain finally put the obvious together: Velasquez had cushioned me and protected me from the blast. The boulder I thought I'd landed on had been his chest.

Above us, the protective shield dissipated. Velasquez helped me roll off him and I pushed to a sitting position, gasping when a fiery jab of pain shot through the top of my right shoulder. Tentatively, I investigated the pain with my fingers, sucking in air through clenched teeth when I encountered a splinter protruding from my skin. I craned my neck to see, setting off a fresh wave of pain.

"Hold still." The two words were the only warning Velasquez gave me before he yanked the splinter free. Groaning, I studied the twisted shard he held up for my inspection. It looked like a frozen ribbon of blood; then I recognized the thin carnelian shape of my earring. I touched my earlobe. The delicate strands had all broken into jagged pieces. I patted at my neck, feeling the wetness of several cuts but no more embedded pieces.

"Did you get cut?" I asked, turning to check Velasquez as I took the back off the earring and let it drop.

"Not from those." He brushed the front of his gray shirt, shedding sparkles of carnelian as he turned to help Seradon. She sat with her head in her hands, elbows on her knees, her posture an eerie echo of Elsa's when I'd first seen her.

"I'll live," she said, blotting blood from her upper lip with the hem of her shirt.

"Look at me," Velasquez said, touching my chin. He knelt in front of me, leaning close, and I hadn't seen him move. His blue eyes filled my vision. They weren't a flat color; rather, they had striations of darker agate and flecks of onyx. Lapis lazuli, I decided, arrested by their unexpected beauty.

The thought snapped my brain back into focus. Worry pinched Velasquez's full lips. With unexpectedly gentle fingers, he pulled the skin down beneath one of my eyes, then the other. Impatiently, I tracked his finger. When he shifted to examine my shoulder, I resumed my search for Oliver.

The blast had thrown us over ten feet beyond the pentagram, into the dirt. The others had been flung farther and were scattered around the pentagram plateau. No one appeared gravely injured, but everyone moved gingerly.

Elements hung heavy in the air, or more precisely, earth shimmered thick enough to give the illusion of being tangible. A wall of fire and earth hung on invisible strings to my right.

The blood drained from my head. It was more than a wall; it was the same barrier I'd seen inside the purifier's loops. Elongated and distorted and arching twice as tall as Grant, hundreds of helixes spun in an interlocking weave to create an impenetrable barrier between the two elements. The wall extended over thirty feet beyond the marmot before dipping down to touch the ground, but the complex braid of helixes that had previously been linked to the loop inside the purifier shot in a straight line toward the horizon. Four other evenly spaced elemental braids speared outward from the marmot like spokes on a wheel, and I didn't need to move to know the magic in between each would look equally dense and singular.

"You'll be fine," Velasquez said. "You're not as fragile as you look."

I wasn't paying attention. I'd spotted Oliver.

He lay in a crumpled heap below the pillar where he'd been perched. I lurched to my feet, catching myself with one hand on the ground when the world dipped and my legs buckled. Pushing back to my feet, I half crawled, half ran to the gargoyle, passing through the purifier's fire-earth and air-fire walls without resistance.

"Oliver!" I fell beside him and slapped a hand to his side, gathering magic to examine him. Air leapt to my call, but the other elements I needed to balance the magic felt as if they existed on the other side of a mountain of sand. "Oliver, come on. Wake up."

Bright red-orange eyes popped open, and Oliver lifted his head. His square jaw fell open in a dragon's smile. I sucked in a full breath, releasing it with a breathy sob of relief. Scooting back, I gave him room to right himself. Together we examined his wings and limbs, equally relieved to find him whole. I tried again to pull the blend of elements necessary to test Oliver's internal health, but once more only air responded.

"How do you feel?" I asked.

"Drained."

"It's no wonder," Seradon said, stopping beside me and wriggling her jaw to pop her ears. "I'd be toast without you. If you ever want to join a squad, you can be part of my team anytime, Oliver."

The half-grown dragon preened. I watched his movements closely, pleased not to see any stiffness or tenderness.

"His extra boost of magic right before the explosion gave me the strength I needed to cocoon us both," Seradon said to me. "The purifier—and we really need a better name for this monstrosity—seared through my shield and drilled into my head like it knew where to look. Without Oliver, we'd both be burned out."

I shuddered. "Thank you."

"Yep, that's what we do." Seradon gave me a gentle pat on the back before striding to Grant's side.

Burned out. My fingers trembled as I tightened my ponytail, and it took a moment for me to process the red sparkles tipping my fingers when I examined them. Carefully, I reached for my left earring. A few shards remained fused to the post and powdery pieces of orange-red quartz clung to my neck and scalp. I used my shirt-sleeve to protect my fingers as I pulled the earring out; then I dropped it to the ground next to the pillar.

"Thank you, too, Oliver. You're amazing."

"Yep, that's what I do." Oliver grinned at his almost perfect imitation of Seradon's inflection. I smiled, feeling my world right itself. One gargoyle safe, one to go.

I rose with a modicum of grace this time, but my legs were wobbly and I braced against the pillar until I felt steady enough to walk. Flexing the fingers of my right hand hurt, and I examined the swelling around my middle finger's second knuckle. Blood oozed from a scrape, but it was coagulating. Considering I could have been nullified, a hurt knuckle seemed trivial.

Pushing away from the pillar, I headed for the marmot. Oliver yelped and stumbled into me, knocking me sideways. With a weird hopping kick, he jetted forward, then spun back toward me.

"What was that?" I rubbed my calf, where his alula had clipped me.

"That hurt!" Oliver pointed to the purifier braid separating the air and fire sections of the expanded bubble of polarized magic. I'd passed through the weave without feeling anything. I reached for the elements to test him, but now only fire responded. Frustrated, I had to rely on Oliver's assurance that the pain had been temporary.

"Okay. Stay here until we get this sorted."

Oliver nodded and curled his tail tight to his body. Hunched, he looked half his normal size, and I wished I'd insisted the young gargoyle wait outside the park, or better yet, at the library where he'd be safe.

I skirted a dirt-churned crater, realizing only when I saw sparkles of carnelian glinting in the indent that the divot was from the impact of Velasquez and me, or more accurately, the impact of Velasquez's body as he shielded me. I had more than Seradon and Oliver to thank for my relatively unharmed state.

From a distance, the marmot looked the same. He stood in the same position on his haunches, wings draped down his back and antlers arching skyward. Scraps of metal, wicker, alabaster, and glass littered the surrounding area and caught in the gargoyle's antlers. The horrific purifier had been reduced to nothing more than loose trash. A breeze lifted shredded phoenix feathers into the air, and I waved a hand in front of my face to keep them out of my eyes.

The elements swirled through an elongated vortex stretching from the marmot's toes up past his antlers. I tilted my head, trying to make sense of the chaotic magic through the dense swirl of fire element. When my brain made the belated connection, I sidestepped into the earth zone to double-check. My heart beat in my ears as I crouched to run a finger through a bright white radial line on the ground. A fine powder of quartz gritted against my fingertip. The explosion had pulverized my five quartz barriers, but perversely my inverted pentagrams had inflated to dwarf both me and the marmot. Worse, they appeared to be working as anchors for the purifier, holding it in place. Not only had I made the purifier explode, but I'd also made it stronger.

Just peachy.

I couldn't tell if the mutated pentagrams rested against the marmot or if the infinitesimal gap remained between the gargoyle and the purifier. At least magic no longer pulsed from the marmot.

I scrabbled for the elements to heal him, and this time earth tumbled into me but nothing else.

I'd worked all the elements right after the blast. Why couldn't I touch more than one at a time now?

Because I wasn't cocooned inside Velasquez's protective ward, I reasoned. He must have trapped the elements inside the shield when he'd created it, before magic polarized around us. That explained why fire had been the strongest element at the time. I'd thought I'd injured the metaphysical pathways in my brain, but standing in the earth section, I could draw on as much earth as normal without strain.

Frustrated, I shoved my hands through the vortex of magic and planted them on the marmot's chest, ignoring the swirling magic pricking my skin with a thousand sharp needles. Again, I felt nothing, but even live gargoyles could be as still as stone and equally as cold to the touch. I needed magic to get inside him. I needed to fix the damage the purifier had caused before it was too late.

Out of options, I held on to earth and refined it down to the thinnest strand of quartz possible. The destructive cycle spinning around my wrist made me clumsy, jolting earth into the tortured gargoyle when I meant to feather it against him. A delicate echo of the marmot's essence pushed back against the foreign intrusion, and I withdrew as gently as possible. His life signs were faint enough to be alarming, but he lived.

I couldn't help him, not with magic like this. I glanced to the horizon. The polarization had to wear off soon. The balanced elements on the outside of this bubble would eat through the divided magic and degrade the purifier's pattern. Until that happened, I had no way to assess the marmot's injuries or right the internal damage the purifier had wrought on the helpless gargoyle.

Yet somehow, the bubble looked larger than it had before.

"He's alive?" Oliver called from where he huddled several feet away.

"Yes, but it's like he's asleep."

"That's because he's dormant," Grant said. The squad convened around us, everyone looking at the marmot.

"A lot of gargoyles do this," Seradon said. "It's like they check out for a while. They still give power, some more freely than gargoyles who are awake, but they don't interact with anyone. They become sort of like quiet statues."

"For how long?" I asked.

Seradon shrugged. "I don't know. You haven't encountered this before?"

I shook my head, feeling like a hypocrite. I should know more about gargoyles than anyone. I was the gargoyle healer, after all.

"This guy's been dormant for years. Probably a decade or two, maybe longer," Grant said.

"He hasn't moved that whole time?" I shared a glance with Oliver. The young gargoyle looked as confused as I felt. The squad seemed to believe the marmot's catatonic state was normal, but I couldn't think of a reason a gargoyle would opt to mimic a statue, passively feeding *everyone* magic in the vicinity. They were usually more picky than that. Plus, gargoyles needed to eat at least a few times a month. "Can he move, if he wants to?"

"I guess so. Being dormant is probably what saved him from being torn apart by the purifier," Seradon said. "Don't fret so much. This is all part of a gargoyle's life cycle."

I frowned and nodded. She sounded confident, but in my healer heart I knew she was wrong. Nothing about the marmot's lifeless state was normal, but it explained his pockmarked skin. I suspected his internal health would have looked poor even before Elsa's interference. It also explained how she'd been able to surgically attach the abominable purifier: The marmot had been helpless to stop her. That hadn't prevented him from feeling the pain of the implants, though.

"Are there more like this? Dormant?" My swollen knuckle protested, and I relaxed my fisted hands.

"A few," Seradon said.

Shame burned in my veins. I'd been concentrating on sick gargoyles who came to me or who contacted me through their chosen families. I hadn't paid any attention to the welfare of the public gargoyles or those who couldn't even speak for themselves. I needed to step up my efforts as a healer. I couldn't leave gargoyles helpless to be preyed upon by psychopaths like Elsa, who saw them as tools and not living creatures.

"This is bad," Winnigan said. She walked around the marmot, eyes on the horizon.

"I'm done messing around," Grant said. "Form up a link."

"The damn thing did its best to burn me out, sir. I'm mud and won't be much use for hours," Seradon said.

Mud? Fresh guilt welled up on a wave of gratitude, and I tried to think of a more adequate way to thank her for saving me from being nullified. "I'm sorry" tumbled out.

Seradon chuckled. "Aww, civilian guilt. That's cute."

Velasquez snorted, but his expression was blank when I looked at him.

"We don't have hours," Grant said.

"Good thing we have Mika. She can take my place."

Grant pinned me with his sharp brown eyes. "It's not ideal but I can make it work."

I wasn't half the earth elemental Seradon was, as the explosion I'd unleashed just proved. With a sinking stomach, I looked around the group. They assessed me with neutral expressions, telling me without words that no one was happy to be stuck with me. I felt acute relief when Grant spoke and everyone shifted their attention to him.

"The polarized magic isn't dissipating on its own. Since the blast, it's gained at least ten feet in every direction. We need to break the constructive pattern."

I hugged my stomach. It hadn't been a trick of my imagination. Even the spokes looked longer, stretching far beyond the dome of polarized magic and disappearing into the park. They didn't need the marmot to feed from any longer; the purifier was self-sustaining and prepared to assimilate the entire city.

"I don't get it," Marciano said. "The purifier should have torn itself apart once it didn't have the gargoyle to feed on."

"I think it might be my fault," I said, waving a hand at the intact inverted pentagrams. Grant had to be regretting allowing Velasquez and Seradon to talk him into letting me save the gargoyle. If not for the flicker of life in the marmot, I'd be regretting it, too.

"Placing blame or feeling guilty won't get us anywhere," Grant said. "We need to—"

The polarized fire section rolled over a lit gas pit. Raw elemental magic roared from the flames, surging into the polarization field. Even from over fifty feet away, the backwash of heat tightened my skin. The influx of energy flared against the seam between fire and earth, built up, then surged through the looping pattern of the stretched helixes, feeding into earth. Earth spewed energy into water, water sloshed into wood, wood shot into air, and the entire polarized bubble bulged outward in a powerful push that covered another five feet in every direction.

"That's going to be a problem," Velasquez said.

I studied the park with fresh eyes. Elemental magic was always strongest around the physical source, and Focal Park had been designed as a place of natural enhancement. Its pentagon shape reflected the five elements, and each section represented a dominant element, all radiating from the center of the park in a natural constructive order. Elsa had aligned her purifier exactly along those lines, so each polarized segment ate through the matching element section of the park.

"That woman couldn't have made a bigger mess if she tried," the captain said, echoing my thoughts.

Air and earth passively fed their polarized sections, but soon the wood section would reach the entrance to the botanical gardens, and a dozen more gas torches and fire pits aligned with the fire field's path. If the polarization fields reacted to those as they had the small fire pit, this bubble of messed-up energy would expand in alarming leaps. Currently the only obstacles in the purifier's way were the smaller pieces of balancing elements in every section—a fountain in the fire section, a wind chime in the earth section—and us.

"If this reaches the river, it could swallow the city," Winnigan said, staring off into the distance where sunlight glinted off Lincoln River directly in the path of the polarized water section.

"Or it could negate it," Velasquez said. "That much water at once could overwhelm everything and cause the whole mess to collapse."

His words gave me hope, but if Winnigan was right and the city's elements divided into five separate sections, Terra Haven would fall apart. Everything from basic housekeeping magic to the complex structural patterns of the city's communication and transportation networks would collapse.

Not to mention the devastation to lives. We were proof that humans could function in the polarized fields, even if magic wasn't working right, but some creatures depended on the blended elements for sustenance. Stuck in this divided energy, gargoyles throughout the city would sicken from the imbalance and be forced to flee the city or die.

"We're not letting it reach the river," Grant said. "We're countering this now. Spread out to your element and link."

The squad traded glances and hustled to their sections. Seradon strode to my side and gave me quiet directions.

"This is different than what we did before, and it's going to hurt. Since you can't access all the elements, the link will have to act as one person. Grab earth and push it to Winnigan, then let Velasquez push fire to you."

Earth element burrowed into me, sharp as shale without another element to buffer it, but no matter how much I drew or how hard I pushed, I couldn't penetrate the barrier between earth and water. The magic I fed into the wall of helixes warped and transformed into water, exiting the barrier in a useless splash. Around the circle, the captain, Marciano, Winnigan, and Velasquez were each haloed in an impressive display of elemental magic, but everyone had the same problem I did. Worse, our efforts fed the purifier, and the bubble pushed outward.

Grant cussed. "Stand on the dividing lines and try again."

We all shifted to the right. Sweat trickled down my neck, stinging my cuts. Keeping my eyes on the marmot, I aligned myself in the middle of the purifier's wall, with polarized fire encasing the right side of my body and earth the left side. The helixes moved harmlessly through me—until I tried to grab an element. I reached for earth first, and magic pounded out of control against my brain. Refining my draw down to a slender strand enabled me to manipulate the element, but the moment I opened myself to more, earth crashed through me, breaking my hold and leaving my metaphysical pathways bruised. Reversing tactics, I reached for fire. It roared into me, overwhelming and unchecked, then guttering to a mere flutter too soft to grasp. Heat beat against my right side and charred my elemental senses. Through sheer determination, I clung to a whipcord of fire and yanked it to me.

Between one second and the next, the fire element morphed into earth inside me. With a cry, I threw the wild energy from me before it ripped me apart. I staggered into Seradon, gasping for air. Pain speared through my skull, subsiding to a dull headache as I clutched my temples. Elements didn't do that. It would have been like having a real flame in a fireplace turn spontaneously into molten lava. The elements could feed and support each other, but they didn't transform.

"You okay?" Seradon asked.

I straightened and nodded. To the right, Velasquez collapsed to one knee, a beam of raw fire shooting from his palm into the sky. Shaking his head, he surged to his feet. Marciano knocked himself flat on his back, and grass sprang up around the left side of his body, covering him in seconds. Around the circle, the polarized bubble surged and churned, eating across more parkland.

"Stop!" Grant ordered. "This is useless. We need to be on the outside where we can get some damn control."

The squad convened in the earth section. Sweat matted Velasquez's shirt to his chest and ran down his neck. He stuck an arm back into the hot air of the fire section, then retracted it.

"That's not natural," he muttered.

"We can't predict how this'll mutate, but we should be safest in our element," the captain said. "Divide up and get to the outside. We'll link up once we're clear."

"I prefer not to cook," Velasquez said. "I'll go with Mika."

"Good. She'll need your help. Seradon, you're with Winnigan until you're clear, then get to a healer and get back here ASAP."

"Aye, sir."

I fervently hoped Seradon's recovery could be sped up by a healer. With any luck, she'd be back to assist with the link, because I was far out of my league. So far all I'd managed to do was buy the marmot gargoyle a little time, and in the process I'd unleashed a diabolical energy intent on unraveling the very structure of magic. I hadn't exactly proven myself to be a competent stand-in.

Oliver paced the purifier's braid between earth and fire, working himself up to jump through. He'd been hanging back out of the way since he couldn't assist us. I wished I could do the same.

"Captain, I'd like Oliver to go with you," I said, motioning the young gargoyle to stay put. I was tempted to keep Oliver at my side for our mutual comfort in this bizarre situation, but I had to think of his safety. With access to only one element, we were all vulnerable to unknown dangers. Oliver would be a lot safer under Grant's protection than mine. A person didn't become captain of an FPD squad without learning how to defend himself with and without magic. If things got dangerous, Grant would be able to take care of the adolescent gargoyle.

Grant gave me an assessing look, and his nod said he approved. "Oliver, you're with me. Clear out."

"Mika?" Oliver asked, and the confusion in his tone made my heart hurt.

"It's okay. You'll be safe with Captain Monaghan."

"What about you?"

"Are you really doubting this guy?" I hooked a thumb in the direction of Velasquez's broad chest. "We'll meet up on the outside. Hurry but stay safe."

The squad split into their elements and moved out at a jog. Oliver darted through the braid between the air and fire section and shook off the pain, then broke into a lope, easily keeping up with the captain.

As much as I wanted to watch them until they disappeared, I forced myself to turn back to the marmot. Planting a hand on his cool stomach, I said, "Hang in there. I'll be back for you."

Shaking the tingling pain of the inverted pentagram from my hand, I pivoted to face the expanding front line of the earth section. "Let's get out there and break this thing once and for all." My attempt at bravery made my words come out harsher than I intended.

With a faint smile curving his lips, Velasquez saluted me.

5

Once we cleared the sycamore trees around the central pentagon, the ground flattened into bisecting stone pathways and gravel mazes shaded by cottonwoods. The paths to the right led to the arched bridges and meandering trails of the water section, where willow trees lined the banks of intertwining streams. To the left, the shallow slope of the fire section Kylie and I had run down shimmered with unnatural heat.

Velasquez steered us up the middle toward the shallow-tiered rock gardens, and we jogged up the steps, me huffing, Velasquez silent. The polarized bubble had advanced over a hundred yards from the center of the park, and at the rate we were moving, we'd clear it in a few minutes. Earth weighted my skin, shard-sharp and oppressive. I drew on it just to touch it. Even unlinked and unaided by a gargoyle, I held double the amount I normally could. The element was so pure it could pull the dust particles from the very air. I could reshape the ground with it as easy—

I jumped when Velasquez touched my arm.

"Hold up. It's reached the reflection pool. I want to see what happens."

Velasquez pointed to the fire section, but I scanned the air section beyond it, looking for Oliver. I found Grant first. He ran against a crosswind, and sand lifted and eddied around his ankles, partially obscuring Oliver loping at his side.

In the fire section, the leading edge of the polarized magic touched the edge of a shallow pool of water almost twenty feet across, and the magic stuttered around us. Water element rising from the physical liquid clashed with fire, extinguishing a patch of polarized element. The influx of fire magic feeding into the earth section slowed, and the advancing border of the entire polarization bubble halted. The weight of earth against my senses eased.

I spun. On the opposite side of the earth section, water still drank down the earth element through the earth–water seam. Magic continued to push through the constructive weave—water into wood, wood into air—draining the magic from each section. Before I could celebrate, the built-up energy hit the air–fire border and whooshed through, strengthening the fire element. The calm waters of the reflection pool burst into a boil. Steam gushed into the air as the entire pool evaporated. Fresh fire magic fed into the earth section, constricting earth around my skin again, and the outer rim of the bubble jumped several yards, negating the progress we'd made to the border.

"So much for that," Velasquez said, turning back toward our goal and setting a ground-eating pace.

I fell in behind him, gasping when I caught sight of his back. Long rips in the shirt of his gray uniform exposed bleeding cuts and pebble-embedded abrasions.

"Good thing I came with you," he said. "Otherwise it would have been Marcus flambé." When I didn't respond, he shot me a look over his shoulder. "What, too graphic?"

"Your back. I thought your uniform had protection weaves in it."

"It did. That blast, this"—he gestured to the polarized energy around us—"burned through it."

My hand lifted to my own torn sleeve, the only damage my unspelled clothing had taken during the explosion. My skin beneath it was unharmed. "Ah, did I thank you for . . ." Would it be too dramatic to say *saving my life*?

"Letting you use me like an air cushion?" Velasquez grinned.

I caught my breath. The man needed a permit for a smile like that. Maybe that's why he didn't pull it out much. He should, though.

"I couldn't invite you to the party, then let you get hurt," he said.

"You have a weird idea of a party." I stepped around a bench seat and into a well of pain.

Invisible bonds wrapped around my legs to my waist, and agony welled from my bones, burrowing outward through my joints and my skin. I screamed and wrenched to free myself. Nothing held me, yet I couldn't move. I folded forward to clutch my legs—

"No! Don't!"

—and the trap slid over my head. Pain pulled from my pores, and I flailed against the invisible bonds, gasping on air too thick to breathe. My foot shifted. I clawed for magic, but even earth didn't respond. A hollow nothingness pressed back where magic should have existed, stunning me. I could see the element eddying above my head, but I couldn't reach it and none penetrated the invisible spherical barrier holding me.

Velasquez thrust his arm into the air beside me, fingers splayed. Thick bands of earth pushed from his fingertips, the movement of the element the most beautiful magic I'd ever seen. The trap eroded and distorted the magic, flattening it and almost extinguishing it before feathery tendrils brushed the inside edge of the invisible sphere. It imploded, and magic sucked into the void, the raw earth sharp and welcoming.

I collapsed sideways, rubbing the fading cramps from my legs as the pain ebbed from my body.

"What *was* that?" I asked, accepting Velasquez's help up.

"A null pocket. When the purifier exploded, this nook of balanced elements must have canceled each other out."

I glanced around. The five elements were equally represented in a tight circle around the stone bench. Dozens such setting existed throughout Focal Park. "Why didn't it get consumed by the earth?"

Velasquez shrugged. "We're dealing with bizarre magic. Somehow that tiny explosion took down the ward, too, which doesn't make any sense."

I was so used to seeing the park without the ward, I hadn't noticed it was missing.

"We don't know what we're dealing with, so watch where you step." He resumed his march toward the front edge of the polarization field.

"Sure. I'll keep my eye out for invisible pockets of nothing," I muttered as I trotted to catch up with his long-legged stride. I fell into step beside him. "Why did it hurt?" I asked, speaking loud enough for him to hear this time. I'd been cuffed with null bands before, and they'd slid a barrier between me and the elements, but they hadn't inflicted pain.

"It was pulling the magic from you."

"But why? Why couldn't I walk through it?"

"Nulls are balanced voids. When you bungled into it, it reacted as if you were the enemy. It couldn't let you keep walking. It had to destroy the magic inside you, so it trapped you."

"You make it sound like it had the ability to think."

"A poor analogy, then. It reacted to the magic in you the same way fire reacts to paper: You were consumable."

What a pleasant thought.

"Usually null pockets deteriorate on their own, and pretty fast, but I don't trust the elements to act normally right now."

As if to reinforce his words, the earth moved beneath our feet like a blanket being shaken out. A low rumble rolled up the hill, drowning out the creaking protests of the cottonwoods. I flung out my arms for balance, managing to keep my feet beneath me. Velasquez widened his stance and rode the undulating ground like he'd done it a dozen times before. My legs continued to tremble even after the granite resumed its characteristic inert state.

"Stay close and stay behind me."

Velasquez's matter-of-fact tone snapped me into motion. Following in his footsteps, I jogged across sun-warmed rocks, my feet slapping the hard stone in tandem with his. We had at least another twenty feet to go before we reached the edge of the polarization field, all of it uphill, and I couldn't shake the feeling that we were moving too slowly. It was all well and good to be safe and conserve our energy instead of making a headlong dash, but the longer we were inside the polarized magic, the more my skin crawled with the need to escape.

The granite shivered beneath my feet, the smooth wind-worn rock growing rough and uneven between one step and the next. I glanced around. None of the other rocks in our section were moving or reshaping. The earth was responding to our footsteps.

"Velasquez..."

"I see it." The fire elemental altered his stride, his footsteps landing softer without him slowing. I tried to do the same and fell behind.

Velasquez jumped to a wide boulder a step above us. I'd barely cleared the step behind him when the boulder sprouted a short wall in front of Velasquez, solid rock reshaping as fast as a blink. With speed I'd never have accredited to the large man, he sprang to the right. A crest of speckled gray granite swirled behind his feet, the dense rock moving and re-forming like water but sounding like a landslide. When he landed, a sheet of schist shot skyward at his right side, dwarfing him. Velasquez slammed into it, the impact bouncing him back a half step. Schist bulged from the wall and frothed up the smooth surface, coating it in short, jagged peaks.

I slammed a knee into the protrusion Velasquez had avoided and windmilled my arms to counter my forward momentum. The granite beneath me lifted, carrying me toward Velasquez. He grabbed my arm, balancing me as the rocks ground to a halt.

Neither of us moved, our ragged breathing filling the space between us. Velasquez was a foot shorter than me, standing in a knee-deep hole and hemmed in on two sides by rock walls where moments before there'd been a flat expanse of granite. I swallowed hard.

The earth growled behind me, and I twisted to look. A ridge of brown-and-black-banded hornfels pushed upward along the dividing line between the earth and fire section in an inches-high mountain range, with a few peaks sprouting as high as my thighs. Up and down the helix wall, the earth rumbled in an ever-growing and shifting barrier.

"What the—" A heavy crack louder than ten gargoyles landing on marble drowned out Velasquez's curse. We both spun toward the sound. A waist-high block of granite large enough for me to stand on punched from the dirt at the leading edge of the bubble. In rapid succession, three more burst from the soil like jagged teeth in the mouth of the polarized bubble.

"The air," I said, swallowing twice before I coaxed sound from my throat. "It's damming it. Or trying to." In the destructive cycle, earth stopped air. Based on the twisted logic of this polarized magic, it made sense that the raw earth wouldn't tolerate the movement of air. When Velasquez had jumped, he'd created a breeze, and the granite had grown to halt it. When he'd jumped the second time to avoid the sudden growth, he'd created even more air displacement, and the rock had boxed him in to cut it off.

"Look." I crouched. It hurt the cut on my shoulder to maintain my grip on Velasquez's arm and bend down, but I couldn't make myself let go. Leaning forward, I huffed out a sharp breath. Schist bubbled out of a vein in the granite and formed a shallow bowl around the puff of air, effectively stopping the wind.

"Crap," Velasquez said.

"Yep."

"Okay. I'm going to get out of this hole before it closes in on me."

I straightened and braced myself. Velasquez planted one foot on the granite next to me, then eased himself free of the earthen trap. A sharp spiral of granite shot upward from the base of the hole, counteracting the downdraft of air Velasquez displaced. I yanked him toward me before the sharp tip could puncture his back.

Velasquez stumbled against me, catching me in his arms before I could move my feet.

"Maybe we should move to the water section," I said, my nose pressed against his broad chest. He smelled of sweat and dirt, and it wasn't a bad combination.

"I don't think it would help."

We eased apart without moving our feet and I leaned to look around him at the water section. The ground had risen to create a crenelated wall along the water–earth boundary, damming over-flowing streams that had previously lazed throughout the earth section. Deeper in the water section, a pond burbled, then foun-tained, fed from an underground geyser. It overflowed its banks and flooded the breadth of the water section. Seconds later, the magic influx cycled around the purifier's constructive bubble and hit earth.

Velasquez and I staggered as the density of our air thickened with unnatural gravity. At the edge of the central pentagon, a sycamore tree toppled, and the ground rose up to break its fall. Cascading ridges of earth halted the rush of air up the tiers, curling back over the fallen tree and toppling a few cottonwoods, restarting the process. I pressed one ear to Velasquez's chest, clapping a hand over the other to muffle the cacophony. Beneath us, the ground quaked and I rode it out on trembling knees.

Thick black smoke billowed into the sky where the top of the sycamore had fallen into the fire section. In rapid succession, three more smoke columns joined the first and heat tightened the air even as more power flooded into the earth section and the leading edge of the polarization jumped several yards.

I lifted my head from Velasquez's chest to watch Winnigan and Seradon wade into the growing pond, then dive beneath the surface. Both women emerged a few feet away, arms paddling as they swam. A current pulled them away from us toward the wood section, where the pond cascaded down a waterfall that hadn't existed ten minutes ago.

"What's happening to the ground in the wood section?" I asked. The earth eroded under the falling water as if it were sand, not hardy granite, hornfels, and schist.

"The same thing that's happening here. Wood destroys earth."

With growing horror, I examined the wood section. The ground around the central pentagram was pockmarked with holes like empty graves. Farther away, the ground disappeared as if sheared off at the front edge of overgrown creosote bushes, and the gnarled roots of the botanical garden's red maples twisted in the open air. The trees' trunks were twice as thick as they'd started the day, and I realized the movement of the visible roots wasn't caused by the wind; I was seeing the trees grow.

Through the trunks, I caught a glimpse of two figures. Marciano and Grant slogged through the boggy ground. Marciano carried a branch he used to prod the ground before advancing, like a man moving across snow, looking for hidden crevasses.

Oliver wasn't with the captain.

I whipped my head the other direction, blindly grabbing Velasquez's forearms to steady myself as I squinted to see the air section through the bordering fire section. Heat waves bent the light and made the horizon dance. I couldn't make out any of the park's tall sculptures or windmills, and my knuckles tightened on Velasquez's sleeves.

My breath whooshed out when I finally spotted Oliver. He flew above what looked like a smear of khaki. Sand. The heat of fire wasn't distorting the view; the growing winds had kicked up a sandstorm.

Oliver flapped his wings, then retracted them, plummeting into the sand before flapping slowly aloft again. His long body jerked against the wind before he dropped out of sight again.

"What's he doing?"

"Conserving energy," Velasquez said.

Oliver emerged from the sand again, long wings beating almost too slow. As he rose, the air barrier near him flared and blew magic into fire.

"He's trying not to stir up air," I said. *Damn it, I should have brought him with me.*

Oliver couldn't land, because he'd be blind. He hadn't been able to go with the captain because he would have been swallowed by the eroding soil. If the wood section was anything like the earth, he wouldn't have been able to fly through it. Gargoyles were made of stone; they required air magic to stay aloft, and the wood section with its polarized magic wouldn't have had any air for Oliver to use.

"We need to get moving. Slowly," Velasquez said.

A thunderous crack of rock lifting against a breeze coming from outside the polarization field echoed the urgency in his tone. Velasquez turned and took a cautious step. Small peaks of granite lifted on either side of his foot from the push of air, but the bulk of the boulder beneath us remained still.

"Follow close," he said.

Every rumble and clatter of moving earth grated against my nerves. In between the unnatural earthen shifts, the only sound audible was our footsteps. The lap of water against the growing dam on the right, the waterfall cascading into the wood section, the windstorm Oliver battled—all the destruction reshaping the park should have raised a racket.

"I think the air is getting denser," I said. It was harder to draw a breath, and it wasn't because we were walking up an increasingly steep incline.

"All the more reason to hurry," Velasquez agreed as he took another careful, agonizingly slow step. I tried to laugh, but it came out as a breathy whimper.

We hiked up the middle of the earth section more than thirty feet from the fire section, but heat radiated against my left side and sweat rolled down my spine. I focused on Velasquez's feet, doing my best to step exactly where he did. Every ripple he caused doubled with my passing, building a ragged sluice into the boulders. After a handful of steps, narrow blades popped up between my feet when one foot passed the other. High-pitched but soft squeaks accompanied each sharp formation.

A few steps later, the earth crumpled and sharpened beneath my boots in response to the puffs of air stirred by Velasquez's feet. Moving gingerly, I tiptoed after him, every step becoming increasingly sharp and uneven. I'd stopped checking our progress against the leading edge of the earth section. It was too depressing. Everything that slowed us down only increased the strength of the purifier, and the bubble pushed outward at a steady, ground-eating pace. Despite the distance we'd covered, we were still a dozen yards from escaping.

Lightning split the sky beside us in the fire section, sounding like it exploded against my eardrums. I jumped. The granite beneath me reacted, spearing straight into my foot.

I screamed on an inhale, the sound sucking into my throat.

6

"What? Are you okay?"

Unable to speak, I pointed to my left foot. Velasquez twisted without shifting his feet, then cussed.

"Did it go through your foot?"

The sharp pain radiating from my sole scrambled my thoughts, and I fought the urge to yank my foot free. Any sudden movements could cause the granite to reshape around or *inside* my foot.

"I don't think so," I gasped. "Into but not through." Pain climbed up my leg until it felt like everything from my knee down had been pierced. I pictured the bottom of my foot and the rock penetrating it, and white noise rang in my ears, clouding my vision. A sharp snap next to my nose brought me back to myself.

"Hey. Stay with me. You need to lift your foot. Slowly. Then you're going to climb on my back and I'm going to carry you, okay?"

"No."

"No? What's your plan?"

"Your back. I can't—"

"My back is fine. Two steps will cause fewer rock ripples than four."

I shook my head. Arguing helped distract me from the compulsion to rip my foot free. "You're bleeding."

"So are you. If you're not afraid of getting a little of my blood on you, I'm not afraid of getting a little of your blood on me."

I shifted, biting my lip when pain shot up my leg.

"Okay," I said.

Velasquez offered me his arm and I clung to him while I inched my foot from the rock spike. Sweat coated my body when I was finally free. I crossed my foot over my knee and peeked at the bottom. The thin leather sole of my boot had been sheared through, and blood seeped from the arch of my foot. For a closer inspection, I'd have to remove my shoe, and I wasn't eager to see the wound or to jostle my foot that much.

"You're not walking anywhere on that," Velasquez said.

I nodded, not trusting my voice. The pain had morphed into a pulsing throb, and the thought of putting weight on my foot made me want to whimper.

"Grab my neck," Velasquez said, turning his back to me.

I stared at the dirt- and rock-crusted scrapes in his back. I wouldn't be able to hold on without hurting him.

"Maybe you should go on without me. If I don't move, I should be okay until you guys shut this down."

"You're being dramatic. Hop on and let's get going."

I grasped his shoulders and lifted my left leg toward his hip but hesitated, unsure how to proceed.

"We'll be here all day if you try to do this without touching me."

"I don't want to hurt you."

With a growl, he crouched, grabbed my left thigh, and lifted me, stepping forward at the same time. I squeaked and slung my arms around his neck, pulling my right leg up to squeeze his hips. A solid curl of granite unfurled behind me, slapping my butt and jostling me against Velasquez. He grunted, then took a second cautious step.

"You okay?" he asked after three more steps. The granite shifted and bubbled behind us, folding on itself like a crumpled rug as it halted every current of air Velasquez's footsteps lifted.

"I think so."

Dirt sifted from Velasquez's thick hair when my head brushed it, and the loamy odor was comforting. Clinging to the fire elemental was akin to hugging a warm boulder, and I welcomed the illusion of safety that being pressed up against his strong body gave me.

"Good. Because I know we're trying not to move the air, but I need to breathe."

I felt him swallow against my forearm and hastily relaxed my stranglehold. Belatedly remembering his back, I did my best to shift my weight to the vise grip of my thighs around his hips while concaving my stomach away from his wounds.

"What are you doing?" Velasquez asked.

"Trying not to hurt you."

"Cut it out. You're making it worse." His footsteps hadn't slowed or altered during my adjustments.

"Sorry, Velasquez."

"Call me Marcus. And relax. I'm about as fragile as the gargoyles you heal."

"Modest, too, Marcus," I muttered, knowing he'd hear me.

He flexed, and his shoulder muscles hardened like stones beneath my arms in a silent testament to his boast. I reminded myself that he had to be made of tough stuff to be in an FPD squad. A lot tougher than me. More tears than I was proud of had escaped while I'd been extricating my foot. I hoped he was too preoccupied to notice when they dripped from my chin to soak into his shirt.

"Hold tight. I'll have to take these stairs faster," Marcus said. His voice rumbled against my chest, and I realized I'd sagged against him. He'd made good time across the boulder field and had already reached the first unnatural block of granite. The front line of the polarization field expanded half as fast as a normal walking pace, with alarmingly frequent jumps as various parts of the massive constructive weave encountered fresh elemental magic to feed on. The crack and snap of growing rock had become a constant, and what had started as a handful of jutting teethlike pillars along the front edge of the field had expanded to a series of uneven steps building toward the sky. The leading edge was already taller than Marcus. Only the rise of the hill naturally dampening the wind currents had prevented the pillars from shooting up higher.

I tightened my grip on Marcus as he powered up the first steep steps. Granite scraped and grated behind us, sounding as if the rocks were chasing us, a great attacking stone monster perpetually one step away from hamstringing Marcus and taking us both down for the kill.

Marcus let go of my right leg to use his hand for balance. I did my best to remain still on his back, both because it was the only way I could be helpful and because every time my foot was jarred, pain spiked all the way to my knee.

For several steps, Marcus moved parallel with the outer edge of the bubble and I could see the air section. I looked for Oliver, but I couldn't find him through the haze of the fire section. Lightning skittered through the polarized fire with increased frequency, held at bay by the flimsy-looking wall of the purifier's helixes. The bright flashes left afterimages on my vision; the thunder deafened me.

"Almost there," Marcus said through ragged breaths.

The leading edge of the polarization bubble stretched a few feet in front of us. Outside it, the interlocking helixes narrowed to a mass no thicker than my waist, and from our new height, I spotted the end of the fire–earth braid.

"Look! The purifier stops there." I pointed to a pile of boulders ahead of us and to our left. The fire–earth braid fed into the rocks, but it didn't come out the other side. "Maybe it's weakening." Given the oppressive stillness of the air and the swelling cacophony of the granite around us, I amended my hope. "Or it has a finite reach."

Marcus hopped to a higher pillar, sidestepping the curl of granite that followed his foot.

"Or it found another patient for you," he said.

I spotted the gargoyle among the boulders. The foxlike gargoyle's dull tigereye body and dirt-brown wings blended into the rocks—or they would have if a massive malicious braid of magic hadn't speared into her.

"Oh no! Hurry!" If she'd been subject to the purifier's dividing magic this whole time, it had to be tearing her apart.

"Working on it," Marcus grunted.

The ground beneath us rumbled. The pillars close to the edge of the field shifted and rose. Marcus cursed and danced across the top of the rocks, fighting for footing on the shifting tops. We were close to escape, but the leading edge of the bubble crept forward, pulling taller pillars into our path.

"I'm going to have to jump," Marcus shouted over the near-constant booming.

"Okay." If he could angle toward the hillside, the drop would be only a few feet, but first he had to clear the ever-rising cliff steps.

Marcus grabbed both my legs in a crushing grip. I tightened my arms around his shoulders.

"Here we go."

He sprinted up the shifting rocks, and I jounced on his back, eyes locked on the perpetually advancing edge of the field. Just as Marcus planted his foot on the last rising pillar and pushed off, the bubble shifted and grew by several feet at once. Granite burst from the inert ground beneath us, shooting toward our plummeting bodies.

I yanked earth magic to me and sheared off the top of the growing pillar before it could break Marcus's legs. His right foot clipped the edge of the pillar, but his left hit the top solidly. Working blindly on the rock beneath his feet, I drove pure earthen strands into the granite and stretched it the same way I would manipulate quartz. The grainy rock reshaped, as malleable as dough. Lifting the rock beneath Marcus's foot, I launched us toward safety.

We catapulted through the barrier, and my connection to the raw earth magic snapped. Blinded by the backlash, I lost my grip on Marcus and braced for impact with the rocky ground. It never came. Soft strands of air cushioned my fall. I opened my eyes, closing them just as quickly as the light refracted into a thousand razors inside my head.

I sucked in a breath, then another, savoring the light texture of the air in my lungs despite by body's conflicting pains.

"Am I dead?" I croaked.

"Mind blasted."

Clutching my head, I squinted in the direction of Marcus's voice. When the sunlight didn't slice my brain this time, I opened my eyes wider.

I sat on a large boulder a few feet up the hill from Marcus, and once he saw I could support myself, his bands of air and wood magic holding me up dissipated.

"Good move with the rock wave."

In a sea of pillars, one column of granite looked like it had melted toward us before being sheared off by a colossal blade. With the backlash of magic reverberating in my brain, it took me a moment to process the sight. I'd reshaped a couple hundred pounds of pure granite as easily as I might have a grape-size quartz seed crystal. That kind of strength couldn't be matched even by a full-spectrum earth elemental. Yet inside the polarized earth section, it'd been easy.

Mind blasted? Not fried, right? I scrambled for the elements, going limp when they responded. Reverently, I spun the five harmonious elements together, forming a basic pentagram and floating it in the air in front of me just to admire the beauty of the combined elements. The amount of earth I could hold was paltry compared to what I'd wielded inside the bubble, but I didn't care. Buffered and mixed with the other elements, earth felt smooth again, not sharp and raw like it had in the polarization field. It felt whole, and so did I. Out here, with all the elements working together, we had a chance at stopping Elsa's monstrosity.

First things first, we had to save the fox gargoyle.

I pushed to my feet—and fell back to the ground with a strangled gasp. The wound in my foot caused nauseous waves of pain to pulse through me, and I took shallow breaths until the urge to vomit subsided.

"Have you ever had a field patch?" Marcus asked.

I shook my head, keeping my lips pressed together.

"Oh, goodie. A virgin."

I jerked to check his expression. Marcus winked at me with an exaggerated leer obviously designed to distract me. I would have rolled my eyes, but he chose that moment to unlace my shoe. My fingers clawed into the soil, but I managed to contain most of my whimper as the shoe peeled from my foot. A fine slice of fire cut away my sock and it dropped to the rock.

"Hey, you'll live," Marcus said with irritating cheer. Something cold settled against my skin, then crept *into* the wound. It should have hurt or grossed me out, but the pain abated until only a cold spot remained, and I decided I'd never felt anything sweeter.

"What was that?"

"A field patch. A little water cooled to ice to block the nerves, a little earth to dam the bleeding, a little fire to counter infection. You'll need a healer and proper healing when we're done, but this will tide you over."

"It doesn't hurt," I said, awed. I shifted to pull my foot up to take a look, but Marcus captured my ankle.

"No. If you see it, you'll think about it too much. Let me wrap it."

Marcus knelt and spun tiny bands of fire around his midsection, slicing strips from the bottom of his shirt. With his pants riding low on his hips, the shortened shirt revealed a tanned stomach and a sculpted V of muscle veering into his waistband. I looked away. Having spent the last ten minutes clinging to his back, I knew Marcus didn't possess an ounce of fat—I didn't need to ogle the man for proof. Even if the view was a good deal more pleasant than anything else in my sight.

"If you teach me how to repeat the patch, I could put it on your back," I said.

"Just get some of the rocks out, and we'll call it even."

I waited for Marcus to say he was joking, but he didn't look up from my foot. He wound the strips of his shirt into a makeshift bandage, his speed silently reminding me that we didn't have any time to waste.

"Turn so I can see what I'm doing," I said.

I grimaced at the raw texture of Marcus's back. Carrying me had reopened the wounds, and they looked far worse than I remembered.

My civilian guilt, as Seradon had called it, welled up stronger than ever. I glanced at the blood drying on my shirt, all his, and then got to work.

Wrapping a band of earth with soft layers of water, I dabbed the elements across his back. The water loosened the grit caked in the wounds and the earth pulled on all like matter. Bloody pebbles rolled down his back to the ground.

If he'd been as similar to a gargoyle as he'd boasted, I would have slid magic into him and healed him from the inside. Unfortunately, my earth elemental skills were useless on human physiology, and if I tried to push magic into him, I'd likely do more damage than good. My clumsy efforts were the best option, but it must have felt like I was picking at the cuts with my finger. I winced with the extraction of each tiny rock, but Marcus didn't react.

"I think that's the worst of it," I said as Marcus tied off the wrap on my foot.

"Good. We need to get moving. Here's your shoe."

The leather fit snug around the bandage, making me grateful I couldn't feel the puncture. When I stood, I put my full weight on my foot and all I felt was the cool press of Marcus's magic.

I looked for Oliver, and the view took my breath away.

Beyond the misshapen wedge of the earth section we'd escaped, an expanding triangle of the park lay scorched and strewn with embers. Flames belched from pockets in the ground and lightning crackled brilliant streaks through the shimmering hot air. Viewed through this, the air section beyond looked to be one giant sandstorm, and dirt hazed the sky above it. Oliver's slender orange-red body had been swallowed by the storm, and I fought the urge to run to find him. I should never have sent him with Captain Monaghan. Oliver was my responsibility, and now he was all alone and fighting through a sandstorm created by powerful, unpredictable magic.

Logically, I knew his humping lope would have been a disaster in the air-sensitive earth section. Oliver wouldn't have been able to fly to even out his gait, and while Marcus was strong, I doubted he could have carried me *and* Oliver out. It wouldn't do any good for me to get trapped in the sandstorm with Oliver, either, as much as I yearned to go help him.

Telling myself I wasn't abandoning Oliver, I hobbled a few steps toward the fox gargoyle. When the numbness in my foot held, I hurried to the base of the pile of boulders.

From this angle, the gargoyle was hidden. While I hunted for a foothold, I kept an eye on the leading edge of the creeping polarization bubble. At best, we had ten minutes to free the gargoyle before the field reached us.

"Here." Marcus indicated an almost natural staircase up the rocks on the other side of the boulders. I clambered up, trying not to rely on my injured foot. Just because I couldn't feel the wound didn't mean I wouldn't make it worse by stressing it.

I forgot about my foot when I reached the gargoyle. Hardly larger than a bear cub, she lay curled in a tight ball in the narrow bed of rocks, her long tigereye fox muzzle partially hidden under her thick tail. Up close, I could see her wings weren't dusty brown; they were a smoky citrine so gritty and scarred and covered with dirt that they looked brown. Her eyes were dim, as if she'd been sleeping when the purifier exploded and locked on to her. Or knocked unconscious. Her magic passively fed into and boosted the atrocious polarizing magic just as the marmot gargoyle's had. No quartz had been necessary to forge a connection between the purifier's braid and the fox, either; it'd burrowed in using raw power.

"I think if I can remove the braid, it'll be like unhooking an anchor," I said. "It might cause the purifier to unravel. Having another gargoyle to feed off of must be strengthening it."

"Okay. I'll check on the others."

Almost on top of his words, an air message opened above us and Winnigan's voice emerged. "We're out. Seradon's going to get healed. I'm headed your way."

Marcus responded as he continued to climb up the boulders toward the peak. Movement in the periphery of my vision pulled my head up. Seradon and Winnigan jogged across the flat sunbathing grounds, skirting the expanding polarization field. When she reached a natural path, Seradon peeled away, angling toward the tunnel exit. Despite having been magically stunted from the initial blast and then swimming her way out of the water section, she managed a cheerful wave and smile before she disappeared out of sight. In her place, I would have been dragging myself on all fours toward the nearest escape route. For all our sakes, I hoped a healer waited just outside the park, ready to repair Seradon's metaphysical pathways so she could rush back before the captain was ready to link.

Maybe the link wouldn't be necessary if I could break the purifier's hold on the fox.

Forming a basic mixture of elements, I slid it into the gargoyle. As I expected, I had to adjust the elements immediately. The purifier's braid of fire and earth had warped the fox's insides, and it was pulling her apart. I wasted precious seconds trying to sever the braid where it tunneled into the gargoyle's neck. The massive bands of elemental energy were too strong for me, so I switched tactics. Laying my hands on her wings, I drove my magic deep into the gargoyle, hunting for the tip of the purifier's magic where it anchored to her body. If I couldn't cut the purifier off before it entered her, maybe I could stop it from digging any deeper.

I found the end of the braid less than two inches from the gargoyle's opposite side. The purifier's magic twisted and churned inside the gargoyle, corkscrewing her innards and creating a rift inside her as if she were just another rock, not a living creature. Only her innate magic bound into her tigereye body kept her alive, and it was failing.

While I examined it, the braid of fire and earth tunneled through another half inch of her body. It wasn't anchored in her; it was boring through her! If it managed to push out her other side, it'd shatter her body.

Knowing I had mere minutes to save her life, I gathered counterelements—water and wood—and threw them against the fire and earth of the purifier. I anticipated the backlash of pain that resonated into me, and I didn't let up. The forward progress of the braid halted; then it began to swell inside the gargoyle, opening physical fractures.

Cursing, I released my countermagic and grabbed quartz-tuned earth. As fast as I could, I healed the fresh wounds; then I shifted my focus to the fox's neck. The divisive magic of the purifier had polarized the magic inside the gargoyle, and I patched the large fractures just under her skin, hoping it would thwart the purifier. Undeterred, the fire and earth braid passed seamlessly through my magic and continued to burrow into the gargoyle.

While I wracked my brain for a solution, I countered as much of the purifier's advancement as I dared. Anything more would have injured the fox.

I couldn't form an inverted pentagram in front of the purifier's braid as I'd done with the marmot. For starters, I didn't have a convenient quartz crystal to embed the pentagram in or glass loop to contain the bulk of the purifier. The braid was also exponentially larger than before, and without the combined magic of the full spectrums at my disposal, I doubted I could create a pentagram large enough to absorb the incoming fire and earth elements. Furthermore, though no one had confirmed it, I was pretty sure my inverted pentagrams around the marmot were strengthening the purifier, and I didn't want to give this monstrosity any more power.

At a loss, I did the one thing I knew how to do: I healed the gargoyle.

Splitting my attention, I sewed minute quartz stitches deep inside the fox, bridging the dichotomous elements tearing her apart. While she continued to resonate with earth on one side and fire on the other, the divided elements no longer physically split her. It was probably wishful thinking, but I thought her faint life signs might have strengthened, too.

I'd patched up the gargoyle from her neck almost to her hip before I realized why the purifier's magic wasn't interfering with my healing: It didn't fight or overpower my gargoyle-tuned magic because it recognized it as part of the weave.

"She tuned the purifier to gargoyles."

"What does that mean?" Marcus asked.

I glanced up to where he perched on the top boulder, standing on the narrow peak of rock as if it were solid ground. The sight of him that high made my legs feel funny.

"I think there's a gargoyle at the end of every purifier line, feeding it magic."

"Shit."

Elsa hadn't just embedded her original contraption to the marmot gargoyle through the quartz; she'd tuned the magic to feed off the gargoyle. And when the purifier had exploded, it'd still been tuned to lock on to gargoyles. That's why the fire–earth braid ended here, with the fox, while the other four braids stretched out of sight. They'd locked on to the closest gargoyles in their paths, and all the others were outside the park.

I had no way of knowing how far away the gargoyles were, either. I was almost certain this fox had been dormant before the purifier wreaked havoc on her. Otherwise she wouldn't have remained in the park when everyone else evacuated. Were the other trapped gargoyles dormant, too? How many dormant gargoyles existed in the city? Was it an epidemic? Why hadn't I known about them? I didn't deserve the title of gargoyle healer—

Oliver landed heavily next to Marcus, claws digging into the boulder, and the sight of him snapped me out of my self-recriminations. His long body drooped beneath heavy wings, tail limp. Sunlight sat heavy on his dull red-orange scales where normally it glistened, and he was breathing so fast it had to hurt.

"You're okay?" he asked.

"I'm okay."

There wasn't enough room for him on the small landing with me and the fox gargoyle; otherwise I thought he would have climbed down. He settled for reaching one stubby leg toward me. I lifted my hand to rest it on his paw, then immediately jerked it back. He wasn't dull from fatigue; his entire body had been scratched a thousand times over. The sand. He'd been scoured in the sandstorm when he'd flown through the air section.

"Does it hurt?" I asked even as I slid my magic into him.

"Not much."

He lied. It felt as if someone had taken sandpaper to his skin. He stung from the tip of his nose to his tail, more so along his wings. Internally, his body rioted in a nauseating imbalance. Using so much pure air to fly had altered his internal systems far worse than if he'd helped me work exclusively with air magic for weeks.

"Feed from me," I ordered. Seeing Marcus beside him wielding a hefty amount of water, I added, "Feed from both of us." I followed the direction of Marcus's magic and saw he'd linked with Winnigan. The red-haired water elemental stood at the base of the boulders, and together the two full spectrums pummeled the polarized fire section with water.

Magic blossomed inside me, opening a wellspring of strength that more than doubled the amount of elements I could hold.

"Good." I could feel his body begin to stabilize, but I still experienced an echo of the pain of each breath stretching his chapped sides.

Wishing I had more time *and* my bag of seed crystals—a gargoyle healer staple, I'd learned—I fanned fire in gentle waves across the carnelian just beneath the scratched outer layer of Oliver's skin, taking special care around his muzzle and eyelids. My patchwork healing sped his natural regeneration on the worst of his wounded flesh, coaxing his skin to grow fractionally. Oliver shuddered, then stilled as I worked, and I stopped after less than a minute and well before he was fully healed.

"I'm sorry. I have to—"

"Help her," Oliver said, finishing my sentence. He opened his glowing eyes to study the fox gargoyle. "Is she . . . dormant, too?"

"I think so. Whatever you do, don't get close. The purifier is tuned to gargoyles. It might jump to you." I knelt by the fox and slid magic back into her. My quartz stitches were holding, but they weren't doing anything to balance the energy within the gargoyle. Half of her body swirled with fire magic, the other with earth, and her body thrummed with a constant, cramping pain that alternated between her left and right sides.

The leading edge of the polarized energy inside the fox broke through the skin at her hip and shot toward Oliver.

"No!"

I sliced the feeble strands, shocked when my desperate ploy worked and the polarized magic broke and disintegrated.

"Oliver, you've got to get out of here." I tried to close the braid's exit wound on the fox's side, but the moment the braid became trapped inside her, it started swelling, crushing her insides.

"I can't hold it inside her. It'll kill her. You have to go. Get out of the park. Out of the city."

"What will happen to her?" Oliver asked. He hadn't moved, and I hacked through two new shafts of the purifier's magic as they speared toward him.

"I'll save her. She's going to be fine as long as the magic doesn't build up inside her. Which is why you have to leave. I can't keep holding it back."

"Where will that magic go if I leave?" Oliver asked.

"Out. It'll go out."

"To another gargoyle?"

Yes. But not to *my* gargoyle. I couldn't say that out loud, though. "Oliver, please. Go. I need to concentrate."

With an unreadable look, Oliver launched from the rock and disappeared. Praying he didn't stop flying until he reached the edge of Terra Haven, I turned back to the fox gargoyle.

Larger and larger bands of Elsa's hideous polarizing braid escaped from the gargoyle's hip. Dividing my focus, I slid a feeler into the fox and continued to hack and slice any escaping magic. My patches held despite greater amounts of fire and earth feeding into and out of the gargoyle. The purifier showed no signs of weakening.

I no longer nursed the marginal hope that the river would stop the polarized magic's expansion. Winnigan's prediction of the bubble swallowing the city seemed more plausible, and when it did, the divided magic would decimate Terra Haven and any living creatures in its path. Everything in the wood section would erode; everything in the water section would drown. The air section would choke everything with dust and erode anything left standing. The earth would tear apart homes and offices; the fire would consume anything in its path.

A wall of heat pressed against my back and sweat dripped down my nose, but the polarized magic escaping the fox grew stronger each time I cut it, and I couldn't spare an ounce of concentration to blot my face.

"We've got to move," Marcus said, suddenly standing beside me.

"It'll swallow the gargoyle," I said, glancing up. The wall of polarized magic pushed close enough to touch.

"And us, too. It was hard enough getting out the first time." He grabbed my arm.

"Wait." I fumbled to assemble fresh quartz patches and stitch them into place where the purifier cut into and out of the gargoyle. The polarized magic slid through my elemental bandages as easily as it did through the fox, but my magic might lessen her pain.

I slashed through a helix of fire larger than the fox as Marcus lifted me. Air exploded from my lungs when my stomach crashed down on top of Marcus's shoulder; then he leapt from the pile of boulders to the ground ten feet below.

I tried to scream, but without air, no sound came out. His thick arm held my legs as I jounced helplessly when he landed. He set me on my feet and I whirled to check the fox, but the tall rocks hid her from sight.

Seconds later, the fire–earth braid burst over the rock, and the polarized field swallowed the boulders where we'd been standing. Marcus grabbed my arm and propelled me up the hill to safety, but my eyes were riveted on the gargoyle-tuned braid.

A sinuous shadow intercepted the braid as it shot straight as an arrow across the ground toward the city.

"Oliver! No!"

The young gargoyle dove into the purifier's questing magic, and it burrowed into him, slamming him to the ground.

7

"Oliver!" I flung myself toward his crumpled form, falling over my own feet when they couldn't keep up. My magic reached him first, and I drove it into him and slashed the purifier's twisted weave. Unlike the other two gargoyles, Oliver fought back with me, and our combined magical assault pushed the insidious braid from him. Immediately, it dove back into his chest.

"We need to roll him. I'll push the magic out of him and then we'll get him free of its path."

"No." The weak protest came from Oliver. He couldn't move; the braid had paralyzed him, and continuing to fight off its intrusion left him no strength to move his limbs, but he managed a few words. "Me, not others," he rasped.

Oliver, not another gargoyle. He didn't want me to spare him just to sacrifice another gargoyle.

"No. Not you." I bounced the purifier's strands from Oliver before they could take root. "You're young. I don't know if you have the strength."

"You'll save me."

My chest caved in at his trusting look. Then Oliver closed his eyes to concentrate on fighting the purifier's intrusive magic. No matter how many times we thrust it from him, cut it off before it could enter him, or tried to blockade against it, the strong braid plowed back into Oliver's chest.

All our actions were a stopgap measure. Eventually we'd tire and the purifier would take root in Oliver. It'd divide him just as it had the fox gargoyle, and it'd tunnel through him with the same ruthlessness, only to jump to the next gargoyle.

The polarization field crept closer. What would happen when it reached Oliver? I couldn't abandon him. I couldn't leave him to face the pain and terror alone and paralyzed.

I swiped tears from my cheeks.

Two bundles of elemental energy wrapped in air rocketed over the top of the bubble and dropped beside Marcus and Winnigan. The outer layers peeled back, revealing twin images of Captain Monaghan. He looked as if he stood underwater, his image reflected in the wavy lines of thin water layers.

"Status report," both captains barked, their voices crystal clear.

"We're together and linked," Winnigan said. She hadn't halted her assault on the fire section even as we'd retreated; she'd merely changed tactics, sending crushing waves of water and wood into the braid that attacked Oliver—with minimal results. Speaking and wielding massive amounts of complex magic didn't appear to challenge her.

"That explains the echo," Grant said. One of the mirror spheres disintegrated. The remaining floating head moved, spinning until the captain looked at me. "Good. Oliver found— Crap. Is the purifier connected to him?"

"Elsa tuned the purifier to gargoyles," I said.

"That means there are five gargoyles feeding this thing?"

"We think so," Marcus said. "I think that's what broke the ward around the park. This fire–earth line already overwhelmed one gargoyle. We weren't fast enough to save it. Then it jumped to Oliver."

"Oliver jumped into it," I said.

"Why would he do that?" Grant asked.

"To save another gargoyle." I slashed at the evil burrowing magic, pushing it out of Oliver. The small dragon balanced the disruption to his internal magic, but the fire and earth braid forced its way back into him before he had normalized. I blocked it with swift strokes of wood and water.

"Mika's keeping the purifier from taking root, but she won't last much longer," Marcus said. I gritted my teeth. It was the truth, but I didn't appreciate hearing it.

"It seems to be helping," Winnigan said. "Velasquez and I have been throwing everything we've got at the fire section, trying to weaken it, but I don't think it's made a difference, Captain. Mika preventing the purifier from feeding off Oliver has done more to slow the tide than anything we've done."

Really? I checked the polarization field. It had swallowed the boulders where the fox gargoyle lay trapped, but it hadn't advanced more than a foot up the hill beyond it.

"Marciano and I tried the same thing against wood with similar results. We're going about this wrong. We need to use this freakish magic against itself."

"A destructive pentagram?" Winnigan asked. "How are we going to get a mix of elements through this field?"

"Any way we can. Link up."

A massive bundle of elements shot from Winnigan and flew out of sight over the curve of the polarization field. I watched it go in amazement. A thousand yards had to separate us from the captain, yet these full spectrums acted like linking across such a huge distance was nothing new. For a woman who was proud of being able to work earth a mere five yards away from her, what they did seemed incredible. Seconds later, the magic swelled in Winnigan and Marcus, proving they'd made their connection with Grant and Marciano.

"You, too, Mika," the captain said. "We need a full five for this."

What they needed were five elementals with full spectrums, not four full spectrums and a midlevel earth elemental. I glanced back up the trail toward the tunnel, hoping to catch sight of Seradon returning, fully healed.

"I need to stay focused on Oliver."

"You need to multitask."

I glared at the mirror sphere. "If I stop, even for a minute, it's going to take root. And if it does, this whole field is going to get stronger." And Oliver would be trapped.

"If you don't link up, it won't matter. The field is getting stronger with or without Oliver's contribution. If we want to stop it, we have to work together."

"You can still protect Oliver after you're linked," Marcus said.

I remembered how easily the squad had yanked control from me when I'd been working to save the marmot. This time, they wouldn't be controlling a small containment ward. They would be creating an acre-size pentagram through the polarized magic. That seemed like it would take everything we had and then some. How much magic would I have left to use to keep Oliver safe?

I shifted to sit beside Oliver, laying a hand on a patch of wing I'd healed. Four other gargoyles were trapped throughout the city, and by focusing all my efforts on saving Oliver, they were suffering, slowly being torn apart. I was delaying because I didn't want to see *my* gargoyle hurt, and that wasn't fair to the rest—or to the fox and marmot already engulfed in the polarization field.

"Some party this turned out to be," I grumbled, trying to sound brave.

Winnigan looked at me like I was crazy, but Marcus grinned.

"That's the spirit," he said.

"Winnigan, fan out," Grant said. "This'll be easier if we're not so far apart."

"Right. Let's destroy this monster." Winnigan ceased her water-focused onslaught, clapped Marcus on the shoulder, and jogged back toward the water section. The pond Winnigan and Seradon had swam through less than a half hour ago now spanned the entire polarized wedge, accelerating the erosion in the neighboring wood section. A hundred yards remained between the river and the leading edge of the polarization field, but the spontaneous lake would soon bridge the intervening land. We were running out of time.

The captain's mirror sphere remained beside Marcus, but from the jostling of Grant's image, I guessed he was running to the air section.

The polarization field pulsed, and the moment the braid connected with Oliver, it inched toward us. Oliver fought back, but his efforts weren't as effective as mine.

I bent forward to whisper into Oliver's ear. "Don't give up. I'm going to be right here, fighting for you. And for all the gargoyles. We're going to free you, but you have to fight it with me."

"All you have to do is link with me; I'll do the rest," Marcus said. He squatted in front of me.

I slashed through the baneful braid, temporarily freeing Oliver, then forced myself to pause long enough to gather a balance of elements and thrust them to Marcus. For a second, I could feel only the two of us, and the power radiating from Marcus wrapped me in comforting warmth. Then he dropped open the barrier between us and the rest of the squad.

I fell into the pool of linked magic and unraveled.

The elements buffeted me, shaving away bits of my identity until I couldn't tell where my body sat or what held me together. Panicking, I flailed for control. The elements flowed around me, cocooned me, battered me, but I couldn't hold a single strand. I was part of the magic, fluid and shifting. Drowning.

"Open your eyes."

Seradon must have held me together last time. She'd buffered me through the whole process, not just when the purifier had exploded.

Damn it, I had no business working with these people. Every one of them was three times as strong as me and mountains more talented. I couldn't even find myself in the link. I was alone. Lost. Where was my body? Where was *I*?

"Look at me."

Marcus's harsh growl rumbled against my eardrums. My body shook, and the movement pulled me back to myself with a snap. I opened my eyes.

The fire elemental held both of my shoulders in crushing grips, and he jostled me again, snapping my head back and forth.

"Are you with me?"

I nodded when I couldn't find my voice. Two of me were here: one looking into his eyes, the other floating in a conglomeration of magic.

Thinking about the link widened the rift between my two selves, pulling me back into the nebulous expanse of elements. I grabbed Marcus's forearms and squeezed, using the tactile sensation to ground myself.

"You have to hold yourself separate. You're a part of the link, but you're not *the* link. Think about what makes you, you."

What made me, me? I'd never had to think about it. I just was me.

"How?" I croaked. "Can't you just . . ." I hunted for the right word. "Isolate me? Like Seradon did?" Every second of delay cost Oliver and strengthened the purifier. We didn't have time to teach me fancy tricks. I needed to get back into Oliver to protect him.

"If you're going to be any use, you have to be in control of yourself. Focus." His serious lapis lazuli eyes bore into mine. "You're an earther."

Yes. I was an earth elemental. I tested the thought, and all the earth available to me through the link tumbled into me, burying me.

Marcus shook me. "You're a gargoyle healer."

Earth magic refined to quartz at my thought, snapping into a shape I could use to heal gargoyles. I held the thick elemental band separate from myself without falling into it. Progress. The resonance of four powerful people on the other end of the magic jarred me, but I clung to my identity. I was a gargoyle healer, an earth elemental with a specialty in quartz—

In the middle of a magic catastrophe that required the skills of someone far more talented than me.

Doubt and fear separated me another step from the link. The fate of Terra Haven depended on me being the earth elemental in this otherwise competent FPD squad. It was enough to make me want to vomit—a sensation unmatched in the link.

I settled back into my body with a feeling akin to waking. I was me, unique and separate, a part of something larger but not the linked energy itself.

I relaxed my control, and the linked magic swirled through me, pulling me back into the immense mixture of elements. I teetered. *I am a gargoyle healer. I am an earth elemental,* I chanted while watching the bubble of polarized magic expand. *I am terrified.*

I dropped a hand from Marcus's arm to Oliver, and contact with the gargoyle crystallized the separation between me and the link.

"Okay. I've got this."

Marcus scanned my face, then released me. I let go of his other arm and flexed my fingers. My knuckles popped. I'd probably left bruises.

Turning back to Oliver, I peeled a slice of magic from the link and cut the purifier's braid. It resisted and when I added more counter-magic, rather than severing the intrusive magic from Oliver, my elements sliced into him. I jerked back and hastily patched the wounds, murmuring an apology to the unresponsive gargoyle. More gently, I countered the fire and earth, pushing the purifier back as far as I dared. It clung to his chest an inch under his skin, rooted in his stone flesh. The time it'd taken me to orient myself in the link had cost Oliver his chance at freedom. If I'd made the wrong call, I'd doomed Oliver to unending pain.

"Settled?" Grant asked. I jumped, having forgotten about the mirror sphere floating beside me.

"Yes." Tears blurred my vision.

"Good. I need an anchor of solid quartz."

"Really?" Surely they had a better anchoring system for pentagrams.

"Unless you can create a wind funnel in the ground."

I glanced at Marcus in confusion.

"Seradon usually makes our anchors," he said. "She can reshape the earth to harness our elements' strengths: a miniature wind funnel for air, a molten pit for fire, that sort of thing."

Oh. Right. Seradon could do things with earth I only dreamed might be possible. The captain had asked me for quartz because it was what I did best. "Where do you need it?"

It took precious minutes to pinpoint *over here*. With Marcus instructing me through the process, I located Grant standing in front of the expanding air section. Distinguishing the captain from the vat of magic required recognizing his signature, which Marcus described as a cold firestorm but to me looked and felt like the leading edge of a thundercloud, a harnessed forefront of natural violence. After I pinpointed the captain, making the anchor at his feet was easy. With all the magic of the squad at my fingertips, I quested into the soil and yanked a vein of quartz to the surface. A few modifications removed the flaws from the quartz, and I molded it into a head-size sphere.

"That'll work," Grant said. His magic slid into the quartz. In less time than it'd taken me to separate the quartz from the surrounding rock, Grant wove a constructive pentagram, anchored it in the quartz, and grafted a powerful band of air to it. He shot the air straight through the polarized sphere, bisecting the wood section and angling for the apex of the water section.

The impressive display of power would have been distracting under different circumstances, but I had Oliver to worry about. I yanked my awareness back to my body and worked to combat the creep of the purifier's magic into Oliver. It had rooted deeper into the gargoyle while my attention had been elsewhere, doubling his pain.

"Hang in there," I whispered.

"Place another anchor *there*, Mika," Grant ordered through the mirror sphere.

Finding the indicated location was easier this time: I simply followed the straight band of air Grant had created to a distance beyond the center of the water section's arc. The selected location happened to be underwater, but that didn't matter. I reached into the earth below and drew out more schist, then refined a tall finger of quartz to protrude above the waterline. A cool, smooth presence in the link locked on to the new anchor. Winnigan. She built a constructive pentagram into the quartz just as Grant's air element slammed into the anchor, and she deftly wrapped the incoming magic into the quartz, locking it in place. One branch of the pentagram was set.

I switched back to fighting the purifier's encroaching tendrils in Oliver and didn't look up until Marcus called my name. When I did, I felt the strain in the link as Grant shoved raw water magic across the wedge of purified earth and out through the fire section. Setting the air line had been relatively easy; both the wood and water sections contained plenty of physical air to bolster Grant's magic. But shoving water through the damming energy of earth and then through the dry fire section taxed the considerable strength of all the squad. Grant had almost forced his way free of the polarized field, but at this rate, we wouldn't have enough power to finish the last three lines of the pentagram.

"Watch, Mika," Marcus said.

He reached into the polarized fire section and shaped a funnel of fire around Grant's line of water, softening the heat and molding a pathway for the captain. The line of water surged to punch through the polarization field.

"Now you," Marcus said.

"Anchor first," Grant barked.

I'd barely finished forming the quartz outside the fire section when Marcus and Grant took hold of the crystal. Marcus shaped a pentagram, Grant slammed the water into the anchor, and Marcus locked the second line of the pentagram in place.

"Wrap the water with earth, Mika," Marcus said. "Buffer it. We need to free magic for the next line."

I grunted, too busy countering the fire and earth braid in Oliver to respond. He was weakening, and I did my best to shore up his strength even as I fought the burrowing magic.

"Now, Healer," Grant ordered.

"Just a minute."

"*Now!*"

With a snarl, I forced my attention from Oliver. Mimicking Marcus's tunnel, I spun earth around the line of water. I hadn't compensated for my strength when working the purified earth inside the purifier's sphere, and the ground leapt upward into a rock tunnel through which the water magic slid unchallenged.

"Nice," Marcus said in approval.

I barely heard him, having returned to protecting Oliver. Only now I had to split my attention between maintaining the earthen tunnel and fighting the malicious braid. Oliver fought, too, but he couldn't prevent the braid from dividing his internal magic. Already, fire swirled on his right, earth on his left, and the unnatural divide sapped his strength. Every task that forced my attention from Oliver enabled the purifier to bore farther into him, and I despaired at the increasing difficulty of battling the mindless magic. Worse, the magic in the link was dwindling. Winnigan required a chunk to lock the incoming air and outgoing water lines to the anchor in her section, and Marcus required twice as much to lock down the incoming water and outgoing fire lines as well as maintain his protection around the water line inside the polarized fire wedge. On top of that, the captain required the majority of our linked magic to build the remaining lines.

I jumped ahead of Grant to build a quartz anchor at the apex of the wood section and Marciano lashed the incoming fire element to his anchor. Not stopping, Grant plowed a wood line across the wood and water sections toward us. I built the last anchor a few feet to my left, in front of the earth section, but before I could turn back to Oliver, Grant thrust rough-hewn wood magic across the earth section, and I had to scramble to build a new tunnel through the rocks all the way to the anchor to protect his magic. At the last second, I remembered to make a constructive pentagram in the quartz anchor.

"Brace yourself," Marcus said.

The wood magic slammed into the anchor and me at the same time as the captain transferred control to me. I fumbled to grab the fraying ends of the wood line and wrap it into my constructive pentagram inside the quartz. Grant gave me barely enough time to lock it in place before he shoved a fresh band of earth through the anchor. I held tight as Grant shot the final line of the pentagram across the park toward his air anchor.

Magic pulled me in four directions at once, and when I reached for Oliver, all the pieces I held started to unravel.

"Hold it!" Marcus said.

I lurched for the anchor, squeezing the wood and earth lines back into place, only to have my earth tunnels crumble. The entire pentagram trembled under the strain as I righted my fortifications.

"Just a little longer."

My world narrowed to holding my four pieces of magic. If I failed, the pentagram would collapse, the purifier would continue to grow, and Oliver would die.

I shook with the need to get back to defending Oliver.

Marcus said something, but his words garbled against my anxiety. The braid tunneling into Oliver had thickened to span his chest. Without magic, I couldn't tell how far through him it'd burrowed, or how much damage it had done. If I didn't mend the rifts of the dichotomous magic, he'd be torn apart.

Magic blossomed through the link, doubling its strength. I gasped, looking around for what I already knew I'd find.

Gargoyles! We had help!

I spotted four winged shapes against the bright sky and my heart soared.

Through the link, I felt everyone shore up their defenses. Grant connected the earth line to his anchor and a surge of power swept through the five overlapping lines. Yet even with the influx of magic, when I attempted to split a fifth layer of magic toward Oliver, the four others I held quaked.

Far too slowly, the captain took control of the anchors, and when he had mine, I spun immediately for Oliver. The purifier had burrowed more than halfway through him, and I fought it back with precise ferocity, looking up only once I'd reduced the purifier's magic to the weakest hold possible.

I saw Kylie first. Her white-blond hair streamed behind her as she ran down the hill at Seradon's side. The crack of rock feet landing on granite announced the arrival of the gargoyles. Not just any gargoyles, either. *My* gargoyles.

Oliver's four siblings landed in a semicircle around him, and my heart sank to my toes.

"Back up! Get away from Oliver." I shooed them with a frantic arm, and they hopped aside, Herbert jerking back when I almost bopped his toucan nose. "This isn't safe. What are you doing here?"

"We had to come. You need us," Anya said.

An outsider would never guess the five adolescent gargoyles had been born in the same clutch. Quinn looked like a small citrine lion with the scales of a dragon instead of fur; Anya resembled a panther, though one with a navy dumortierite and mint-green aventurine body rather than black; Lydia's purple, pink, and orange agate swan-like body glowed like a flying sunset; and Herbert's pink quartz armadillo body and toucan beak were shot through with cobalt dumortierite. Aside from Lydia's two lionlike feet vaguely resembling Quinn's, no two siblings shared the same animal characteristics— other than wings, of course, but all gargoyles had wings.

"Is Oliver okay?" Quinn asked, creeping closer again.

"No." I fought the purifier's magic even as I waved him back.

"Whoa! What happened to the park?" Kylie asked as she pounded to a stop near us.

"Sir, I'm back with reinforcements," Seradon said, speaking to the captain's mirror sphere.

"Hold tight. I'm going to loose the destructive magic." Grant's sphere flickered and disintegrated.

"Grant!" Kylie cried.

"Hush. He's fine," Seradon said, grabbing Kylie's arm and holding her in place without looking away from the park.

A perfect half-sphere of polarized magic cupped the middle two-thirds of the park, transforming the once beautiful terrain into five nightmarish wedges of destruction. Thick lines of the largest pentagram ever created inside the bounds of Terra Haven bisected the dome, the five quartz anchors at the pentagram's points now barely two feet from the leading edge of the creeping magic. Ignoring all normal laws of magic, four bands of looping elemental pairings speared arrow-straight across the undulating grounds and disappeared into the city. The fifth bore into Oliver.

Grant stabilized the magic flowing through the enormous park-spanning pentagram. Drawing on the boost of magic from the

gargoyles, he fortified the bonds connecting each tip of the pentagram, then freed them from the anchors.

The pentagram shrank until the tips rested against the underside
of the purifier's sphere. I held my breath.

"Come on," Seradon said. "Work, damn it."

Magic surged through the pentagram as each element branch
drank from the polarized magic on one end and destroyed it on the
other, using the purifier's magic against itself.

The polarization field shrank, slowly at first, then faster,
retreating in a rush toward the center of the park and the marmot
gargoyle where it all began. A wave of heat escaping the fire section
washed over us, whipping my ponytail against the side of my face and
drying the sweat in my scalp. The incessant rumble and cracks of
earth died down, and the snap of tree branches and the muted roar of
the new waterfall filled in the silence.

My relieved sigh caught in my throat when I reached for Oliver.
Magic gushed from him, the thick braid sucking down his life as fast
as the pentagram destroyed the purifier's polarized magic. The traumatic drain ripped fissures through Oliver's insides, and pain fractured my skull, an echo of the agony Oliver experienced.

I tried to stop the purifier from feasting on his magic, but it was
too strong. My only option was to hack the braid from him,
inflicting more cuts into his tortured body to sever its tendrils.
When I sliced the last of the fire and earth strands from his chest,
the braid snapped toward the dwindling dome of polarized magic,
its slingshot speeds unchanged when it passed through the fox
gargoyle.

The moment I freed Oliver, I wove patches through his body,
mending all the cuts and evening his internal magic with gentle
brushes of magic. I didn't let up until he'd stabilized, and then only
because I didn't want to add too much strain to his body.

He opened his eyes, blinking up at me, and even managed a small
smile.

"We did it. You're going to be okay," I said.

"The other lines aren't retreating," Kylie said, pointing to the four remaining braids stretching beyond the horizon. At the center of the park, the dome of polarized magic shrank out of sight.

"Oh no," Seradon said.

The other gargoyles. They didn't have a healer on hand to cut the braids from them. The destruction of the purifier would drain the magic from them and kill them.

"I've got to help them!"

I sprang to my feet. I needed transportation. A pegasus or gryphon or flying carpet, something fast and—

The severed fire–earth braid rebounded, hurtling up the slope on its previous trajectory. I lunged for Oliver, but it reached him first, burrowing back into his chest with renewed vigor.

8

Oliver whimpered and stilled. I fell to my knees, fighting cable-thick bands of fire and earth. Through sheer will and with the backing of all the power of the link, I forced the purifier's braid from Oliver. It wormed back into him the moment I slackened my defense.

Seradon crouched and examined Oliver. "She tuned it to gargoyles," she said, recognizing the problem instantly. "Damn that woman!"

A dome of polarized magic sprang to life at the heart of the park, then swelled with alarming speed as the five divided elements rebuilt. Thanks to the earlier remodeling of the park, each section was sculpted to support a singular element and all the counterelements had already been eliminated.

Grant yanked magic through the link, setting fire to the over-grown groves in the botanical gardens and funneling water across the park to the fire section through a huge trough he cut into the earth in front of the expanding polarization bubble. The field stuttered as it battled destructive elements, its expansion reduced to a slow creep. The captain had bought us time, but not much.

A new mirror sphere rocketed across the park and opened in front of Marcus.

"This isn't going to work until we can disconnect the gargoyles," Grant said.

Everyone turned to look at me. When Grant spotted Kylie behind me, his face tightened, but he didn't say anything.

"I don't know if I can," I said, keeping up a steady counterattack on the purifier's braid in Oliver. Quinn crept closer to his brother on almost silent rock paws, and I shooed him back again.

"We don't know how far away they are," Marcus said, eyes on the horizon. The water–earth purifier line extended across Lincoln River and disappeared into the city beyond. The others looked equally long.

"It's not just the distance," I said. "Even if I could reach them all, I don't think I could break the purifier's connection. Once it gets a firm hold, I can't force it out without tearing the gargoyle apart. All I could do for the fox was patch her insides so the magic didn't kill her."

"The fox?" Seradon asked.

"Another gargoyle was connected to this line, there, in the rocks," I said, pointing. I wished I could get back to the fox now and check on her, but until the purifier was destroyed, I wasn't leaving Oliver's side. "This corrosive braid channeled through her."

"Then it jumped to Oliver?" she asked.

"In a way. He put himself in its path. It would have kept going until it found another gargoyle. Oliver thought . . ." He thought I could save him, and I was doing a miserable job. "I'm barely staying ahead of the braid in him."

"I see that," Grant said.

Of course. Through the link, he'd know exactly how I fought the purifier in Oliver, just as I knew he continued to feed fire into the trees across the park, drawing on magic from the link. A huge column of smoke rose into the sky, matched in the fire section where the captain's river of water doused flames and molten embers alike.

"If it bore through the fox that quickly, the other lines might have already slid through the first gargoyles they encountered and be on to the next," Seradon said.

I felt sick. *Slid* didn't come close to describing what would have happened to those gargoyles. Without my patches to hold them together, the dual polarized magic would have shattered their bodies, killing them before embedding itself in the next victim.

"So you can break the purifier lines from the next gargoyles before they have a chance to take root?" Grant phrased it as much as an order as a question.

"Maybe." If I was close to the gargoyle. If the timing was just right. If I let the four currently trapped gargoyles die first.

"We couldn't link that far apart," Marcus said. "Even if Mika broke one or two of the purifier's lines, she wouldn't be able to hold them from all five gargoyles at once over that distance, either."

"She might not need to. We could each take a gargoyle and defend it after she's broken the purifier's hold," Winnigan said, her voice faint through Grant's mirror sphere. He must have a similar sphere next to Winnigan and Marciano, conferencing us all into this conversation.

"That's some complex quartz manipulation she's doing," Seradon said. "Look at how she's holding Oliver together while countering the purifier. She's perpetually healing and fighting at the same time. Do you think you could do that?"

I didn't know who she directed her question toward, but I couldn't believe she doubted her teammates. They could do mind-boggling things with the elements; surely they could work quartz at this scale.

"Maybe. No. Not like that." Marcus squinted at my weaves. "But if the purifier wasn't embedded in the gargoyle and I only had to hold it back, I could do that."

Grant shook his head. "No. Seradon's right. We need the gargoyles to be closer. Can we move them?"

"That'd take time," Marcus said.

"It might be our only option."

"We could hold the lines closer," Anya said.

"What? No!" I whirled to face the gargoyle. She flared her wings at my outburst. Seated next to Oliver, I was marginally taller than the blue and green panther. When I'd first met her, she'd been barely as large as a housecat, but she'd always possessed the same determined look when she made up her mind.

"Let her speak," Grant said.

"No." Anya was proposing likely suicide for her and her siblings. It was bad enough Oliver was suffering through the purifier's attack.

"My siblings and I could hold the divisive braids here, close enough for Mika to reach." Anya glanced at her siblings, and they all nodded in complete agreement. I bit off another protest. "Mika would be able to keep them from burrowing into us as she's doing with Oliver."

Fight this same battle on five fronts against five different elemental braids of polarizing magic? Even with the full power of the link behind me, I doubted it was possible.

"If I fail, you'll all be trapped. You might die." It was hard to force the words out, but Anya needed to know.

The gargoyle panther shook her head. "You will protect us."

"I *am* protecting you by telling you not to do this."

"We have to. For Oliver. I know you won't let us die."

I swallowed against a lump in my throat. I didn't deserve that kind of blind trust, but against such unwavering confidence, there wasn't anything I could say to change her mind.

"It might work," Seradon said.

"It *will* work. Mika is strong," Anya said.

"It will only work if the purifier will lock on a closer gargoyle and let go of the one farther away," Grant said.

"I will try," Lydia said. She spread her wings to launch, and I grabbed for her.

"Wait! Let me try something."

I fumbled with the elements, my panic making me clumsy, and I teetered into the vast magic of the link. *I am a gargoyle healer. I am terrified.* The thoughts anchored me.

After pummeling the braid back far enough to give myself a breather, I used a hook of earth to lift a vein of quartz from the soil in front of Oliver. I separated a solid bar of purified quartz from the rest and dropped it onto my palm. Then I shoved the earth smooth again while shaping the quartz into a disk. I made it the exact same size and shape as the disks I'd used to protect the marmot, and I placed it against Oliver's chest. A few layers of the elements and a twist to invert the pentagram, and I had a duplicate blockade.

The purifier's thick magic passed through it as if it didn't exist and burrowed into Oliver.

"It was worth a try," Seradon said.

I wasn't ready to give up. Stripping the quartz of all elemental magic, I started fresh, feeding it a combination of elements that resonated with gargoyles. If I could make the purifier think the quartz rock was a gargoyle, maybe I could trick it into locking on to a piece of rock instead of a living creature.

This time when I held the disk in front of Oliver, the fire and earth braid reacted, unraveling my magic too fast to follow and pulverizing the quartz to dust before leaping into Oliver.

I slumped even as I blocked the deadly braid. I could tune quartz to harmonize with a gargoyle, but I couldn't infuse the complexity of a living being into the lump of rock to make it strong enough to withstand more than a second of the braid's attack.

Smoke blew into my eyes, and Kylie casually pushed it aside with a brush of air, her magic stronger thanks to the gargoyles. The expanding raw earth stifled the river Winnigan continued to funnel from the newly formed lake along the path Grant had cut, and steam hissed louder than a geyser as the water evaporated in the fire section. Across the park, new green growth smothered the burning trees. It wouldn't be much longer before the purifier's divided magic retook the ground we'd gained and continued its inexorable push toward the city. I couldn't think of any other options to try, and we were running out of time. We had to stop this.

I forced the words through numb lips. "We have to use gargoyles."

Seradon rested her hand on my shoulder, her eyes troubled. "If you can keep the purifier's invasion to a minimum, you'll be able to break them all free. This should work."

If and *should* were not words I wanted to use in tandem with gargoyle lives.

"You'll have to free all the gargoyles simultaneously when I activate the destructive pentagram again," the captain said. "This is powerful, unpredictable magic. If your timing's off, the backlash could leave you scarred. Or nullified."

Now he tried to talk me out of it?

I slashed the hungry tendrils of fire and earth as they tried to root into Oliver, but my eyes swept over the other four gargoyles. If we didn't give this a try, the city would be consumed and torn apart by the polarized magic. That thought alone should have been enough motivation, but I wasn't thinking about the city. I was thinking about the countless gargoyles who would suffer or die. Out in the city, four other gargoyles were currently being used as amplification tools for the purifier, helplessly being fed upon. They didn't have anyone fighting the purifier for them. My little gargoyles were willing to try to save them, and their bravery humbled me. I didn't relish taking the chance of being mentally scarred; the possibility of being nullified made my hands shake.

"I won't be any help with the pentagram," I said.

"We already laid the ground work. We'll manage without you this time," Grant said.

I turned to Lydia. She cocked her agate head, and when I reached across Oliver, she rubbed against me. "You'll be paralyzed the moment you touch the magic. Don't fly into it."

"Okay." She backed up to give herself room to extend her wings.

"Be careful."

Lydia launched into the air and flew toward the purifier's braid of air and fire on the other side of the fire section. I watched her go with my heart in my throat, wishing I could call her back.

No one spoke as she dropped to the ground a few feet from the thick helix cables flowing out of the park in an unerringly straight line. Lydia examined the braid, her long neck snaking back and forth in agitation; then she flared her wings and dove into the flow of magic.

The instant it touched her, she froze, paralyzed. Polarized air and fire drilled into her body, and I dove in with it. Pain exploded in my mind, almost jostling me from the gargoyle, but I clung to her and threw my magic against the purifier. Earth countered air and water countered fire. Dividing my efforts, I patched Lydia's insides with fresh gargoyle-tuned weaves of quartz, and I didn't let up until the purifier's hold had weakened to mere tendrils. Then I bounced back to Oliver and checked the steady creep of the purifier into his body.

"It worked," Marcus said.

The purifier's braid now ended at Lydia. Whatever gargoyle had previously been pinned on the end of the esurient magic had been freed, leaving Lydia as trapped as Oliver.

"Praise the skies," Grant said in a rare display of emotion.

"Captain," Seradon said. The warning in her tone made me look. The polarization field bulged, consuming three feet of ground in every direction, extinguishing the last of the water in the fire section. A crack and grumble of shifting earth dammed Winnigan's rerouted river.

"Looks like it's going to be a race," Grant said. "The rest of you gargoyles, move out."

"Wait!" I grabbed for Anya, Herbert, and Quinn, and they stumbled to a stop, turning to look at me. "Drop in one at a time around the circle. And fight with everything you've got."

Quinn ran back to me to nuzzle his broad lion head against my arm; then all three were airborne, flying high over the purifier's bubble to sacrifice themselves, secure in their beliefs that I could save them.

ANYA FUSED WITH THE PURIFIER FIRST, STEPPING INTO THE LINE OF wood and air between Marciano and Grant. I thought I was prepared for the purifier's swift attack, but it still caught me off guard. For several harrowing minutes, I grappled with the ferocious braid, patching Anya as I could until I forced the purifier *almost* out of her.

Then I had to leap to Oliver to fight the encroaching divisive magic in him, then in Lydia, before I could check on Anya again. A few quick snips kept the purifier in place.

I took a steadying breath. I could do this.

"Herbert needs somewhere to land," Seradon said. "Velasquez, build him a platform. Make it strong. If he falls into the water, he might drown before we can save him."

I struggled to focus on the physical world. Where Herbert needed to land between the water and the wood sections, the ground had eroded, and a waterfall cascaded along the purifier's braid. The moment the line touched him, Herbert would be paralyzed and he'd plummet to the bottom of the churning water.

A platform of granite lifted from the ground, growing until it cleared the water by five feet. I felt for the magic creating it, surprised to find more than the cables of earth reshaping the rock—I could distinguish Marcus's magic signature, a steady heat wrapped around a core of rosewood and sparking with lightning like a living jewel. It was a signature as impressive as the man himself. He wasn't half bad with earth, either. I should have expected nothing less from a full spectrum, even if he was a fire elemental. Nevertheless, I wasn't taking any chances with Herbert's life.

Any more *chances,* my guilty conscience accused.

"It needs to be stronger." I twined my magic through Marcus's, reinforcing the granite with a cage made from quartz I located from near the base of the pillar. Nothing short of a fire-fused thunderbolt would break the platform.

"You're getting bossy," Marcus said.

My rebuttal was cut short when Herbert landed on the platform and the purifier's polarized wood and water magic sliced into him. Methodically, I beat it back, layering familiar patches to lessen the pain. His acute agony had barely faded to a dull ache when Quinn fell into the line of water and earth.

"Too fast," I gasped, but he was too far away to hear, and it was too late anyway. The purifier drew strength from all five gargoyles, eating into them. I siphoned magic from the link to combat it on five fronts, frustrated by the lag in the magic. When I tried to grab more, Grant growled.

"Work with what you've got," he said, his voice coming from over my shoulder in the mirror sphere.

I growled right back, too focused on saving Quinn to form words. A giant shaft of air speared between one anchor and the next, consuming the magic in the link as Grant rebuilt the destructive pentagram. The extra boost the four gargoyles had given us had been cut off one by one as they'd sacrificed themselves to the purifier.

I seized all available remaining magic, and even though I wielded more than I could normally hold even when a gargoyle boosted me, it still didn't feel like enough.

As soon as Quinn was safe, I hopped to Oliver, then Lydia, Anya, Herbert, and back to Quinn. Cycling through the gargoyles wasn't fast enough. The purifier ate into them with mechanical relentlessness, and every time I slowed to fight it out of one gargoyle, it gained a deeper hold on the others.

Dividing my magic, I countered air in Anya and Lydia at once, then shifted to counter fire in Lydia and Oliver. Working my way around the circle fighting the purifier in two gargoyles at once proved more effective, but it still wasn't enough. I split my focus again. Since earth was my strongest element, I kept a steady onslaught of earth against air in Lydia and Anya while countering an additional polarized element in a third gargoyle. Oliver, Quinn, Herbert, and back to Oliver, then to the fire in Lydia, the wood in Anya, and back to Oliver.

I lost all sensation of my body, dizzy inside the magic and unable to slow for even a second to gain my bearings. My world narrowed to the noxious rooting braids and the purifier's unrelenting attack.

"Is she breathing?" Kylie asked. Her words bubbled out of the space between the gargoyles, and I dismissed them. They had nothing to do with saving the gargoyles.

"Don't touch her. Don't break her concentration," Seradon said.

I wouldn't break. I'd shatter. Or disintegrate. I existed in three places at once, fighting three different battles, and every so often, I found a spare thought for a fourth division of magic, and I wove a healing patch in a gargoyle. I was beyond being able to differentiate between them. They were simply five points, five homes for my consciousness. Five pieces of me, and all of them hurt.

The pain echoed through my magic, throbbing aches layered atop sharp stabs in discordant pulses that became my rhythm of movement. Jump to the sharp pain, fight, soothe, move on to the next.

Magic stuttered to me, its strength varied and always less than I needed. The only way I'd get ahead of the purifier was to work faster, and to work faster, I needed more magic.

As if in response to my thought, a rush of magic filled me, and I jounced between the gargoyles so fast it felt as if I touched them all at once.

"I'm ready to activate the pentagram."

The words struck like a gong in my head. I struggled to speak and managed, "Gnnnaaa."

"She's not ready, sir," Seradon interpreted.

"I can see that, but she needs to get ready. Mika, can you hear me? The field is going to overwhelm those gargoyles if you don't free them. Now."

Trying. I'm trying, I thought, but I couldn't get the words out.

With the influx of magic, I reversed my tactics and grabbed a braid, pulling it from one gargoyle—Lydia. Huge coils of air and fire ripped from her chest and writhed in my grip. The elements divided, some seeking a way back into Lydia, some angling over her. Like it had a mind, a predatory consciousness, the purifier's braid hunted for the next life to suck dry. I strained to hold it in check, and it took all my concentration to box in the raw power. I wouldn't be able to hold all five braids until the destructive pentagram destroyed them. Even if I had control of all the magic in our link, it would have been beyond me. As it was, I couldn't even spare enough magic to grab another.

Yet I couldn't make myself release the corrupted magic back into Lydia. She was free, but the moment I let go of the purifier, she'd be pinned and paralyzed again. We'd be right back where we started.

My heart squeezed. Lydia, Anya, Quinn, Herbert, and Oliver had all entrusted me with their lives. If I couldn't break the purifier's hold on *all* of them, they'd die. Because I wasn't the healer they needed me to be.

Unless...

Unless the purifier wasn't attached to Lydia. Unless I gave the purifier something else to latch on to.

I had already fractured into pieces. I could feel my five gargoyles more clearly than I could distinguish my body. I felt their pain and their lives as if they were my own. All it would take was a reversal. Not quite a swap. More like a transplant.

I released the air and fire braid, holding it at bay against Lydia's skin, letting it hook into her only enough to prevent it from jumping to a more distant gargoyle.

"Mika. I'm activating the pentagram. We can't wait."

No. I'm not ready.

The purifier's magic trembled, then surged tighter and stronger into the gargoyles, latching on and pulling magic from them as the pentagram drained the magic from the polarization fields.

I flung myself from gargoyle to gargoyle, tearing the purifier's hooks from each one. I didn't try to be gentle, and I forced myself to ignore the wash of pain echoing from them. I focused on myself. Me. The gargoyle healer.

I thought about the link, about how I'd felt when Marcus had coached me through finding myself. I paused my assault long enough to pull myself into one place; then I split my essence again and again into five perfect copies.

"Mika, what are— No! That's a terrible idea," Seradon cried.

My singular connection with the link fractured to five points, and I spun at the end of those points like five kites at the end of cobweb strings. Seradon was wrong. This was the only option, the only way to protect the gargoyles. It might not be the way the FPD squad would do things, but I wasn't part of the squad and I wasn't a full spectrum. I was a gargoyle healer, and I wasn't going to let a gargoyle die, not when I could prevent it.

"Mika, stop!" Marcus bellowed.

I flung myself in five directions, latching each piece of my essence onto a separate gargoyle. Burrowing into them, I reshaped my selves to resonate with each gargoyle.

My body fractured. Knives of pure fire cut through my skull. I screamed, or someone did. Someone felt that pain, but it wasn't me. It wasn't all of me.

My five selves grabbed hold of the purifier in its five different forms and wrapped each in bands of countermagic. I was pure water and earth fighting fire and air. I was fire and air fighting wood and water. I was all five elemental pairings at once, and I was gargoyle, too. I was quartz and fire and a sprinkling of water and wood and air lifting my wings.

My teeth chattered. I could hear but not feel them clacking together. No, they had to be someone else's teeth. My mouths were closed. My bodies were paralyzed.

The purifier's hold on us weakened. It couldn't pierce our magic. It retreated. Slowly at first, then it suctioned away from us, pulling free of our bodies. We clung to it. If we released it, it would find another gargoyle. It wouldn't stop. Only we could stop it.

The purifier fought us, tried to escape, but we held. We just had to hold.

"Let go, Mika. You've got to let go."

"What did she do?"

"She's going to kill herself."

"Mika! Let GO!"

Marcus's voice boomed against my eardrums. *My* eardrums. I jarred back to the tiny neglected sixth part of my self and snapped my eyes open.

Lapis lazuli eyes filled my blurry vision.

"Can you hear me? Break the link. Let go. Let the pentagram work."

I fractured to pieces, most of me sucking toward the center of the park, pulled by the vortex of destructive magic in Grant's pentagram and the purifier braids to which we—no *I*—clung.

If I released them now, would I survive the backlash? Would I be nullified?

I hesitated, my terror echoing through all the pieces of me.

"Shit, Mika. Break the link. Pull yourself together."

My head jostled on my neck. Marcus was shaking me, and I wanted to tell him to stop. It hurt. All of me hurt. The pain seared through my brain, eating through the cobweb strings. I broke from the purifier and scrambled to reel myself in, but the cobwebs had morphed to razor wires, and each tug sliced through my skull.

My body convulsed in Marcus's grip, the sky spun above me, and my consciousness imploded.

9

Warmth unfurled. I hadn't known I was cold until I felt the heat's steady, solid presence. I drifted closer to it, then burrowed into it, pulling it tight around myself. It expanded to cradle me.

An expansive hollowness opened inside me. It should have been terrifying, but I recognized it and the potential it represented. It wasn't love, but it was something close.

A web of elements unfolded around me, each line of magic beckoning. I reached out and tentatively touched one. It hummed like a violin string beneath a bow. I strummed another element, and another. Each resonated through me, reshaping me.

A jagged line of fractured magic pulsed among the elements. I shied away, but the gentle warmth solidified around me, a cocoon of heated rosewood. Emboldened, I reached for the magic around the fracture and carefully knit it back together. Earth and fire and breaths of air made it whole.

I spotted another anomaly. This time water and earth mended it. Again and again, I repaired the broken magic, bolstered by the solid heat holding me and the familiar hollowness engulfing it.

When I sealed the last fracture, I recognized the hollow sensation. Gargoyle. But not just any gargoyle. Oliver.

The cocoon trembled with my excitement. Oliver was alive. He was boosting me, which meant he wasn't trapped in the purifier. He was safe.

My thoughts tumbled together, and I jolted to full consciousness.

I stared up at Marcus, the hard lines of his face haloed by the clear blue sky. Magic eased from me, taking with it his warmth.

"What happened?" I rasped.

"You were stupid."

"What?" I squinted at those lapis lazuli eyes, then rolled my head to the side. Oliver hunched beside me, his muzzle pressed to my arm. I tried to reach for him, but my fingers only wiggled. Oliver nuzzled me, returning my pathetic attempt at a smile with a grin.

"You divided your spirit—a *very* stupid thing to do," Marcus said, pulling my gaze back to him. "Then in a stroke of sheer idiocy, you anchored each piece separately to another living creature. But that wasn't enough for you. You had to prove you were a master dimwit and you changed your resonance to match the gargoyles'."

"That part was pretty impressive, if astronomically dumb," Seradon said.

"You could have torn your brainless head to shreds with that stunt," Marcus continued, talking over Seradon. "You would have. You would have killed yourself. You would be a splintered null vegetable right now—"

"She doesn't need you to yell at her," Seradon said, stepping into view as she patted Marcus's tense shoulders. "I'm sure her hearing is perfectly fine."

The fire elemental took a deep breath and continued in a rough growl. "You'd be a meat sack right now if your gargoyles hadn't buffered you."

"It took all five," Seradon said. "It was incredible. I didn't know it was possible. They held you inside them. Like they wrapped you in magic. I think it only worked *because* you changed your resonance."

"They're all safe?" I asked.

"Yes, they're all safe," Seradon said.

Relief lifted me from my body. I closed my eyes until the dizziness passed. "If I sit up, are you going to shake me again?" I asked Marcus.

He huffed a breath, then relaxed his grip on my shoulders and helped me up. Stone feet cracked against the granite boulders as Lydia and Quinn landed nearby. Quinn galloped to me, skidding to a stop when Marcus blocked him from barreling into me.

"Are you okay, Mika?" the young gargoyle asked, his goofy lion face scrunched with concern.

"I'm fine." Okay, that was a lie. My head was going to split open if I moved too fast, and my entire body ached. The only part of me that didn't hurt was my left foot, and that was because it was still wrapped in Marcus's field patch.

Lydia snaked her head around Oliver, her glowing purple eyes scanning my body. "The fire elemental is right. That was stupid."

"Lydia!" Kylie scolded. She pushed Marcus aside and knelt in his place. I missed the support of his hands on my shoulders. I hadn't realized how much I'd been leaning on him. It hadn't been just the gargoyles who had saved me. It'd been his warmth, his magic cradling me while I recovered.

"How long was I out?" I asked.

"Five minutes. The longest five minutes of my life, too. You scared the crap out of me." Kylie brushed a wisp of hair from my face with shaking fingers.

"Sorry about that."

"But you did it. You saved Terra Haven."

The way she said it made me groan. She was going to try to make me into a hero again.

"No, *we* did it. Marcus and Grant and Winnigan and Marciano—"

"And you," Kylie insisted.

"And the gargoyles."

The captain's mirror sphere whirled through the air and halted less than a foot from my face.

"I specifically told you to stay out of this, Kylie Grayson. Who let you back in here?" Grant barked.

"And I've told you I answer to the public, not you," Kylie said calmly.

"Journalism does not trump the law."

"Sir, I recruited her," Seradon said.

The mirror sphere shot back several paces so the captain could take in all of us. "Explain."

"I knew you would need help and I figured our healer would have gargoyles who owed her a favor or two. I asked Kylie to contact them for me."

"You called the others?" I asked.

Kylie nodded proudly. I curled my fingers into the rock. She'd meant well, but her rash decision had endangered all my gargoyles' lives.

My swollen finger protested, the pain cutting temporarily through my headache, and I relaxed my hands. It'd all worked out. Berating Kylie now would be pointless. She couldn't have predicted how dangerous the situation would be for the gargoyles.

"This still doesn't explain why Kylie is back inside the park," Grant said.

"Have you ever tried to argue with a mule?" Seradon asked.

"Hey!" Kylie protested. She had risen to her feet beside Seradon, and the mirror sphere rose with her so it floated well above my head. I let their words wash over me and turned to the gargoyles. I thanked them, knowing my words were inadequate. Quinn burrowed into my left side, and Lydia bustled around Oliver to rest against my thigh. I ran my fingers over their smooth sides—careful of Oliver's rough patches—and it seemed like enough for them. I closed my eyes for a moment, savoring the peace of being surrounded by gargoyles, all of us safe.

"Where are Anya and Herbert?" I asked.

"With the captain," Quinn said. He'd begun to purr, and it garbled his words. A tiny smile cracked my lips.

"How did you recover enough to provide a boost?" I asked Oliver. He'd curled his tail around my back and pressed up against my right side, so close that he had to tilt his head all the way back to look me in the eye. "When you got out of the air section, we hardly had time to balance you, yet you feel stronger than ever."

"I opened myself to your link," he said.

"While you were pinned by the purifier?"

"It was the only way to keep fighting," Lydia said. She ran her beak through the long feathers of a wing, straightening ruffled rock quills.

I reached for the elements, gratified when earth came easily to my call. It was just my strength, no link or gargoyle enhancement, and it'd never been so wonderful to hold such a small amount of magic. I formed a basic test pentagram, refined it to resonate with a gargoyle, and slid it into Oliver. Pain echoed along the link from the laceration made by the purifier. The raw patches on his skin stung and a general soreness soaked his body. None of the injuries were serious, and he would heal from them all with time, but I planned to speed up his recovery. As soon as I felt stronger.

Lydia and Quinn were better off, not having suffered through the sandstorm and having been trapped in the purifier a shorter amount of time.

"You guys are incredible."

"We're heroes. We saved the other gargoyles," Oliver said.

"You saved the whole city. That should be the title of Kylie's next article: 'The Gargoyles Who Saved Terra Haven.'"

Oliver trilled in agreement. I'd have nightmares, but he didn't appear to have any regrets after the traumatic ordeal.

"You like this kind of excitement, don't you?" I asked Oliver.

"Yes."

"Even after everything you went through?"

He shrugged. "We saved lives."

It was the kind of answer I would have expected from a member of the FPD squad.

The wind shifted, bringing with it the dry heat dissipating from the fire section along with an acrid scent of charred earth. If possible, the park looked worse than before. I sought out the rock boulder holding the fox gargoyle, relieved to see it unaffected by the magma bubbling against the base. I'd have to wait to check on the fox until the area cooled. The marmot needed my help, too, as did the other gargoyles who had been trapped at the end of the purifier's braids. But first I had to convince my legs to move.

"Something's wrong," Marcus said. He stood a few feet away on a tall outcropping of rocks, surveying the park. "The magic doesn't feel right."

"Of course not," Seradon said. "It's going to take—"

"Squad. Convene on my signal," Grant barked through the mirror sphere. A shaft of light shot upward from the center of the park, the captain hidden by the landscape.

Marcus hopped down and strode to my side. "Can you stand?"

"Yes." *Maybe.* The gargoyles gave me space and I struggled to get my feet beneath me. Marcus gripped my arm and tugged me upright as if I weighed no more than a doll.

"What about walking?"

"No problem," I said, all bluff. My legs were rubber. I wanted to lie down and take a nap and not wake until the pain in my head abated.

"Maybe you should stay here," Kylie said. "I'll go get a healer. You're in no condition to—"

"No." Grant's tone brooked no argument. "Mika needs to come here."

My heart sank. We weren't linked, and the captain wasn't likely to want to use me in a link again, anyway. A gargoyle had to be in trouble, and from Grant's location, it had to be the marmot.

I took a step. My knees wobbled but didn't collapse.

"I could carry you again," Marcus offered.

"Again?" Kylie echoed.

I was tempted. My foot was still cut, even if I couldn't feel it through Marcus's field wrap. I was exhausted. I hurt. But he had taken injuries, too, and I wasn't going to add to them if I didn't have to. Plus, I was afraid that if I allowed myself a moment of weakness, my remaining willpower—the only thing holding me upright and conscious—would evaporate. The marmot gargoyle needed me; I'd be weak later.

My steps evened out, but Marcus kept a hand under my elbow. I must have looked as bad as I felt if he expected me to collapse at any moment. Quinn, Lydia, and Oliver trailed us for a few feet, then took flight when we started climbing the granite teeth. I would have preferred the flatter ground of the former fire section, but embers smoldering among the magma flow nixed that option. A small lake flooded the water section, and it would have taken too long—and too much energy—to circle around to the air section, where the dust cloud was settling to reveal a sand-blasted landscape a great deal smoother than the one through which we climbed.

Marcus lifted me up taller steps and carried me down the steep descent on the other side. I grumbled my thanks and pretended I'd managed the whole earthen obstacle course on my own. Marcus's lips curled in a small smile. I was doing my best to appear stoic and strong, and he found me amusing. Great.

"Okay. We get it. You're a tough little healer," Seradon said when I paused to catch my breath. She grabbed my left arm and looped it over her shoulders, circling my waist with her right arm. "But it's time to move."

Marcus grinned and lifted my right arm around his shoulders, clutching the waistband of my pants with his left. Between the two of them, my feet touched the ground only every third or fifth step, and we covered the rest of the distance to the central pentagon at a run that somehow left me more winded than either of the squad members. Kylie ran in our wake, and I caught fragments of her panted words as she described the park to herself. I didn't need to look to know she captured her words in a bubble of air that she'd use as notes when she wrote her article.

At the heart of the park, the central pentagon plateau had suffered the most drastic alterations. The ground on the wood side was simply gone. The hole dropped away in a triangular wedge heavily eroded on the right by the air section and on the left by water. The plateau would have been submerged without the outlet the sinkhole provided, judging by the amount of water filling it. A V of ankle-high, razor-thin marble and granite defined the tip of the earth section, ending at the marmot's toes. It cut a ridge straight through the broken marble pentagram, and below the plateau, it dammed the water on the left and the cooling ripples of magma on the right. The ring of sycamore trees around the pentagram had been reduced to two, both with roots submerged in the receding pool. The others had burned or toppled.

The marmot had survived better than I feared. A little water and heat couldn't hurt him. The ground remained stable and flat under his feet. Only his side that had been exposed to the sandstorm had suffered.

But it wasn't my need to heal the raw length of his body that spurred my steps. A sphere encased the marmot, and the elements swirled around the outside like the rainbow on a bubble of soap, only this bubble was twice my height and equally as wide. Inside, the elements simply didn't exist.

Grant, Winnigan, and Marciano stood to one side, and above them, Herbert and Anya perched on the same pillar where Oliver had sat hours earlier when we'd first arrived. Short-lived relief flashed through me at the sight of them, safe and whole.

"What's going on?" I asked, struggling free of Seradon and Marcus. I thought I knew the answer, but I didn't want to be right.

"That's the largest null pocket I've ever seen," Seradon said, confirming my fear.

"Damn!" Marcus stopped short, steadying Kylie when she tripped into him.

I stared at the nothingness around the marmot, fighting back a tide of helplessness. The agony of just my legs trapped in a null field had been overwhelming. When I'd foolishly submerged myself in the tiny pocket, I had felt like I was dying. Gargoyles lived and breathed magic. Existing without it wouldn't simply be agony; it'd kill the marmot. I didn't know how much time he had left, but it couldn't be long.

"We've got to get him out of there. How do we break it?"

"The same way I broke the one that trapped you," Marcus

answered. "We have to push magic from the center outward to desta-bilize the field."

"We don't have much time," Grant said, taking the words from my mouth.

"It's expanding!" Kylie gasped and backpedaled from her close examination of the null's surface. Her wide eyes darted to Grant's. "That's not how a null field works. They dissipate."

"In a normal world, yes, but this park was overwhelmed with pure elements. When the destructive pentagram drained it, it pulled all the balanced energy into one spot, and they negated each other."

In a massive way. The gargoyle sat at the center of the null field, too far inside for me to reach, but I had to try. Every second of delay could cost the marmot his life.

"Boost me," I ordered, glancing toward the gargoyles. Oliver, Lydia, and Quinn had joined their siblings, perching on nearby pillars. Magic from all five opened inside me, filling me with almost as much strength as I'd had in the link. I grabbed it all and stepped into the null sphere.

10

Pain crumpled me and momentum alone propelled my next slow step deeper into the null field. The air coalesced around my body, tight as molasses and equally hard to breathe. My bones sprouted needles of agony, all pushing outward through my skin as magic leeched from my body. I stretched cramping fingers toward the marmot, pushing all my gargoyle-enhanced magic toward it, willing it to live. The other hand I left flung behind me in the normal air, pulling in every scrap of magic I could hold.

When Marcus had freed me from the small null pocket, he'd been able to direct his magic across the empty sphere to puncture it, but I couldn't push the elements more than a few inches from my outstretched hand. No matter how much I strained, the magic oozed from me, the elements squiggling chaotically before dissipating into the dense air and its all-consuming nothingness.

I shuffled another constricted step, and pain slid up the arm behind me and closed over my fingertips. All magic vanished. It didn't snap in a backlash. It didn't trickle to a thin thread. It ceased to exist, leaving only pain, and I was still a yard from the gargoyle.

I gasped for air, my equilibrium lost in the saturation of agony. I stepped back, reaching for magic, and my fingers crunched against an invisible wall, bending backward, the sting indistinguishable from the stabbing pain invading my entire body.

A strong hand shot through the null field's shell and clamped onto my forearm. Magic, sweet and soft, pulsed into me, and the wall softened. Marcus yanked me free of the null. I fell against him, limp, and he hooked his hands under my armpits to prevent me from collapsing at his feet. Every joint in my body ached as if I'd been sick with the flu for a week, but I could feel magic again. It settled against my skin like a balm, and I could have happily rolled in the feeling if I could have figured out how to work my muscles.

"What were you thinking?" Marcus bellowed.

"He's going to die." My words were frustratingly breathy. I might have sounded stronger if I could have lifted my head from Marcus's chest. Even better if tears didn't thicken my throat. Hadn't the marmot been through enough already? Every second it took us to save him was a moment of endless pain for him. "We have to save him. Can't waste time."

"Well, there goes my plan," Grant said, sarcasm thick in his voice.

"Give her a break. She's a healer. You know how they're never right in the head," Seradon said.

"Some less so than others," Marcus growled.

Clutching my temples, I silently conceded that I'd been rash. Panic and guilt ate at me as I stared at the helpless marmot, but with the slowly ebbing pain forcing me to take a moment to think, I recognized the stupidity of my actions.

Not looking at anyone, I righted myself, only to grab for Marcus's forearm when my left foot contacted the ground and the sharp pain stole my breath as if the granite spear had been driven anew through my sole. The null field had negated the field patch.

Gritting my teeth, I centered my balance on my right foot and finally managed to stand on my own. Marcus squinted at me, then let me go.

"We need to unbalance the null," Grant said. "Velasquez, the hottest fire you've got."

Marcus stepped away from me, and I swayed in place. Kylie darted forward to prop me up. She might have said something, but my whole being was focused on the squad's rescue efforts.

Blue-white flame shot from Marcus's hands, setting fire to a bushel of plants Marciano grew from a crack in the marble. Grant snapped branches thicker than his legs from the downed sycamores, and he and Winnigan used bands of air to pile them atop Marcus's fire. Kylie directed a whirlwind of air through the surrounding area, collecting twigs and smaller branches to add to the flames. In less than a minute, the squad had built an unnaturally hot bonfire twice as tall as Marciano. Kylie helped me hobble backward away from the intense heat of the blue flames. Elemental fire magic flowed from the blaze, and it licked against the null field.

I held my breath, waiting for the first signs that the null was shrinking. Against the building power of the singular element, it should have destabilized.

The null crept across the burning logs, smothering the roaring fire to soft orange flickers. No elemental magic formed around the flames inside the null. Fire without the element? How was that even possible?

"So much for that plan," Marcus said, dampening the fire to coals. Elemental strands shifted above the embers to twine up the outside edge of the null sphere.

"Are you up for linking yet?" Grant asked Seradon.

She shook her head. "Still can't lift a pebble."

"Okay. Mika, sit your ass down before you fall down and link up. We're forming a bridge and getting to the heart of this."

I didn't wait until I was sitting; I thrust an equalized bundle of elements at Grant, and he deftly caught it, pulling me into a link. His thundercloud of magical strength swamped my thoughts; then Marcus's heated rosewood shield snapped into the link, followed by the cool slap of Winnigan's magic and a snarl of smoldering ironwood that must have been Marciano. Practice made it easier to distinguish each elemental in the link, but I didn't take any pleasure in the new skill since it got me no closer to saving the marmot.

I lowered myself to sit on a blob of marble. At one point, it'd probably been a bench, but the polarization had reshaped it into a black-veined lump of rock. Kylie kept a hand on my arm as if she thought I'd tip off the seat. When the gargoyles dropped into the link, opening a seemingly bottomless well of magic, I thought Kylie's concern might be justified. Magic roared through me, and I teetered on the edge of control. Losing myself in the magic was tempting. If I let go and lost myself, I'd be buffered from my pain.

I'd also be useless to the marmot.

I am a gargoyle healer. I didn't really need the words to collect myself this time, but it helped me to hear it, even if it was only in my thoughts.

"Are you okay?" Kylie asked. "Can I do anything?"

I shook my head. At one time, I would have thought this amount of magic could solve any problem. Now I knew better. All magic had its limits.

Grant and Marcus clasped forearms, and Marciano grabbed hold of Marcus's other arm. Winnigan trotted to my side and reached for me. She stood close enough for us to lock arms without me needing to stand; then she and Marciano linked up so we made a human chain. Seradon stood back out of the way, her face a mask of frustration. Not being able to help must have been tearing her up inside.

I glanced at the marmot. I knew exactly how she felt.

The captain eased into the null field, arms splayed, one toward the gargoyle, the other toward Marcus. Tight lines formed around his eyes and his face whitened, but if I hadn't been inside the null myself, I never would have known pain ate through his body from the inside out.

Grant drew on all our magic, and I swayed toward him. I wasn't the only one; the squad tilted toward the captain as the forcible suction of the elements through us tilted our equilibrium.

Grant funneled all the magic out of the palm he stretched toward the marmot. The captain's long arms enabled him to progress a few feet closer to the marmot than I had, but despite the massive level of our combined power, little more magic escaped into the null. With another step, his fingers on Marcus's arm slid past the invisible barrier, submerging Grant in the null field.

The link frayed and magic whiplashed. With a cry, I cut myself free of the wild energy, and an explosion of raw elements burst into the air. A backdraft of wind pressed me to the marble and knocked Kylie to her butt; then it dissipated. Down the line, elements bloomed from the squad, displacing the air with audible snaps and pops. Inside the bubble, the captain stood several feet from the center, not even close enough to touch the marmot.

"Grant!" Kylie picked herself up and darted toward the null field. Seradon intercepted her.

The captain turned, his body hunched, and reached for Marcus, having lost contact in the wild release of magic. Marcus and Marciano both reached into the field, feeding their individual magic into Grant and yanking him free.

The marmot remained imprisoned in the middle of the null, as helpless to free himself as we were to reach him.

"It's not dissipating or weakening," Winnigan said, massaging her temples. "It's *eating* magic and getting stronger."

Chills tingled down my spine. Elsa had a lot to answer for. Her attempt to manufacture her own gargoyle-like enhancement had backfired in the worst way possible—and after having experienced the polarized magic, that was saying something.

"How big could the null field get?" Kylie asked.

I caught the anxious look Winnigan and Grant shared, and fresh dread weighted my stomach. If they were worried, I should be paralyzed with fear.

"It might stop where the polarization stopped," Winnigan said. "It might not. We've never dealt with anything like this."

If the null field got that big, the marmot would certainly die. The fox, too. If it didn't stop expanding, all magic would cease to exist and everyone would die. We *had* to get magic to the center. But how? I looked around, desperately hoping a solution would drop out of the air.

"A bridge," Marciano said. He was a man of few words, and he didn't waste any now.

Grant snapped his fingers and pointed at Marciano. "Right. If we can't be the bridge, we can make one. Something physical. With one of us on the inside guiding the magic, this could work."

"Here." Marciano wrapped wood, fire, and water around the branch of one of the remaining standing sycamores. The limb came free and Marciano's magic stitched the bark together to repair the damage. Even as the limb floated toward us on hefty bands of air, Marciano reshaped it, stretching and growing the branch until it was thinner than my wrist and long enough to span the null field.

"Good," Grant said, plucking the pole from the air.

"It won't work," I said. I'd caught sight of my pack, tossed aside when I arrived and forgotten in what had become the water section when we fled.

I shoved from my marble seat before my doubts could catch up with the impractical hope surging through me. I hopped across the uneven ground and dropped beside the waterlogged bag. Cold mud squished under my knees and soaked through my pants as I fumbled with the drawstring on the bag. When it wouldn't loosen, I snapped it with a sharp twist of earth.

"Mika?" Marcus asked.

"Explain yourself, Healer," Grant demanded.

I yanked Kylie's soggy library books and my ruined notebook from the bag and flung them out of the way, then upended the bag. Clear seed crystals poured into the mud, all twenty-five pounds scattering in front of me.

"Wood is weak," I said. "It's too malleable and the grain in the wood will fracture our magic. You and I both had a hard enough time pushing magic from our bodies; we'd have to work five times as hard to funnel it through a branch. Quartz accepts all elements better. It'll be a stronger, cleaner bridge."

I'd worked with seed crystals a thousand times, a hundred thousand times; effortlessly, I wrapped them in quartz-tuned earth magic and fused them together. When Oliver, then the other gargoyles, dropped magic into me, the crystals flew through the air too fast for my eyes to track, but I didn't need to see what I was doing. I ran feelers of earth across the ground, and every crystal sang to me. I could differentiate the subtle variations in each one and discern how they'd best align together without looking. Even unaided, I could have mustered enough air to lift the crystals into place, but with the help of the gargoyles, the marble-size seeds were as light as grains of sand. The bar grew in a seamless length, complete before I finished talking.

"True," Seradon said. She paused to take in the finished rod. "But you're not the strongest elemental. It should be Marciano inside the null guiding the magic."

"No. I'm the gargoyle healer. I'm going in." I stood, lifting the quartz pole like a staff. It towered over me.

"This is about more than saving the gargoyle," Marcus said.

"Of course. This is about saving magic itself, which includes saving all magic creatures, gargoyles included." *But especially this marmot.* If the null continued to expand, a lot of lives were in jeopardy, but right now, only one was and I was the best person to help him. "Besides, none of you are stronger with quartz than me."

I sounded brave. I probably even looked brave since the quartz rod was helping me stand up straight. I was filthy, bloody, and battered, and I wasn't backing down.

I did my best not to acknowledge how terrified I was. This could go wrong in so many ways that if I didn't keep moving, I'd be paralyzed with doubt. I was counting on my quartz specialty to be enough, but it might not be. And if it wasn't, I could be dooming the marmot gargoyle. I could be dooming everyone. The more times we failed to break the null and the longer it existed, the stronger and bigger it grew. If I failed, it might be too big to stop the next time, even by a stronger elemental. Plus, there was the crushing pain of the null itself and the very real possibility I'd run out of air before I even reached the center.

But I wouldn't back down. Not only had I proven myself capable of doing things today that even these elite FPD warriors didn't know were possible, but also *I was a gargoyle healer.* I was supposed to protect the gargoyles in this city, yet I'd been oblivious to the marmot's needs and he'd been trapped and tortured on my watch. I wasn't going to fail him again.

"Break the quartz into five pieces," Marcus said.

Grant nodded. He turned to Kylie. "Reporter, it's time to do something useful for once."

While I severed the quartz rod into five pieces and gently coaxed them all to the length of the original piece, Winnigan accepted a bundle of elements from Kylie. My best friend would be the fifth person in their link, taking my place on the outside.

Seradon examined the slender rods. Quartz might be one of the strongest rocks in the world, but anything stretched too thin became fragile, and the five rods were now hardly thicker than my pinkie finger. They'd snap if I stepped on them, but they could still support their own weight, so they would have to be strong enough.

"You'll need to use all the magic together, and you won't have a lot of energy left to combine it manually once you're in the null," Seradon said. "If you fuse the bridges together, it'll give you one place to hold and allow the magic to mingle."

"Good thinking." With Seradon's help, I arranged the rods on the ground so the ends made five perfect wedges and the tips formed an apple-size pentagon at the center. A few twists of quartz element and they were fused.

"I never would have called you into this mess if I'd known it was going to be this dangerous," Seradon said.

Surprised, I looked up into her worried brown eyes.

"It should be me going into the null," she said.

"Aww, FPD guilt. That's cute."

Seradon's laugh came out as a bark, and she clapped me on the back.

A rumble of earth shook the plateau as Grant guided the magic of the link into the sinkhole, lifting a slab of mud-covered hornfels to replace the missing chunk of ground. When he finished, the group circled my lines of quartz, each standing at an end. Seradon moved out of the way, a serious expression replacing her momentary mirth. A glow of magic surrounded me, swirling in the link between the others. I shared a glance with Kylie, reading my own fears in her large blue eyes. She managed a tremulous smile, and I tried to return it.

Everyone picked up a rod and I lifted the central pentagon. Together we walked toward the null.

"Kylie, let go and circle around," Grant ordered. Her rod needed to pass through the null and out the other side before she could grab it again. The rest of the rods were long enough for the squad to hang on to the tips without encountering the expanding null sphere.

I slid my hand down the slender quartz as Kylie let it go, lifting the fragile bridge higher so the sagging tip didn't catch on the ground and snap. Kylie darted around the null to take her place on the other side, and the squad and I shifted to align the spokes to avoid hitting the marmot.

Taking a deep breath, I released all magic and stepped into the null.

———

NOTHINGNESS PUNCHED ME IN THE GUT AND THE PAIN BLOSSOMED IN all directions through my body. I fought against panic, striving for even breaths. My lungs pumped dense air, starving on the too-thin oxygen. No matter how deeply I inhaled, I couldn't quite catch my breath.

Leaning into the soupy null field, I locked eyes on the marmot and focused on moving my feet one agonizing step at a time. My heart constricted at the sight of him. No longer blinded by panic and without the film of elements that coated the outer layer of the null sphere muddying the view, I beheld the toll today's numerous traumas had inflicted on the gargoyle. All color had leeched from his former earthy brown and blue-tipped body; he looked like a statue carved from a chunk of slate and as equally devoid of life.

Hang on. I'm coming.

The null drank magic from me, siphoning it from my muscles and knotting my joints until I hobbled on cramped feet and bowed legs. In the oddly thick environment, increasing my pace proved as impossible as jogging at the bottom of a lake. No energy lifted from the earth; no element twined through the air currents. The physical pieces were all in place, but without magic, the world felt dead. Even sounds were muffled and indistinct.

My hand spasmed on the delicate quartz pentagon, and it flexed in my grip. My fingers curled, the pain gnarling them into a fist against my will. I stopped on quivering legs and let go of the unsupported pole to use my free hand to pry my gnarled fingers from the pentagon. If I crushed it, I'd have to start all over, wasting time the marmot didn't have.

I almost dropped the pentagon as I maneuvered the two rods I stood between to rest on my shoulders, with the pentagon pressing against my throat. Afraid to hold the unsupported quartz pole in my cramping hand and risk snapping it, I used the back of my hand to lift the sagging tip. The slender quartz weighed no more than five pounds, but it felt like fifty.

My feet had taken root. I strained forward, pushing into the excruciating molasses, and heaved the lead weight of my throbbing foot. I kept my eyes pinned on the marmot, my entire existence narrowing to reaching him. Five minutes or five hours later, the fingers of my free hand brushed against his cold chest. The weight of Kylie's quartz line lifted and I stumbled the last two steps on what felt like the broken bones of my own feet.

The marmot appeared no better up close. No life pulsed beneath my hand. Even though I'd told myself I wouldn't be able to feel anything without magic, it still came as a shock. He felt like a piece of carved rock.

Please don't be dead. Please don't be dead.

I leaned close to the gargoyle, until the V of the two quartz rods cut into my neck and two separate lines rested against the marmot's slender shoulders. He was the center of everything, and short of climbing him, this was the closest I could get to the heart of the null.

Very carefully, I closed my fingers around the pentagon. Magic trickled into me, soothing the persistent burn of the null in my finger-tips. For a second, the relief swelled through me; then the misery of the other ninety-nine percent of my body overwhelmed my senses again.

I drew the magic to me—and gritted my teeth as the pain in my extremities increased in response. I could feel the others at the end of the quartz lines and the gargoyles inside their link. They held over-whelming magic, but no matter how they strained to shove it to me, the null strangled their copious magic to the merest trickle. It would be enough. It had to be.

I pushed every scrap of magic I could touch into the null. The soft lines of loose elements drifted in the vacuum and vanished a few inches from the quartz.

Black spots danced in my vision as my brain tried to shut down to protect itself from the pain, and I abandoned that tactic. I needed more magic than I could pull, and continuing to use the tiny trickle squeezing through the quartz wasn't going to cut it. In torturous increments, I refined the incoming magic into the five elements, layering them around the pentagram in the constructive cycle: earth, water, wood, air, fire. The magic in the rods shifted to align the incoming elemental energy to match my pentagon as the others caught on to what I was doing.

I planned on letting the constructive cycle do the work for me and build up its strength until it had enough magic to make an impact when I released it into the null, but it didn't increase, or if it did, it wasn't quick.

While I waited, my feet and legs went numb. The pain didn't abate, but I couldn't feel the muscles anymore. I couldn't find my foot to lift or my knee to bend. I couldn't move or escape. Panting, I sucked in volumes of empty null and very little oxygen. At this rate, I'd suffo-cate before the magic built up to a usable level in the pentagon. I needed to create a faster, stronger constructive cycle—the strongest I'd ever encountered.

I needed to use the purifier's constructive pattern.

Oh, the irony.

I'd spent the last hour countering the purifier's powerful helix braids. I knew them intimately. If I'd had a chance to think about it, I would have said I would take the knowledge of those destructive, horrific weaves to my grave, determined to never let them see the light of day again. Yet, less than a half hour later I was reconstructing them and praying it would save us.

Knowing what the weaves looked like and re-creating them with thimblefuls of magic were two very different concepts. To keep the trickle of magic flowing, the constructive pattern along the pentagon had to be maintained, so I was forced to build the helixes into the empty air at the center of the pentagon, unanchored. The elements kept slipping from my grasp and evaporating into the null. Every time I held two elements long enough to twine them together, fire ate through my body as the null tried to pull my skin inside out. The jabbing, pounding pain in my skull should have long since liquefied my brain. Part of me hoped it would. Soon. Just to make the pain stop.

Numbness crept up my hips and abdomen. I clung to the marmot with my free hand, afraid I'd topple. Three braids down and bands of steel nothingness tightened around my lower ribs, constricting my limited oxygen even further. The black dots were back, but this time I couldn't stop. Even if I did, it wouldn't help. The null had me in its jaws and it wasn't going to let me go.

I formed the final helix braid as the paralysis slid over my chest. I'd divided the inner space of the pentagon into five triangles, creating an inverted purifier with all the spokes pointing inward. With a final twist, I connected the free tips of the braids using a minuscule constructive loop, then released it.

Please be alive. I stared into the gargoyle's dead eyes, feeling the life suck from me. Air was a fond memory. *You'd better live. You'd better make this worth it.*

Magic swirled in the pentagon faster than before, but nothing happened. Not even tiny tendrils of magic released to counter the null. I'd failed.

I clung to the marmot, and his statue-like arms supported me under my armpits. My legs must have collapsed, because I was looking at the marmot's pockmarked chest instead of his eyes.

"Hold, damn it!" Grant's order penetrated the void, his voice muffled like it was filtered through a wall of rugs.

My neck went limp, and I remembered to loll my head back, away from the quartz pentagon. I couldn't crush the pentagon.

Kylie stood at the end of her quartz rod, and though her expression was intent, tears coursed down her cheeks. Marcus stood at the next quartz rod, his face beet red and veins at his temple protruding as he shouted over my head at Grant.

"... have to get her ... killing her ..."

Crap. I was dying. I mustered my energy and fought to remain conscious, to draw a breath, to live. The void smacked me down as easily as I might crush an ant. My will petered out.

11

Darkness closed around my irises, narrowing the world to a pinpoint. A compressed cyclone of elements shot from the pentagon in a flat disk, slicing along the bands of quartz. They hit the null's boundary and it imploded. Magic hit me with the slap of a belly flop against my entire body. The elements poured into me, igniting every fiber of my being in fiery agony.

Then air rushed into my lungs, and for a glorious instant, my body was absolutely pain-free. As if in slow motion, the purifier's braids multiplied and swelled along the quartz rods before blasting outward, mindlessly hunting for the nearest gargoyles in their paths.

I'd saved us only to doom us.

No. Not again.

Pain sank back into my body, but it was an echo of the previous crippling agony and unimportant. Yanking the pentagon over my head, I turned my back to the marmot to shield it and smashed the purifier-lined crystal rods against the marble. Shards of quartz exploded and magic ripped from the pieces, bursting apart and slamming me into the gargoyle. His hard paws jabbed my ribs and my head snapped back against the solid rock of his neck. My brain rang like a struck gong between my ears.

Magic unraveled inside me, eating along my neural pathways. My knees gave out and I crumpled to the shard-strewn marble. A pillow of air cradled my head before it hit the ground, and I fought to keep my eyes open. The marmot still needed me.

A rush of warmth cascaded from my scalp to my toes. Fire magic slid into my bones, accompanied by a peripheral feeling of rosewood and traces of lightning. Marcus. Tension uncoiled in my stomach; I was safe. Cool water and veins of wood spun around me, sinking slowly into my skin until they met up with the warmth of the fire in my bones, restoring the magic leeched from me and leaving me blissfully numb.

"It's just a field patch," Marcus said. His voice rumbled against my ear.

He held me cradled against his chest. I was too euphoric from the lack of pain to care that I looked like a complete wimp. I allowed myself exactly five breaths to savor the glorious lack of pain before I struggled to stand. Marcus assisted me, not commenting when I had to brace a hand on his shoulder to stay upright after he set me on my feet.

I reached for magic, and it trickled to me along scalded mental pathways. My legs almost gave out with relief. I hadn't nullified myself.

Oliver dropped from the pillar where he'd perched and landed next to me. He wrapped a wing around my leg, giving me much needed stability. Lydia swooped to land beside Marcus. She gently nipped at his shirt, then bumped his forearm with her rock head and leaned into him. Half grown, she came to his waist. She was going to be a huge gargoyle. The other siblings dropped to the ground and circled the marmot. Herbert flapped ungracefully when the muddy ground of the former water section suctioned to his armadillo paws, and he hopped a few feet to the left.

The five gargoyles opened their magical boost to me, but I didn't accept it. The pain behind what little magic I held told me not to push myself. It felt like I'd sprained my brain, and I needed to heal before I could work magic at full strength, let alone gargoyle-enhanced levels.

I didn't need the boost to form a soft probe, either. I slid the gargoyle-tuned mix of elements into the marmot, holding my breath. He'd been stabbed repeatedly, used as a magic pump, assaulted by polarized magic, and suffocated in a null. On top of that, he suffered from a disease that left him comatose. It was foolish to hope he'd survived.

His fragile life beat deep inside his jasper body. My breath shook when I released it. He teetered on the edge of life, fractured by magic and pain and the mysterious dormancy disease. Using the thinnest, most delicate bands of jasper-tuned earth and soft brushes of fire, I fed him magic. As I moved the elements through him, I wove gossamer-fine patches over his fractures and watched as his body absorbed my magic and used it to begin to heal. His frailty dictated my speed—achingly slow—and the extent to which I could assist him. Well before he was whole, I eased my magic from him. Anything more would overtax his system and do more damage than good.

I blinked at a world washed with muted pink and orange. It took my sluggish brain several seconds to connect the warm lights with the sunset—longer to realize that I stared up at the sky because Marcus held me cradled in his arms.

Again.

How embarrassing.

"Will he live?" Marcus asked when I focused on his face.

"Yes. With more healing." With all the trauma he'd experienced, I hadn't been able to identify the cause of his coma, but that problem would have to wait until tomorrow. Or the next day. I needed to do some recovering of my own first.

"I think I can stand," I said. It felt silly for him to be holding me.

"Mmm." Marcus sat and placed me on the ground next to him. I decided it was a good compromise. "Grant has summoned healers."

"Oh, good." As wonderful as Marcus's field patches were at numbing the pain, I needed true healing. So did Seradon and Marcus.

In the fading sunlight, the devastated park looked like the aftermath of a horrific war between elementals. Winnigan and Marciano stood at the bottom of the plateau, facing Lincoln River. Winnigan had removed her shoes to stand with her toes in the receding pool, and soft bands of the element twined up her legs, absorbing into her skin. Marciano stood behind her, his arms wrapped around the much smaller woman, his chin resting on her head. Silently, they soaked in the sunset. I hadn't realized they were a couple, but somehow the giant and the petite redhead fit together.

Grant, Seradon, and Kylie sat at the end of a shattered line of quartz where Kylie had been standing when we broke the null. Her slumped posture indicated her exhaustion, but it didn't stop her from pestering them with questions.

"You'll recover faster if you don't talk," Grant advised.

Kylie visibly gathered herself to argue, but Seradon spoke first. "I think she's earned a few answers."

Grant scowled, then nodded. Kylie graced him with a triumphant grin, and it made me smile. She couldn't have been hurt if she was still angling for her story. Or at least not *badly* hurt. She looked up and met my gaze, tossing me a wink Grant couldn't see.

"In that case," she said, "let's start at the beginning. You said a concerned citizen reported Elsa. How were you contacted? What was your first impression of the scene?"

Grant's grumpy one-word responses seemed to amuse Seradon. I had no doubt Kylie would coax the whole story from the captain, but I tuned them out. I didn't want to relive today, not now and especially not knowing that my own Kylie interrogation lurked in my future.

"Are you okay?" I asked Marcus.

One dark eyebrow lifted. "Why wouldn't I be?"

"Right, this was just another day in a full-five squad."

"Are you mad?"

I shook my head. I was, but it was petty. I felt like I'd been pressed through a mesh strainer and clumsily reassembled while he merely looked a little tired.

"I wasn't the one inside the null," he said, as if he could read my mind.

"What was it like on the outside?"

His gaze slid down my face to rest on my hand. At some point, Oliver had tucked his sinuous body against my side, and I absently stroked his wings where I'd healed them earlier. The rest of his body still needed attention. *Soon,* I promised us both silently.

The other gargoyles remained around the marmot, and their eyes drooped. I sent soft test weaves through them, reassuring myself that all my gargoyles were okay. The ordeal with the purifier and the null had exhausted them, but they'd recover.

"Like running in quicksand," Marcus said, finally answering my question. "I had so much magic available to me, but no matter how hard I pushed it down the quartz, only a trickle reached you. It felt like I was doing nothing but watching you . . . watching you be drained." He paused, lifting his face toward the sunset. "Useless. Being on the outside felt useless."

I wasn't sure what to say. The sunset turned the high clouds from pink to purple. Nearby, a bird sang a lullaby to the sun and a few crickets added sharp accompaniment.

"The gargoyles were true heroes," he said. Oliver lifted his head, bright eyes shining in the twilight. "I've never encountered a null that big—not even half that big. Without their help, we wouldn't have been enough. As it is, it's going to be days before any of us can work magic at full capacity. Right now, without us linking back up, you're probably the strongest elemental in the park."

Huh. So he was human after all.

"You saved us twice today," I said to Oliver. "Terra Haven owes you a medal of honor."

Oliver hummed, a quiet, happy sound. Despite everything he'd been through, he was more balanced and healthy-looking internally than if he'd spent a week safely ensconced in my apartment. His siblings were listing on their feet, but he was alert.

"You have a warrior's spirit, Oliver," Marcus said.

He was right. I took a deep breath and acknowledged a truth I'd been hiding from myself: Oliver needed more than me. His siblings were all exploring roosting locations throughout the city, places they could call home where they felt a resonance with the inhabitants and environment. But Oliver had remained with me, and it wasn't simply because he liked me better than the others did. He wasn't like his siblings. He wasn't ready to settle into one place. He was more adventurous. He was happiest when we were rushing toward a gargoyle in need. He was a rare gargoyle who thrived on action.

I leaned around Marcus and called to Grant. We were close enough to converse, but he promptly extricated himself from Kylie's conversation and strode to my side. I didn't miss the way he glanced back at my best friend, though, and there was nothing grumpy about his expression. Maybe Kylie didn't bother him as much as he pretended.

"What can I do for you, gargoyle healer?"

"Could you use a gargoyle in your unit?"

Grant's eyes widened and his eyebrows flicked up. "Is there a willing gargoyle?"

I glanced at Oliver. The young gargoyle watched me curiously.

"You'll never find a better group of people to work with, Oliver," I said, my heart breaking. Oliver had been a true hero today, and he'd thrived in the role. I'd been selfish to keep him as my companion. It was time to set him free. "You're courageous and strong—a real warrior, like Marcus said. I don't think you'll ever be happy in just one place. You need adventure."

"We have adventures," Oliver said, his brow furrowed.

"Sure, every once in a while. But the squad has experiences like this every day."

"You were a real asset today," Grant said. "I'd be honored to have you on my team."

Oliver perked up.

"Think of all the important work you could do with them. You could save Terra Haven every day." I wouldn't cry. This was for the best. With the squad, Oliver could do what he loved, and the squad would keep him safe and healthy. He'd be happy. "I think you'd make a great addition to Captain Monaghan's squad."

"Really, Mika? Do you think so?" Oliver's tiny ears quivered behind his carnelian ruff.

"I do. This is your calling, Oliver." A bittersweet ache settled in my chest, partially assuaged by knowing I was putting his well-being above my own needs. This was how a true gargoyle healer behaved.

Oliver leapt to his feet with an excited trill that echoed through the park, and the pressure in my chest eased. This was the right call. I swallowed the lump in my throat, and forced a smile that turned genuine when Oliver launched straight into the air, shouting, "I am a *warrior*!"

12

I limped down the library steps and turned to wait for Oliver to glide down to meet me. Pigeons cooed and bobbed along the roofline, but the blue sky remained empty. I turned away, my heart constricting with familiar soreness. It'd been almost two weeks since Oliver had departed with the FPD, and I'd thought it'd be easier by now. For the twentieth time today, I assured myself that I'd made the right decision in encouraging him to go with the squad. Remembering his excitement helped.

Distractions worked better.

I purchased a copy of the *Terra Haven Chronicle* from a newsboy on the corner and hobbled to lean against the brick wall of a building, out of the way of traffic. The healers had done a wonderful job mending my foot, though it'd hurt worse than the original injury. I had another week of wearing a brace while the freshly knitted tissue and muscle strengthened before I'd be cleared to walk unimpeded. I was counting the hours.

The front page of the paper focused on the recent governor's debate and had nothing to do with me, gargoyles, the full-five squad, or Focal Park. I breathed a sigh of relief. I'd had the dubious honor of gracing the front page again, thanks to Kylie. Sometime before the healers had arrived, she'd snapped a picture of me, Marcus, and the marmot behind us. I'd looked like a disaster victim, not a hero, especially next to Marcus, who even in repose managed to appear ready to rush off to halt a swarming clutch of basilisks. The headline had been equally embarrassing: *Gargoyle Healer Saves Terra Haven*. Kylie had a gift for writing, but she tended to exaggerate my heroism. Thankfully column space had been limited, and after she'd described everything else that had transpired thanks to Elsa's purifier, she'd only had two inches left to recount my destruction of the null. She still managed to make me seem impressive enough to be a member of the FPD.

I found Kylie's follow-up story on page 11 today. It detailed the ongoing cleanup at the park and a few facts about Elsa's career, ending with a simple statement: *Elsa Lansing remains under guard at the Soothing Halls mental hospital, awaiting trial.*

I folded the paper and stuffed it in my bag with my haul of books. I slung it over my shoulder and checked to see if Oliver was—

Releasing a sigh, I limped along the sidewalk and tried to picture a punishment a jury could dole out that would be worse than Elsa's current fate. In her greedy pursuit of more power, she had nullified herself. For the rest of her life, she'd be able to see magic but never touch or use it again.

I shuddered. The few minutes I'd spent inside the null field had been some of the most horrific of my life, even discounting the agony of having magic sucked through my skin from my bone marrow. Cut off from magic, the world had felt dead. I had felt dead. It would be a horrible existence.

Pausing, I searched for sympathy for Elsa, finding none. The dull headache that had been my constant companion since destroying the purifier thumped behind my temples. Drawing magic still hurt, especially in large quantities. The healer had assured me I would make a full recovery, but it would take longer than my foot.

If it had been just me Elsa had hurt, I might have been able to forgive her, but I couldn't forgive what she'd done to the gargoyles.

The day after my adventures in the park, I'd hunted down the four gargoyles in the city who had been trapped in the purifier's braids. Healing them had been simple enough for my overtaxed body and brain to handle; distance had weakened the purifier and limited the internal damage it inflicted. The marmot and fox hadn't been so lucky.

I caught sight of my grim expression in the reflection of a store-front window. My eyes looked harder than I remembered.

Turning away, I resumed my trek back to my apartment. I'd already visited the fox and marmot today. Focal Park remained closed to the general public while it was restored, but I was a gargoyle healer and had received a special guard detail to escort me in and out each day. With daily healing, both the fox and marmot had stabilized even though they remained unresponsive and paralyzed.

I wasn't giving up. I'd worked alongside a full-five squad to destroy an acres-wide mutation of magic. I'd split my spirit among my five gargoyles to save them from the purifier. I'd rescued the marmot from the largest null field anyone had ever seen. If I could do all that, I could solve the mystery of the dormancy disease and heal these gargoyles, too.

My extensive testing and probing in the marmot and fox hadn't revealed the source of the disease, so I'd turned to the library. If I couldn't find the problem within the gargoyles, maybe I could find answers in the manuals of previous healers and in scholarly journals. I'd checked out every book, newspaper, and scroll that even hinted at a dormancy sickness, and when I'd tapped out the resources of Terra Haven's library, I'd special ordered material from around the country.

Between recuperating, doctoring the fox and marmot, administering to more mundane gargoyle sicknesses, and doing research, I had almost managed to keep myself busy enough to not miss Oliver.

When Ms. Zubberie's Victorian came into sight, I sighed with relief. My awkward hobble was tiring and the books in my bag were heavy. I was looking forward to getting upstairs to the room I rented and flopping onto the bed for the rest of the day.

An enormous orange rock plummeted from the roof, unfurling its wings a few feet above the ground. Oliver hit the ground running, using his wings to augment his short legs.

"Oliver!" My heart performed an acrobatic performance in my chest, soaring with elation and dipping back behind protective walls. I couldn't read too much into this. He was probably just visiting or needed a checkup.

I dropped my bag and crouched in time to brace myself. Oliver skidded to a halt in front of me and wrapped me in his massive eagle wings. It was like being hugged by a flexible wall, one that snuffled my hair and made soft crooning sounds of happiness. I hugged him back, patting his cool sides. Life and magic practically burst from him, and though I knew it was only a figment of my imagination, he seemed like he'd grown an extra foot since I'd last seen him.

"I'm so glad you came to visit," I said when he released me, sitting so close to me he was almost on top of me. I shifted my weight to my knees, shocked to notice that even with his stubby legs we were almost eye to eye.

"This isn't a visit," he said.

"It's not?" My heart plummeted. Did he need my help? He looked healthy. I'd healed the bulk of his raw patches before sending him off to his new home, and the intervening time had smoothed out the rest. If I was being honest, he looked better than healthy; he glowed. Life with the squad had been far better for Oliver than life with me, and the realization was a fresh jab to a raw wound.

Marcus stepped from the shadows of the Victorian's balcony. My breath hitched at the sight of him, and I told myself it was because he'd surprised me. He wasn't in uniform, but even in civilian clothing, no one would mistake him for anything other than an FPD man. From his impressive frame straining the seams of his off-white shirt to the graceful way he moved, everything about him spoke of years of training.

He trotted down the front steps, and I searched his expression. Some of my alarm died at the sight of the barely there smile softening the hard planes of his face, but I rose to my feet anyway. I hadn't forgotten how big Marcus was, and I didn't want to be towered over, especially since even once I was standing his height enabled him to pull off some impressive looming. Plus, the last time he'd seen me, I'd been limp from exhaustion and injuries. I wanted to emphasize my strength and recovery. See, the little gargoyle healer can handle herself.

I wanted to impress him. Oh, crap, I had a crush on the growly fire elemental.

"What's wrong?" I asked, hoping my voice sounded normal.

"Nothing. Oliver just wanted to come home. He says his place is here, with you."

I stilled, holding in selfish hope.

Oliver stared up at me with adoration. "I need to help you," he said.

"But what about the excitement and adventure?"

"Life with you is more exciting."

"Maybe the squad had an off couple of weeks." I glanced to Marcus and he shook his head.

"We rounded up a litter of unchained kludde pups invading the blight. It was pretty dicey stuff."

"And I met a manticore," Oliver added.

"You did?" How could life with me compete with that?

"It was fun, but our work is more important," Oliver said.

"'Our work'?" I echoed.

"Protecting gargoyles."

I blinked. Is that how he saw what I did? "With the squad, you have endless magic to feed on. Look at you; you're glowing with good health."

"That's pure coming-home glow," Marcus said. Oliver's tongue lolled out of his mouth and flapped when he nodded vigorously.

"Are you sure, Oliver?"

"Yes. I promise I'll make sure I balance my magic. You won't have to worry about me. Unless . . ." His wings wilted against his body. "Unless you don't want me."

The barrier around my hope shattered, melting my body's stiffness. I'd been so determined to make sure Oliver had a life he loved and a place to call home, I'd failed to see he'd already found it. With me.

"I'd be the luckiest person in all of Terra Haven to have you, Oliver." I blinked back happy tears and knew my grin looked almost as goofy as the gargoyle's.

"Oliver knows where we live. He's welcome to come by anytime," Marcus said.

I ran my fingers across the gargoyle's glossy forehead, and he closed his eyes in bliss, leaning into my leg. Marcus grabbed my arm when I staggered under Oliver's weight. I glanced up, and the warmth in his lapis lazuli eyes stole my breath.

"You're welcome anytime, too," he added.

He stepped back and flashed me his thousand-dollar smile. I closed my mouth with a click.

"You know, Oliver's not the only one with a warrior's spirit. Have you ever considered training to be in the FPD?"

"Me?" Surely he was joking.

"You proved you can think under pressure. You'd be an asset to a team."

I tried to picture myself working alongside Marcus, dealing with rampaging kludde and malfunctioning magic on a daily basis. I shook my head. "I'm flattered but no. I've found my place in life. Healing gargoyles is more than enough for me."

Marcus nodded. "I thought as much. But if you ever change your mind or you're ever in my neighborhood, drop by." He clapped me on the shoulder and said farewell to Oliver. I was pretty sure he also winked at me.

I pivoted to watch him walk away, blushing to my roots when he glanced back and caught me staring.

"Did you miss me?" Oliver asked.

"Every single second. Come on, let's go home."

Oliver fell in step beside me, and the imbalance inside me righted.

"Have you figured out what's wrong with the dormant gargoyles?" he asked.

"Not yet. But we will."

We climbed the steps of the Victorian side by side, as we'd done dozens of times before, but this time was special. My gargoyle was home to stay.

SECRET OF THE GARGOYLES

GARGOYLE GUARDIAN CHRONICLES
BOOK 3

ABOUT SECRET OF THE GARGOYLES

I place the lives of all gargoyles into your hands with what I am about to tell you...

In her brief career as a gargoyle healer, Mika Stillwater has faced some daunting challenges, but none have stumped her—until now. A strange sickness infects a handful of gargoyles in Terra Haven, rendering them comatose and paralyzed. Worse, the cure she seeks is shrouded in the gargoyles' mysterious culture and the secret they guard with their lives.

Gaining the gargoyles' trust is only the first step. To save the sick gargoyles, Mika must embark on a perilous mission into the heart of deadly wild magic to a place no human has ever survived...

1

I fanned a tiny hummingbird feather back and forth, collecting the swirling air element from the breeze before scooping up the soft bands of fire element from a guttering candle flame. An equal mix of water element came from a bowl of spring water, and wood element from a pot of wheatgrass. Splitting my concentration, I kept the four-element cocktail spinning to one side and plucked a quartz seed crystal from my pocket.

I tuned a tendril of earth magic to quartz and used it to flatten and stretch the marble-size crystal. When the tensile structure of the quartz began to give, threatening to crack, I eased my magic out of the crystal. The flattened disk lay across my right palm, barely a foot and a half across and so thin it bent toward the ground around the edges. Hopefully it'd be enough.

"Stand back, Oliver," I said, glancing toward my gargoyle companion.

He undulated sideways, his carnelian Chinese dragon body moving as fluidly as a flesh-and-blood dragon's.

"Is this good, Mika?" he asked, studying the motionless sick gargoyle in front of me. Oliver didn't voice the doubts I read in his glowing sunset-orange eyes, and his magic boost never wavered. He wanted this to work as badly as I did.

"Yep. Here it goes."

The sick gargoyle's marmot body had once been a beautiful brown jasper, with vivid blue dumortierite tipping his reindeer antlers and long wings, but now he was pockmarked and only a few dull shades more colorful than gray. From his lifeless brown eyes to his rigid posture, everything about the marmot gargoyle looked dead, but he was only dormant. Inside him, a spark of life remained, and I was determined to wake him from his comatose state.

Ignoring the chilly morning air that brushed my stomach when I raised my arms, I lifted the sheet of quartz high above the gargoyle. Standing on his hind legs, the marmot was almost eye level with me, and his antlers cleared my head by several feet. Ideally, I would have placed the thin quartz across his antlers, but their points were too far apart, so I settled for positioning the quartz above his head. With exaggerated care, I layered the four-element mix across the surface of the quartz disk, gradually sinking it into the thin membrane until the clear crystal swirled with magic. Hardly breathing, I collected air to cushion the bottom of the quartz, then retracted my hand. The disk remained floating above the marmot.

Crossing my fingers, I backed up, buried my eyes in the crook of my elbow, and dropped the quartz onto the marmot. The fragile sheet shattered, tiny grains spraying against my thighs. I lowered my arm. The five elements rolled down the marmot, coating his crown and ears, then muzzle, neck, wings, and stomach before sliding off his bottom toes and the tips of his stone feathers. The moment it touched the ground, the spell dissipated.

A fine glitter of quartz dust circled the marmot, and it crunched under my feet when I stepped closer to examine him. The gargoyle's eyes remained dull. His ears didn't twitch. Weaving a basic five-element pentagram, I tuned it to the gargoyle's resonance and tested him. His life pulsed against my magic, the reedy sensation encased in muted pain.

"No change." I brushed quartz dust from the marmot's upraised paws, then blew more from his forehead with a heavy sigh. It'd been silly to get my hopes up.

Many people believed gargoyles went through a dormant phase as a normal part of their lives, opting to check out for decades at a time, but my healer instincts said otherwise, and one test of the marmot's failing health had backed up my suspicion. Gargoyles typically enjoyed a sedentary life, choosing to remain near specific buildings for most of their days, but they still moved. Frequently. They were also picky about whose magic they enhanced, yet this paralyzed marmot gave a magic boost to anyone in the vicinity, as if his powers were as out of his control as his limbs. He was trapped inside his own body—and he wasn't the only one. I'd found six other dormant gargoyles in Terra Haven stuck in an identical dormant state.

"What now?" Oliver asked.

"We try something else," I said, which was better than saying, *I don't know.*

I slumped, dropping my forehead to rest against the marmot's. I'd already tried everything I could think of. I'd attempted healing him with and without Oliver's enhancement, beneath new and full moons and all the days in between, using exotic, expensive resources and basic seed crystals. I was running out of ideas—even the desperate ones, like today's modified, outdated spell originally designed to heal lethargy in humans—and the marmot was running out of time. Never strong to begin with, his life signs grew fainter every day. Even the other dormant gargoyles fared better than he did, but not by much.

Familiar weariness pulled my eyes closed. In the three months since I'd first learned about the comatose gargoyles, I'd been searching for a cure nonstop, and sleepless nights bent over my table scouring increasingly obscure references combined with a series of hope-crushing failures had sapped my energy.

"We'll find something, Mika." Oliver planted a paw on my hip, nuzzling my side, and I staggered beneath his weight.

"I know. Together we can do anything." The words tasted bitter.

A shouted curse pulled my head up, reminding me we weren't

alone in Focal Park. A few hundred feet away, one of the cleanup crew tumbled into an enormous sinkhole, only to swing back up to solid ground on thick bands of air wielded by her four coworkers. She clutched the arm of the woman who grabbed her while one of the men reinforced the crumbling cliff, using hefty bands of earth element to reshape the granite beneath the topsoil and strengthen their footing.

The eroded crater in the middle of Terra Haven's premier park hadn't occurred naturally. Neither had the mutations in the botanical gardens or the flow of now-cool magma that had decimated a fifth of the grounds. The entire park had been deformed, all thanks to Elsa Lansing.

May she rot in prison.

Elsa had attempted to manually re-create a gargoyle's magical enhancement in an inanimate invention and failed spectacularly, nearly destroying the city along with Focal Park. But that was the least of her sins.

I ran a finger over five smooth patches on the marmot's neck. The clear crystal integrated into his fading brown jasper neck was my healer handiwork, and it'd taken me over a month to coax his weak body to graft enough layers of quartz to seal the five stab wounds. It turned out that to mimic a gargoyle's enhancement, Elsa had required the magic of a gargoyle, and she'd had no compunction against drilling into the marmot and draining his life to fuel her invention. Comatose and paralyzed, the marmot hadn't been able to fight back or even flee.

Rotting in prison was too good for Elsa, and knowing her invention had nullified her, leaving her unable to ever touch the elements again, was only a small consolation.

The earth rumbled behind me where towers of three-foot-wide granite pillars jutted from what had been a smooth slope before Elsa's invention went haywire. One of the taller granite posts snapped off at the base, then flew across the park to hover above the sunken ground. Cables of wood element pulverized the rock, crumbling the entire thousand-pound column into the gaping earth. Magic glowed around all five workers, funneling through the woman who had fallen into the pit, as they selected another pillar to demolish.

If not for my status as Terra Haven's sole gargoyle healer, I would have been banned from the hazardous park with the rest of the city's citizens during the restoration process. Instead, I had special clearance to tend to the marmot and one other dormant gargoyle in the park. The other, a large fox, lay out of the way atop a high granite outcrop, but after righting her internal imbalance caused by the invention's malicious magic, I'd stuck to the more accessible marmot for my healing experiments. He'd had the good sense to be on level ground when sickness struck, not perched at a vertigo-inducing height.

"Let's get this cleaned up, then see if the library has received the journal we special ordered," I said, unable to infuse any enthusiasm into my words.

"She's here," Oliver whispered.

My shoulders stiffened. I didn't need to turn to know he meant the onyx and amethyst gryphon gargoyle. She'd been following me around for the last month, observing from a distance any time I interacted with a dormant gargoyle—a critical witness to my repeated failures.

The first time she'd shown up, I'd thought she'd come to help. Every gargoyle I'd asked about the dormancy sickness refused to talk to me about it except for Oliver and his four siblings, and they were as perplexed as I was—by the disease and by the other gargoyles' silence. But the gryphon was different. She'd helped me in the past: When Oliver had been a baby, he and his siblings had been kidnapped and imprisoned by Walter, a mercenary earth elemental who had tortured them to steal their magic for himself—and for the highest bidders in his black market scheme. While I'd been desperately trying to rescue the hatchlings, the gryphon had convinced the city guards to investigate my wild tale. Without her timely arrival, I wouldn't be alive, and neither would Oliver or his siblings.

I'd been wrong about her intentions now, though. The gryphon refused to let me or Oliver get close enough to talk, and I'd grown to resent her judgmental presence. It was bad enough that I hadn't found a cure after months of research and experimentation; having an audience made it ten times worse.

I ground my teeth and used a soft push of air to sweep the quartz powder into a pile. With Oliver's help, I packed up my supplies, the weight of the gryphon's censure boring into my back the entire time. Irritation made my movements clumsy. I didn't need the gryphon to point out my deplorable incompetence; I lived it every day, watching the dormant gargoyles slowly fade while I tried useless spells. My frustration with today's failure was made worse by the fact that I'd never really expected the spell to work; I simply hadn't had anything better to try—and I hadn't for weeks. But the gryphon's silent condemnation was the final straw.

"I've had enough of this." I spun and locked gazes with the gryphon. She lurked closer than normal, and I could easily make out her glowing lavender eyes, despite her location in the dappled shadows fifty yards away.

"Do you need help?" I called, my tone conveying the *butt out* meaning of my words. I projected my voice through a cone of air to direct it toward the gryphon and away from the cleanup crew. I didn't need them sticking their noses into this, too.

The gryphon's neck feathers ruffled, and sunlight ghosted across the ripple of onyx. Her hard eyes remained expressionless.

"Look, I'm doing my best here." I shrugged off Oliver's placating gesture and stomped up the incline toward the gryphon. "I'm trying everything I can think of, so unless you have any suggestions—"

The gryphon surged forward, leaping into the air on stone eagle wings and hurtling straight for me. I dropped to all fours to avoid being clipped by her massive eagle talons, my heart lifting into my throat. The backdraft of her wings whipped my hair into my eyes as she shot past us. She banked, spinning through the air as if she'd anchored one wingtip in the ether, and swooped back toward us. Her enormous body temporarily blocked the sun before she landed on silent stone feet close enough to snap my head off. Oliver reared up protectively in front of me, but even with his wings flared, his slender body looked fragile next to the gryphon. She ignored him, folding her enormous amethyst-striated onyx wings against her body and glaring at me.

"Stop shouting." The gryphon's voice was that of a lion's, soft and rumbling, despite forming in a rock throat and emerging through an eagle's beak.

"Uh, of course." I straightened on shaky legs and squared my shoulders.

Dismissing me and Oliver, she stalked around us to stare into the marmot's blank eyes. I released a quiet breath and patted Oliver. He dropped to all fours, keeping his wings partially cupped to give himself extra bulk. I shuffled in a wide arc around the gryphon until I could see her face again, and Oliver twined beside me, moving slower than normal. I think it was his version of being tough, and I appreciated the effort.

"I've been watching you," she said.

"I know—"

She turned the full weight of her stare on me, and my mouth clicked shut.

"I have talked with the gargoyles you've healed," she continued, "and I have talked with the gargoyles this cub has been spreading tales to."

Oliver bristled, the orange-red ruff around his face flaring. I crossed my arms. Was this where she accused me of being an unfit healer? If so, she was wrong. I'd been an exemplary healer—at least until I'd encountered the comatose gargoyles. She was welcome to point me in the direction of a more practiced healer or even a book that might provide an answer to the dormancy sickness, but otherwise I wasn't in the mood to listen to her recriminations.

"You risked much to save the hatchlings when they were so foolishly caught. You risked more to save Rourke."

My indignation faltered. She knew the sick gargoyle's name.

"I'm still trying to save him—to save Rourke," I said. "But you know that. You've watched me every day."

The gryphon acted as if I hadn't spoken, observing without

speaking as the cleanup crew broke off another pillar of granite, spun it through the air, and crumbled it into the deep pit on the other side of the park.

I tried to read her expression. She didn't look ready to chase me out of town for being a miserable healer. She looked more torn than angry.

Had I misjudged her? Was it possible she wasn't here to berate me? Something had made her approach me today, and I bit my lip to hold in a babble of questions and demands that might scare her off.

"You have proven yourself twice, Healer, and perhaps you've even earned the honorific this pup has been claiming. It's been centuries since we've known a true guardian."

I twitched as if she'd poked me. Oliver had started calling me *guardian* after I'd saved the marmot and a half dozen other gargoyles Elsa's invention had ensnared while it'd been tearing up the park. I hadn't put much stock in it. He was young and worshipful, and working with *Guardian Mika* sounded more impressive than *Healer Mika*. I hadn't realized the title meant anything, but the gryphon implied it did.

"If I'm going to trust you..." She pivoted on a hind foot and paced away from me and back, tail lashing. "If I'm going to save you..." She paused to peer into Rourke's faded eyes. With a choked roar, she spun away and thrust her beak so close to Oliver's snout that their breaths mingled. My brave companion didn't flinch.

The gryphon's voice rumbled with anguish when she asked, "Is she really a guardian? Is she worthy?"

"My life is hers," Oliver said.

"You are too young to know what you say."

Oliver quivered, wings flaring in anger. "I've held her spirit inside me. My age doesn't matter. I felt her in my heart. I know Mika is a guardian."

I shuddered at the reminder. I'd once transplanted pieces of my spirit into Oliver and his four siblings in a colossally stupid maneuver that would have shredded my brain if it hadn't worked. At the time, it'd been the only option I could use to save the gargoyles from being ripped apart by Elsa's invention, and I hadn't fully considered the ramifications. Nor had I realized Oliver had been able to glean anything from that piece of me, let alone that it was what convinced him I was a guardian.

I was beginning to suspect the title of *guardian* was more than an honorific, too.

The gryphon broke off her staring match with Oliver and straightened to turn her piercing regard upon me. I did my best not to fidget, but my bubbling hope made it difficult. If I guessed correctly, she knew what could save the marmot—what could save all the dormant gargoyles—and she seemed to be talking herself into telling me. I hunted for the right words to convince her I deserved her trust, but the longer I looked into her glowing amethyst eyes, the more certain I became that nothing I could say would be enough. Either she believed me worthy or she didn't.

I crossed my fingers behind my back.

"Guardian." The gryphon paused as if testing the word. "My name is Celeste, and I place the lives of all gargoyles into your hands with what I am about to tell you."

2

Celeste scanned the park and I found myself checking our surroundings, too. The cleanup crew was too far away to hear and no other creatures were close. Nevertheless, when she spoke again, it was barely above a whisper, the rumble of her words mixing with the cracks and groans of pulverized granite.

"Rourke's cynosure baetyl was gravely injured."

Oliver reared back, every spike and feather on his body standing on end as he shook his head. I glanced between him and the hunched gryphon, alarm quickening my pulse.

"His what?" Baetyls were stones believed to be of divine origin, but what did that have to do with gargoyles, and how did a rock serve as a guide?

"That's not possible. Nothing can harm a . . . a baetyl." Oliver barely mouthed the last word and his wide eyes darted in every direction.

"What is a cynosure baetyl?" I hissed.

"Home," Oliver whispered with a shiver. "We shouldn't talk about it."

"A baetyl is where we hatch," Celeste said.

"On a stone?" I pictured a rock nest high atop a mountain where tiny baby gargoyles were born and took their first flight.

"Inside, not on. Baetyls are underground. They're sacred, secret places without which no hatchling would survive. We need our baetyl's magic to be born, and we need it again throughout our lives to rejuvenate our bodies."

"We do?" Oliver asked.

Celeste lowered herself until she lay on the ground to get closer to the young gargoyle's eye level. "It is a compulsion you'll feel when you're older. Your body knows when it needs to return. You're far too young to have experienced it, but if you are too long away from your cynosure baetyl, you will eventually weaken and become unbalanced."

I crouched to hear her whispered words. Baetyls hadn't been hinted at in any book or journal I'd read. For centuries, scholars and healers had speculated on the birthing rituals of gargoyles, but the few who had broached the subject with gargoyles had been rebuffed. I understood their need for secrecy. If unscrupulous people like Walter and Elsa knew where they could find weak gargoyles and helpless newborns, the gargoyles would never be safe.

"Wait! Walter! Did he defile your baetyl, Oliver?" The man still lived, imprisoned, but if even a chance existed that he could get his hands on more baby gargoyles . . .

Oliver shook his head. "No. We were outside the . . . outside home when he captured us."

I relaxed my white-knuckle grip on his shoulder with a sigh of relief. Celeste watched us with unblinking eyes, waiting until we'd focused on her again before continuing.

"Rourke is over a half century overdue to return to his baetyl. The only reason he's survived this long is because of his location."

"What do you mean?"

"He was not the first of his baetyl to sicken. We watched others fade into comas, and some died fast. Some didn't. Survival depended on seclusion; those in public places fared better and lived longer. We hunted out the location with the most concentrated number of humans actively using magic. The park used to be that place before it was destroyed."

"That's why he boosts everyone in the area," I said, the answer to the mystery clicking into place. Gargoyles fed off the magic they enhanced. It was why they gravitated toward busy public buildings and the homes of powerful full-spectrum families. Full spectrums could wield all the elements with a strength I could only come close to with quartz, and when a gargoyle enhanced someone that power-ful, they fed off a wealth of magic. By passively enhancing everyone who came close enough, Rourke and the other dormant gargoyles had been able to continue to feed even as their bodies shut down. I'd been afraid I had missed some dormant gargoyles hidden in less populated areas, but she just confirmed I hadn't. Sadly, any who had fallen comatose somewhere out of the way would already be dead.

Celeste's eyes tracked the cleanup crew as she spoke. "Even if they finish fixing the park tomorrow, I fear that if Rourke goes much longer without contact with his baetyl, he'll die. So many have already wasted away. I may have doomed us all, but I cannot abandon my mate to that horrid death."

"Rourke is your mate?"

Celeste nodded.

"And he's been like this"—I gestured to the frozen gargoyle trapped in his own body—"for over fifty years?"

"He and all the rest from his baetyl. There used to be twenty-three. There's no one left to speak for them, none to judge you for themselves, so I am acting on their behalf."

My heart broke for Celeste. She'd watched her mate's life wither away for decades, unable to do anything to help him without risking the lives of every gargoyle.

"Thank you for trusting me, Celeste. I'll make sure he and the others get home to their baetyl." It couldn't be that simple, could it?

Celeste shook her head as if answering my unspoken question. "They tried to go back years ago. Rourke said his baetyl had been injured and he came back sicker than before. I took him to my baetyl, but it pained him too much to stay."

"A baetyl can't be injured," Oliver said, his voice small and uncertain. He'd huddled into a tight bundle, and for the first time in months, I thought my six-foot-long companion looked little.

"Anything can be hurt, even baetyls," Celeste said.

I finally realized what she was asking of me. "You don't need me to heal Rourke. You need me to fix the baetyl."

"It is my last hope."

Relief washed the strength from my limbs and I sat. I had an answer to the dormancy sickness. *I had a cure.* I even understood why Celeste had taken so long to come forward. In telling me about the existence of baetyls, she'd endangered the lives of all gargoyles. Even Oliver had never mentioned a baetyl to me, and he trusted me with his life. For all Celeste knew, I could publish the information, and then there'd be a mob of unscrupulous scavengers hunting for baetyls and the helpless gargoyles inside. She'd had to extend her trust even further in asking me to fix Rourke's baetyl: To fix it, I'd have to be told its exact location.

I have a cure. I repeated the words again in my head to savor them. This morning I'd despaired of finding a remedy in time, and now . . . *I have a cure.* The words reknit my confidence. My inability to cure the comatose gargoyles hadn't been my fault. I'd been attacking the symptom, and the problem wasn't even a part of the gargoyles. It existed elsewhere, outside their bodies.

The ramifications of that thought dampened my satisfaction. The problem existed *outside* the gargoyles.

"When Rourke said his baetyl was injured, did he mean the baetyl itself or the baetyl's magic?" I asked.

"They're the same thing. A baetyl's magic is the baetyl," Celeste said, confused by my distinction.

"Is a baetyl's magic like a gargoyle's?" I was a quartz savant, but my skills with normal five-element magic weren't half as impressive. It meant I could perform amazing feats with quartz-tuned earth, which was how I became a healer of gargoyles and their living-quartz bodies, but the rest of my abilities were midlevel at best.

"A baetyl's magic is . . ." Celeste hunted for the right word.

"Everything," Oliver said.

Celeste nodded, as if he'd made sense.

I tamped down my frustration, knowing they weren't being purposely obtuse. We were close to saving the dormant gargoyles. All I had to do was figure out how to fix a baetyl, which as far as I could tell was either a cave with magic or a form of magic contained in a cave.

A magic that could heal comatose gargoyles. A magic that was *everything*.

Fixing a cave I could probably do, especially with the help of gargoyles to boost my magic. Fixing a form of magic itself sounded beyond my capabilities.

"How big is a baetyl?" I asked.

"I've never been inside Rourke's, but probably no larger than this park," Celeste said.

I struggled to keep my expression blank. Focal Park covered over a square mile. I was hopelessly out of my depth.

"Are you asking me only because you don't think you can trust anyone else? I can find you others—" *Stronger elementals*.

"No. No one else has a chance of helping," Celeste said. "You're the closest thing to a gargoyle who can work magic. If any human can integrate with the baetyl's magic, it is you, Guardian."

Oliver nodded in agreement.

I stared at them both in astonishment. They saw me as a pseudo-gargoyle? It was flattering and perplexing all at once.

"You're sure this is the only answer? Maybe I could replicate a baetyl's magic here," I suggested.

"You couldn't even come close. This is the only way."

Of course it was. "Once I fix the baetyl, Rourke and the others will recover?"

"After they've spent long enough inside it, yes."

I took a deep breath and modified my previous plan to include finding the secret location of Rourke's baetyl, carting over three thousand pounds of frozen gargoyles inside, and *then* repairing a form of magic I knew nothing about in a cave larger than several city blocks.

Because I was a guardian or because I was the equivalent of a human gargoyle, Celeste believed me capable of all three impossible tasks.

I'd have to be, too, since seven lives depended on it.

"You don't happen to know where his baetyl is, do you?" I asked.

"Of course."

My spirits lifted. "Really? Where?"

"Waupecony Ridge."

Her words punched my gut and I deflated. "You mean Reaper's Ridge?"

3

The Native Americans hadn't been poetic when they named the white quartz–laden peak Waupecony Ridge, or White Bone Ridge. They understood the perils of the mountain, but early settlers wouldn't listen to their warnings, especially not once they saw the veins of gold lacing the snowy quartz. From the beginning, there were reports of Waupecony Ridge miners who lost their memory and even more who wandered from the mining camps only to be found days or weeks later, starved, dead, and often the snack of local predators.

Then the Hidden Cache Mining Company had purchased rights to the entire ridge and begun large-scale mining. They pulled a fortune from the mountain for several years—right up until forty-three of their miners were torn asunder in a freak explosion of wild fire and earth magic. It was the first in a battery of elemental storms, and when they couldn't be contained, the federal government had decreed the area too dangerous for continued operation. That hadn't prevented the elemental storms raging across the hillsides from claiming a life or two a year, killing hikers and fortune hunters too foolish to heed the restrictions, earning the area the nickname Reaper's Ridge.

Occasionally, a Federal Pentagon Defense squad would be dispatched to Reaper's Ridge to subdue wayward storms, and even the elite FPD warriors couldn't do much more than enforce a wide perimeter around the ridge.

Why did the baetyl have to be there?

"I can't do this on my own. I'm going to need help," I said.

"I'll help," Celeste said, and Oliver seconded her.

I nodded, not really listening. I would have preferred going to Kylie for assistance. She was my best friend and had helped me in the past, but she was out of town, covering the blooming of the ever-lasting tree for the *Terra Haven Chronicle*. Even if she were available, she was a journalist at heart. Dangling exclusive information about gargoyle birthing grounds in her face, then telling her she had to keep it a secret, would be pure torture. More practically, she didn't have the physical strength, magical know-how, or warrior training I'd need to survive Reaper's Ridge. I needed the help of seasoned full-spectrum elementals. I needed Captain Grant Monaghan and his squad.

When I said as much to Celeste, she leapt to her feet and loomed over me. "You can't tell anyone, especially not *five* more people."

Despite her menacing stance, she didn't scare me this time. I knew her posturing was born of fear, not a desire to hurt me. Nevertheless, I stood up, walking to Rourke's side to put some space between myself and the incensed gryphon.

"You said you don't know how much more time Rourke has. We need to work quickly, and I trust Captain Monaghan and his squad with my life. He was the one who led the efforts to save Rourke and the park." He'd done more than that: It'd been Grant and his team of FPD warriors who had saved the city, and they'd trusted me to work alongside them to help injured gargoyles. If anyone could get us through the storms on Reaper's Ridge, it was Grant's team.

Grant also happened to be the only leader of an FPD squad that I was on a first-name basis with and the only one who would believe me if I said my perilous mission was necessary. More important, he and his squad were the only people I would trust with this secretive mission.

"They are not guardians. They cannot help," Celeste insisted.

"I wouldn't suggest we go to Grant's squad unless I thought they were necessary *and* trustworthy," I said. "Think about it. How would I get Rourke to the baetyl by myself? I can't carry him, and even if I could, what about the others? How would I protect them from the wild storms? As much as I'd love to do this on my own, I need help. This isn't a one-woman mission."

Lacking the muscles to carry a gargoyle didn't bother me, but admitting to being too weak as an elemental to protect them rankled. The gargoyles of Terra Haven depended on me. If I couldn't be everything the gargoyles needed, then it was up to me to make sure I found others who could shore up my shortcomings.

It took an hour of circular arguments before I convinced Celeste, and when she finally agreed, she insisted we leave immediately. I concurred; we didn't have any time to waste.

We exited the park together, with Oliver and I staying well clear of Celeste's snapping tail. In the early days after the destruction of Focal Park, Oliver and I had drawn a lot of attention. Few gargoyles left their rooftop perches and fewer still walked the streets with a human companion. With Kylie's front-page "Gargoyle Healer Saves Terra Haven" article fresh in everyone's mind, complete with a picture of Oliver and me, we couldn't have been more recognizable if we'd carried signs. But after a few weeks, the small crowds we'd drawn in our wake had faded. We'd become neighborhood fixtures and recipients of friendly waves and greetings, which I much preferred.

With Celeste stalking at my side, we were back to spectacle status. I ignored the stares and pointing fingers and concentrated on what I'd say to convince Captain Monaghan to help us.

Every few blocks, a fresh wellspring of gargoyle-enhanced magic burst open inside me. The unexpected gush of available magic repeatedly caught me off guard, tripping me mentally and physically even though I should have been used to it by now. Ever since the incident in Focal Park, gargoyles had started providing magic boosts for me whenever I was in range, whether or not I was using the elements at the time. Since gargoyles were particular about who they enhanced and typically didn't attempt to boost an elemental who wasn't actively using magic, it was flattering. Oliver claimed it was a sign of respect for a guardian, but up until today, I'd dismissed his explanation as a by-product of his hero worship. I couldn't help but notice that with Celeste accompanying us, the frequency of the boosts had increased threefold, as if her presence added weight to my reputation.

I acknowledged the offerings with waves and nods to the serious gargoyles who watched us pass from their high perches, for the first time in a long time feeling worthy of their favor. I had a real plan to help the comatose gargoyles, not just desperate hopes and ineffective remedies. Thinking about Reaper's Ridge, I amended the thought: I had a plan *and* desperate hopes.

Oliver was the only one of us who'd ever been to the squad's home base, so he led the way. None of us spoke as we left behind the bustle of downtown and climbed the gentle hills on the east side of Terra Haven. Enormous mansions jutted along the tops of the rolling crests, but we turned onto a flagstone pathway halfway up a slope and stopped in front of a bright yellow two-story stucco house with a nine-foot-tall wooden door. Celeste flew up to the roof, landing soundlessly on the terra-cotta tiles and disappearing. I steeled myself and knocked.

No one answered. I waited a minute, counting the seconds, then tried again, pounding the iron knocker against the wood with all my strength. Eleven seconds later, the door burst open and Marcus Velasquez loomed over me. I fell back a step, then caught myself. Cold blue eyes burned into me, and a muscle bunched in his anvil of a jaw. Recognition dawned a second later, and the rugged fire elemental's intimidating pose relaxed fractionally, but his forbidding expression didn't alter. Without saying anything, he crossed his tan arms—a move that emphasized his thick biceps and wide shoulders—and leaned against one side of the door frame, obviously waiting for me to speak.

A flurry of bubbles rioted in my stomach.

"I . . . Is Grant here?" I squeaked.

Sometime during the catastrophe at Focal Park, I'd developed a crush on Marcus. The last time I'd seen him, I'd even convinced myself that he was interested in me, too. But I'd been too busy hunting for a cure for the dormant gargoyles to devise a casual way to bump into him and reassess my feelings for him under more normal circumstances—like when he wasn't saving my life—and he'd never sought me out. After a few months, I decided I'd made everything up, my crush included.

Up until five seconds ago, I'd believed myself, too.

"Hi to you, too, Mika Stillwater." His deep voice rolled through me.

"Hi, uh, Marcus." I flushed. *Get over yourself. You're not here to ask him out. You're here to help Rourke and the other gargoyles.*

"Hi, Marcus," Oliver said.

"Hey, Oliver." The gargoyle got a small smile.

"Is Grant here?" I managed to get the words out without sounding strangled this time. Bully for me.

Those cool blue eyes fastened on me again, and I wondered what had ever made me think he might have been interested in me. It'd clearly all been a euphoric side effect of my near-death experiences. Marcus was an accomplished fire elemental in an FPD squad. He was so far out of my league he may as well have been on another continent.

"He's out."

"Seradon?" I asked. The squad's earth elemental had liked me. She'd help.

"Out."

"Winnigan?" My voice came out too high.

Marcus's lips twitched and he finally took pity on me. "Everyone's on vacation. I only stuck around because . . ." His eyes scanned over me and he exhaled with a rueful chuckle. "Because I'm an idiot waiting for something that's never going to happen. Come on in."

Before I could protest, he turned and padded barefoot back into the house. Oliver loped over the threshold and across the tile floor, and his puzzled glance over his shoulder prodded me into motion. I stepped into the house Marcus shared with the squad and shut the door behind me, hurrying to catch up with Oliver. We trailed the fire elemental across a wide room filled with couches and tabletop games and through open French doors into a sun-drenched courtyard. Marcus settled into a cushioned bench, stretching one leg along the entire length. Oliver hopped onto the wide rim of a fire pit and curled his body around the cool coals. I stood awkwardly at the edge of the courtyard.

"How long until they're back?"

"One, maybe two weeks."

"Two weeks!" Celeste dove into the courtyard, blocking out the sun with her enormous dark wings.

Marcus rolled off the back of the bench, sprang to the wall, and spun back with a slender sword in one hand, a ball of fire in the other. My heart lurched into my throat, and I leapt forward, shoving through wicker furniture the large gargoyle had carelessly scattered, but by the time I'd forced my way between Marcus and Celeste, he'd extinguished the fireball and the sword hung loose at his side.

"Anyone else I should know about?" Marcus asked, his tone casual but his body still tense.

"We can't wait that long," Celeste said, ignoring him.

"I know. Is Grant close?" I asked. "Can we reach him? Maybe an air message? What about the others?"

"He's not in Terra Haven. He went to see the everlasting tree bloom, and the others decided to tag along."

Of course they had. I'd be there myself if I hadn't been busy with the dormant gargoyles. It wasn't surprising that the captain just happened to be in the same place as Kylie, either.

Marcus narrowed his eyes at me and stalked back into the

sunlight. "You clearly didn't drop by to tell me you've missed me. What have you gotten yourself into, Healer?"

"It's better this way. No one else needs to know," Celeste said.

"We can't do this alone. We already agreed—"

"Fine." She examined Marcus from head to toe. "One person is better at keeping a secret than five."

"But to fix the . . . the *thing*, I need more than just his help. I was counting on being linked with five full spectrums." Linking meant I'd be able to draw on the combined strength of all five powerful elementals. With all their magic plus a boost from Celeste and Oliver, I had a chance of fixing a baetyl the size of the park. With just Marcus, our odds of success plummeted.

"Mika . . ." Marcus growled.

"You won't need to link," Celeste said.

"How can you be sure?"

Celeste shrugged. "A link wouldn't do you any good. You're a guardian. They aren't. They probably won't be allowed inside."

My throat constricted, and I forced myself to take a deep breath. Celeste's assurances did nothing to ease my trepidation, but I'd already agreed to do everything in my power to help Rourke and the others. Maybe she was right and I wouldn't need the might of five FPD warriors backing me. Maybe one would suffice.

But before I could fix the baetyl, we had to get there.

"Are you sure we can't contact Grant?"

"Tell me what's wrong," Marcus said.

I met his steely gaze. Experience had taught me that Marcus was calm under pressure and highly skilled. If I suppressed the embarrassment of my crush, we'd work well together; we'd done so in the past. Plus, one full spectrum was better than none.

"I know how to heal the dormant gargoyles, but it's complicated and requires something outside Terra Haven. I need help," I blurted out. "And if you agree to help us, I need your sworn oath that you will never reveal anything I tell you. Not even to Grant."

Marcus's expression closed down, and as he studied me, he twisted his wrist, swishing the sword back and forth around his leg.

"Please," I added when the silence became unbearable.

He stalked to the wall and returned the sword to its hiding spot in the rafters. When he came back, he sat on the bench, legs stretched in front of him and crossed at the ankles. "Tell me."

"Swear first, human," Celeste said.

Marcus arched an eyebrow at her. "I swear."

I accepted a boost from Oliver and formed a soundproof bubble of air to wrap around the four of us. Marcus crossed his arms but didn't say anything.

"Do you know about cynosure baetyls?" I asked.

He shook his head, and despite his superior knowledge of the world and magical creatures, I wasn't surprised. The gargoyles had guarded this secret with their lives.

In a few short sentences, I summed up everything I knew about baetyls for Marcus, finishing with, "It's been decades too long for all of them. If the dormant gargoyles don't get to their baetyl—their repaired baetyl—they'll die."

"Why have I never heard about baetyls before?" Marcus asked.

"You shouldn't know about them now," Celeste growled, her lashing tail slowly pulverizing a wicker chair. Marcus didn't seem to notice.

"Celeste only told me because I am a guardian." I stumbled over the title.

"I take it that's different than a healer."

"Vastly," Celeste said.

"How?"

"That's like asking what the difference is between fire and a fire elemental," she said, and Oliver nodded sharply.

Obviously Marcus had never heard of a gargoyle guardian, if he had to ask. Judging by his grunt, I didn't think he was impressed.

"What's the catch?" he asked.

"The broken baetyl is on Reaper's Ridge."

"No." Marcus stood, forcing me to tilt my head back to maintain eye contact.

"So you won't help me?" I hadn't expected him to leap for joy, but I hadn't expected him to refuse, either.

"No, I'm telling you *you're* not going."

"You...you're *telling* me," I sputtered. Planting my hands on my hips, I curled my fingers into the fabric of my shirt to control my rising temper. "I'm not asking for permission."

"That's not permission; that's advice. If you go, you'll die."

I leaned forward, matching him scowl for scowl. "Wrong. I only *might* die." Okay, that had sounded better in my head. I plowed on. "But if I don't go, all seven of the dormant gargoyles *will* die. I can't stand by and let that happen, not when I can save them."

"When you *might* save them. There's no guarantee. Do you even know how to fix a baetyl?"

A year ago, I hadn't known how to heal a gargoyle, and now I was a gargoyle healer. If Celeste thought I could fix a baetyl, then I'd figure it out. But I was smart enough not to say as much to Marcus. Fortunately, he didn't wait for a response.

"FPD squads have attempted to tame Reaper's Ridge multiple times and have paid for it with their lives. Those were hardened groups of linked full-spectrum elementals. What makes you think you could survive five minutes?"

He wasn't telling me anything I didn't know, but I'd been doing a stellar job of burying my dread by focusing on the cure. Now all my fear clambered to the surface. I could tell he saw it in my eyes, and it pissed me off.

"Why do you think I'm here? I know I need help. You know what, though? This was stupid. Forget I said anything. While you're at it, forget I ever told you about baetyls."

"Mika—"

"No. I'll do it without you."

I spun toward the exit but Marcus stepped into my path before I made it two steps. I had the option of running into him or stopping. If I'd thought I stood a chance at moving him, I might have considered ramming him. Instead, I settled on the best glare I had and aimed it at his throat.

"You don't understand." I tried to sound calm, but I only managed to sound like I was holding back tears. "I don't have a choice. That's where the baetyl is; that's where I have to go. I can't let the gargoyles die, not without trying."

His pulse bounced in his throat and his Adam's apple bobbed when he swallowed.

"Move. Please. I have a lot to do."

Oliver whined, jumping down to stand beside me. Celeste loomed in my periphery.

"You're really going, even alone, aren't you?"

"Yes."

"We'll be there," Oliver said.

I glanced at Marcus's face. The man could tunnel through a brick wall with that scowl.

"This is the most idiotic idea I've ever heard."

"No one asked your opinion."

Marcus snorted. "Fine. I'm in."

"You're coming?"

"Someone with brains needs to be on this venture."

I swayed in place with the intensity of my relief. I wouldn't be doing this alone. I'd have preferred the whole squad, but Marcus's abilities were nothing to scoff at. Maybe, just maybe, we'd survive.

"When do we leave?" he asked.

"Today," Celeste said.

"Then we've got a lot of work to do."

We were really going to Reaper's Ridge. I swallowed against the urge to vomit.

4

I strained to hold my bands of air under the seated sardonyx tiger. Even boosted as I was by Oliver and Celeste, I wouldn't have been able to lift the large statue-like gargoyle much more than a foot off the ground by myself. She was one of the largest of the dormant gargoyles and outweighed me by at least five hundred pounds. It didn't help that I was already tired from moving the other six, first from their locations throughout the city and into the quarry cart Marcus had rented, then into the freight car. My magic quivered like an overworked muscle, loose and too flimsy for one more repetition.

Marcus swooped a thick basket of air under my strands and the swan-winged feline floated from the back of the cart and through the wide loading door of the freight car. Together we settled the gargoyle onto the wooden floorboards, maneuvering her between a warthog-headed bear and Rourke. Once I determined she was stable, I released the elements and collapsed against the side of the metal car, swiping sweat from my forehead.

Seven lifeless-looking gargoyles filled the floor of the freight car, leaving enough room at the front for two canvas-lined cots and little else. The gargoyles' frozen forms had made squeezing them into the tight space a bit like assembling a puzzle—one where the lightest piece weighed over a hundred pounds.

Marcus had impressed me with how quickly he'd mobilized everything. In the time it'd taken me to rush home and pack, he'd hired a quarry cart and driver; then we'd spent the last few hours riding around Terra Haven, collecting the dormant gargoyles. Somehow, he'd also booked us a private freight car on the last train out of the city, and we'd finished loading the gargoyles with a few minutes to spare. It would have taken me an entire day to collect the gargoyles on my own, even if I could have lifted them by myself, and I didn't know the first thing about renting freight cars. I started to thank him, but he dismissed me with a flat look and turned to pay the cart driver. Marcus had been helpful but about as pleasant as a bee-stung bear. He hadn't complained once or attempted to talk me out of the trip after he'd agreed to go, but his attitude made his opinion about our quest perfectly clear.

I did my best to ignore him and focus on being grateful for his help. Standing in Emerald Station helped.

Eight tracks and four loading platforms fanned across the station, all protected by an arching canopy of vines. Honeysuckle and wisteria blossoms scented the air, mingling with the baser smells of grease, metal, and sweat. People milled around the open shop fronts of the station or lounged among the wooden seats, and a talented fire elemental wove elaborate scenes of pure flame as he told stories to enraptured children. Too many people were in the way for me to get a good view of his show as I caught my breath, but I saw a few spectacular birds made of fire.

I hadn't been on a train since a middle-school field trip, when we'd embarked on an exciting overnight stay at a sister school a city away. I'd lived for months in anticipation of the adventure. The same bubbly excitement stirred in my stomach now, mixed with anxiety and fear. This wasn't a fun excursion to another city; we were headed straight into forbidden territory, and the lives of these seven gargoyles depended on me not only surviving but also somehow restoring a place I'd never seen to specifications known only to comatose gargoyles.

A heavy rumble and clanging pierced by the shrill whistle of steam brakes announced the arrival of another train on the opposite platform. The bittersweet odor of burning grass and clouds of cooling steam billowed from the engine before the soft elementally enhanced evening breeze dissipated them. Up and down the train, coach attendants opened passenger doors with timed precision and identical flourishes, and men and women poured out. Grabbing bags, they jostled their way through the passengers hurrying up the platform to board our train.

I glanced up to where Oliver perched atop the freight car. He stood with his back arched and tail high, his carnelian orange-red body glowing in the lights of the massive hanging chandeliers. His head never stopped moving, taking in the busy scene below him. He had an adventurer's spirit, so unique in a gargoyle, and I was grateful every day that he chose to be my companion.

Situated at the prow of the freight car, Celeste stared straight down the tracks toward our destination. Where Oliver preened when he noticed people pointing at or admiring him, she appeared to have tuned out the world. As a rule, gargoyles didn't ride the trains. Why would they when they had wings to fly? The sight of two on a single freight car sent ripples of curiosity through the crowds.

Most people didn't look twice at the dormant gargoyles we'd loaded, though. To the casual observer, they could have been confused with statues, and if anyone noticed a moderate boost to their magical strength when they walked by, they probably attributed it to Oliver and Celeste.

I pushed away from the freight car and brushed the front of my pants, dusting off a layer of dirt. The heavy staccato bangs of a gong growing closer pulled my head up. The conductor swaggered through the crowd holding the line to the train's khalkotauroi, a massive bull too tall to see over with heavy bronze feet and a bronze muzzle. He followed the slender woman docilely, chewing his cud, and when he exhaled a belch of fire, the conductor caught the flames in a ball of water element and reduced it to a hiss of steam.

All without taking her eyes from Marcus.

"I'd heard some jerk made a last-minute addition to my train," she said, her husky voice cutting through the cacophony of conversations around us. "I should have known it was you, Velasquez."

Marcus turned, his face lighting up with The Smile. Ruggedly attractive when he wasn't trying, when he smiled *that* smile, he transformed into breathtakingly handsome. I'd been the recipient of The Smile a time or two. It was powerful enough to knock my thoughts sideways. The conductor merely quirked an eyebrow.

"You better not delay our departure," she said. Her chin-length black hair swung into her face when she stopped, and she tucked it behind her ear. Standing between the khalkotauroi and Marcus, she looked fragile and elfin, but her sultry dark eyes swept over Marcus as if she were sizing him up for dinner.

"Naomi, when have you ever known me to slow things down?"

A sour flavor coated my tongue, accompanied by the visceral churn of jealousy in my gut: They were flirting. Ugh.

I grabbed the edge of the open freight car door and hoisted myself inside. Lacking coordination after the long day, I tripped on the tiger's tail and stumbled into Rourke, hugging him to regain my balance.

"Is she okay?" Naomi asked.

"She's fine, just a little slow in the head," Marcus said.

I glared at him over my shoulder, but he and Naomi missed it, both too busy looking into each other's eyes.

Face flaming, I gave Rourke a pat and twisted through the rest of the gargoyles to my cot at the front of the car, only then sneaking a peek out the open door again. The beautiful conductor radiated confidence, which wasn't surprising; she had to be a strong fire elemental to do her job. Plus, she and Marcus had *history*. It was there in her body language when she casually touched his arm and echoed in his relaxed posture. And The Smile. The one that reappeared with nauseating frequency. Here was a woman in Marcus's social stratum. Viewing my crush alongside Naomi made it all the more pathetic.

I growled at myself, imitating the noise I'd heard most frequently from Marcus today. It didn't matter what the man thought of me. It mattered how helpful he was with saving the gargoyles.

Pushing the squirmy ugliness of jealousy down, I reached for my bag. I'd stowed it earlier under my cot, and I had to stand back up to get the leverage to budge it now. Underneath my change of clothes and snacks rested forty pounds of a gargoyle healer's best tool: seed crystals. Pure quartz and infinitely malleable, the seed crystals could be used to heal all manner of physical injuries, including being grafted onto a gargoyle to replace chipped or severed body parts.

Four fit comfortably in my hand and I rolled a few more into my pockets. Then I walked among the gargoyles, checking them with gentle probes of magic. Their life forces flickered with the same muted strength as they had before we'd carted them from their resting places, with little variation between each gargoyle. The years had been equally cruel to them all, pockmarking their skin and eroding rough patches. I could feel the peripheral ache of these wounds when I delved into each gargoyle, but I didn't know how much awareness the dormant gargoyles possessed.

For Rourke's sake, I hoped it wasn't much.

I don't normally have violent feelings, but I'd entertained a lot of fantasies in the last months of stabbing Elsa so she could see how it felt. She'd viewed Rourke as nothing more than a tool to be used. She hadn't seen him as a living creature, and she hadn't cared about hurting him. With people like her in the world, it was no wonder gargoyles were more willing to let the dormant ones die rather than risk exposing their vulnerabilities to humans.

"I'll never tell," I whispered to Rourke. "You're safe with us."

"Oliver, Celeste, do you want to come inside?" Marcus asked, swinging up into the freight car. Behind him, the massive khalko-tauroi plodded toward the engine, his copper hoofbeats reverberating through the station. A cart piled high with hay bales trundled behind him, pulled by a pair of station stable boys. The giant fire-breathing bull would need a lot of fuel to power a train this size through the mountains.

"I'm going to stay up here," Oliver said, hanging over the edge. His tongue lolled from his mouth, his grin looking twice as goofy upside down.

"Come down through the front if you change your mind," Marcus said, pointing toward the human-size door at the front of the freight car.

Celeste didn't answer. She'd been quiet all day after we'd convinced Marcus to help. I didn't know if she was naturally recalcitrant or if her worry kept her silent.

The train released three shrill whistles, and coach attendants repeated the signal with their smaller silver whistles. A few more people rushed by the open door, racing to board before we pulled out of the station.

Marcus tossed two balls of fire into the brass lanterns, using quick flicks of air to close the glass shields around the lit wicks, and then swung the enormous loading door shut. It rumbled on its runners and closed with a deafening clang of metal on metal, locking me inside the windowless container with seven mostly dead gargoyles and one grumpy fire elemental.

———

I SPENT THE FIRST HALF HOUR ON THE TRAIN SITTING STIFF AND SELF-conscious on my cot, pretending to read a novel about a courtesan spy. Or maybe about a princess con artist. I couldn't keep the story line straight, but I kept turning the pages and trying to look natural. I'd fretted over getting the gargoyles to their baetyl and surviving Reaper's Ridge. I'd pictured all types of caves buried in the mountain and had run through dozens of techniques I'd used on gargoyles, hoping one of them would suffice for the baetyl. But I'd failed to consider the actual night spent on the train. Alone. With Marcus.

He'd lain down on his cot after we'd pulled out of the station and we'd checked to ensure the rocking motion of the train wouldn't topple any gargoyles. He hadn't opened his eyes since. I didn't think he was asleep, but I couldn't be sure.

With the rhythmic *clack-clack* of the tracks beneath us and the gentle sway of the freight car, it was hard to maintain the level of urgency that had hounded me in Terra Haven. Without that sense of dire purpose, the terrors of Reaper's Ridge filled my thoughts.

The storms that tore it apart were composed of raw, wild magic, completely unpredictable and impossible to control. If we got trapped inside a storm of pure fire element, we'd be burned alive in seconds, and it would be the most merciful way to die. I'd heard the horror stories of the bodies found—from drowning victims lodged in trees to frozen remains discovered in the middle of the summer. There'd even been a few instances of people who had seemed to explode, as if the wild magic had burst them apart.

Snapping my book shut—which elicited nothing, not even a twitch, from Marcus—I bounced to my feet and yanked open the door at the front of the car. A rush of roasted grass–scented air swirled into the freight car and lifted my hair from my neck. I stepped out onto the small platform and shut the door behind me. Two steps took me to the iron railing, and I leaned out to put my face in the wind.

Terra Haven had disappeared behind gently rolling hills covered with yellowing grass and dotted with trees. Through gaps in the hills, I spotted the glint of Lincoln River and the lush fields of crops along the banks, but our route took us northeast around the mountains, and the river wouldn't be in sight much longer.

I pushed away from the railing and hopped the slender gap between cars, then opened the door to the overnight car in front of our freight car. When I closed the door, my footsteps slowed in the hushed atmosphere. Most of the right side of the car was walled off into a dozen smaller quarters for privacy and sleeping, and the empty walkway was weighted with silence. The faint aroma of lavender and thyme lifted from the thick carpet with each of my steps, and I lingered by the tall windows on the left to watch the hills roll past before the growl of my stomach urged me on.

When I opened the door to the passenger car, a dozen faces turned to stare at me before dropping back to their papers and books. I patted the overhead railing to keep my balance in the rocking car as I walked up the length, and I did my best not to touch anything else. The car was immaculate. Plush red velvet seats with small brass buttons and armrest accents were set in groups of four around marble-topped tables complete with place mats folded into fans, crystal goblets, and real silverware. Most of the car's occupants were dressed fine enough for a temple ceremony, not in dusty jeans and a T-shirt like I was. Even the black and gold carpet was swept clean, and when I passed him, the coach attendant tsked and used a soft brush of air and earth to erase my footprints. I mumbled an apology and rushed through the door.

I crossed the gap between cars again and pulled open the next door, relieved to find the dining car. I made use of the washing fountain in the corner, which had its own attendant who cycled the water and cleaned it with a complex weave of air, water, earth, and wood to remove the grime I'd added to the basin.

A galley kitchen ran along one wall and dining tables along the other. A group of women decked out in leather flight gear and colorful tunic tops lingered over drinks at a table set against the window, talking animatedly about the differences between flying dragons and pegasi, but otherwise the car was empty. I purchased two roasted vegetable potpies, which were made fresh for me while I watched, and half a loaf of rosemary sourdough bread. The chef presented the meal on a silver tray, the potpies in porcelain bowls, and the spoons were silver and wrapped in cloth napkins. He added a saucer with several pats of butter, two teacups, a fan of tea bags for me to select from, and a pot of boiling water. Staggering under the unexpected bounty, I wove carefully back to our freight car, exerting the full strength of my air ability to keep everything on the platter and upright when I navigated between cars.

When I stepped into the freight car and closed the door behind me, Marcus cracked an eye.

"Are you hungry?" I asked. It seemed like a rhetorical question since we hadn't stopped for food all afternoon, and Marcus must have agreed. He sat up and silently helped me with the platter. We didn't have a table, so we set it on the floor between us and braced it between our bags so it wouldn't slide when the train leaned around a curve.

"We're attached to a first-class train," I said.

Marcus grunted and reached for the bread, tearing it in half.

"You got a freight car attached to a first-class train," I repeated.

First-class trains were the fastest on the line and given top priority, which meant all other trains were shunted to the neighboring track or were held at a station to keep the track clear for this train. Used almost exclusively by the wealthy, first-class trains didn't haul freight, and they didn't make stops at abandoned stations.

"You said it was urgent," Marcus said.

"It is, but I can't afford this." I could barely afford the dinner I'd bought us.

"The FPD is picking up the bill."

Really? That was news to me. "Thank you." I couldn't make my words flow together, and they came out in stilted phrases. "And for helping me. With the gargoyles. Even though it's going to be hard."

He watched me while he chewed, face unreadable. Finally he swallowed. "I said I would help."

"I know. And I hadn't thanked you. So . . . thank you."

"I haven't done anything yet."

That sounded like the start of an argument I didn't want to have, so I looked away from his intense stare and took a bite of the potpie. The crust melted on my tongue, flaky and buttery, and the sauce of the cooked vegetables was so delicious that I stopped chewing to savor it. Swallowing a moan of delight, I forgot about Marcus and concentrated on enjoying the gourmet meal. Far too soon, I swept the final drops of sauce from my bowl with the last bite of bread. I stuffed the morsel into my mouth and leaned back, eyes closed, indulging in a moment of pure satiated bliss.

When I opened my eyes, Marcus's unreadable gaze lingered on me. Self-conscious, and reminding myself how out of my league

Marcus was and how mortified I'd be if he ever found out I had a crush on him, I stood up and squeezed into the middle of the dormant gargoyles. I knelt beside the tigereye fox from the park. Hardly the size of a bear cub, she lay curled into a circle, all her feet and her nose hidden under her fluffy stone tail.

I gathered a soft mix of elements to test her health—

Something heavy slammed into the front door, denting it inward with an explosive thunderclap of sound.

5

Marcus launched to his feet, a coil of magic swirling against his hand as he shoved the door open.

Celeste stuck her head in, but her wide shoulders caught on the door frame, halting her forward momentum with a shriek of protesting metal. Cool evening wind whistled through the open door, blowing my hair into my eyes.

"Rourke needs magic! He's fading!" she yelled, grabbing the frame with her massive eagle feet and wrenching. The metal screamed but held.

"Calm down!" Marcus barked. His authoritative posture was ruined a moment later when Oliver catapulted from Celeste's back through the door above her head. Marcus ducked and threw himself against the wall with a curse. Oliver's slender body fit easily through the narrow doorway once he tucked his wings tight, which meant he plummeted like a rock to the floor, shattering our dinnerware. Immediately, he unfurled his wings and launched over the gargoyles straight for me.

I flung myself to the ground, covering my head with my hands. Oliver clipped the side of the freight car with a wing, deafening us all with the metallic reverberation. He landed heavily on the back of the black and white onyx wolf next to me, scrambling to maintain his perch on the gargoyle's slick fish-scale sides and smooth flying-fish wings. His long tail struck me in the shoulder, knocking me sideways, and I scrambled to a safer location under the large tiger.

"Mika! They need help!" Oliver shouted.

"Everyone, *CALM DOWN!*" Marcus bellowed. "Celeste, let go of the door. Oliver, get your snaky butt over here." He pointed to the empty floor space between our cots, kicking the dented silver platter out of the way and scooping the broken porcelain of our dishes into a net of air before tossing them out the open door. Oliver tried to take off, slipped, and crashed onto the fox. The impact shook the floor of the freight car and made my ears ring. Before I could check to make sure he was okay, he squirmed to his feet and wriggled to the location Marcus indicated. I crawled out from under the tiger and checked the fox. Bits of her tail had flaked off and a dull pain radiated through her body, but it was the weakness of her life signs that alarmed me.

"What's the problem?" Marcus demanded.

"We're too far from the city. Damn it! I'm an idiot." Celeste had told me the only thing keeping these seven gargoyles alive had been their location in prominent, magic-laden places of Terra Haven. We'd removed them from the only thing sustaining them. I explained as much to Marcus even as I opened myself to the magic boost all the dormant gargoyles offered so they could feed off my magic. Compared to the magical enhancement of a normal, healthy gargoyle, their boosts were a mere trickle, but the amount of magic they offered wasn't important.

"We have to use magic for them," I said. "They need to feed on it. They've basically been starving for decades, surviving on the scraps they could consume indirectly from people who used them for magical boosts. If they don't get more magic, and quickly, they'll waste away."

I hooked my heavy bag with a band of air and tugged. It wiggled in place, but I couldn't lift it. Then fresh magic gushed into me, and I felt Oliver in the enhancement—his eager energy and the coil of excitement that never dimmed inside him. A moment later, even more magic poured into me from Celeste, but I wouldn't have been able to distinguish the signature of her enhancement the same way I could Oliver's. Months of working closely together had tuned me to him in a way I hadn't known was possible.

Filled with magic, I wove cables of air and levitated my forty-pound bag more effortlessly than if I'd lifted it with my hands. As soon as it was in reach, I removed a seed crystal and began reshaping it to patch the fox's wounds. Fortunately, they were minor enough that I could knit her tigereye flesh into the new quartz, closing a half dozen nicks without overtaxing her delicate system.

"What can I do?" Marcus asked.

"Use the elements—and use their boost to let them feed off you."

A few seconds later, the pummeling wind abated and the car quieted as Marcus coated the opening with a solid sheet of air, wrapping it around Celeste's head when she refused to back up. A glow of fire element swept through the freight car, countering the cold air with a gentle heat. I stepped among the dormant gargoyles, checking each of them. The flicker of their lives stabilized, but they were all frighteningly weak.

"We can't keep this up indefinitely," Marcus said.

"I don't think we'll have to. As long as we make sure they get regular doses of magic, they should be okay."

"How regular?"

"I don't know. I've never done this before." I wasn't even sure I was right, but I hoped I was. Neither of us could sustain a steady volley of magic from now until we reached the baetyl, not even Marcus and not even if we took turns.

Once I was sure no other dormant gargoyles had been injured, I squeezed through them to Oliver's side.

"I'm sorry. I got scared. I didn't mean to hurt her," he said, head drooping. "I wanted to help."

"It's okay. She's fine, but you're not." A ragged patch had chipped from the ruff around his square face like a bad haircut, and the orange carnelian wound was sandpaper rough.

"It's no big deal," he said, despite flinching away from my delicate touch.

"Nothing we can't fix in a few seconds," I agreed. "And you're always an incredible help."

Oliver didn't say anything, but his wings relaxed and he lost his hangdog expression.

I floated a seed crystal to my hand and reshaped it as I knit it into Oliver's injury. At one time, it would have taken all my concentration to mold the crystal and weave the complex elements to mesh the inert quartz with Oliver's living carnelian body. Now I could do it almost without looking.

"Can you feel how much stronger the others are already?" I asked when I finished.

"No."

"You can't?"

"He is not mated," Celeste said. She no longer looked ready to rip apart the freight car, so she must have been able to feel Rourke's increasing stabilization.

Marcus floated the abused silver platter in the air in front of him, rotating it over an intense blue-white cone of flame. While I patched Oliver, he reshaped the softened metal, removing the claw-foot dents Oliver had embossed in it. Then Marcus meticulously re-etched the swirling leaf design through the cooling silver until the platter looked better than when I'd taken it from the dining car.

He glanced my way, and I snapped my mouth shut. Of course Marcus could do the precise work of an artisan. Just because he looked like he was built to run through granite walls, had the elemental strength to match, and spent his time fighting the worst magical creatures and problems in the city didn't mean he couldn't do delicate work with his magic, too.

"How much longer do we need to keep this up?" he asked.

I looked to Celeste. The gryphon stared over my head at her mate, worry sitting strangely on her eagle face.

"Awhile longer," I finally said.

"Are you done there?" he asked.

"Yep. But we need to keep using magic." I gave Oliver a pat and he snuggled against my legs. The clear quartz I'd used to rebuild his chipped ruff to its previous shape looked peculiar among his orange-red rock fur, but in a few days, his body would absorb the crystal and replace it with carnelian.

"It doesn't matter what we do with the elements?"

I shook my head, hunting for ideas. I could blow wind around the freight car and maybe pull a few drops of moisture from the air, but neither would keep much magic moving for the dormant gargoyles to passively feed from.

"How about a game of Elemental's Apprentice?" Marcus asked.

"The kid's game?"

"Got a better idea?"

I sighed. "No."

Elemental's Apprentice was a game of humiliation. The premise was simple: Using only magic, two people tossed raw elements back and forth, sometimes with physical items included. The person who dropped the elements first lost. The easiest way to win was to toss your opponent more element than they could handle. Since I'd always been only a midlevel earth elemental with even weaker skills with air and water, I'd almost always lost, usually getting drenched with water in the process. Against a full spectrum, I didn't stand a chance.

"Let's start with air," Marcus said. He sat on his cot, his back to the wall with the broken door and his legs stretched out. Everything about his posture said he was relaxed and expected an easy victory.

"Sure." I shifted to sit cross-legged on the floor and Oliver curled around me, eyes glowing in anticipation. Pulling on my connection with the gargoyles, I collected a massive bundle of air, weaving the element into a tight vortex and plucking a few strands loose so it'd unravel the moment Marcus caught it. I wasn't going to make this easy on him.

"Whoa. Hang on," he said. "I didn't mean a battle to the death, and I see what you're doing there with that trap. It wouldn't work, but that's not the point. We just need to keep magic circulating, right? Let's keep this friendly."

I shifted the vortex to the side so I could study him. He looked sincere—and amused.

"For the gargoyles," he added.

Still not trusting him, I dispersed my wind-funnel trap and made a small fist-size bundle of air, then wrapped and tied it off so it would hold its form once I threw it. I tossed it to Marcus and immediately prepared a wall of earth magic in front of me in case he hurled it back five times as big and too fast for me to catch. Instead, he lobbed it back, scoffing when I had to drop my barrier to catch it.

"Not a fan of the game?" he asked.

"I've played with a few poor sports."

"The kind who set traps in their first throw?"

I didn't appreciate the implication. "The kind who enjoy humiliating those weaker than them. You know, typical full-spectrum superiority crap." I threw the air back to him with more force than necessary.

Oliver tilted his head against my thigh as he tracked the air ball's flight back to me in the heavy silence. I rested a hand on his side and let out a long breath.

"Sorry, that was uncalled for," I said, reminding myself Marcus had never done anything but help me.

We threw the element back and forth a few times before Marcus asked, "Do you know a lot of full-spectrum elementals?"

"Personally? Just you. And Grant and the rest of the squad," I added quickly. "But as a kid, there were a few in my school. I wasn't sad when they got transferred." Some of my friends had been jealous of the more talented students and the special school they'd been whisked away to in their early teens. I'd been relieved to see them go.

"You're lucky. I know a lot of full-spectrum pricks."

My gaze snapped to Marcus's, and he winked.

"I was one of them for a while. I could teach you some dastardly tricks some other time. Beef up the air, then add water."

"Are you testing my control over the elements I'm weakest with?"

"Yes."

"Why?"

"Because tomorrow we're going to Reaper's Ridge, and I want to see what you've got."

I frowned. "You know what I've got. This isn't the first time we've worked together." Even if he'd forgotten when we'd fought together in Focal Park, we'd spent today linked. The intimate combining of our magic would have left Marcus with no questions about how weak I was in every element.

"Which is why I didn't agree to come with you just because you gave me puppy-dog eyes. I know you're not going to flip out, but you're handicapped by that whole everyone-else-first healer thing."

"What's that supposed to mean?" *Puppy-dog eyes?*

"Tomorrow will be about more than throwing yourself in front of every threatened gargoyle. You'll actually have to try to survive." His scowl was back in full force.

"That's the plan," I said, confused by the turn in his mood.

His mouth flattened. "Grab some water and let me judge if you're capable of two things at once."

"And here I thought it was just a friendly game." He'd seen me do far more complex divisions of magic than handling two elements at once. I'd hoped having a little food in his stomach would offset his sour mood, but it'd been too much to ask of a single meal, even one as spectacular as the potpies.

I wound together a bundle of water element strands and prepared to throw it to Marcus.

"No. With water."

"What water?" I asked, looking around. Oliver had smashed the teapot.

"Gather it up."

I examined the spray of moisture staining the floor, then Marcus. He raised a challenging eyebrow. Gritting my teeth, I got to work.

Pulling the droplets together took more of my concentration than I would have liked. I fumbled the air ball, dropped it once, and had to shave it in half to keep it under control before I finally wrapped strands of water element around a collected handful of water, encased it in a bubble of air, and floated the wobbling blob off the floor.

"Bring it on," Marcus said, not commenting on my sloppy work.

I lobbed the water inside my thin barrier, hoping it'd break apart and drench him. Instead, Marcus caught it, combined it with a separate perfect sphere of water I hadn't noticed him collect, and tossed it back to me as I released the air ball toward him. I caught the water, wrapping it in thicker elemental bands to stabilize it.

In between throws, I sent tiny probes of magic into the dormant gargoyles, checking their health levels. They hadn't gained much strength, but they were no longer weakening. Celeste had relaxed, too, and the worry had eased from her expression. She'd curled up on the open threshold, but her head remained high and she watched Rourke like, well, an eagle.

"Why do you feel more comfortable with water than air?" Marcus asked, breaking the silence and startling me into almost dropping the air ball.

I'd half resolved not to speak to him again, but his tone had lost its bickering edge, so I responded. "My parents are both water elementals."

"Really?"

"Pretty strong, too. They spent a lot of time working with me to help me perfect my limited ability."

"Where'd you get your knack for earth?"

"I don't know. No one in the family had an affinity for quartz like I do."

"Add in some earth. No. Make it quartz. I should get some practice."

As easily as thinking, I'd collected earth element and tuned it to quartz. For reasons I'd never been able to explain, I was stronger with quartz than I was with untuned earth. I used to assume it was because I'd practiced with the element so much, but lately I'd been considering I might have been born with a specialized strength. Quartz had always been easier for me and more accessible. It was only as an adult that I'd thought to use it to make a living. Then I'd met Oliver and his siblings, and my life had been completely changed.

For the fun of it, I wrapped the quartz-tuned earth around three seed crystals, then tossed them to Marcus. He caught it and fumbled, the crystals clattering against each other like castanets, but recovered quickly. I took petty delight in his lack of perfection.

"Wood, too," he said.

I dutifully wove pure wood into a knot and bounced it to him. Marcus added a cotton rag from his bag to give the element weight. If not for the gargoyles' extra magic, I would have had a hard time holding all the separate elements together with air, but with their help, keeping four elemental balls alight wasn't even tough.

"Now fire," Marcus said.

I made a glowball. Marcus returned it with a two-inch flame fluttering at its heart. I caught it delicately, looping it back to the fire elemental from a safe distance. Schools forbade playing with real flames. Losing control of a bucket of water was messy but easy enough to clean; losing control of naked fire could cause permanent harm. That didn't mean I hadn't tried—and walked away with singed eyebrows.

"It won't bite," he said.

"I'm rather partial to my hair," I muttered.

Marcus chuckled. The warm light of the lanterns and the bouncing flame softened the hard planes of his face, and his mirth held a hint of The Smile. I pulled my gaze away before he caught me staring and focused on the arcs of elements between us.

For a while we let the muted *clack-clack* of the metal wheels across the seams of the rail fill the silence. Outside, the sky had darkened, and the scenery through the gap of the missing door had become lost in the shadows. Reaper's Ridge and all the dangers it presented were still a day away, and for the moment, no urgency pushed against my thoughts. In this warm environment so far removed from the real world, it seemed perfectly natural to strike up a conversation with Marcus. We skirted around discussing tomorrow and the dangers awaiting us, sticking to innocuous topics like our pasts—my rather ordinary upbringing in a known-for-nothing town, his adventurous military experiences and exciting missions with the FPD—our favorite places to eat in the city, and the best temple for the summer solstice.

While we talked, we tossed the elements back and forth until our moves were so synchronous I didn't have to think about them, which was probably Marcus's intent. The whole game was likely a strategic plan designed to familiarize me with working with him and vice versa. I didn't care. I enjoyed the moment of comfortable normalcy— something I'd lacked during the frantic months I'd searched for a cure. I also monitored the dormant gargoyles. When their life signs had been stable for over an hour and Celeste had fully relaxed, I reluctantly ended our game.

"You should get some sleep. You'll want to be rested for whatever we face tomorrow," Marcus said, tossing the water out the open door and resealing the air barrier. He let the other elemental bundles dissipate, and the cotton cloth fluttered to his hand. I caught the seed crystals with a scoop of air and dropped them into my bag.

Oliver had fallen asleep tight around me, and I had to wake him to free myself from his stony embrace before hobbling on stiff legs to my cot. Stretching out, I toed off my boots and pulled the scratchy wool blanket over myself. Marcus dimmed the lanterns and settled on his cot. The cozy atmosphere morphed, turning the friendly energy into something intimate and awkward as I listened to him arrange his covers. Tension crept back into my muscles, and I thought it would keep me awake, but the rocking of the train lulled me to sleep minutes later.

———

I woke looking into Celeste's glowing amethyst eyes. Marcus breathed softly on his cot, asleep, and Oliver lay stretched out and sleeping on the floor beside me. I couldn't tell how long I'd been asleep, but I guessed it'd been a few hours. Softly, I reached for the dormant gargoyles, testing them. They'd weakened. Not as much as before, but I didn't want to take any chances.

Rolling quietly to my feet, I tiptoed into the middle of the gargoyles, where I'd left my bag of seed crystals. I sat and wriggled my chilled toes into my boots, then opened myself to the gargoyles' boost. After carefully heating the air in a weak version of Marcus's spell, I decided to do what I did best: work with quartz.

Before I'd become a gargoyle healer, I'd had ambitions of being Terra Haven's preeminent quartz artisan. Now that goal felt juvenile and shallow. Nothing compared to the joyful rush of healing a sick or injured gargoyle, and the most prestigious artistic accomplishment couldn't compete with saving a life. However, I still enjoyed creating beautiful objects with quartz and it kept my skills sharp, and the money I made selling quartz jewelry and figurines at a gallery in the city augmented my sporadic healer income.

Drawing as much as I could hold of all the elements to help feed the dormant gargoyles, I separated delicate strands of earth, fire, and air to combine several seeds into a blob. With practiced ease, I twisted the lump and stretched it into the most popular figurine I sold: a replica of Oliver. Normally I used carnelian to match his distinctive body, but the clear quartz did a good job of catching the light and refracting it through the small details of his eyes, ears, and folded wings.

As soon as I finished, I started the next figurine, making one for each of the dormant gargoyles, then a few of Celeste. I strung together ten crystals and created the train, complete with miniature people on the inside and the khalkotauroi in the engine car, clear hay strands scattered around his feet, clear flame breathing from his nostrils to heat the water. I left out Conductor Naomi.

Sleep weighted my eyelids, and after a while, I reclined on my side with my head propped on the curled fox. I planned to doze for only a few minutes, but when I woke, indigo sky was visible through the open door and the glow of the sun lit the edge of the horizon.

Today was the day—either I was a guardian, capable of fixing a baetyl and saving the comatose gargoyles, or I wasn't, and everyone in our party could die for my hubris. I prayed I wasn't handing Reaper's Ridge its next victims.

6

"Naomi agreed to let us use her private bathroom, but you'll need to be quick to make it through the train without disturbing the passengers," Marcus said when he noticed I was awake.

I grimaced, not needing the reminder of the gorgeous conductor before I'd fully woken; thinking of Reaper's Ridge had made me queasy enough already. But refusing the offer out of spite would cause only me to suffer. Besides, my bladder didn't care how Marcus had convinced Naomi to give us access to her quarters. I grabbed my bag and scurried through the open door. When I returned in fresh clothes and as clean as a sponge bath could get me, Celeste was perched atop the freight car once more. She nodded her head to me but didn't talk, and I didn't linger in the chilly morning air.

Marcus knelt in front of the figurines I'd created last night, holding up a clear replica of Oliver to examine it in the light of a glowball he'd formed.

"The detail in this is amazing," he said without turning toward me.

"You can have it, if you want." Caught off guard by his praise, I tried to sound dismissive, as if it wasn't one of my finer pieces.

The glowball winked out and he closed his long fingers around the figurine. "Thanks." He grabbed his bag and squeezed past me on his way to the bathroom.

"He's smart," Oliver said after Marcus had left.

"Because he picked the one that looked like you?"

"Yes."

Chuckling, I checked on the dormant gargoyles. They were all weak but stable. It pleased me to see the fox's injuries were healing nicely, and when I checked Oliver, his new patch of clear ruff had striations of red carnelian stretching to the surface. By the time we returned to Terra Haven, all signs of his injury would be healed.

I glanced around at the dormant gargoyles and tried to picture the return trip. Would they be with me? Would they remain in their baetyl? Would they all live through the trip?

Would I?

Marcus returned wearing brown leather pants, thick leather boots, and a lightweight fitted gray cotton shirt with a tiny flame stitched at the high collar. The shirt was regulation FPD attire and woven with protective magic, but the leather pants were new. They hugged his long legs and creaked when he sat on his cot. I glanced down at my unspelled jeans and long-sleeved T-shirt. The comparison between us said more obviously than words how unprepared I was for traversing Reaper's Ridge.

Marcus's attitude had changed to match his clothes, the camaraderie of last night chased away by the sunrise and his familiar scowl back in place. He silently handed me an apple stabbed with a paring knife, half a loaf of bread, and a hunk of soft white cheese. I jerked the knife from the apple and ate the fruit, then concentrated on cutting slices of cheese for each bite of bread. Across from me, Marcus methodically consumed his identical breakfast, seemingly unaffected by the heavy silence choking the air and making it hard to swallow.

"Repairing the baetyl is your job. For everything else, you'll do what I say, when I say it."

I lifted my eyebrows at his high-handed order. Marcus gave me a hard stare, no emotion behind his eyes.

"Is that clear?"

I stuffed a bite of bread into my mouth to choke off a dozen flippant responses and made myself nod. Marcus had experience, training, and more magic than me. It made sense for him to be in charge, especially in the wild magic of Reaper's Ridge. Besides, telling him I'd follow his orders only if I agreed with them wouldn't appease him, and I couldn't afford to have him back out of helping me now.

I'd barely finished eating when the train began to slow.

"Are we there?" Oliver asked.

"Almost."

My stomach tightened around my half-digested breakfast and I ran damp palms down my thighs. I tried to push my fear aside, but it wasn't as easy as last night, when the danger was still a distant prospect. Oliver didn't share my trepidation. The young gargoyle undulated out of the freight car with an excited trill and leapt to the roof. The metal popped under the combined weight of two gargoyles but didn't dent.

Trying to calm myself, I focused on mundane tasks. I tucked my bag up against the larger loading door, folded my blanket on my cot, and laced my boots. The boots were the only part of my outfit that I was sure met Marcus's approval. After our last adventure together, during which a spear of granite had skewered the bottom of my foot straight through my boot, I'd purchased the most heavy-duty pair I could find. They'd been advertised as guard boots and I wore them daily. I hadn't expected to need them, having bought them mainly to counter the remembered pain of the wound, but they'd come in handy twice so far when injured gargoyles had been in too much pain to heed where they stepped.

By the time I'd adjusted the laces from the toe up to the calf on both boots, the train's brakes were squealing and we'd slowed to a crawl. Marcus dropped the air barrier across the broken door, letting in a gentle breeze and the train's perpetual burning-grass odor. I followed him out to the railing, my gaze lifting immediately to the mountains.

Lightning split the clear sky in the distance and thunder rumbled overhead a few seconds later. The tracks ran through a valley filled with sparse, dead weeds and scraggly brush, but a few hundred feet to the west, a dense pine forest blanketed the steep landscape. A gorge dipped into the hillside, revealing a barren ridge of quartz beyond it, the ragged white peaks glowing in the early-morning light. A thick shaft of fire belched from the hill, charring the rocks in its path and extinguishing in a bright explosion made soundless by the distance. Then the train rolled past the gap, and the tree line obstructed the view again.

Pain pinched my hand, and I uncurled my fingers from the railing to examine the red crescent marks of my fingernail imprints in my palm. When I looked up, Marcus was watching me. I tucked my hands into my armpits.

"We're close. Any change in the gargoyles?" he asked.

I shook my head. "They need to get inside the baetyl." If being near it had been enough, all the gargoyles from this baetyl would have stayed nearby until they recovered.

"Looks like we're really going to Reaper's Ridge, then," he said. "The captain is going to skin me alive when he gets back. Unless we die first."

A falling-down lean-to marked the once bustling Hidden Cache Station. Broken shards of glass lay around the base of the sunken ticket window, and paint flaked from the illegible sign and rotting siding. Weeds grew over extra lines of track that split out into the meadow to multiple neglected loading bays now defined only by thinner patches of weeds. Hidden Cache Station was no longer listed on any rail line, and I had Marcus and his connections to thank again for getting the train to stop here and not another fifty miles up the line at the nearest small town.

The station wasn't empty. A rugged mountain air sled sat well clear of the dilapidated building, a pack of cerberi resting in the sled's shade. The driver hopped from the padded seat to the ground as the train came to a stop. If the station's run-down ticket booth and the mountain range had birthed a human child, the driver would have been their offspring. Wind and sun had weathered his leathery skin into a crush of wrinkles around high cheekbones, a prominent nose, and thin eyes. Dirt caked his heavy pants, and streaks of grime coated a threadbare shirt covering his bony chest and stomach. The old man moved with unexpected agility, though, and clapped a worn cowboy hat to his head before shoving the air sled into position using brute force and a sizable amount of air magic.

Marcus walked back to open the large loading door, and I hopped down to join him. Unlike Emerald Station, this forgotten stop didn't have a platform, which worked in our favor since the air sled hovered at a height only slightly lower than the freight car. We wouldn't have to lift the heavy, dormant gargoyles far to get them loaded.

"The driver's name is Gus," Marcus said, his voice pitched low so only I could hear him. He had arranged for the sled driver to be waiting for us at the station, just as he'd arranged for the freight car to be hitched to the back of the first-class train. I opened my mouth to thank him again, but he continued without giving me a chance. "He's not going to let us load the gargoyles until you pay him."

"The FPD isn't picking up this tab?" I asked, trying to keep the hope out of my voice.

"The FPD has a don't-touch policy regarding Reaper's Ridge. They're not going to fund any portion of any harebrained expedition involving it."

I clamped my mouth shut before I pointed out the flaw in his logic, since the FPD had already paid for our trip here. If he made me reimburse him for the train car and trip, I'd be in debt to him for the next five years. Besides, I recognized the verbal jab for what it was. Marcus wasn't going to try to talk me out of going to Reaper's Ridge, but it appeared he was done with making things easy.

I grabbed my bag and pulled out a neatly folded bundle of cash, then walked to the front of the sled where Gus was coiling thick bands of earth around twin stone anchors to hold the floating sled in place.

"Hi, I'm Mika," I said.

"Yep." Gus spat to the side.

"How much do I owe you?"

"This'll do." He swiped the cash from my hand and pocketed it without counting the bills.

"But . . . how much—"

"Oh, pardon me, ma'am. Did you want to shop around first?" He swept his arm toward the empty meadow and cackled, the dry sound turning into a wheezy cough.

I'd spent my life's savings when I'd rescued Oliver and his siblings from Walter at the black magic auction, and Gus had just snatched up every last dollar I'd managed to save since then, including what I'd set aside to pay next month's rent. Unless I sold a record-breaking amount of jewelry in the next week and a half, I was going to have to rely on the goodwill of my landlady to maintain a roof over my head. The thought set my teeth on edge.

I spun on a heel—

And came face-to-jowl with a giant dog's head.

The cerberus huffed a soft bark, its foul breath washing over me and ruffling my hair. Its second head whined and the third sniffed my crotch.

"Whoa, back up," I said, pushing the muzzle from my groin. The whining head licked the side of my face, its tongue as wide as my palm. "Ew!"

Gus guffawed, no help whatsoever.

Oliver coasted from the freight car's roof to my side, and the cerberus backed up a few steps to watch him land, giving me a better look at the three-headed dog. She looked like a Polish hound, with the standard black saddle pattern over an otherwise rich brown coat, but that's where the similarities ended. Aside from having two more heads than a normal dog—all three of them larger than mine—the cerberus was also as tall as a pony and twice as heavy, her body corded with muscles and ending in a whip-long tail that was doing its best to start a windstorm as she crouched to snuffle Oliver. She whined again, or one of her heads did; the other two panted with excitement.

Oliver reared up on his hind legs, which still didn't quite put him at eye level with the cerberus when she stood up.

"Don't be afra—" I started.

Oliver released a trill so high my ears barely registered it, but it made the cerberus go on point. Then the gargoyle rolled onto his back and wriggled his feet at the three-headed hound. She pounced, nipping at his rock body without actually touching him. I ducked the flail of her tail and ran to the far side of the sled. With a few spry steps, Gus joined me.

"Um," I said.

"Never seen a gargoyle play before."

"Is the cerberus playing?" I didn't think her enormous teeth could harm Oliver, but I didn't want to take a chance. I also didn't want her to chip a tooth on Oliver. I couldn't heal a cerberus, and I figured Gus would expect a monetary reimbursement I couldn't afford if she was injured.

"Ginger's gentle as a lamb," Gus said. Ginger growled, three throats in harmony, and snapped her teeth in a fast chatter like bone castanets. Every hair on my body stood on end and I fought to ignore the primitive part of my brain insisting I needed to flee. Oliver wriggled in a circle, trying to imitate the cerberus's eerie chatter. He sounded like a drowning turkey.

Gus watched them tussle for a moment longer before he barked a foreign word. The cerberus leapt to his side and planted her butt nearly on his foot. Gus patted each of her heads. Oliver shook dirt from his back and flapped his wings, giving me a goofy smile I could read far too clearly.

"Cerberi are not city animals," I told him.

"A little help here," Marcus said.

I turned back to the freight car. He'd already transferred two of the lighter gargoyles onto the sled by himself. I scurried to help him with the rest. Gus didn't make a move to help, despite being far stronger than me with air. Sweat ran freely down my face and soaked into my shirt by the time we'd finished, and when Celeste retracted her magical boost, I slumped against the high side of the sled, feeling like I'd run a mile uphill. Marcus looked like he'd taken a stroll by the beach.

He formed a pocket of air and spoke into it, and the weave caught his words, absorbing the sound. After rocketing the air message to the conductor, he shut and latched the freight car. The message zipped into the open side of the engine, where two attendants shoveled manure out the door. Naomi leaned out around them, slinging a message back down the train to Marcus. Her words were for his ears alone, and whatever she said made him grin. I turned away.

The train pulled out of the station while Gus hitched the cerberi to the sled. All six were marked similar enough to Ginger to have been born in the same litter, though the two at the front looked older. Wider than horses—at least from the necks up, where their three heads fanned out from their bulky shoulders—the cerberi had to be staggered along the towline, three to each side. Lined up noses to tail, the pack stretched longer than the freight car, and they looked sturdy enough to pull the sled-load of heavy gargoyles without breaking a sweat.

I started to grab my bag from where I'd tossed it beneath the sled, but when I caught sight of Marcus, I froze. He'd strapped a broadsword to his back, and the black hilt protruded over his right shoulder. The leather harness holding the hilt bisected his chest, and a handful of brass null traps were affixed to the thick straps. A sturdy elemental anchoring rod made of twined copper and quartz hung from a loop at his belt and two slender knife hilts protruded from sheaths in his boots.

He was an FPD fire elemental whose muscular frame topped six feet by several inches. His scowl could cower a kludde. He'd always been intimidating, but I'd gotten used to him. Now he looked like a stranger, and a scary one, at that.

Marcus's hard blue eyes lifted to mine and I forgot how to breathe. A predator looked back at me, but instead of fear, heat washed through my limbs. When he smiled, all teeth and little mirth,

I jerked back toward the sled, hefting my bag to the wooden floor-boards and climbing in after it. I pretended to double-check the stability of the frozen gargoyles while trying to remember how to breathe normally.

Marcus hopped up to the driver's bench seat beside Gus and settled a crossbow across his lap. Celeste circled on lazy updrafts above us, so high she looked no larger than a thunderbird, but Oliver remained with me. He flapped to the front of the air sled and wormed his way through the dormant gargoyles into a small space behind the driver's bench. I squeezed into the limited space at the back of the cart and sat just as Gus unraveled the earth strands holding us anchored. He loosed a shrill whistle that bumped through five octaves, and the cerberi leaned into their harnesses.

The sled eased forward so smoothly that if my eyes hadn't been open, I wouldn't have known we'd moved. The cerberi transitioned from a walk to a trot to a canter in perfect harmony, enormous paws pounding across the hard soil. Wind whipped through the gargoyles on the open sled, slapping my hair against my face and neck and carrying Gus and Marcus's conversation back to me.

"What's wrong with these ones? Why are they frozen?" Gus asked.

"It's just something that happens to them."

"Must be the rocks for brains." Gus chuckled at his own joke. I scowled at his back.

Gus guided the cerberi to a dirt path at the edge of the long meadow and they veered to follow it, picking up speed. It'd once been a road, but now weeds and trees choked the edges. Sunlight gave way to dappled shadows as the forest closed in around us. Pine and the musky scent of the forest floor filled the air, and above the thunder of paws, I could hear the raucous calls of crows and the occasional shrill challenge of a hawk. The cerberi took the turns of the old road at a gallop, and the sled slid smoothly through the air behind them. It would have been a pleasant experience if not for our destination or the lives of the gargoyles depending on me.

Or Gus.

"How'd a smart FPD man like you get stuck with this tarred-feather task?" Gus asked.

"Wrong place, wrong time."

I switched my glower to Marcus.

"Last I heard, the FPD wised up about Reaper's Ridge."

"This one"—Marcus tossed a thumb in my direction—"has a plan. She's going to use all these gargoyles to tame the wild magic." His tone said what his words did not: that I was a moron.

I gritted my teeth. Marcus had come up with the cover story. He claimed it was something Gus would believe, was far enough from the truth to keep the baetyl a secret, and would enhance the reputation of gargoyles and gargoyle healers if I "managed to crawl back off this mountain alive."

I waited for Gus's shock or outrage that anyone would think to use a half-dozen helpless gargoyles in such a dangerous manner.

"Why not bring more live ones?" Gus asked. "The boost coming off these is useless."

"Live ones wouldn't come."

Oliver growled, the sound more musical than menacing. I caught his gaze and shook my head. He knew the cover story. He knew Marcus didn't mean what he said. It didn't make it any easier to listen to, though. I stuck my tongue out at the men, and Oliver gave me a weak smile.

"You think it'll work?" Gus asked.

Marcus laughed, and it wasn't a pleasant sound. Gus joined him, shaking his head.

"There's always some crazy city folk who think they can tame the ridge," Gus said. He spat out the side of the wagon, and I threw a shield of air up to block the splatter from hitting me. "Shame they're sending a good company man like you, though."

"I'll be okay. I get paid either way. I just have to get the fool set up, then stand back and watch the fallout."

Gus thought that was hysterical.

I tuned them out and gathered a test pentagram, sliding it into the nearest dormant gargoyle. Her life guttered faintly, with nothing to feed on since the sled's magic was crafted into it and static. I gathered more of the elements, pulling them through the unfocused boost of all seven dormant gargoyles, and grabbed a handful of seed crystals from my bag. The magic I did was less important than letting the gargoyles feed, so I threaded earth through the quartz, reshaping the seeds into a singular sphere, then a diamond, then a snowflake. I kept the quartz in perpetual movement, and to use more magic, I worked as fast as possible, holding the quartz in front of me on a cushion of air that I constantly had to adjust to compensate for the movement of the sled beneath me.

It worked to distract me, too—from Gus and Marcus and anything else they talked about, and from the dwindling distance between us and Reaper's Ridge.

"Stupid girl! Knock that nonsense off before you get us all killed," Gus said.

A wallop of air swung toward the quartz I was working, and I countered it with earth without thinking. Gus's air slapped against my barrier and shattered. He grimaced at the backlash, shooting me a hateful look over his shoulder.

"Get your charge in hand," Gus barked at Marcus.

"Mika. The wild storms are drawn to any active magic. No more for a bit."

I let the quartz drop to my lap. Marcus held the cross-bow loose in his hand, a brass null trap affixed to the tip of the notched arrow. His eyes scanned the horizon, the sky, the broken patches of forest, never settling on one place for too long.

Reaper's Ridge rose beside us twice as tall as the road we traveled and separated by a single canyon and a few hardy trees. Storms crawled across the ridge and exhaled from the rocky mountainside into violent snow flurries, explosive lightning and downpours, and fire. Under a cloudless piece of sky, a flash flood gushed across a few hundred feet of hillside before dissipating as suddenly as it had formed. The muddy ground rolled, and new boulders pushed to the surface.

Chills rushed down my body. It was the disaster at Focal Park all over again, only instead of the ridge being divided into five sections of predictable polarized magic, the elements clashed and twisted together in a violent mishmash.

I clutched the edge of the sled and scanned the visible parts of the ridge, hunting for clues to the baetyl's location, but the mountain guarded its secret well.

Gus whistled two short notes, and the sled slowed. I glanced past the cerberi. The overgrown road continued down into the canyon, unobstructed by anything larger than weeds.

"Why are we stopping?" I asked.

"This is as far as I go."

"We're not even to the base of the ridge," Marcus said.

Gus spat over the side of the sled. "This is as far as I go," he repeated.

7

"**I** hired you to get us to Reaper's Ridge," Marcus said, his voice a menacing rumble as he loomed over the wrinkled old man.

Gus clicked his tongue, and all the cerberi turned toward us, eighteen throats growling in unison. My skin tried to crawl. Oliver stood on his hind legs to see over the driver's bench seat, wings flared in alarm. The cerberi raised their hackles and inched back toward the sled. Gus had dropped an anchor, and we remained in place as they stalked closer.

"Really?" Marcus let out an exasperated breath. "Don't threaten me, old man. I'm not in the mood. If you don't want to go any farther, how much to borrow your team and sled?"

Gus shook his head. "I wouldn't send my least favorite hound to Reaper's Ridge."

"Fine. How much to *buy* the whole pack?"

"Not for sale."

"Not even one?"

"Nope."

Marcus's profile tightened, his standard scowl becoming threatening.

"Get out or I'll dump you out," Gus said. He used a trickle of air to activate a spell woven into the sled, and it began to tilt to the right.

Marcus smacked the spell with a whip of air and the cart righted itself. Gus's gnarled fingers tightened on the reins, his eyes darting across the canyon to the riotous magic. A band of fire and air quested toward us, crackling into fiery lightning before it stretched across the canyon.

"Suit yourself. We're heading back," Gus said.

Marcus clapped a hand over the driver's mouth before he could signal his cerberi.

"How much for the sled?"

When Marcus removed his hand, Gus's grin revealed a few missing teeth. He named an exorbitant price. My heart dropped. I didn't have any more money, let alone the small fortune Gus demanded. Maybe if we carried the gargoyles one at a time, we could make it work. We'd have to move them in stages, making sure we did enough magic around them to keep them alive without doing so much magic as to attract a wild storm.

I eyed the wolf gargoyle. He weighed more than Marcus and me combined. Without using the elements, I wouldn't be able to move him. We needed the sled.

Marcus had already reached the same conclusion, because he was haggling. "Tell you what: I'll accept your price, but only if you agree to pay me half again as much when I sell it back to you."

Gus's eyes shone as he shook Marcus's hand enthusiastically. He snatched up the wad of bills Marcus pulled from his pocket and leapt agilely from the seat to the ground. After unhooking a slender board from the front of the sled, he unhitched the towline from the sled and attached it to the board. When he activated the board's spell, it floated a foot or so off the ground. Gus stepped on, grabbed the reins, and signaled the cerberi with a sharp whistle. They folded back down the line in the direction we'd come. By the time the last cerberus squeezed past the cart, they were galloping. Gus rode the floating board like he'd been air surfing his whole life, and he and his cerberi disappeared back into the forest. In less than a minute, the sound of the cerberi's enormous paws faded and an unnatural silence settled around us, broken only by the rumble of rockslides and thunder across the canyon.

"I don't think he expects you to live long enough to return his sled," I said.

"Easiest money I ever made." Marcus jumped from the driver's seat.

I tried to match his nonchalance as I scrambled to the ground. No birds chirped or called, no squirrels jumped through the branches above us, no lizards scurried through the fallen leaves. If any animals lived this close to Reaper's Ridge, they stayed hidden.

An eagle's shriek echoed off the hills, chased by a clap of thunder. Celeste dove through the trees to land next to me, folding her wings to her black sides as she trotted the last few steps.

"Where is the driver going?" she demanded.

"It doesn't matter. We need to move the sled ourselves," Marcus said. "Mika, set us a new towline."

Gus had taken the original towline with him, but a spare coil of rope was clipped to the underside of the sled. I tied the ends to the eye hooks in the front of the sled, creating a loop of rope.

"Can you pull it?" Marcus asked. He never ceased scanning the surroundings, crossbow and null trap at the ready.

I stepped into the circle of rope and leaned my weight into it. The sled shifted a few inches. Oliver loped to my side and reared to grab the line with his front paws, but his sinuous shape prevented him from getting any leverage and the sled didn't budge. We all turned to Celeste.

"Well?" Marcus asked.

She gave him a hard stare. "I am no animal of burden."

"It's you or me, and I think we'd both prefer me standing guard."

"This is debasing," Celeste grumbled, but she allowed me settle the rope around her broad chest for the same reason she'd trusted me with the secret of baetyls: love. She would do anything to save her mate. With Celeste pulling and me leaning against the back of the sled, we got the platform in motion.

The road switchbacked down into the canyon, and the slant helped us keep momentum through the increasingly dense undergrowth choking the unused path. After flying across the countryside behind the cerberi, our walking pace chafed. It also gave me too much time to think, and a snarl of doubt twisted my thoughts into knots. What if I couldn't repair the baetyl? What if we couldn't find it? How would we feed the gargoyles magic without attracting the storms? What good was my paltry magic against the massive collections of wild, raw elements? Every storm I'd caught a glimpse of could overwhelm me on sheer power alone. What had ever made me think I could do this?

Concussive explosions echoed through the narrowing canyon, the source hidden in the crevices of the mountainside. Every so often, wind howled through the trees, a different temperature every time. I twitched and jumped as I walked, trying to suppress my growing nerves, but the ridge never gave me a quiet moment to gather my wits.

By the time we reached the base of the canyon, I'd switched from cursing Gus for leaving and Captain Monaghan and the rest of the squad for being on vacation when I needed them to counting my blessings. I had Marcus with me, an air sled to move the gargoyles, and Oliver at my side. I wasn't alone. It would be so much worse to face this by myself.

A solid granite bridge arched above the shallow river at the base of the gorge, and Marcus made us wait while he examined it before he allowed us to cross. I would have preferred to test it with earth, but since we didn't want to attract storms, Marcus's visual inspection had to suffice.

I stood at Celeste's shoulder while we waited, studying the thick foliage overgrowing the road on the opposite side.

"You know the way, right?" I asked.

Celeste nodded, and when Marcus gave the go-ahead, she surged up the bank on the other side. I threw my weight against the back of the sled, scrambling after her. After a few dozen feet, she found a marginally clearer path through the dense undergrowth. Another hundred feet up the mountain, it revealed itself to be a real road, widening and clearing as it curved in a switchback.

My footsteps faltered when a wave of dizziness shoved through me. I glanced around, looking for a source. Beside me, Oliver whined.

"It's the ridge," Marcus said. He'd stopped up the trail to let us catch up.

"It feels . . ." I tried to put a term to the irritation grating against my elemental senses. My head felt like I'd been gritting my teeth for hours, the ache at my temples faint but grinding.

"Like a warning against trespassers?" he suggested.

Exactly. The entire mountain hummed with menace.

"We could turn around."

I ran my eyes over the comatose gargoyles. "No. We have to keep going." I stiffened my rubbery knees and pushed back into motion.

No one spoke again, as if being silent could keep us safe. The farther we climbed, the more bizarre and twisted the landscape became until the forest bore no resemblance to the hill across the canyon. Barren patches of scorched earth butted up to sections of woodland so overgrown the trunks of the oaks were bloated and cracked and the underbrush was impenetrable to anything larger than a mouse. Rows of pine trees lying as flat as plowed oat stalks and numerous rockslides only added to the difficulty of traversing the increasingly indiscernible road. Above us, clouds formed, rained, and dissipated in minutes instead of hours or days, often interspersed with lightning and fire. Through it all, the grumbling, cracking, grating sounds of shifting rocks and thunder never let up. I walked on nerves strung so tight I quivered inside my own skin, and when Marcus called a halt, I bounced on my toes.

He raised his crossbow, eyes on the sky and the wild snarl of energy ghosting closer. I jerked around, looking for cover, but we were caught in the middle of a meadow. The safety the trees might have provided was illusory, but being in the open felt foolishly vulnerable.

"What do we do?"

"Nothing. Just be quiet."

Comforting.

The storm was composed of fire wrapped in swirls of air and wood. In other words, it was a perfect firestorm in the making. Flames licked from the raw elemental tangle as if testing the air with a dozen blistering tongues as it swept above the tree line. The pine boughs swayed in its wake, the rustle of needles lost beneath the crackle of the uncontrolled elements.

Holding my breath, I cowered next to the air sled, useless. I couldn't pull magic to protect us without attracting the storm. I didn't have a single nonmagical weapon. I was supposed to be a gargoyle guardian, but I had no way to defend the helpless dormant gargoyles.

"Nobody move," Marcus said, his voice soft. "We might get lucky."

The magic storm slid past us on the outer rim of the meadow. At its current trajectory, it would pass us by without—

The storm kinked on itself, changing course and spearing directly toward us.

"Damn it!" Marcus shot a null trap into the wild energy. It should have neutralized all active magic in the vicinity, but the magic storm swallowed the trap with an infinitesimal hiccup. "Mika, to me!"

I lurched to his side, tripping over my own feet in my rush. Marcus had planted himself between the cart and the storm, and he shoved the anchoring rod into the ground in front of us.

"Link with me," he ordered.

The storm had us in its indifferent sights; hiding our magic had become moot. "With gargoyle help?"

"No gargoyles."

I drew as much as I could hold of water and air, my two weakest elements, then added a balanced amount of earth, fire, and wood and shoved the bundle to Marcus. If I hadn't been so scared, I might have been self-conscious about the pathetic level of magic I offered him.

The link between us snapped into place and Marcus's magic roared through me, so much more powerful than my own. The rush of power tipped my internal awareness into the link, pulling me into the slurry of elements. If I allowed it, the link would consume me, and I'd be as helpless as a dormant gargoyle, just a vessel to pull magic through.

"Relax. You've got this," Marcus said.

I teetered on the precipice of control, then fell back into my body. Magic still flowed between us, but I could separate my core self from the magic.

I opened eyes I hadn't realized I'd closed. Marcus leaned close enough to fill my vision.

"Ready?"

"Ready."

Not a moment too soon. Marcus threw our combined might into a huge shield of water and earth, wrapping it around the sled, the dormant gargoyles, Oliver, and Celeste and tethering it to the elemental anchor he'd pounded into the ground. The magic storm slammed the shield a second later. The impact would have thrown me from my feet, but Marcus grabbed my arm without even looking at me, holding me up.

Water countered fire; earth countered air. The wild magic folded back on itself before twisting for a second attack. Fire and air pounded the shield and burst, unraveling with a thunderous boom. The remaining snarl of wood flared across the shield, feeding from the water, devouring the earth. Fast as thought, Marcus wrapped the wood magic in fire and squeezed. The elements canceled each other out with a clap I barely registered over the ringing in my ears.

Marcus released the link, and I sagged to the ground, drained. He stalked across the quiet meadow and picked up the null trap with a pinch of air. The brass basket was blackened, the previously round shape melted and disfigured. Shaking his head, Marcus tossed the deformed mess into the back of the air sled.

Oliver loped under the sled to my side, rubbing against my forearm with a whine.

"I'm okay. Just catching my breath," I assured him. That hadn't even been a big storm. I tilted my head to peer up the mountain. "Are we close, Celeste?"

"No."

My heart sank.

"That's not going to work many more times," Marcus said, yanking the anchor from the ground and shaking the dirt from it before sliding it back into its loop at his waist.

"We can help," Oliver said, including Celeste in the offer.

"It might be dangerous if the magic backlashes to you," Marcus said before I could.

"No more dangerous than if you burn out before we reach the baetyl," Celeste said. "Rourke is getting weaker. We need to keep moving." She leaned her chest into the rope and dug her back paws into the soil. Marcus pushed the sled until she got it in motion again. I braced my hands on the dirt and shoved to my feet. Another ten minutes' rest would have been preferable. Marcus picked up his crossbow and notched another null trap—whatever good it would do us.

"If we use the dormant gargoyles, it'd help them at least," I said, falling into step with him. "The anchor worked, right?"

Everything had happened so fast, I had only an impression of the anchor funneling some of the wild magic harmlessly into the soil.

"More than the trap."

"What about the sword? Does it have any special properties?"

"Against raw elements, no. But if we encounter something with a body, it might come in handy."

"Do you really think anything could live here among the storms?"

He shrugged. "I've seen stranger things."

We climbed the switchbacks as fast as Celeste could pull the sled. My thighs ached and my stomach sat heavy with fear and doubt. Marcus sent Oliver to scout the way in the air, and I bit my tongue to hold in my protests. Oliver was smart and fast; he wouldn't put himself in danger. Even so, after he flew off, I spent so much time looking at the sky that my neck knotted and my toes bruised inside my boots from tripping over unnoticed rocks.

Our luck held for almost a half hour, until a small storm of raw water and air spinning as tight as a tornado veered off its previously straight course and whirled toward us. It switched directions so rapidly, we didn't have time to move from where we were pinned between a steep outcrop of ragged milky quartz and a washout. Already past the storm, Oliver circled back, wings beating so fast they blurred in his effort to reach us.

"No, don't let him—"

Marcus formed an air message and curved it around the storm. I half expected the wild magic to snatch it out of the air or change course in attraction to the magic, but it didn't alter its headlong rush for us.

I thrust my magic toward Marcus without taking my eyes from Oliver. Our linking was rough but fast, and in my worry for Oliver, it didn't unseat my equilibrium. When the message reached Oliver, he pulled up, his long body sagging beneath his spread wings. I let out a shaky breath.

"Thank you." Oliver was clear of the storm. He would be safe.

If Marcus replied, a gust of wind took his words. He formed another shield, this one fire and earth, and anchored it in the copper and quartz rod he stomped into the ground. I could feel the dormant gargoyles in our link this time, but Marcus didn't include Celeste despite her silent offer of enhancement. I could have accepted her boost and pulled more magic into the link, but I trusted Marcus to have a plan.

The storm dipped, coating the ground beneath it in ice and lifting rocks and weeds into a funnel. Wide-eyed, I watched the frozen front race toward us. Marcus locked my wrist in his hand and drew a wallop of power from our link, altering the fire in the shield from the basic elemental form to the weaves for a white-hot heat. When the storm hit us, it melted into nothing with an anticlimactic *shush* of released air.

"That's more like it," Marcus said. He released me from the link at the same time he let go of my arm, and I sagged against the sled. My heavy breaths fogged the chilled air, and between ragged pants, I could hear the tinkle of the ice crystals melting in the sunlight. Marcus rolled a weak band of heat across the ground in front of Celeste, thawing it, and we pushed back into motion.

Before following the sled, Marcus stooped to grab something from the icy ground. It wasn't until he held it up that I recognized the frosted twist of metal as a null trap.

"How did that get there?"

"I tossed it. I hoped if it was grounded, it would work. I think it's safe to say they're useless."

"That storm should have passed us by," I said, pulling the grounding rod from the ground. It burned my palm, and I bounced it between my hands to cool it until Marcus took it.

"It's as if someone is guiding these damn things toward anything living," Marcus said.

I shuddered at the thought. "Not anything. It ignored Oliver."

In unison, we glanced at the sled of dormant gargoyles.

"It's them," I said.

I couldn't believe I'd missed it. It was so obvious. The mining explosion, the broken baetyl: They were the same thing.

"Because the gargoyles are basically leaking magic?" Marcus guessed.

I shook my head. "Celeste, why haven't any of the other baetyls been accidentally discovered?"

"Baetyls protect themselves."

Exactly. The Native Americans had avoided Waupecony Ridge long before the storms. The baetyls must have some form of a ward or protection spell to scare off anyone who ventured too close. But the lure of wealth had spurred the members of the Hidden Cache Mining Company to ignore the dangers.

"The early miners, they merely lost their memories, right?" I said, without giving Marcus a chance to respond. "They must have gotten too close, and the baetyl's protective measures kicked in. The storms didn't start occurring until the incident with the Hidden Cache mine. Baetyls have their own type of magic—"

"They *are* magic," Celeste interrupted.

"What if the miners broke *into* the baetyl and fractured its magic? All these wild storms have to be coming from somewhere. What if it's coming from the baetyl?"

"That would explain a lot," Marcus said.

"I think so, too. And if the dormant gargoyles are tuned to this specific baetyl's magic, then these wild storms might also be tuned to them. The gargoyles might actually attract the storms."

"Well, doesn't this day just keep getting better," Marcus said to no one in particular.

———

THE THIRD MAGIC STORM WHIRLED ACROSS A BARREN SLOPE OF Reaper's Ridge and headed straight for us less than five minutes later. Oliver whistled a warning, giving us time to stop on a plateau of sandstone before the storm rolled over a gully into view, its snaking coils of earth and water covering over eighty feet of ground and moving so fast we had no chance of escape. It ripped up the ground, spewing gravel in its wake and hurtling hail in every direction. The few spindly trees in its path cracked and splintered.

"It's too big," I said. My knees felt like wet sand, and I locked them. "If we try to shield against it, it'll flatten us."

"We need to weaken it."

"How?"

"Unravel it. Come on." Marcus grabbed my hand and pulled me into a stumbling run *toward* the oncoming storm.

"What are you doing?!"

"Giving us a head start. Link up."

I thrust magic to him as I finally got my feet under me. He didn't slow our sprint until the pebble-size hail stung our faces.

"Concentrate on earth," he said. "Anywhere it's wrapped around water, loosen it."

"Me? Don't you want to do it?"

"It's your element. Get to work."

"But . . ."

"Unless you want to let it hurt the gargoyles."

I grabbed hold of the link. The elements flooded me, enhanced by the dormant gargoyles and Marcus. His magic signature—a shield of rosewood wrapped in flames and sparks of lightning—sat in my head with the same solid, comforting presence as his fighter's stance at my side.

Reaching for the first cable of wild earth felt like sticking my hand into a fire and trying to grab a particular flame. The raw element writhed around my magic, eating away my control. I sliced it, cutting a piece of earth from the bundle. The severed end dissipated.

"Just like that. Keep going. Don't stop, no matter what."

Working on the outer perimeter of the storm where I had a remote chance of seeing what I was doing, I hacked twists of earth as fast as I identified them. With the snarl of water and earth swallowing the hillside, I had no shortage of options, but no matter how fast I sliced through the earth strands, more always took their place, many of which were too tightly bound to the writhing water to budge.

I faltered for only a second when Marcus scooped me up, then redoubled my efforts as he retreated.

"It's not going to be enough." We were almost to the sled, and though I'd reduced the storm to one-tenth its original size, it loomed twice as large as the first storm we'd tackled. It hadn't slowed, either. Hail battered us, the tiny beads of ice sharp as finger flicks against my exposed face and hands. I squinted against the dust and sand, holding a hand over my eyes to shield them.

Dipping into our linked magic, Marcus enclosed our upper bodies in an air bubble, shielding us from the elements. Without setting me down, he pulled the anchor rod from its loop at his waist and hurled it into the ground, stamping it into place.

"My turn," Marcus said, tugging on the power of the link. I relinquished it in time for him to wrap a shield of fire and water around us, Celeste, and the cart of gargoyles. It wouldn't be enough, but we didn't have another option.

8

The storm slapped against the shield and shattered it in a single blow, hurtling Marcus and me into the air. We slammed to the ground a half-dozen feet from the sled.

Wild magic pinged between the helpless dormant gargoyles, battering them with stones and hail. Celeste fought free of the rope and the storm, scrambling up the hillside to safety.

The storm should have swept over the cart and continued across the ridge, but it didn't. With almost predatory focus, it attacked the dormant gargoyles. Desperate, I seized control of the magic in the link again and resumed my assault on the storm, slashing and yanking on the tangles of earth.

When I grabbed a strand that pulsed like tainted quartz, I dropped it, shocked. The rest of the wild magic had been pure, undiluted earth. This was tuned—malignant and sharp, but tuned. I scrambled to find it again, and this time I cut through the flawed magic with a sharp slash.

The last of the wild water flattened, and the storm billowed above the dormant gargoyles like a fluffed sheet, then settled onto them and disappeared.

I collapsed. Marcus grunted when my head hit his chest. I froze, taking a quick assessment of my location. Crap. I'd landed on top of him when the storm blasted us.

"Oh! Are you okay?" I asked, rolling to the side. Gravel bit into my hands and knees.

"Fine." He groaned as he sat up. I pushed to my feet and gave him a hand to help him up. Considering he weighed twice as much as me, it was more a token offering than actual help.

"Sorry about that. Again." This wasn't the first time an explosion had ended up with me using him as a cushion. I circled him, remembering the injuries he'd sustained when he'd protected me in Focal Park. The spell in his shirt had held this time, and his back was merely dirty. "I didn't plan on making it a habit."

He snorted and drew his sword, checking its length. I winced in sympathy at the bruise its sheath had probably left on his back. His shirt wouldn't have protected against that.

I stumbled back to the gargoyles, two inches of hail crunching underfoot. I tested all seven twice before I believed my readings.

"They're okay," I said. Cut up and abraded from the flying rocks, but their internal balance wasn't skewed, as I'd feared.

"They're better than okay. They're stronger."

I glanced at Marcus, surprised by his accurate guess, then realized we hadn't broken our link. Letting our connection unravel, I said, "I felt something in the storm. At the end. Did you catch it?"

"The repulsive bit of earth?"

"I think it was the baetyl's warped magic."

"That makes sense. If all these storms are coming from the baetyl, they should be tainted with it."

"It fits with our theory of why the storms are attracted to the dormant gargoyles."

"Rourke hasn't been this healthy in years," Celeste said, showering us with sand and ice when she shook out her wings.

After getting her permission, I checked her with a tuned blend of the elements. Celeste had a few scratches but was otherwise unharmed.

"You can heal me when Rourke is safe," she said when I reached for a seed crystal.

"She's right. Conserve your strength." Marcus scanned the broken terrain. "Are we close, Celeste?"

"About halfway there."

I slumped against the side of the sled, eyeing the steep ascent ahead of us.

"This is good news, Mika," Marcus said, taking in my tired expression. "The energy in storms doesn't hurt the gargoyles, not like it would us. Plus, the gargoyles do a great job of making the storms predictable. That means we can switch strategies, which is damn lucky. Defense isn't working; we're going on the offense."

We put Marcus's new plan into action with the next storm—this one a whirlwind of water, wood, and air. It barreled down on us in the middle of a scorched gully where burned stumps and fallen logs had slowed our progress to an aggravating creep. Celeste ducked out of the rope and took to the air before the storm reached us, and Marcus used the anchor rod to pin the sled in place. Then we sprinted toward the storm again, angling up the hill out of its path.

"Same as last time: Cut the storm apart, but this time focus on air," Marcus ordered.

I nodded. He was playing to my strengths: In the destructive cycle of the elements, earth destroyed air. He could use fire against water and wood with more efficiency than I could.

"Should we link?" I asked.

"No. We'll be more efficient apart."

Holding a stitch in my side, I watched the seething magic tumble across the ground. Chunks of ash puffed into the air whenever the storm touched down, lifted by the storm's wind and the plants bursting from the soil. Sporadic showers fell from the midst of the energy, and the rich aroma of freshly churned soil and rain drifted through the air. It was almost a shame to break apart this storm; it left a string of plants in its wake, rejuvenating the otherwise barren hillside.

Well before the storm was close enough for me to reach, Marcus tore into its outer edges, burning through the wood element. I tapped a foot impatiently, useless until Celeste landed close enough to offer me a boost. I grabbed at the magic she offered and flung earthen blades into the vortices of air.

Despite our assault, the storm bounded toward the dormant gargoyles, picking up speed until it pounced, frothing around their frozen shapes. Plants erupted from the soil, growing taller than the sides of the sled in seconds, but they couldn't obscure the wild magic from us. Methodically, we slashed it to pieces until it weakened enough to unravel on its own. I jogged back to the sled even as I tested the gargoyles. They all felt the same as before: stronger than they'd been in Terra Haven but still comatose.

"Not too shabby," Marcus said with his first real smile of the day.

The storm had shifted a few gargoyles on the sled, and we set them back in place. Then Marcus cut through the vines and small trees choking the sled, and we pushed onward.

We weren't so lucky with all the storms. Most were more violent, tearing up earth, striking with lightning, belching flames and ice alike. But our strategy was sound. Fatigue proved to be a greater obstacle. The higher we climbed, the more frequently we were forced to stop to deal with the storms. Oliver returned to my side to give me a boost, but even with his help, every encounter drained my energy, and my sprints toward the oncoming storms became jogs. In between storms, my feet dragged along the path. I ate the snacks Marcus handed me. I drank the water he gave me. I focused on not tripping. Only the dormant gargoyles and their improved health kept me going.

The dead gargoyle beside the trail caught me completely off guard. She was small and looked like a cross between a hedgehog and a wolverine, though twice the size of either animal. Her butterfly wings were spread as if to catch the sun, but her body had faded to gray and her right side had eroded into the dirt. I fell to my knees beside her and tried to help her anyway, but my gargoyle-tuned magic didn't penetrate the dead rock.

With trembling fingers, I brushed a layer of dirt from her face.

She had been so close to her baetyl, and she had died. Alone. Her life fading until nothing but the husk of her body remained.

I'd begun to hope that if we unraveled enough wild magic, the pieces of baetyl inside it would fill the dormant gargoyles on the sled with life and they'd wake, but staring into the lifeless gray eyes of the dead gargoyle, I knew it wouldn't be enough. Nothing short of fixing the baetyl would be enough.

Oliver whined and twined around me, tugging me from the corpse.

"Come on. There's nothing we can do for that one," Marcus said.

"Shouldn't we do something? I don't know—bury it?"

"It is customary to scatter the body," Celeste said. I glanced toward the old gargoyle. She hadn't stopped. The trail was steeper here and momentum was precious. She plodded past, head bowed.

"Is it okay if I do that?"

"It's part of your duties as a healer and guardian," she said.

My heart squeezed. I gathered earth and wood and wrapped the deceased gargoyle. The body crumbled under the weave, the once life-filled quartz disintegrating into pieces no larger than sand. With a boost from Oliver, I lifted the remains on a current of air and scattered them across the hill. Oliver hummed a sorrowful note, and Celeste added high-pitched harmony.

Swiping tears from my lashes, I pushed to my feet.

The hedgehog-wolverine was only the first of many dead gargoyles we found along the ridge. I stopped counting them after a dozen, and it sickened me how quickly I perfected the magic to decompose their bodies and scatter them. I began to look forward to the storms. Those at least I could do something about.

Heart weary and exhausted, I didn't understand why we stopped under a clear sky with no storm on the horizon until Celeste spoke.

"This is the entrance to the baetyl."

We'd made it? We'd survived Reaper's Ridge? Relief swamped me, followed by a wave of nausea as I realized that deep down, I hadn't expected to make it. I bent in half, taking deep breaths until my innards settled back in place.

When I was sure my shaking legs would hold me up, I fumbled around the sled to look at the entrance. Cut into the steep hillside and shadowed by a rocky overhang, the crooked opening was no wider than my outstretched arms and thoroughly unimpressive. I would have walked right past it without noticing if Celeste hadn't pointed it out.

"This is it? It's so . . . accessible. Anyone could walk right in." All gargoyles had wings. Why wasn't the entrance somewhere only they could reach?

"Normally, humans wouldn't be able to get this close. Thank you." The last was for Marcus, who had lowered anchors on the sled to take the burden from Celeste.

Summoning my energy, I jogged up the incline. A ledge of unnaturally flat ground lay in front of the opening, and the rest of the hill above us was too steep to traverse. The baetyl entrance itself was nothing to look at, but when I turned around, the view took my breath. Reaper's Ridge fell away beneath us, ravaged and misshapen, giving way to a view of the lush rolling foothills and the valley farther away. If I had wings, it would have been easy to launch into the sky.

Oliver landed next to me and peered inside the dark opening. His ruff flattened and he backed up so quickly he tripped over his hind legs and crashed to his side.

"Oliver!" I reached for him, but he'd already scrambled to his feet. Turning, he barreled into me, knocking me to the side of the entrance and pinning me against the slope.

"Something's coming! Something big!" he cried.

I sprawled against the rock slope, trying to catch my footing. Before I found my voice to ask what he meant—nothing big would fit through the opening—Marcus sprinted to the opposite side of the entrance, tossing the null traps into the cave. Using a spear of earth magic to drill a hole, he plunged the battered anchor rod into the rock in front of the cave.

"Celeste, to me," he ordered. He flattened himself against the rock face across the baetyl opening from me. "Storm or beast?" he demanded.

"Storm," Oliver said, releasing me. I staggered at my sudden freedom and braced a hand on the hill to steady myself.

"I can feel the energy building," Celeste said.

"Do we have time to move the sled?" Marcus asked.

As if in answer, the ridge shook, raining pebbles onto our heads. Beneath my hand, the rock heated and reshaped. Fear flooded me with a burst of energy and I scrambled back, Oliver at my side. When I reached for the elements, his boost was already there, waiting for me.

Marcus threw a five-element ward across the opening, anchoring it into the rod and tying it off.

"Ready?" he asked. Anticipation tightened his features and lit his eyes.

"I hope so."

Wild magic burst through the ward, tearing it to shreds and shattering the rod. The concussion knocked me to my butt and robbed me of my hearing. Marcus caught himself on a knee and stayed there, ripping into the magic as it emerged. It swelled from the baetyl to fill the sky, endless writhing bands of destructive raw elements building into a deadly monstrosity.

In a stomach-dropping rush, it dove back to the earth and swallowed us.

9

The earth pitched beneath me, and I rolled to the right, narrowly avoiding being swallowed by the shifting ground. Without rising, I slashed through twists of earth and wood, destroying the elements nearest me. The hillside stabilized, but I couldn't catch my breath; fire and water rolled in a tight mass of lung-scalding steam. Lashing out, I cut the loose coils of writhing fire. A deluge of water spilled from the storm, soaking me, and I sucked in cool oxygen.

The storm dwarfed all we'd encountered along the way. It wasn't two or three elements but all five bunched together, creating mayhem. The violent magic wouldn't boost the gargoyles until we could unravel it, and in the meantime, it ricocheted between them, knocking their frozen bodies into each other. I struggled to rise and protect them, but layers of wild magic pinned me to the hillside.

Rocks surged and grew behind me, burying Oliver in a pile of sand and stones. Frantic, I snapped a dozen strands of earth where they touched the ground around him, and he burst free, shaking grit into the air. A spear of wood element lanced from the storm as if aiming for me. I lurched to the side, narrowly evading the wild magic. It plowed into the soil, sprouting a two-foot sapling in a spray of rocks and dirt. Shielding my eyes with a hand, I burned through the tangle of wood before it could bury the ledge in a new forest, then rolled back to Oliver's side. His eyes were as wide as an owl's and he trembled as he curled around me.

Seeing his fear cut through my own panic. He was depending on me for protection. If I continued to react instead of attack, we wouldn't survive. I needed to think like a guardian.

"I'll keep us safe," I promised. "Stay close."

I concentrated on our immediate vicinity, unraveling earth and dousing fire, refusing to let any of the storm touch the ground near us. Across the ledge from us, Marcus did the same, holding a storm-free bubble around himself and Celeste. He wielded massive bands of the elements, slicing through fire more often than any other element. Taking my cue from him, when I had a chance to pick my next attack, I struck at earth; it was my strongest element and, after fire, the most deadly.

Snow and sand blinded me, winds knocked me flat and lifted me from the ground, and fire scorched me more than once. I fought through it all, hunting for the disharmonious quartz-tuned knot of earth holding the whole storm together. The wild magic blurred into a huge, shape-changing monster, and my control of my magic slipped and fumbled with weariness. Occasionally an explosive blaze or a sheet of ice forced me to shield Oliver and myself, but I dropped my barriers as soon as it was safe. Defending would do nothing but tire me out—attacking was the only option.

I whittled away the storm's power with increasingly clumsy strokes, and when I found the snarl of quartz-tuned earth, it was pure happenstance. I pounced, clinging to it with strength born of desperation. As fast as I could finagle my fatigued magic, I tore it apart. The wild elements collapsed and dispersed in a harmless gust of warm air.

A hush fell over the ridge, broken only by the harsh sounds of my panting followed by the chatter of my teeth when a chilly breeze plastered my soaked clothes to my body.

It took a moment for me to focus on Marcus. Dark circles cupped his eyes and exhaustion weighted his shoulders. He swiped mud from his leather pants as he stood, hail falling from his shoulders when he bent forward. The spell in his shirt had kept his torso dry and clean, a fact I envied as my body convulsed in another shiver. I'd managed to get to my knees at some point, and dirty snow melted around my calves. With reddened fingers, I sluiced slush from my thighs.

Plucking at my shirt to peel the wet fabric from my skin, I sought out Celeste. She'd flown to the sled where it sat on the ground, the spells previously holding it aloft destroyed by the wild magic. The taller gargoyles had toppled, including Rourke, and she used her talons to right him. Her lack of alarm told me most of what I needed to know—he was okay.

For now.

"Are you hurt?" Marcus asked. He loomed over me. I tilted my head back to look at him, but the muscles in my neck didn't cooperate and my head lolled toward my shoulder. Damn, I was tired.

"Sleep would be nice." If there were time. We didn't know how long this reprieve would last. Reaching deep into myself, I found the strength to stand. Oliver squirmed to his feet, stretching his wings, and I realized he'd been propping me up. I reached for him, and he brushed his head against my fingertips before coasting down the short incline to the dormant gargoyles.

"We need to go into the baetyl now, before the energy has a chance to build again," I said. I wouldn't survive a second megastorm.

Marcus's jaw muscles bunched. Grit pulled his dark hair into wayward spikes, and I thought the tousled look suited him far more than his scowl.

"You think that's wise?" he asked.

My head pounded. "No. But I don't think we have a choice. Let me check on the gargoyles, then we'll go."

"You can't even walk."

He issued the statement like a challenge. Giving him a scowl as fierce as the one he leveled on me, I straightened and took a step. My boot caught in the mud and the suction threw off my fragile balance. Marcus caught me when I stumbled into him. I glared at his Adam's apple, daring him to say something. He didn't. Shifting his grip to my bicep, he marched me down the slope to the gargoyles. I forced some rigidness into my backbone and dredged up the rest of my reserves so I could stand unaided when he released me. Unimpressed, Marcus crossed his arms, as if waiting to watch me face-plant.

I tottered between the gargoyles, checking for injuries. Internally, they all were remarkably strong, and their renewed health breathed a modicum of energy into me. I couldn't run a mile, or really even run at all, but I could do this; I could repair the baetyl. For them. To save seven lives.

I had to.

The gargoyles' physical injuries were minor—nicks and scrapes where their paralyzed bodies had slammed and rattled into each other during the storm. Normally I would have pulled out seed crystals and healed them, but saving my strength was more important. I could feel the sluggishness of my magic; expending it now, even to ease the small pains in their bodies, would be foolish. I didn't right those who had toppled for the same reason.

I checked Oliver, then Celeste, relieved to find them basically unharmed. Celeste had the equivalent of bruises along her hip and back and Oliver felt weary, but they would both survive without any assistance on my part.

Taking a deep breath, I turned to face the baetyl opening. The ledge had been completely reshaped by rockslides and new stone and plant growth, but the baetyl's opening was unchanged. I took it as a good sign. At least some of the baetyl's powers remained to protect it.

"Okay, I'm ready," I said.

"Really."

It wasn't a question, and when I met Marcus's gaze, I found anger rather than skepticism.

"Can you even get back up to the ledge?" he asked.

Frowning, I wrapped my arms around myself for warmth. What

had put a burr in his britches? "Are you going to test me every step of the way?"

"I'm not here to carry you." His hands flexed into fists, then relaxed. "Why didn't you contact me before yesterday?"

My eyebrows shot up at the non sequitur. Maybe I'd misheard him. "What?"

"After Focal Park. I can tell when someone is interested in me, so don't try to lie. You were interested. I made it clear all you had to do was come find me, but you never made a move."

"You want to talk about . . . about if I like you? Now?" My face heated under his glower.

"Yes."

"But—" I glanced toward the baetyl, willing to attempt a jog up the hill if it would extricate me from what was fast becoming an embarrassing conversation.

"I want an answer."

"Of course I liked you, but I was searching for a cure for the dormant gargoyles. There wasn't time . . ." My reason was perfectly valid, but telling Marcus to his face that I hadn't had time for him seemed callous. Besides, after the first few weeks of nonstop searching hadn't unearthed a cure, I thought I'd already missed my chance with him. A man like Marcus didn't have to wait around for women, and I'd told myself that whatever he'd seen in me that day in Focal Park wouldn't have been enough to hold his attention after the excitement died down. His ambivalence toward me on this trip had confirmed my prediction. Except now he acted as if I'd offended him. Had I hurt his feelings?

"Right. I should have realized that," he said.

"Thank you." The knot in my stomach eased.

"I mean, why bother making time for a life when you're so intent on killing yourself?"

He delivered the question in such an understanding tone that it took me a moment to process the words.

"What are you talking about?"

"This. This is what I'm talking about." He jabbed a finger at me and frustrated disdain replaced all the false sympathy in his expression. "You can barely stand up straight, but you're ready to rush off to the next danger. You've got no regard for your life."

"That's nonsense. I'm not trying to kill myself. I'm trying to save lives."

"Then act like it."

"What's that mean?" The wind no longer felt quite so cold, and I shifted from hugging myself to mirroring Marcus's crossed-arm stance.

"You hunt out ways to throw yourself into danger. You want examples? We're standing on Reaper's Ridge—"

"We just defeated Reaper's Ri—"

"And what about that stunt you pulled in Focal Park?" he asked, his words overpowering mine. "You were so eager to meet death, you practically ran to it."

"Someone had to break the null."

His ugly chuckle set my teeth on edge.

"The null. Right. I hadn't even gotten to that. I was talking about when you split your spirit among five different gargoyles and nearly liquefied your brain. But you just made my point. You think saving others means rushing into every dangerous situation you see—"

"Isn't that your job?" I shot back, irritated that he made me feel like I needed to defend myself. Of all people, he should understand.

"I'm a Federal Pentagon Defense warrior. I have training. I have full-spectrum strength."

"So that makes it okay? I'm a guardian. The *only* guardian these gargoyles have. Of course I'm going to take risks to save their lives."

"Taking a risk is one thing; swapping your life for a gargoyle's is another."

I clenched my jaw. Some people valued human lives more highly than gargoyles', but I never expected the elitist attitude from Marcus. "Is your ego so fragile that you would have preferred I let gargoyles die so I could have spent time fawning over you?"

"Don't pretend you believe I'm that shallow."

"You don't have a monopoly on being a savior, Marcus. The

gargoyles need me. I'm the only person who has a chance at saving them. And you know what? If it means my life—*one* life—has to be sacrificed to save *seven*, then so be it." Hearing my own conviction sent a tremor through my knees, but I didn't take the words back.

"That's just it. Being a healer—being a *guardian*," he corrected before I could, "doesn't mean your life is a bargaining chip."

"It means I'll do whatever I have to to save the gargoyles."

"This is why I said no," he said softly, making me realize we'd been shouting. "You don't have the good sense to save yourself. And it's why I said yes, because I couldn't let you kill yourself without trying to stop you."

"Are you saying you're going to try to prevent me from going into the baetyl?" I glanced around, locating Oliver and Celeste. They watched from a few feet away. Celeste's face was unreadable, but Oliver looked scared.

Marcus shook his head. "No. I'm not stopping you. Just..." He rubbed his hand across his mouth and jaw, his stubble rasping audibly in the charged silence. The tension left his shoulders and a pitying look replaced his scowl. "Just think about what I've said. The gargoyles don't need a martyr; they need a guardian *and* a healer."

He turned away to rummage in his pack, and I glared at his back. I couldn't decide what pissed me off more: the fact that he thought the lives of gargoyles weren't worth as much as mine or that he thought my actions to save them were rash.

Another breeze swept the hillside, and I ground my teeth together to stop their chattering. Every single scrap of me had been soaked, and even though it felt as if my blood were boiling, I wasn't getting any drier.

"Here," Marcus said, his voice as flat as his expression. He poured an unmarked packet into a canteen, swished it, then thrust the canteen into my hands. "Drink it all."

I sniffed the opening and pulled my head back with a grimace when a nauseating odor of brine, algae, and something bitter made my nostrils try to pinch together. "What is it?"

"A stimulant."

I glanced up at his cold eyes and took a sip, gagged, and doubled over coughing.

"It's not wine. Chug it. Try not to breathe between drinks and it won't be so bad."

Eyes watering, I forced myself to raise the canteen again and took a massive swallow. My throat threatened to close, but I powered through.

Marcus dumped a packet of the pungent powder directly into his mouth. With a band of air, he pulled a water bottle from the sled to his hand, took a gulp, swished, and swallowed. My tongue curled in sympathy for his assaulted taste buds.

"Ugh. I have the breath of a swamp monster," I muttered. I rubbed my tongue against the roof of my mouth, but it didn't alleviate the nasty flavor.

"Better than the breath of a burned-out null."

I rolled my eyes, but my frustrated comeback evaporated as energy surged through my veins. I raised my hands to stare at them, half expecting to see them glowing, but they remained reddened and dull. I took a step on legs that had transformed from pudding back to muscle and experimentally pulled the elements to me. They came in a rush.

"This is amazing." I jumped up and down. My mind, body, and magic felt as fresh as if I'd had a week off.

Without warning, Marcus sent me stumbling with a blast of heated air that pulled the moisture from my clothing and dried me at the same time. I closed my eyes against the stinging wind but didn't protest. When he finished, I was chapped but dry and warm. My smile seemed to irritate him, if the tick of his jaw muscle was any indication. I grinned wider.

"Stop bouncing," he ordered. "This isn't a game. We still don't know if you can fix a baetyl. We could be walking into a trap, so keep your wits sharp."

"Oh, good advice," I said, my voice heavy with cheery sarcasm. Being flippant was easier than letting his words sink in. The scary unknown of the broken baetyl loomed in my imagination, feeding my fears. Psyching myself out about it wouldn't help. "You know me. Always running into danger without a thought. But since you're telling me to be cautious . . ."

Marcus swiveled his head to glare at me, and the words died in my throat. I spun on a heel and marched up the incline to the tunnel entrance.

Peering into the dark opening, it was harder to maintain a sense of detachment from my fear. The wild storms had all but drained me. My arms were cut, my legs and feet bruised. I'd been burned and frozen. And that had only been what had escaped the baetyl. What horrors lurked inside?

———

MARCUS INSISTED ON GOING FIRST AND CELESTE FELL IN AT HIS HEELS. Oliver and I trailed after them, and I wondered if Marcus could feel the heat of my glare between his shoulder blades. Our moody leader also insisted I conserve my strength for whatever was ahead, so all five glowballs illuminating the tunnel were his. The walls were rough and asymmetrical, run through with veins of quartz and shale. Only the floor was smooth, polished by thousands of stone footsteps. I expected a challenge around every bend—a physical obstacle or more storms—but we strolled into the mountain without issue.

The cool air grew more humid the deeper we went, until moisture clung to the rock walls and dripped on our heads from the ceiling.

"It's too cold," Oliver said, his chiming voice hushed. I shivered at the creepy *shush-shush* echoes of his words.

"Is it supposed to be this wet?" I asked.

"Yes."

Marcus's back stiffened and he halted at a turn in the tunnel. Celeste crowded up next to him and he stepped aside to make room. My feet ground to a halt beside her. We'd found the baetyl.

Marcus's glowballs illuminated a field of citrine crystals barely as tall as my hand and packed more densely than blades of grass across the sloped floor. Darkness swallowed the rest of the cavern to our left and right, but bulky shapes loomed beyond the light. Squinting, I could make out flat planes and sharp angles, and when my brain put the pieces together, I gasped in wonder.

The baetyl was *filled* with crystals.

Six-sided prisms longer and thicker than a freight car crisscrossed the baetyl at the edge of the light, overlapping compact crystals no larger than Celeste. Even smaller crystals filled the gaps, and everywhere I looked glistened as endless facets caught and reflected the glowballs' fiery light.

"It's so dark. It's worse than I feared," Celeste said.

I reached for fire to form a glowball, and it flickered and wobbled before steadying into a sphere of light. Even then, the element stretched, skewing the light.

The warp of the baetyl was in full effect.

"Careful," Marcus said when I pushed the glowball into the cavern.

The light twisted, the element growing harder to control across the distance. Shadows guttered along the geometric lines of the baetyl, giving shape to crystal-coated alcoves and ledges of every color and type of quartz. The shifting golden light made the tigereye and agate crystals appear to ripple like liquid, and the jewel-bright spears of amethyst, citrine, prasiolite, and rose quartz refracted their colors across smoky quartz and shimmering clear crystals. The alien structure looked like the inside of a mountain-size geode, and the beauty of it stole my breath.

Even the air felt different, smooth and ancient. The humidity of the tunnel gave way to a cooler texture with a scent as unique as the baetyl. Part undisturbed earth, part weighted air, and part mineral, the odor pooled in the back of my throat, and I took deep breaths to savor the aroma. It was the smell of pure quartz—and up until that moment, I hadn't even known quartz had a smell, let alone that I had been craving it.

In the clutter of quartz and dense shadows beyond my glowball, I couldn't determine the boundaries of the baetyl, but Celeste's comparison of its size to Focal Park seemed about right.

The glowball twisted out of my grasp and imploded in a burst of sparks. Darkness coated the baetyl once more, hiding all but the tiny bubble of space Marcus's lights illuminated. I smoothed my hands down my thighs.

"Now what?" Marcus asked.

I don't know, sprang to my lips, but Marcus already knew I didn't know what I was doing. I wasn't going to give him the satisfaction of saying it out loud.

"We keep going," I said.

I contemplated the lawn of jagged crystals covering the floor. The baetyl had never been intended for fragile human bodies. Every surface had a sharp point. Tentatively, I tested the sole of my boot on the uneven peaks. When the crystals didn't puncture the tread, I settled my weight onto my foot and took another step. The crystals held firm.

Oliver stepped onto the quartz and hissed. Beside him, Celeste touched a crystal with a talon and narrowed her eyes.

"It hurts," Oliver said. He spoke so softly that I didn't think he meant for me to hear.

"You can wait—" My words died in my throat at Oliver's fierce glower. He must have been learning that look from Marcus.

"I go where you go," he said.

His tone was pure Marcus, too. I glanced to the fire elemental to see if he noticed.

"Like guardian, like companion," he said.

Oliver hissed as each foot hit the crystals for the first time; then he quieted. I didn't need to test him with magic to know he was in pain; I could see it in the hunch of his shoulders and the droop of his ruff. Clamping my mouth against a protest that would only offend the brave young gargoyle, I waited until Marcus and Celeste caught up before mincing deeper into the baetyl.

We ducked under a slender rose quartz crystal bar, then climbed over a carnelian crystal a few shades lighter than Oliver and so thick Marcus and I couldn't have spanned it with linked hands. Marcus kept rigid control over the glowballs, eliminating all but two, so we moved in a tight halo of light. After ten steps, I lost sight of the entrance.

"Oliver, how's your night vision?" I asked, wishing I couldn't hear my apprehension in my voice.

Marcus shot me a sharp look, then glanced back the way we'd come. He stopped while we waited for Oliver's response.

"I don't know."

"Can you see where we came in?"

"Yes. You can't?"

I let my breath out slowly. "No. What else can you see? Are there any obvious problems?"

"The roof has caved in," Celeste said, emerging from the darkness ahead of us.

"A cave-in? Would that be enough to break a baetyl?"

She shrugged. "Maybe. It's small."

Small or not, it was a place to start. "Lead the way."

She hadn't finished turning around when gargoyles burst from the shadows. They charged from every direction and dive-bombed from above, teeth bared, claws raised, and spikes distended in attack.

I froze in shock, but Marcus spun into action, drawing his sword in a fluid motion.

"Get behind me," he ordered.

I dodged to the side to avoid being flattened by a stampeding quartz porcupine, and Marcus lurched in the opposite direction when a gargoyle dropped out of the shadows above him. His sword flashed through the air, just missing the gargoyle's canine tail.

"Wait! We're here to help," I shouted, waving my arms ineffectually.

A life-size jasper hippopotamus barreled down on me, his wide bat wings slicing through the air like blades. I jumped to the side, leaping across a broad, horizontal amethyst crystal. The hippo pivoted on thick lion legs, clawed paws shoving effortlessly against the jagged floor to follow me.

"Mika!" Oliver cried.

The hippo's jaw unhinged on a silent roar. I screamed and

grabbed the elements, but they squirmed from my grasp. Frantic, I rolled under the amethyst crystal, ignoring the sharp cuts and stabs of the baetyl's crystal floor.

"Run, Oliver!"

The hippo fell upon me mouth-first, crushing me between his stone jaws.

10

I floated, a spark in pure inky onyx. I couldn't feel my body. I tried to wriggle a finger or shake my head, but there was only darkness and the rapid pounding of my pulse.

Was I dead?

Why would I be dead?

The massive stone teeth of the hippo flashed across my memory, then all the attacking gargoyles. They'd come out of nowhere, and we hadn't had a chance to fight back.

My pulse fluttered faster.

I opened my eyes.

I lay in a narrow plaster tunnel. Not just any tunnel. It was the hidden back room of the temple in New Hope where I'd rescued Oliver and his siblings from Walter's black market auction. *How did I get here?* I had been in the baetyl . . .

When I sat up, I saw Oliver. He was tiny, hardly larger than a house cat. I frowned at his small body, trying to pinpoint why my brain insisted his size was wrong. That wasn't the problem. The cage of elemental magic pinning him to the stone floor was the problem. He was trapped. And injured. His left two feet and wing tip had been burned with acid, leaving jagged patches of raw pain. Oliver's magic, his life, leaked from the wounds into the cage, strengthening it. His golden-red eyes whirled with agony, but the cage smothered his cries.

I lurched to my hands and knees, heart pounding. This was exactly how I'd found Oliver when Walter had tortured—

Walter.

Walter was in prison.

Darkness closed in on us, until all I could see was Oliver, trapped and in pain. The baby gargoyle locked eyes with me and his muzzle opened and closed in muted misery. Fingers trembling, I gathered the elements and thrust them into the first quartz anchor, countering the trap. It didn't matter how this had happened. I'd sort it out later. After I freed—

Agony pumped through my veins, cording my muscles. Magic leeched from me. I had to free . . . someone. Fear clouded my thoughts and the elements slid from my grasp. The pain abated. Oxygen filled my lungs, flavored with quartz. I sucked in another deep breath, centering my thoughts.

Myself. I had to free myself. I opened my eyes to a view warped by the elements. Magic wrapped me in a twisting cage, siphoning my life. If I struggled, the pain would return, so I held still and tried to think. I couldn't remember anything before the pain. How long had I been caged? Who was holding me?

Walter walked toward me. Once I saw him, I saw the rest of Focal Park spread around us, the dome of blue sky and puffy white clouds above me and the etched-marble pentagram beneath me. I'd been positioned in the center and seed crystals locked the elements in place at all five points. My head went light on my shoulders. Stuck in the center, I'd be the focal point of the spell, my life drained to feed whoever controlled the pentagram. I needed to escape or I'd be killed.

I gathered magic, gritting my teeth against the rush of pain, but no matter how hard I clung to the elements, they kept slipping from my control. Walter smiled. He used brushes of air to shove the crystals holding the net closer around me, tightening the magical cage until I couldn't move.

"Good." Elsa stepped up beside Walter. The inventor looked as insane as the day she'd unleashed her gargoyle-enhancement replication invention upon Focal Park. I panted against the elemental restraints, tasting quartz in each breath.

Walter hadn't been at Focal Park, and I hadn't been alone—

Silver cracks split the air around Elsa like lines of tinsel opening into nothing but silver light.

Elsa leaned close, breathing on my face, pulling my attention back to her feverish eyes. "This will change everything."

I strained to move, but my body wouldn't respond. Elsa wove a spear of wood tempered with water and drilled into my neck. Pain like fire erupted from my throat and seared across my brain in white-hot agony. I screamed inside my head, but no sound escaped my frozen lips.

I could feel the hole in my neck.

A hole in my neck.

I should be dead. I couldn't survive a *hole* in my neck.

I wasn't made of stone . . .

Silver cracks fractured the air around the inventor as she readied her next wood and water attack. I tried to study the fissures, but Elsa filled my vision. She plunged her barbaric elemental weave into me again. Scorching pain burned through my brain, but I clung to my last thought. It was important. *I wasn't made of stone. I wasn't made of stone.*

I wasn't a gargoyle. I could fight back.

I grabbed for the elements. Like grains of sand, they trickled through my grasping mental fist. All but earth.

I refined earth to pure quartz, and the magic solidified in my grip. Elsa loomed, another wood and water spear poised to stab me. The silver lines around her faded. My instincts demanded I defend myself. I could block her, shatter that damn magic spear before it hit my stone—

I wasn't made of stone.

The silver lines burst back into existence, and with a soundless roar, I drove the quartz into the shimmering fractures with every ounce of my strength.

Focal Park, Elsa, the trap—it all shattered. My magic hurled through the baetyl, burrowing into an amethyst cluster five feet away. The crystals shattered and reshaped, falling to the baetyl floor in perfect amethyst snowflakes.

"Mika?"

Oliver loomed in my vision, his head as large as mine, his body the appropriate size. I grabbed him and wrapped my arms around his smooth ruff. He whuffled my face with soft, relieved breaths. When I let him go, he pulled back far enough for me to see Celeste. Light fractured across the crystals around her, defining her dark outline more than illuminating her.

"She is herself?" Celeste asked Oliver.

"I am me," I said, taking comfort from the simple statement. I looked for the source of the light, surprised to see it coming from the crystals. When had they started glowing?

"What happened?" Oliver demanded. "You were fine; then you were both screaming and collapsed."

"Where's Marcus?" I sat up, hissing when the movement woke the pain in a dozen cuts on my arms and hands. Marcus lay a dozen feet away, sprawled on his back across a bushel of mint-green prasiolite crystals. His head lolled off the edge of a sturdy crystal and his hands and feet twitched, but the light underneath him left his face shadowed.

I staggered across the crystal floor to him, Oliver so close to my side that I had to grab his wings to prevent myself from being knocked down.

"Marcus." His eyes moved behind his eyelids, and he mouthed unintelligible words. I prodded his arm, and when he didn't respond, I added more force to the next poke. He twitched and moaned but didn't wake. His sword protruded from the baetyl wall a few feet away; he'd managed to wedge the tip of it between two crystals. The scabbard remained strapped to his back, but his fall had broken the rigid bamboo, and splinters of it dusted the crystals below him.

"He's trapped in the nightmare." I reached for magic—maybe a jolt to his senses would wake him—but it was as if I were in the nightmare again. The elements slid from my grasp, all but earth. Its jagged edges vibrated against my skull until I tuned it to quartz; then the element stabilized and smoothed out. Unfortunately, I couldn't do anything with quartz to wake Marcus. Growing alarmed, I lightly slapped his cheek. He swung a halfhearted punch without opening his eyes. I danced out of reach. "Marcus, wake up!"

"What nightmare?" Oliver asked.

As if his confusion summoned them, gargoyles seethed from the baetyl's geode-like walls. They swarmed over the crystals and rushed us. An enormous green aventurine bear with delicate dragonfly wings led the charge, a half ton of rock galloping on clawed feet to demolish me. I widened my stance and threw a quartz shield around Marcus, Oliver, Celeste, and myself, bracing myself for impact.

"What are you doing? Mika, what do you see?" Oliver stood on his hind legs, flaring his wings for balance, and squinted in the direction of the charging bear.

My legs trembled. If not for Marcus, I would have run, but I couldn't abandon him and I couldn't carry him.

The bear skidded to a stop just beyond my shield and reared up on her hind legs, releasing a soundless roar. I frowned. A mute gargoyle? My brain tried to make sense of it but was too distracted by her massive paws. They were larger than my head and tipped with finger-length claws; with one blow, she could kill me, yet she only waved her paws in front of her as if testing the air.

If she had been a real bear, I would have been scrambling for Marcus's sword and making as much noise as possible to drive her off. But she was a gargoyle, a reasoning creature.

"I'm here to help," I said.

She shook her head, denying my words.

"Who are you talking to?" Celeste asked. The gryphon perched on a wide tigereye crystal behind me, her sharp eyes scouring the shadowy baetyl.

"Her."

"Who?" Oliver asked, squinting at the massive gargoyle.

"You don't see her?" Frowning, I glanced to Oliver and back to the bear. She hadn't moved, and next to my gargoyle she looked . . . less. Less substantial. Weak.

"See who?"

"The bear? The other gargoyles?" Only there weren't other gargoyles now, just the bear, Oliver, and Celeste.

"I don't see anything," Oliver said.

Confusion muffled my fear, helping me pick out details I'd overlooked in my panic—like the fact that I could see the geometric shapes of the baetyl *through* the bear gargoyle. Her paws also made no sound on the crystals—none of the gargoyles' feet had. Frowning, I settled back on my heels, relaxing enough to unclench my fists, but I didn't lower the shield.

The bear dropped to all fours, nose snuffling the air around my shield; then she turned and faded from sight. Trapped air gusted from my lungs. I dropped my shield without releasing my grasp of quartz magic and rubbed my hands together, wincing when I roughed up cuts on my palms.

"It was an apparition," I said. I explained the gargoyles pouring out of the baetyl and the hippo swallowing me and sending me into a nightmare. I didn't describe the nightmare.

"I think Marcus is trapped in a nightmare, too. I got out by using quartz magic." If that was the only key to escaping the trap, Marcus wasn't going to wake from his nightmare any time soon. He was a big, bad FPD fire elemental. He had oodles of training for all kinds of dangerous situations, but he'd never think to use something as simple as quartz-tuned earth magic to escape whatever madness he was likely seeing right now.

"The baetyl must be trying to protect itself," Celeste said. "Humans aren't meant to be here. If it were whole, you wouldn't have made it this far. So it's fighting back the only way it can."

"The baetyl is sentient?" I glanced around, imagining all the crystals sprouting eyes and watching me. The thought chased a shudder down my spine.

"It is magic unto itself," Celeste said with a shrug that whispered the rock feathers of her shoulders together.

I'd had plenty of time to think about the nature of the baetyl on the way up Reaper's Ridge. I'd abandoned my earlier hope that it might resemble gargoyle magic on an immense, advanced level. A gargoyle, no matter how enraged or injured, could never create magic storms. The apparitions and nightmares only confirmed it: I was dealing with very foreign, very dangerous magic like no other I'd encountered before. Even if it wasn't sentient, it had some level of awareness—enough to tell when it had been invaded and to deploy honed defenses.

I rolled my shoulders against the urge to hunch, as if I could hide myself by making myself smaller.

"Why didn't it attack me the second time? Why did the bear walk away?"

"Maybe it recognizes you as a guardian," Oliver said.

I doubted it; otherwise it wouldn't have attacked me in the first place. If I could trust any part of an apparition, I'd say the bear gargoyle had been confused by the shield. Not many humans could manipulate the earth element through only quartz. It'd taken me years of practice to make it feel natural.

I remembered something Anya, Oliver's sister, had told me when we first met. She'd said my magic smelled like a gargoyle. Could holding a quartz shield have been enough to confuse the baetyl into thinking I might be a gargoyle?

"Do I . . . Does my magic smell like a gargoyle?" I asked, half afraid the question would offend my companions.

Oliver shrugged. "You are a guardian."

I looked askance at Celeste. She padded closer and pressed her beak to my chest, inhaling deeply.

"Your magic smells like a healer, but there are notes of a baetyl in it." She backed away, eyeing me with fresh wonder. "My sense of smell is not good, otherwise . . . I waited so long out of fear . . ."

When I interpreted her wondrous expression, a zing of shock jolted through me. Up until this moment, she hadn't fully believed I was a guardian, but there was no mistaking the certitude in her eyes now. Celeste rolled her shoulders and fluffed her feathers, and when she settled, she looked as if someone had lifted a heavy load from her back.

Oliver saw the change in her and smiled smugly.

"Your magic is a bit like a baetyl's and it's what makes you a guardian," Oliver said. "Or maybe because you're a guardian, it's why your magic smells so good."

"Just mine? Not Marcus's?"

"Just you, Mika. Only you."

A seed of hope sprouted in my chest, nurtured by the thought that maybe, just maybe, having magic even remotely similar to the baetyl would enable me to fix it.

I took a deep breath, tasting the quartz air as I watched Marcus's hands clench into fists and feebly box at nothing. He looked helpless and vulnerable. Even his scowl was weak. No amount of prodding had stirred him, either.

"The baetyl's not going to let me help Marcus until we fix it, is it?"

Celeste shrugged. "He might be beyond help. But Rourke is not, and we are wasting time."

My stomach twisted. She was right, but it didn't make her words more palatable.

Celeste and Oliver helped me move Marcus, shifting him until he lay as flat as possible on the bed of sharp crystals. His leather pants and spelled shirt did a much better job protecting him than my clothing had. It was his head I was worried most about. I didn't have a spare piece of cloth to put between him and the bladelike tips of the crystals, so I removed one of his leather boots and used the leg of it to cushion his head. He might get some cuts on his exposed foot, since I doubted his socks were spelled, too, but it was a fair trade-off.

I tried folding his arms over his stomach, but he flailed and fought me, smacking his hands into the crystals around us. I gave up and backed away, and he calmed. Blood oozed from nicks and cuts on his hands and wrists, and I let them bleed. If I knew more about healing people *and* could grasp more elements than quartz, I would have healed him, but quartz wasn't going to do him any good.

Instead, I did the only thing I could: I turned my back on him and walked away. He'd been a true friend, helping me when there was no incentive for him, risking his life to get me this far, and I abandoned him.

11

From the shadows of overhanging crystals, the gargoyles swarmed, but when they drew close, they turned, parted, and let me pass. A braver person would have been able to walk confidently through the bombarding apparitions, but my steps faltered and shook, and I flinched when the gargoyles darted out of the shadows, mouths agape and faces contorted with killing rage. The baetyl might be temporarily confused by the flavor of my magic, but once it realized I wasn't a gargoyle, it'd crush me.

Behind me, Marcus wasn't as lucky. I turned, watching helplessly as the apparitions dove into his body, their ghostly forms disappearing when they touched his flesh. He thrashed and moaned, feebly slapping the air. I almost ran back to him, but I knew it would be pointless. I could stand over him and guard his body or I could fix the baetyl and save his mind.

I wasn't stupid enough to test the baetyl's crystals with so much as a grain of quartz element, but the deeper I crawled and climbed through the maze of crystals, the more heavily its magic pressed against my skin. Its jagged disharmony set my teeth on edge. A headache unfurled across my skull, the pain a dull pound compared to the sharp sting of the cuts on my arms.

I examined my wounds in the glow of an especially bright, clear crystal. Blood oozed through my shirt at my left bicep, caking the rip in the fabric. I didn't think peeling the cloth from the cut would help at this point, so I ignored the gash. A series of nicks spiraled down my forearms, with one long scratch on the underside of my right arm. Most had stopped bleeding already, and my shirt was doing a decent job soaking up the rest of the blood. My hands hurt the worst. Lacerations crisscrossed my palms, oozing blood.

Oliver and Celeste walked across the crystals without being cut, but the tension in them reminded me of their first steps. Not only was this baetyl broken, but it also wasn't their cynosure baetyl. The magic in here was not theirs, and every step hurt them in a different way. I picked up my pace.

Celeste led us to the cave-in. Amid all the flat planes and jewel tones of the crystals, the mound of soil and rocks lay like a physical insult on the otherwise pristine floor. High above us, a jagged dark patch marred the lines of the ceiling.

It wasn't a natural collapse. The sturdy beams of enormous crystals spanning the breadth of the baetyl should have prevented any part of the cavern from caving in, but if the structural integrity had been destroyed from above by the Hidden Cache miners, it wouldn't have mattered how strong the crystals inside the baetyl were.

We paused as I assessed the ugly gap in the crystals and waited for inspiration. I had hoped that when I encountered the problem, I'd see the solution. Obviously, the cave-in needed to be mended, but the scope of it worried me. Even from a hundred feet below it, the hole looked large enough to drive two trains through side by side. Enhanced by Oliver and Celeste, I could probably do it—if I had a few days *and* control of all the elements.

Which meant I needed to get started right away. For Marcus and for the dormant gargoyles waiting outside, none of whom had time to spare. Except . . .

I couldn't focus on the cave-in. I peered into the gloom of the baetyl, straining to see . . . to hear . . . something.

"What's that way?"

"The heart," Celeste said.

Yes, the heart. "Take me there."

The crystals grew denser the deeper we traveled, and their internal light increased until a dozen different shades of soft twilight lit the cavern. Celeste was forced to find her own way, not fitting through the same spaces as Oliver and me. I spent more time crawling through gaps than walking, with Oliver helping me over the larger crystals. The blood from my palms blended into his carnelian sides when he let me use him for handholds rather than the sharp edges of the quartz.

We passed two other cave-ins, both smaller than the first but not by much. I examined them without really seeing them. The baetyl's magic had grown stronger, the broken and pure notes shredding my senses like a cheese grater, disrupting my ability to concentrate on anything else.

I lost track of time. My sense of direction narrowed to the painful-sweet siren song of the heart. If I'd thought about it, I wouldn't have been able to find the exit, but leaving had lost all sense of importance. The heart was all that mattered.

I slid down the slope of a citrine crystal as wide as my shoulders and landed softly on a bed of onyx peaks, then paused in surprise. The network of crystals opened, creating a gap that stretched to the ceiling. Another twenty feet in front of me, a massive wall of interlocking crystals wove from the ceiling to the floor. I scanned the surface, hunting for an opening in what looked like an impenetrable maze of quartz.

Celeste coasted to my side from a large gap higher up, and I stepped aside to give Oliver a place to land when he slid down the crystal behind me.

"The heart is inside," Celeste said.

I'd assumed as much. "How do I get through the wall?"

"There are openings up higher," Oliver said.

"How do you know?" He'd been at my side the whole time; he hadn't had the opportunity to scout ahead to check for gaps in the wall.

"This baetyl shares similarities with mine."

I waited for him to elaborate. He ducked his head and looked away, and I realized he didn't want to say anything else. The fact that I was here, inside a baetyl, didn't make a difference. Baetyls were private, even from gargoyle guardians. Only the extreme extenuating circumstances had forced Celeste to reveal their existence, but it hadn't changed the gargoyles' instinctive secretive nature. Not even for Oliver, my stalwart companion.

"How high up?" I asked.

"The biggest should be near the top."

I tilted my head back. The ceiling here was at least twelve stories high. Contemplating that height, even while standing on solid ground, made my legs weak. I pressed my fingertips into my stomach to quiet the butterflies.

In an ideal world, Celeste would have been able to carry me up and through the wall. She outweighed me by at least four hundred pounds and was larger than most mules. If she'd been a real gryphon, she wouldn't have had a problem. Gryphons and gargoyles both used air magic to fly, but the differences in *how* they did so was the speculation of scholars. All I knew was that for gargoyles to use their stone feathers to lift their solid rock bodies, they couldn't also carry anything much heavier than their own heads. Even a gargoyle as large as Celeste wouldn't be able to lift me. Her magic wouldn't support both of us.

"You'll have to climb," Celeste said.

I worried my bottom lip, eyeing the crystal wall. The smallest branch of quartz was thicker than my thigh; the largest could have fit three of my studio lofts inside. All were packed so densely at the base that I couldn't fit more than an arm through the gaps.

"To the top?" I asked.

"Not that far. You might fit through about halfway up."

I closed my eyes and swiped sweat from my forehead with trembling fingers.

"I'll go with you," Oliver said.

I gave him a tremulous smile. He knew how scared I was of heights, even if he didn't understand why.

"Thank you."

"I'll try to guide you through from the other side." Celeste walked a few paces away to give herself room to unfurl her wings, then launched into the air. She had to fly back the way we'd come first to give herself time and room to gain the necessary height. I lost her among the crystals, her dark black and purple body disappearing in the shadows. When I spotted her again, I almost mistook her for an apparitional gargoyle swooping out of the dark gap between a dumortierite crystal and a shadowy cluster of smoky quartz crystals. Her flight path should have looked erratic and cumbersome as she wove through the crystals; instead, her movements were organic. Every flap of her wings and turn of her body was timed for her to soar gracefully through the upper reaches of the baetyl.

Observing her, I saw the baetyl's design with fresh understanding: I'd been traversing the baetyl as a human, clumsy and crawling, but it had never been designed for two-legged movement. It was a place for wings and flight.

When Celeste closed in on the wall near the ceiling, she tucked her wings and plummeted into an opening not visible from where we stood. I waited to hear the sounds of her progress, but if she had to touch down, none of her footsteps were loud enough to reach us.

I glanced back through the crystals behind us, ignoring the pull of the baetyl telling me I was facing the wrong way. Overlapping quartz of every color and size disguised the way back, hiding the cave-ins and the exit. I tried to picture how deep we were inside Reaper's Ridge. A half mile? A mile?

If Marcus were at my side, he would have already started climbing the wall and finding a way through for us. But he wasn't with me. Lost amid the crystals, he lay helpless and tortured by nightmares, dependent on me to save him.

I stopped stalling and turned back toward the wall.

"Let's see if we can find a way through."

Oliver scampered across the sharp crystals to the left and I walked the opposite direction, taking great care with my footing. When neither of us spotted any openings near the bottom, I selected an accessible-looking section near the right wall and began to climb. The crystals comprising the wall were some of the largest in the baetyl, and their girth meant not every angle was razor sharp. Unfortunately, it also meant I had fewer handholds on the slick surfaces.

Oliver had a harder time than me, lacking the traction provided by fingerprints and leather boot soles. After falling off twice, he flapped to a narrow ledge above me and guided me up the wall.

I did my best not to look down. Sweat and blood slicked my hands, and the tips and edges of crystals cut into my stomach and hips as I scaled the uneven surface. In a few places, the crystals were wide enough for me to walk along like uneven stairs, but more often, I clung to fragile toeholds and inched my way higher.

I almost cried when I reached the first opening large enough for me and looked through: Beyond the gap crisscrossed another layer of interlocking crystals too tight for me to navigate.

"How thick is this wall?" I asked, eyes closed. A tear escaped after all, but I didn't have a spare hand to brush it from my cheek.

"I don't know," Oliver said. He draped from a rose quartz crystal above me, brows furrowed with sympathy.

"Guess. More than two feet?"

"Definitely. Probably more like twenty to forty."

Another tear slid down my face. "Okay. We keep going up."

I balanced precariously on the slanted edge of an agate crystal thirty feet above the sharp baetyl floor when I finally found a promising hole large enough to wiggle through. I squirmed through on my stomach, then lay there, panting, savoring the reprieve for my tired arm muscles. When I'd regained my breath, I pushed myself to my feet and carefully stood.

Crystals jutted from every angle around me, and when I looked down, I forgot how to breathe. I stood on an aventurine ledge, and despite its almost jade color and the glow it emitted, I could see through it to the crystals below it—and the crystals below those, as if I stood on a plane of glass three stories in the air. My head went light.

My heart beat its way up my throat. I crouched and closed my eyes. Vertigo tilted the crystal beneath my hands, and I jerked my eyes open and stared straight ahead.

"Are you okay?" Oliver asked, peeking at me from the other side of the opening.

I nodded, my throat too dry to form words.

"The crystal is strong. You won't fall."

I nodded again and forced myself to look around. The opening wasn't a dead end—I could go up.

Lucky me.

Oliver tried to squeeze through the opening with me, but his inchworm way of walking bunched his body up too tall to fit through the gap. He shot me a worried look.

"Maybe if I fly and use my momentum to slide in," he suggested.

I shook my head, but it took me two tries to get my voice to work. "You should take a safer route. Like Celeste."

"Are you going to be okay without me?"

I thought about Marcus lying helpless near the entrance, being bombarded by the baetyl's fractured magic. I thought about the dormant gargoyles growing weaker, depending on me to save them.

"Yes." I pushed to my unsteady feet, almost grateful for the pain of my injuries to focus my thoughts. "I'll see you on the other side."

Through a beam of smoky quartz, I watched Oliver launch into the air and fly away.

I'd never felt so alone and foreign in my skin as I did while inside the crystal wall. I'd worked with quartz my whole life. I'd identified as an earth elemental since grade school, but I found myself missing wood. A blade of grass, a patch of moss—any hint of growing greenery would have soothed my taut nerves. There wasn't even dust. Surrounded by all the shiny, glowing geometric planes, my flesh looked strange, too pink and rounded. I couldn't even take solace in the elements. I continued to hold quartz even though I hadn't seen a phantom gargoyle since I'd touched the wall, but the element had grown brittle and fragmented. Knowing it was a reflection of the baetyl was no comfort. I'd never had a place change the nature of the elements, and being perpetually in touch with the flawed magic screwed knots into my shoulders. Only fear of not being able to take hold of it again and being powerless against the apparitions prevented me from releasing the element.

I hurried and it still took a century. Sweat dripped down my face and stuck my shirt to my back. The cuts in my hands stung in a peripheral way until I slipped and grabbed for purchase on the slick crystals. Most of the time, I was forced to crawl, contorting myself around the overlapping branches of quartz. With the crystals so close together, I no longer feared falling to my death; instead I developed a new phobia of getting a foot or arm stuck and being trapped until I starved to death.

When I heard Oliver and Celeste, I thought it was a hallucination. I inched through a gap so tight I couldn't lift my head, moving mostly by gravity on the smooth slant with a little help from my feet. Then stone paws wrapped gently around my wrists and pulled me through.

Oliver curled around me, halting my descent with his body. I lifted my head, spotting Celeste first. She stood beside me, fitting easily on the rose quartz ledge. Gratefully, I got to all fours, then grabbed Oliver's wing when I caught sight of the drop-off beyond him.

"I've got you," Oliver said.

"Thank . . ." I forgot my own words as I took in the heart.

The wide open, perfect sphere of the heart was defined on all sides by thousands of crystals of every size, as if it were an enormous woven quartz basket—one that could fit two or three city blocks with room to spare. Hundreds of crystal ledges like the one we stood on protruded from the walls all the way around the heart, the enclosure designed to fit droves of gargoyles.

The structural beauty of the quartz sphere was surpassed only by the central crystal. It thrust from the floor nearly to the twelve-story ceiling, its girth so broad a dozen gargoyles could have stretched out on the sloped top. Unlike all the other crystals in the baetyl, which were each made of a singular type of quartz, the towering heart crystal swirled with every variety of quartz in a riot of color, the pattern never repeating.

I was so mesmerized by the beauty of the heart that when I spotted the enormous crack running through the multicolored crystal, I physically recoiled. The culprit was obvious: Another cave-in had split the ceiling directly above the crystal. I followed the length of the crystal back to the floor, spotting the pile of dirt and boulders near the base.

I didn't need to look further. I'd found the crux of the problem.

A laugh bubbled out of me. We'd made it. After months of fruitless searching and experimentation, I had a cure. I was finally going to save the dormant gargoyles.

Excitement overrode my vertigo, and I crouched to search for a way to the floor.

"There's an easy way down over here," Oliver said.

Thanks to the frequency of the protruding crystal ledges, descending was almost as simple as walking down stairs. Oliver stayed at my side, between me and the drop-off, and Celeste trailed behind us. I did my best not to notice the empty space below the see-through crystals, but I didn't take a full breath until I stood on the floor that was so densely packed with evenly sized crystals it was almost smooth.

Oliver touched down beside me, then hissed, flapping back up to a ledge.

"It hurts worse here," he said.

"I feel it, too." The hum of energy emanating from the heart crystal hammered spikes into my skull, all but drowning out the sweeter notes I'd heard earlier.

When I looked up, I spotted the eggs. Lying atop the multicolored crystalline floor, the drab spheres struck me as insultingly ugly. There were nine, each no larger than an ostrich egg, and all were the same dead gray as the gargoyles we'd encountered on the mountain.

Several were cracked open, and I looked away from the lifeless husks inside.

A flare of earth and air boiled out of the crack in the heart crystal high above me, the elements snarling together as they drifted through the crystal wall. I gaped at the newly formed magical storm. Anywhere else in the world, I would have said the spontaneous creation of wild magic was impossible. The elements existed all around us, but it was people or creatures who called them forth and put them to use. They didn't burst unguided from inert stone.

But this wasn't ordinary quartz. It might have been sedentary, but if the heart crystal could use magic to rejuvenate gargoyles and protect itself, it wielded magic as adroitly as any walking, breathing creature. Broken, it'd lost control of its own powers and the elements escaped, warped and deadly.

If saving the lives of the dormant gargoyles wasn't a worthy enough cause, stopping the formation of more wild storms would have been more than enough reason to heal the heart crystal.

I strode across the sloped floor, conscious that I moved alone. I expected my headache to get worse with each step closer, but it remained a steady, pounding pain. Still, I hesitated before touching the enormous crystal.

Without a blemish or even a seam between the different types of quartz, the smooth surface felt as soft as silk. I petted it as if it were a gargoyle, and when nothing happened, I formed a hair-thin strand of quartz element and tested the surface. My magic met the resistance of the other four elements, and I grabbed fire, water, wood, and air to balance my probe. The elements responded to me as easily as if I stood outside the baetyl. Whatever had limited my magic earlier didn't apply in the heart.

I shouldn't have been surprised to find the heart crystal's elemental chemistry to be almost identical to a gargoyle's. A little more water, a little less air, but otherwise the same—if on a much grander scale.

I widened my probe, reassured to find the crystal's elements harmonious at the base.

"Okay, Oliver. I could use a boost."

When I pushed deeper, the baetyl's magic reacted. Faster than thought, it latched on to the line of my magic and burrowed back along the elements, flowing into me as smoothly as a gargoyle's boost.

Alarmed, I gathered myself to fight off the invasion, but the baetyl's magic was already inside me. It didn't react like a gargoyle's, either. Rather than passively enhancing the amount of magic I could use, it reversed the rules and pumped the elements into me.

I gasped when Oliver's boost opened a fresh well of potential magic inside me, and before I could utter a warning, the baetyl's magic rushed to fill the void, spilling through the link and diving into Oliver. With a pained scream, he severed his enhancement. A whiplash of displaced elements jerked from my control and shattered the baetyl's grasp. Liberated, I fell backward, landing on my butt and hands. A dozen new pinpricks pierced my palms, but I barely registered the pain above the explosion inside my head.

I stared in horrified awe at the heart, swaying in place until the agony abated to a throbbing in my temples and my blurry vision cleared. When I decided movement wouldn't induce vomiting, I gingerly rolled to my feet and tottered to Oliver's side. The gargoyle clutched his head with both front paws, his body curled tight.

Cautiously, I reached for the elements again. They responded naturally, and I breathed a soft sigh of relief as I tuned them to the proper blend and tested Oliver. Aside from a headache, which I could do little more than buffer with gauzy weaves of carnelian-tuned quartz, he was fine.

"Let's not do that again," I said, trying to inject a smidgen of levity into the moment.

"I would advise against it. This is not our baetyl," Celeste said, coasting down to land on the same crystal as Oliver. Her wings closed over her back with a soft rustle. After almost a year of working with gargoyles, it still amazed me that their heavy quartz feathers could sound so soft.

"I shouldn't have asked," I said. It hurt Oliver just to be inside this baetyl; I should have realized asking him to open himself up to the elements here would have been a bad idea even if I couldn't have predicted the baetyl had the ability to use my connection to the elements to overpower me.

"I'm okay," Oliver said, lowering a paw from where he'd been stroking his temple. "But can you hurry?"

Despite the urgency, my footsteps lagged as I walked back to the heart crystal, and I stopped before I was close enough to touch it. The baetyl had exploited my lightest brush of magic, burrowing *into* me. I hadn't known such a thing was possible, but even prepared, I doubted I would be able to prevent its invasion a second time. It had pushed magic into me and filled all the extra space of Oliver's boost without effort. The power it'd given me hadn't been malevolent, but it hadn't been mine, and I hadn't been able to deny it—or control it. The baetyl's magic hadn't been passive, and opening myself back up to an aggressive, semi-sentient magic terrified me. If I wasn't strong enough to seize control, the baetyl would crush me. No one would come to my rescue, either. Marcus was incapacitated; Oliver and Celeste were helpless against this baetyl.

I swallowed and shook out my arms and shoulders. For the dormant gargoyles, for Marcus, for Celeste and Oliver—for all their sakes—I had to risk it.

Marcus's accusations of throwing my life away echoed in my thoughts, and I shook my head to dispel them. He was wrong; I valued my life greatly. Even knowing the number of lives at stake, my arms shook as I raised my hands, and I couldn't uproot my feet. I didn't want to die. If there were any other option . . .

"I'm not trying to kill myself," I whispered. "I'm trying to save lives."

Before I lost my courage, I took a step and slapped my palms to the crystal's smooth surface, simultaneously sliding my magic into the heart.

The baetyl's magic bowled into me.

12

I curled my fingers against the flat surface, straining for control. The baetyl's magic battered me, swelling through my body and questing to push further, to explode through my skin and outward. I stared at my blood-splattered pink knuckles, the tendons rigid outlines. Next to the beautiful glossy surface, my blotchy skin was an atrocity.

I shook my head. The thought wasn't mine. It wasn't the baetyl's, either. The enormous geode didn't have anything so easy to comprehend as thoughts, but I could feel its *distaste*. My blood-and-sinew body was a foreign abomination that did not belong.

I'm here to help. I didn't know if I said it out loud or only thought it, but it didn't matter. The baetyl wasn't listening. It pushed magic through me, using me, and fire and water burst from my fingers, flaring up the sides of the crystal. Droplets fell back to splatter my face, but the flames roared upward until they touched the crack and splintered into a burst of sparks.

I closed my eyes and grabbed for dominance over my own magic. I felt as vulnerable as the first time I'd linked with the FPD squad in Focal Park, when I'd nearly lost myself to the overwhelming magic— only this was a hundred times worse. The baetyl's copious magic threatened to pull me into its undertow and destroy me. I fought back the only way I knew how: by grounding myself in my own individuality.

I am an earth elemental. I am a gargoyle healer. I am a gargoyle guardian, I chanted, reasserting my control bit by bit. I focused on the earth element, and the more I held, the more the baetyl quieted. When I fine-tuned it to quartz, the baetyl's magic shifted to a contained pulse inside me.

I peeled my hands from the crystal, leaving bloody prints behind. Magic sat inside me, quiet as a sleeping dragon and more powerful than twenty-five gargoyle-enhanced full-spectrum elementals. The world bounced in my vision as I pivoted to locate Oliver and Celeste. I kept my movements slow and careful, as if I balanced fine china on my head, afraid a sudden movement would wake the baetyl's magic and it'd annihilate me.

"Mika?" Oliver asked, his chiming voice high with worry.

"It's alive," I whispered, and the wonder of the realization threatened my internal balance. The baetyl's magic quivered, and I repeated my mantra, idly manipulating the quartz element without releasing it. The baetyl quieted.

"Can you fix it?" Celeste asked.

With this amount of magic, I could do anything . . . if I could maintain control.

"Whatever happens, don't open yourselves to me," I said, and waited until they both promised before turning back to the heart crystal and covering the bloody marks with my hands again. Disguising the ugly blotches helped me concentrate.

In infinitesimal increments, I drew the other four elements to me and wove a filament to match the elements inside the heart crystal. When I pressed the blend into the crystal, the baetyl's magic stopped testing me and unfurled, as unresisting as a gargoyle's enhancement.

I took a breath and forgot to exhale. Time stilled. The serene magic held the weight of the baetyl's ancient life, and *ancient* had a texture: a velvet stillness of centuries of patience wrapped in the glassy-smooth sides of crystals that grew a few millimeters a decade.

It had strength, too. Power akin to the boost of a hundred gargoyles breathed inside that vast sensation, a singular entity of immense power.

And I was linked to it.

I turned my attention up, sliding my magic through layers of tigereye and amethyst, prasiolite and carnelian, onyx and jasper and agate all wrapped in a honeycomb of elements. I lost myself in the purity of the shifting quartz varieties, and when I encountered the crack, the serrated edge splintered the velvet glass power inside me.

My breath exploded from my lungs and I sucked in another one. In my chest, my heart beat like hummingbird wings, a blur cocooned in eons, pulsing ninety times in a single minute. The baetyl's magic recoiled from the fluttering sensation, frothing inside me and threatening to spill through my skin. I gulped in another breath and held it, willing my heart to calm. If I lost control of the baetyl's power, I'd drown. Fighting was useless. I couldn't combat the strength of the baetyl; I could only work with it.

Keeping my eyes screwed shut, I nudged my magic back in line with the healthy quartz of the baetyl, then reached for the crack. I was prepared for the jagged texture this time, and I let it flow over me. As carefully as I would heal a gargoyle, I knitted the broken seams back together. The quartz reshaped beneath my magical touch, closing the base of the wound, but it didn't heal. The jangle of broken magic buffeted me, refusing to be calmed.

Pulling back to the base of the crack, I searched the enormous crystal until I found the problem. The honeycomb of elements had been shattered along with the physical quartz. I could mold the physical seams back together, but if I didn't fix the magic inside the crystal, it would tear itself apart again.

One problem at a time. Sweeping my magic up the crystal, I pulled the fragmented pieces of the quartz together and sealed the top.

My eyes snapped open in shock and I fell back from the heart crystal. The enormous pillar was wider than a house and composed of every variety of quartz possible, but I'd healed it as easily as I'd replaced Oliver's broken ruff on the train. I stumbled to the spherical wall for a better look, eyes locked on the upper reaches of the crystal. My elemental senses didn't deceive me; it was whole.

"Whoa," I breathed.

The baetyl's power pulsed inside me, waiting, ready.

On wobbly legs, I returned to the base of the heart crystal. I didn't need to touch it, but I did anyway. I needed the reminder that I had hands.

Feeding elements back into the crystal, I studied the honeycomb, slowly working my way up as I memorized the pattern, then faster as I grew more confident. The heart crystal's internal structure was incredibly intricate, but at its core, the honeycomb was gargoyle. Not *a* gargoyle, but a conglomeration of the pattern of the elements inside all gargoyles: the variances between quartz types, the shape of air element lifting their wings, the fire of life in their stone chests. All of it melded together into a complex design inside the heart—right up until the split.

Where the elements had been severed, the quartz lay dormant, no different or more magical than my seed crystals. The wrongness of that lifeless quartz stirred the ancient magic inside me. Fury not completely my own curled my fingers into fists, but the pain of my nails gouging into the cuts on my palms brought me back under control.

The baetyl's magic vibrated a warning when I grasped the tattered edge of a severed line of earth magic. I added to it as I stretched the fragile thread through an elaborate knot of fire, water, wood, and air before reconnecting it on the other side of the mended fissure. The baetyl quieted.

It approved.

After that, I worked faster. Healing the enormous multi-quartz heart crystal tested everything I'd learned as a gargoyle healer. The baetyl was alive without being a creature. It both used magic and exuded magic—and *was* magic. It was the only explanation for how the baetyl could supply me magic without weakening itself. Against all logic, I used the baetyl's own magic to heal it, and it grew stronger.

The farther up the crystal I magically mended, the more my

awareness of the baetyl expanded. I could sense that the heart crystal extended as deep into the soil as it protruded, and the roots of the other crystals riddled the soil in every direction.

At the edge of my perception, I caught glimpses of a pattern in the placement of the crystals and the location of the types of quartz around the heart. I strained to comprehend the sophisticated arrangement, and the baetyl's magic slid into the open door of my curiosity, stretching inside me. I protested, a murmur of sound too round and wet. Fear fluttered weak in my chest, vibrating around the frantic pulsing beneath my ribs. When the velvet-glass power buffered me from the fear, I experienced a flicker of relief; then that, too, was soothed into calm acceptance.

By the time I finished looping and knotting the honeycomb of elements into perfect harmony, I no longer needed to use the existing edges of the torn elements as a guide. The pattern had become obvious. It was in the shape of the entire baetyl and the placement of the crystals that grew in it. It was in the location of the baetyl in the mountain. It was the essence of *new* and *always*, birth and renewal.

The flaws in the baetyl's perfection stood out as if on fire. Once the heart was healed, I dove toward the first problem. Dead baby gargoyle skeletons inside powdery eggs were not part of the grand design. I tore apart the lifeless rock and scattered the grains across the crystal-studded floor, then pulled the fine granules through a thousand tiny gaps I created between the crystals, sweeping the remains into the soil below.

The cave-in rubble went with it, pulverized and scattered into the mountain. Growing the quartz in the gap in the ceiling took time, but I accelerated the process by flinging the elemental pattern of the heart into the gap. The ridge leapt to obey my command, shaking around us. I didn't let up until crystals glittered across the ceiling, lit with the internal glow of the pattern. The crystals were small, but given another few centuries of growth, they'd match the rest. In the meantime, they completed the arc of the roof, connecting the broken magic again.

A wash of power swept through the heart, bringing pain and

taking it away again. The baetyl breathed around me, more than a pattern now. I could feel the crystals in my bones, the three remaining gaps in the roof like wounds in my own flesh. I turned to examine them, only to stare, befuddled, at the wall of crystals blocking my way.

Walking took all my attention. I watched my feet lift and clop across the crystal floor, confused by the texture of my boots. When I reached the wall, I looked away from the flat brown leather with relief and pushed a hand flat against an amethyst crystal. My limb was pink and *squishy*. That wouldn't do. I pulled quartz from the amethyst and spread it across my hand, growing little crystals to coat the doughy flesh.

The quartz looked right, but it *hurt*.

Movement in the heart spun me around. Gargoyles! I reached for them but pulled my magic back before it touched their bodies. They weren't *my* gargoyles. They beat their wings, gaining altitude, then dove out of sight into the crystal wall high above me. The sinuous movement of the smaller gargoyle was familiar, but I'd never created a gargoyle in that shape.

I've never created a gargoyle at all.

I plucked at the thought, examining it. It felt important, yet it made about as much sense as the pain in my hands.

I'd figure it out after the baetyl was whole.

Facing the wall again, I shifted the crystals and walked unimpeded along the floor, bending the crystals back into place behind me without looking. Outside the heart, the remaining wounds pulsed with insistent urgency. Walking was taking too long; I unfurled my—

Where were my wings? A frantic pat down my back revealed smooth flesh and no wings. How had I become this loathsome malformation?

I quested into my body with the elements, tuning them to match the foreign liquid and meat materials. When I encountered the earth, water, and wood blend of my shoulder blades, I grafted my elements to them, converting them to quartz as I grew them.

My body spasmed, and I screamed when two blades formed

beneath my skin and burst out my back. The baetyl screamed in unison, every crystal shrieking. The sound terrified me, bringing me back to myself.

I lay across a waist-high crop of variegated onyx, the sharp tips gouging into my stomach and armpit. The fingertips of my left hand hung a few inches above the baetyl floor, and I watched blood drip from my ring finger onto the prasiolite below.

Breathing hurt, but as my vision darkened, I forced myself to take sips of air. Or maybe it was the baetyl that powered my lungs. It pulsed inside me more intimately than any gargoyle's boost and sweet with possibility. I'd just moved twenty feet and untold tons of crisscrossing quartz as easily as I might push aside a gauze curtain. Stitching it back together should have taken the strength of every full spectrum in Terra Haven working all day, and I'd done it without thinking.

I'd modified my body's blood and bones and skin to grow quartz as easily as I'd reshaped the heart crystal. And it'd been easy.

I'd have grown myself wings if it hadn't hurt too much.

I whimpered when I realized I wanted to do it again. The power swelled inside me, waiting to be used, waiting for me. With the baetyl backing me, I could do anything. Fusing human and gargoyle physiology was only the start. I could level this mountain and build a new one. I could reshape the world in the design of the baetyl, making it all a perfect place for gargoyles. I could cure any disease. It wouldn't have to be only gargoyles, either. With the baetyl sitting in my head, the complexity of my own body became remarkably simple. I could be a healer of all creatures—the greatest healer who ever lived. I could perform the kind of magic people would talk about generations from now. No one would match me. I'd be more powerful than any full spectrum in the world—than *all* of them linked.

In doing so, I'd destroy the baetyl. It wasn't a gargoyle that would boost me until tired, then cut me off. The baetyl would feed me magic until it ran out.

Would that be so bad? I could cure a thousand ailments before the baetyl was tapped out. It wasn't as if this was an active baetyl.

Only seven gargoyles who'd been born here remained alive. Seven lives against the hundreds, thousands, I could save. The gargoyles would approve. They'd lived out their time, and their deaths could mean something. Their deaths could help me and the world become better.

All I had to do was reach for the baetyl's magic again. It sang inside my head, offering itself. I had healed its heart. The baetyl would give me whatever I asked.

If I accepted and used all that power, I'd be no better than Walter or Elsa. Even with my head swimming with pain and addled by the baetyl's magic, I knew it was wrong to throw away the dormant gargoyles' lives in the name of using the power to save others. It was a palatable excuse to embrace the almost limitless power of the baetyl, but it wasn't morally sound. Letting the gargoyles die wasn't saving anyone. It was murder in the name of a nebulous greater good.

On the heels of that thought, my argument with Marcus flashed through my mind, followed by a zing of understanding. Marcus had been right; I'd been flinging myself into danger to save others, more than willing to sacrifice myself to save the gargoyles. With blood pooling beneath me and my body broken and weak, the irony of the timing of my epiphany wasn't lost on me.

My actions might have been noble if I'd been at all discriminating. I'd been so focused on rescuing gargoyles, I'd forgotten to treat myself with the same reverence. Worse, I'd been ignoring my own value. Just as the baetyl's power was needed here to heal the dormant gargoyles and give life to generations of new gargoyles, my life and magic was needed to heal all gargoyles, not just the ones in front of me.

I weighed my logic against my conscience. Was I being egotistical to claim my life was more valuable than any one gargoyle's? Than the lives of the seven gargoyles? The answer came quickly: Sacrificing myself to save a life or seven lives was shortsighted and foolish. I deserved better. The gargoyles deserved more of their guardian.

Just as clearly, I knew the same logic couldn't be applied to healing the baetyl. If my death was necessary to repair the baetyl, my sacrifice wouldn't be a shortsighted waste of life; I'd be saving generations of future gargoyles.

Envisioning the baetyl filled with gargoyles, healthy eggs hatching in the heart once more, I found the courage to open myself to the baetyl's magic again. It roared inside me, buffeting me with its eagerness, filling my head with its knowledge. Gritting my teeth, I severed the crystals from my back and mended my flesh. Shards of bloody quartz rained down around me, and I helped the baetyl absorb them, burying all traces of my hopeless wings. Then I rolled my fragile human body off the onyx crystals and straightened.

Oliver perched twenty feet away on a bright citrine crystal hardly larger than him but glowing twice as bright as it had before we'd entered the heart. The baetyl examined him through my eyes and gathered itself. He wasn't a gargoyle who belonged here, but together, with a few tweaks, we could make him one of ours.

It wouldn't be hard to alter him to resonate with us. The baetyl played images through my head, showing me the process. Altering his pattern would kill him, but then we'd bring him back and he'd be better than before. And bringing him back . . .

For a breathless moment, a pattern more intricate than anything I'd yet encountered lay before my inner eye, thousands upon thousands of glowing elemental strands laid *just so* and compressed into a single spark. It was the pattern of life itself and the root of every living creature. Tears of awe dripped down my chin, and I blinked to clear my vision. To have the chance to use the baetyl's power to create *life*—

I forced myself to look away from Oliver. To make him a gargoyle of this baetyl, I'd have to kill him first, and I wasn't going to do that.

Denied, the baetyl's power receded, taking with it the knowledge of how to shape life from the elements. Gasping, I scrambled for the memory, but it slipped from my mind. I lifted my gaze back to Oliver, seeing only the gargoyle and not the elemental design of his life inside him. My chest ached, and telling myself I'd made the right decision didn't make me feel any better. I'd had *life* in my hands, and now I couldn't remember more than a fragment of the pattern.

"Don't come near me, Oliver." I didn't trust myself; if he came closer and the baetyl offered me the chance to create life again, I didn't think I could say no twice.

Swiping tears from my cheeks with shaky fingertips, I crawled over a large jasper crystal. It would have been simple enough to move the quartz out of my way using the baetyl's power, but the more I held the power, the more I wanted to use it. If I gave in just to shift crystals out of my path, it wouldn't take much to convince me I really did need wings. Or that Oliver would be better off sharing this baetyl with me. Or that the power in my hands was worth more than the lives of the gargoyles I'd come here to save.

So I climbed over and through the crystals and up the sloping floor back to Marcus, telling myself I wanted to be human and to heal the baetyl and leave. I didn't want wings or to fly. Flying was scary because it meant leaving the ground. Heights were scary.

I didn't believe any of it, and that alarmed me. I was scared of heights, but the baetyl wasn't. Fear wasn't a concept it understood.

I scrambled down the glowing side of a tigereye crystal that wouldn't reach its full potential for another three centuries and spotted Marcus. He stood, sword in hand, gaze assessing and steady, and relief made me stumble. He rushed to my side before I fully caught my balance, but he didn't reach out to steady me. Up close, I could see the worry in his lapis lazuli eyes, and behind them, I caught hints of the pattern of elements that made him, him.

"So you're scared of heights," Marcus said.

"What?" I squinted, trying to map his pattern, unexpectedly warmed by his voice.

"It's a good fear. It'll keep you safe. Fear is good." He used a soothing tone, as if he expected me to bolt.

"What are you talking about?" I demanded. The nightmares had twisted a few thread-thin strands of elements out of place inside him, making snarls.

"You've been chanting about being scared of heights," he said.

I blinked. "I have?" Damn it, I lost the snarls. I let the magic I'd kindled in my fingertips flow back into the baetyl.

"Come on, let's get out of here." Marcus gestured for me to

precede him toward the exit. Blood soaked through his shirt at the shoulder. Sweat beaded and rolled down his face.

"Are you hurt? I can heal you," I offered.

"You can heal me? Since when?"

I opened my mouth and realized I couldn't explain eternity in words. It didn't even make sense to me, at least not when I tried to define it. But I could feel it in the silence in my mind and in the baetyl's strength.

"I need to finish healing the baetyl," I said instead.

"Finish?"

I turned unerringly to face the closest cave-in. Marcus inhaled sharply, and in the periphery of my vision I saw him stretch a hand toward my back, but he dropped it before he touched me.

"Mika?"

"Hang on."

"Oliver said you'd healed the heart," he said, using that soothing tone again, but I barely heard him. The quartz that had hummed inside me while I'd been in the heart grated here near the giant gaps in the roof. Magic pulsed from the heart, perfect and pure, then fractured over the broken ceiling and misshaped crystals. That had to be fixed or the discordant magic reverberating back to the heart would eventually damage it and the entire baetyl again.

"It's still flawed. Can't you hear the disharmony?" I asked, reaching for the baetyl's magic.

Marcus swung back in front of me. "You're not repairing the ceiling by yourself." The tip of his sword etched a short scratch into an aventurine crystal with his exuberant gesture. I wrapped the blade in air, yanked it from Marcus, opened a fissure in the ground, and threw the sword into the depths before I remembered embracing the baetyl's magic. Contemplating the shadowy hole barely large enough to fit the broadsword, I tried to remember the elements I'd just used, but couldn't. Had I been in control of the magic or had the baetyl? Deliberately, I stitched the floor back together, sealing the sword in the earth. The satisfaction of eliminating the threat to the crystals wasn't mine, but the fear that chased it was.

Marcus watched me with wide eyes. He'd gathered a thimbleful of elements, and I wondered what he planned to do with that paltry amount of magic.

"Are the gargoyles boosting you?"

"There are no appropriate gargoyles. She—I—refused." I blinked and looked around for the foreign, unwelcome gargoyles. There had been two in the heart.

"Oh, Mika, what did you find?" he whispered.

I refocused on Marcus, confused by the concern pinching his brow. "It's broken," I said. "I have to fix it. I have to." If he was going to stand in my way, I could send him the same direction as the sword.

"Okay. Okay, we'll fix it. That's what we came here to do. Just link with me first."

"I don't need to."

"Yes, you do."

"I'm strong enough without you." Magic trembled in my grip. It would be so easy to open the ground at his feet.

"I can see that. But you asked me to protect you. At least let me try."

I sucked in a deep breath, grounding myself in the quartz-flavored air. "Okay. Link."

Marcus thrust his pathetic amount of balanced elements toward me, and I accepted it, closing my magic around it. He groaned and fell to one knee, but he'd ceased trying to stop me, and that was all that mattered.

I strode around him to put him out of my sight. I'd spared him because . . . because . . . I shook my head and put him out of my mind, too. He didn't matter.

We pulverized the fractured crystals beneath the broken roof and swept their remains and the rubble from the cave-ins into the mountain below the baetyl. A few layers of elements spread in the baetyl's pattern laid the groundwork for new crystals along the floor before we turned our attention to the offending holes in the roof. Unnatural tunnels bisected the mountain above, and we collapsed them all. They were the reason we'd been weakened. They were the reason all our gargoyles had died and our magic had mutated. For good measure, we grew solid beams of quartz to bisect every previous tunnel. The mountain had plenty of quartz to work with, and it was a simple matter of encouraging it to grow solid and strong.

Crystals sprouted from the gaps in the ceiling under our careful guidance, brightening the cavern with their inner glow. When the last one burst into place, healthy magic swept through the baetyl, and we listened to it chime. Every time we encountered a sour note, we adjusted the crystals, mending a crack here, smoothing erosion there. The two unwelcome gargoyles sat like ugly deformities near the exit, vibrating at the wrong elemental frequency, and we scooped them up and tossed them out.

The baetyl hummed with perfection, and contentment spiraled through us until we felt a singular entity that didn't belong. We turned to face it, scoop it up, toss it out—

It clung to us! It was inside us! Foreign magic pulsed within us, hot and unbalanced.

Panic flared, rumbling through the baetyl, setting the crystals rattling and squealing against each other.

"Mika, fight it. You're strong. Let it go."

It—*his*—voice rasped unnaturally in the hallowed air of the baetyl. He didn't belong. He wasn't a gargoyle. There was no quartz in him, not in his magic or his body. He was a nuisance.

And yet . . .

We looked down at his hand on our arm. None of it looked right, not the thick brown-pink bands of his fingers, not our curved and doughy forearm.

"Fight it. For me."

We gathered ourselves to sever his connection with us and crush him before he poisoned our purity. Lapis lazuli eyes locked with ours and alarm spiked inside us. In me. The baetyl faltered, not comprehending. His presence was wrong. He didn't belong. But the thought of crushing the life from him repulsed me.

Fear and revulsion widened the gap between me and the baetyl, helping me find and define myself. This was Marcus, a fellow human.

The man I had a crush on—another emotion the baetyl couldn't understand.

I seized upon the feelings, rolling fear and attraction in my mind to distance myself from the baetyl. I stopped trying to pull myself free of Marcus's grip and really looked at him. Sweat ran freely down his face and soaked his clothing. He was on his knees in front of me, his face pinched with pain. I frowned. I wasn't fighting him now, but he looked like he still struggled.

"Fight it," he said through clenched teeth.

The baetyl surged back through me. He was an affront to its restored perfection. He must go.

No.

I grabbed for control, but it slipped from me. The baetyl's magic roared inside me, filling my body and readying itself to bury Marcus. The amethyst crystals on the back of my hand lit up, singing in harmony with the rest of the baetyl. I belonged; he did not.

No.

I gritted my teeth. I couldn't best the baetyl's strength; nothing could. So I let it go.

It hurt. Loosening my connection with the transcendent power of the baetyl gave space for all my weaknesses: my fragile flesh split open in so many painful places; my frantic life beating away too fast; my tiny, mostly useless body gasping for oxygen in the muggy air.

Through tear-blurred eyes, I sought out Marcus, surprised to find him so close, still clinging to my arm. His features looked crude and misshapen where once I'd thought he was strikingly handsome. The crystals around us were the true beauty, so perfect and geometrical and glossy.

I caught my reflection in the side of a dark crystal. Bulbous. I was bulbous and hideous like Marcus. I didn't belong here, no matter how much I wanted it.

Aching with the loss, I shattered the amethyst crystals on my hands and reknit my flimsy, inferior flesh, then released the last pieces of the baetyl. It receded from my consciousness, its magic pulling back to the heart and the walls and the crystals all around us.

I clung to the knowledge of the baetyl's pattern as long as I could, seeing it around me and in my mind's eye stretching through the mountain, so perfect and gorgeous. When it faded, I crumpled, empty and small and so very alone. Hiccuping sobs rocked my body, suffocating me, and I couldn't bring myself to care.

"Mika, we need to go," Marcus said, his voice thick.

His magic burned inside me through our link—fire, too strong; earth, too generic. After the baetyl's purity, his imperfect magic revolted me. Lashing out, I tried to sever the link between us. Elements so slender they may as well have been made of silk trickled from me. Marcus's magic clamped down around the link, locking us together and seizing control. Panicked, I jerked my arm from his, stumbling to catch my balance when my wrist snapped free. The baetyl hummed at the edge of my awareness, an invitation to link extended as soft as a gargoyle's offer of enhancement. All I had to do was open myself to the power, all that glorious power . . .

Marcus slumped to the side, eyes closed. "Fight, Mika," he mumbled, his words slurred.

Confused, I sidled closer. Did he want me to fight him? I tentatively slid my awareness down the link between us, jerking back when I encountered the knot he'd made around our link. His usually sparking, fiery signature flickered, fuzzy around the edges despite how hard he held on.

I lifted my fingers and swiped sweat from my eyes. *When had it gotten so hot?* As if waiting for me to notice, the heat grew oppressive, the air thick with humidity. I sucked in a breath, my lungs laboring to pull oxygen from the moist air. Oliver had said the baetyl should have been warmer—

Oliver!

I spun toward the exit. It was barely visible through the weave of crystals, but I remembered sweeping Oliver up and Celeste with him. I'd helped the baetyl kick them out, and we hadn't been gentle.

My body tilted and I crashed into the crystals next to Marcus. I managed to lift my right forearm to protect my head, but the impact jarred my brain, knocking my thoughts askew. When I refocused, I was staring at Marcus. He looked awful, but it was only my assessment this time, untainted by the baetyl's perception of beauty. Pain pinched his mouth into a tight line, and his eyes were sunken, the skin around them tinged with gray and the rest of him flushed an unhealthy shade of magenta. The veins in his neck stood out with strain.

"We need to leave," I croaked.

He dragged his gaze to mine, and the relief in his expression centered me. Then his eyes rolled back in his head, and he fell backward onto the sharp crystals.

13

I scrambled to his side, lifting his head to feel for cuts on his scalp, cursing when sticky blood coated my fingers. Fragments of how to heal human tissue floated through my memory, utterly useless, and the more intently I tried to remember, the more the pieces slipped away. I wouldn't be able to heal him, and the closest healer was back in Terra Haven.

Oh, gods, we'd never make it.

"Wake up." I tapped Marcus's cheek. Heat weighted my already spent body, and I choked on each moist breath. I slapped him harder. "Wake up, lummox. I can't haul you out by myself."

The baetyl's magic sang to me, welcoming me back into its embrace. I wouldn't have to do it by myself. All I had to do was open myself to its tremendous power; then lifting Marcus's puny body would be no problem.

I shook my head. There was nothing puny about Marcus. That was the baetyl whispering in my thoughts. If I let it back in . . . The thought of relinquishing all that power a second time dredged a sob from my chest. I didn't think I could do it twice, and once I was reconnected with the baetyl, I couldn't guarantee it wouldn't take over and bury Marcus in the mountain.

Struggling to ignore the baetyl's siren song, I slapped Marcus, holding nothing back. His head rocked and his eyes fluttered. I leaned closer, hand raised for another strike. Sweat and tears dripped from my chin to his chest.

Marcus's eyes snapped open and he lashed out, crushing my wrist in his fist while his eyes searched mine.

"We need to move," I rasped.

He released me with a ragged breath.

It took us four tries before we both got our feet beneath us. Marcus's eyes lost their focus and he sagged against me as we stumbled toward the exit, his breathing labored. I wrapped my arm around him and did my best to support him on quivering legs.

"I'm sorry. I'm so sorry," I babbled. "You've got to hang on. A few more steps. You're too strong to give up now. I need you to stay with me. I want you to. You were right: I like you. You can't give up on me now before I have a chance to get to know you. You can't let me have blown my chance with you. Just keep going. I'm so sorry. A little farther."

We were five feet from the exit of the baetyl when Marcus toppled again, taking me down with him. Blood trickled from his nose, and I couldn't wake him. Whimpering, I pulled my leg out from under him, scraping my knee on the sharp crystal floor.

I rolled Marcus onto his back, then fell across his chest when my body gave out. With the tiny crystals packed together like so many teeth and the strangling, moist heat, I couldn't shake the illusion that we were inside a monster's mouth, waiting to be crushed. Waiting. Waiting . . .

Marcus's ragged breathing finally prompted me back into action, and I crawled to crouch at his head, wedged my hands under his armpits, and heaved. He inched across the jagged floor. When Marcus's mangled sword sheath caught on the crystals, I used a knife from his boot to cut it free, then left both behind.

"Mika?"

I tugged Marcus another three inches and collapsed. My butt felt like it'd been beaten with a porcupine, but the pain was distant. The only thing that mattered was getting Marcus out of the baetyl.

"Is that you?"

I glanced down at Marcus. His eyes were closed but his mouth gaped open. I stared at his slack mouth, uncomprehending as the voice repeated, "Mika?"

Finally I thought to look up. Oliver hunched inside the tunnel at the edge of the crystals a few feet away, eyes so wide they looked like circles.

"Oliver!"

He flinched, and my heart fractured. I'd given him reason to fear me.

"It's okay. I'm me," I said, my voice raspy and foreign. "Are you okay? Where's Celeste?"

"It's you!" Tension lifted from his shoulders and his wings settled against his back. "Hang on." Face set in firm lines of determination, he slunk across the intervening crystal floor, whimper-growling with each step. He leaned forward as if pressing against a great wind, and I wondered what sort of pressure the baetyl pushed back against him.

Shadows danced around my vision. The heat had increased to oven temperatures while Marcus and I had climbed toward the exit, and my swollen skin ached. I grabbed Marcus's armpits again and hauled him a few more inches. Then Oliver was beside me, twisting to grip Marcus's shirt with his back paw. Together we tugged, and the large man moved a foot. I would have cheered if I had the breath.

In a few more pulls, we cleared the crystals and the ground smoothed. Oliver stopped making pained sounds. I sagged against the tunnel wall, gulping humid air.

Light from the baetyl bathed us in the cool glow of golden citrine, mint prasiolite, sunset-orange carnelian, cerulean dumortierite, and shimmering combinations of so many other crystals. I swept my gaze over the glorious shapes, memorizing the deadly beauty of the baetyl. I'd never see another again, and I'd already forgotten so much; I didn't want to forget this.

Then I turned my back on the baetyl's divine splendor, grabbed Marcus's shirt, and helped Oliver drag him up the dirt path.

———

I MADE OLIVER STOP ONCE I COULD BREATHE WITHOUT FEELING LIKE I was drowning. The baetyl pressed into me, calling to me, but its voice had changed.

I lowered myself to the ground next to Marcus, who remained alarmingly unconscious. Oliver whined, but the baetyl sang inside my head, drowning him out. Too tired to remember the reasons I had for avoiding it, too tired to resist it, I opened myself to the power, but the baetyl didn't try to link with me; it tried to talk to me.

Once I felt its magic, I felt its need. The baetyl was healed—mostly. The last gap existed at the mouth of the tunnel, where the wild magic storms had torn apart the pattern beneath the crystals. Following the baetyl's guidance, I layered elements across the opening, and when the last element settled into place, a wash of magic gusted through the tunnel, toppling me and sending Oliver rolling.

The baetyl receded from my mind, and I let it go without regret this time. I'd done it. I'd healed the baetyl. No one but a gargoyle born in those crystal-lined walls would be allowed in or out now.

I collapsed to my side in the warm tunnel, shifting so Marcus's head rested on my stomach. I needed to get him out. The humidity had decreased and the air was warm rather than stifling, but we had a ways to go. At the very least, I needed to clean his wounds and send Oliver for a healer. I needed to check Oliver, too. I needed to finish my mission and get the dormant gargoyles into the baetyl. I needed to bandage myself back together.

I cobbled together my energy—

And passed out.

———

SOMETHING BIT MY ARM, AND I JERKED AWAKE.

"Easy there," Marcus said.

I grabbed the elements before I recognized his voice, confused at the infinitesimal amount I could hold. The space was wrong, too dark and cool, and the glowballs didn't illuminate much. Where were the crystals? The baetyl—

Memory returned in a rush. I tried to sit up, but a warm hand on my shoulder held me down.

"Relax, Mika, we're all okay."

"The gargoyles?"

"Celeste says they're weak but fine."

"Celeste's okay?"

"She's fine. Oliver, too. Now hold still." He slathered a compound of kachina greenthread across my forearm, covering a dozen cuts. I hissed at the sting, then relaxed as the plant's numbing agents took the pain away. Oliver peered at me over the top of my head, smiling, and my heart eased. Marcus shooed him back, and the young gargoyle took flight across a star-speckled sky, landing a few feet away on a flat boulder. His entire body glowed as if lit from a fire within, reminding me of the crystals inside the baetyl, but it was only a trick of the firelight on his carnelian body.

I'd lifted my free arm to pet Oliver before he'd flown away, and I examined it now. Ragged fibers at my shoulder were all that remained of the shirt's sleeve, and lamb's ear bandages crisscrossed my bicep and forearm. The rest of my shirt was bunched around my chest, and the numbness of my stomach told me Marcus had already tended the cuts there. I turned my arm toward the light and stared at the back of my hand. The crystals the baetyl and I had grown into my flesh were gone. In their place was a series of six-sided scars trailing up to my wrist, the flat scar tissue lavender and sparkly like it'd caught amethyst dust inside it as it healed. I flexed my fingers, relieved when they all moved stiffly.

"Your back is similar," Marcus said. He didn't look up from my other arm, using slender strands of air to tie the lamb's ear leaves into place.

"My back?" I echoed. *My wings.*

"There was so much blood on your back, I started there, but the wounds had been sealed. It took me a while to figure out the red was part of the scars."

"What does it look like?" I wished I had a mirror or could move to feel my shoulder blades. I was lying on my back without pain, but I still wanted confirmation that I was whole.

"Like you've been run through with a sword on both shoulder blades, and the scar tissue is the color of Oliver."

Carnelian. I'd always secretly believed Oliver had the most beautiful wings of any gargoyle. I must have tried to give myself a similar pair. I heard the question in Marcus's voice, too, but I wasn't ready to try to explain the baetyl's power and the way it'd warped my thoughts.

The silence prodded my self-awareness, making me conscious of my prone position, of wearing little more than flimsy bandages and a strip of cloth across my breasts, of Marcus kneeling over me, close enough for me to count his lashes. I felt small and alone, unfamiliar with my own identity after sharing the baetyl's ancient presence, and even my body, covered in ointment and bandages and new, alien scars, was a stranger's.

I breathed through the vulnerability, focusing on Marcus's face to ground myself. He looked good, his skin golden in the firelight and his eyes alert. I wasn't surprised he'd recovered first—grateful and relieved, but not surprised.

"How are you?" I asked, hoping he didn't hear the quaver in my voice.

"Alive, thanks to you pulling me out of the baetyl." He finally met my gaze, letting me see his chagrin.

"It was the least I could do after almost killing you."

He grunted. "You've apologized enough for that already."

I flushed. How much did he remember of my frantic babbling when I'd been carrying him out?

"What happened in there?" he asked. "The gargoyles swarmed, and then . . ."

"You were stuck in your worst nightmare?"

He nodded. "When it ended, you were gone."

"The gargoyles weren't real. They were a warped version of the baetyl's last attempt to protect itself from our invasion. I escaped the nightmares by using quartz element." Talking grounded me, and my lingering sense of loneliness faded as I explained the fissures that had opened in the nightmare when I'd wielded quartz-tuned earth.

"Such a simple solution. I tried . . . a lot of other things."

"I tried to wake you," I said, seeing his haunted expression.

He shook his head. "You did the right thing. You stuck to the mission. Tell me how you ended up in control of all the baetyl's power."

"I healed the heart."

I did my best to articulate my experience, but I don't think I was successful. Describing the kinship I'd felt with the baetyl proved impossible. It'd been so natural and right at the time, but like the patterns it had shown me, the memory had faded. I settled for comparing it to being linked to an enormous gargoyle, and that seemed to satisfy Marcus.

I didn't tell him about briefly possessing the pattern of life itself. Just thinking about it, knowing I'd lost the most precious knowledge in the world, made my breath hitch with yearning, and I wouldn't be able to talk about it without crying or sounding like an idiot. Or both. I didn't have to explain the power of the baetyl to Marcus. He'd felt it through his link with me, just as he'd been in the link when I'd repaired the enormous cave-ins and collapsed all the old mine tunnels.

"It was addictive," I said. Unconsciously, I reached for my connection with the baetyl, finding only a hollow ache. Staring up at the stars, eyes unfocused, I relived the awe of holding all that power.

"Thank you," I whispered, unable to meet Marcus's eyes. "For not letting me kill myself. I would still be in there if you hadn't linked with me. You saved me from myself, just as you promised."

"Mika . . ."

I dropped my gaze to meet his. "Everything you said earlier was right. I haven't been thinking about the risks or the danger. I've been trying to do what's right, and saving gargoyle lives is *right*."

The beginnings of a scowl clouded Marcus's expression, emphasized by the flickering shadows. I almost smiled to see it, and I hurried to continue before he thought I wanted to resume our previous argument.

"But killing myself to do so isn't in the gargoyles' best interest. It's not the way to protect them. You're right; they deserve more than a martyr. They deserve a guardian who does everything possible for *every* gargoyle, the ones in front of me and the ones I can help in the future."

He blasted me with The Smile. My heart flipped and I closed my eyes. I understood his point of view, and even agreed with it, but that didn't mean it made me happy. I wanted to save every gargoyle. Letting a gargoyle die to save myself would be dreadful, and I prayed I'd never have to face that decision.

"I'm thankful you're exactly the type of person you are," Marcus said.

My eyes snapped open in surprise. He gave me a shrug.

"Not many people would have turned their back on the baetyl's power."

"It would have destroyed me if I hadn't." I would have killed him, too.

"But it didn't. You did what you came here to do. You healed a baetyl."

I smiled, and the triumph chased away my troubled thoughts. "Now we just have to get the gargoyles into it, and we'll be set."

I remembered setting the final barrier, sealing off the baetyl, and my good mood died as fast as it'd risen.

I struggled to sit up and Marcus tried to assist me without touching a bandage, which meant he was limited to guiding me up with a hand on a tiny patch of skin between my shoulder blades. My butt cheeks protested the extra weight on them, but I was pretty sure they were only bruised. Blinking, I stared at my legs. Marcus had cut away my pants, leaving me with barely enough denim to cover my hips for modesty. So many bandages crisscrossed down my legs that I resembled a freshly wrapped mummy. My boots, still on my feet, completed the ridiculous ensemble.

"How long have I been out?" I demanded. How much blood had I lost?

"Awhile. We can probably remove most of those," he said, indicating the strips of lamb's ear leaves on my legs. "Your pants did a decent job of protecting you. Better than your shirt. I still need to get these nicks on your face."

I batted his hand aside. "Have you tended your own injuries?"

"The worst of them."

"Let me see."

Marcus sat back with a huff and pulled his shirt over his head. For an embarrassing moment, my brain stopped working in the face of his broad, muscular chest and the defined lines of his abdomen. I blinked and shut my mouth and reminded myself that I was an adult and the man was injured. Dried blood caked his chest and ran down his side from a gash on his shoulder, which he'd covered with lamb's ear leaves. My brain lurched back into action when I saw the bloody tatters of the back of his shirt.

"Turn around," I croaked.

Mouth tight, Marcus shifted so I could see his back. I sucked in a breath and reached for him, stopping before I touched his flayed back. The abuse of dragging him across the sharp tips of the baetyl floor had been too much for his shirt's protective magic; the crystals had sliced through the spell and fabric, into his flesh and muscles. Blood oozed from a dozen long cuts, staining the waist of his leather pants black. It reminded me of the injuries he'd sustained during the Focal Park fiasco, only so much worse.

"Good. You got the dirt out before the cuts could become infected," I said, my voice empty. I pushed aside my horror and guilt, both of which wouldn't help Marcus. "Got any more greenthread?"

He handed me a half empty glass bottle, then rose to retrieve more lamb's ear leaves from his pack. I glanced around, taking in the campfire Marcus had built on the landing outside the tunnel. A few feet down the hill, the air sled lay on the ground, the dormant gargoyles scattered where they'd tumbled during the magic storms. Celeste crouched among them but she watched me, silently reminding me I hadn't finished my mission.

When Marcus sat back in front of me, I gently applied the greenthread concoction to his cuts. The compound stung before it numbed the wounds, as I knew from experience, but he never reacted. With each lamb's ear leaf I laid across the treated cuts, Marcus relaxed a little more, the subtle loosening of his muscles revealing how much the wounds had hurt. The greenthread would counter the pain and hasten the healing, but I was afraid he'd be left with scars.

We secured the lamb's ear leaves in place by wrapping him in strips cut from the remainder of his shirt rather than using bands of air. Marcus insisted, claiming the shirt was too ruined to be used for anything else.

"But air would be more gentle," I argued.

"The shirt will soak up blood. Air won't," he said, ending the discussion.

When I'd satisfied myself that the wound on the back of his head was superficial and I'd dabbed greenthread compound into his thick hair, Marcus pulled on yesterday's shirt and tenderly dabbed greenthread onto the cuts on my face.

"I'm so sorry," I said. I couldn't have gotten him out of the baetyl by any other means than dragging him, but it was my fault he'd been there in the first place. I should have insisted he wait outside. If I'd known what to expect, I would have.

He laid a blunt finger over my lips. "I knew what I was doing."

He was too close, and I felt vulnerable, covered in wounds and bandages and little else. Ignoring the tingle in my lips, I eased back. I avoided his stunning lapis lazuli eyes and the warmth they held, too discombobulated to distinguish emotion from firelight. Even dirty, bleeding, and frowning, the man was too attractive, and all my emotional barriers had been shredded inside the baetyl.

Marcus shifted back onto his heels, visibly relaxing when the move didn't hurt. "You didn't kill me. That means more to me than any apology."

"You've got low standards," I said, trying to joke.

"I saw what the baetyl did to my sword, and I knew it didn't like me or want me there."

I searched his face. "You could feel that?"

"I could feel how powerful it was, and you held it in check." His voice held a hint of awe. "Even when you looked at me like I was something disgusting caught on the sole of your shoe, you held it back."

"I didn't—" I cut myself off. I remembered thinking Marcus was repugnant and wrong. It'd been the baetyl, but it'd been me, too.

"Thank you for saving my life," Marcus said.

"I should have—"

"Just accept it, Mika."

I swallowed my protest. "I should be thanking you." If I *had* gone in alone . . . I shuddered to think of the consequences.

"You're welcome." He cocked an eyebrow at me. "See, that's how you accept gratitude."

"Ha-ha."

"Note how I'm not apologizing for blacking out and leaving you to cart my hunk of flesh out of there. In fact, you're welcome for that, too. I'm sure it made you a better person."

I threw the remaining bundle of lamb's ear leaves at him. He caught it easily. His grin tugged at my heart, and I found myself wistfully imagining him looking at me with genuine affection.

Shaking my head, I struggled to my feet. While Marcus kept his back politely turned, I pulled on yesterday's pants. Fortunately, most of the wounds on my legs were superficial and the greenthread compound had already sealed them, allowing me to remove the bulk of the lamb's ear leaves from my legs. One puncture on my right thigh and another on my left knee I kept bandaged after peeking at the wounds.

I required Marcus's help to wiggle into yesterday's shirt, which I layered on top of my current one without removing any leaf bandages. Marcus wouldn't let me touch my shoulder blades, afraid I'd open the cuts on my arms, so I made him do it for me. He traced the outline of two hexagons larger than my palm, one on each shoulder blade. I shivered, partially in memory of the pain, partially at the feel of Marcus's rough fingertip across my sensitive skin. The patches tingled even after he lifted his hand, but I wasn't sure if it was from Marcus's touch or the scar tissue.

"Wings," I whispered, finally answering his unasked question. "All gargoyles have wings."

Marcus's eyes widened, but he said nothing, not even when I started to cry. It was just as well. I couldn't explain the jumble of emotions snarled inside of me. I mourned the loss of my connection with the baetyl as keenly as if I'd lost a parent, which made no sense. It terrified me with its impressive, unstoppable power and with how badly I wanted to possess it again. Fear had been a foreign concept for it and ultimately what had saved my life, but for a brief moment, I'd possessed the mental clarity of a truly ancient being, and I'd feared nothing. I'd known how to do the impossible because nothing was impossible. I'd been able to reshape my own body. I'd started to grow myself wings.

I swiped the tears from my cheeks and turned to the dormant gargoyles. While I walked among them and tested their health, Marcus busied himself near the fire. I appreciated the space; my emotions were too raw for me to want anything else.

In the dormant gargoyles, I caught remnants of the baetyl's magnificent pattern. It whispered at the periphery of my magic, but when I shifted my attention to focus on it, it slipped away. Sighing, I returned to the fire.

"They need to get inside the baetyl soon." They were far too weak to leave unattended much longer.

"Maybe if we can get them closer, they'll wake up." He offered me a bowl filled with a thick stew, derailing my denial; the gargoyles were no more likely to wake now than they had been in Terra Haven. They needed to be inside the baetyl to receive its benefits.

My stomach grumbled and I snatched the bowl from Marcus's hand.

"Don't expect too much," he said, indicating the food. "We used up the last of my stimulant earlier. This is trail rations, plain and tasteless, but it'll give us some strength."

I hadn't expected anything other than the jerky and dried fruit I'd stuffed in my bag. To me, the stew tasted more divine than the first-class chef's gourmet potpie.

"Got any more special tricks in your pack?" I asked. Bandages, energy drinks, real food and bowls to eat it in—the man had clearly thought this through. I, on the other hand, had brought a change of clothes, snacks, and seed crystals like I was going on a picnic where I might get dirty. Then I'd marched us into the unknown dangers of the baetyl and nearly killed us both. I was a naive idiot.

"Not unless you consider dry socks a special trick."

"I was hoping for something more like Gus's personal air sled to transport the gargoyles."

"That would be handy."

We both turned to study the toppled gargoyles. "Looks like we're doing this the hard way," I said.

"With you, what's new?"

14

W e stood in the middle of the dormant gargoyles while Marcus wove temperature-regulating spells into our clothing. It was a complex blend of fire, wood, and water, with dabs of air beading the surface. He didn't need the gargoyles' boosts, but he used it anyway; the wild magic that had escaped from the baetyl had sustained them for hours, but it wouldn't last much longer.

My eyes closed as Marcus's spell settled into my shirt, bathing me in warmth as if I stood in the sun instead of atop a chilly mountain in the middle of the night. Most of my body was numb from the greenthread compound, my stomach was full, and as my shivers abated, exhaustion crept back in, urging me to lie down and take a nap.

I snapped my eyes open. I had to keep moving.

We carefully righted all the gargoyles, linking to lift them with thick bands of air and settle them next to the tunnel's entrance. If it would have done us any good, we would have fixed the air sled and used it to carry the gargoyles again, but it was too wide to fit into the tunnel.

"Who's first?" Marcus asked.

Life flickered weakly in all the gargoyles. I wanted to insist we carry them all at once, but we didn't have the strength.

"Rourke," I said, meeting Celeste's worried gaze.

Oliver and Celeste dropped their magic into the link Marcus and I shared, filling us with power. *So little power,* I thought, remembering the enormity of the baetyl's magic.

Marcus lit the way with two medium-size glowballs, and Celeste and Oliver trailed behind us. Heat built the deeper we went, and Marcus's spell cooled my shirt in response, keeping my body at an even temperature. I tried to focus on appreciating that rather than the way my pants tightened on my bandages with each step or how my shirt stuck to the wet lamb's ear leaves wrapping my arms and stomach. Beside me, Marcus walked stiffly, his upper body mostly immobilized by the bandages.

I recognized the curve in the tunnel where I'd collapsed: I hadn't made it as far out as I'd thought when I'd been dragging Marcus.

"Mika." Oliver's chiming voice echoed in the tunnel. "I have to stop."

I twisted to look at him, then stopped fully when I saw his pain-pinched expression. Celeste had stopped a few yards behind him. "What's wrong?"

"The baetyl doesn't want us any closer."

The moment he said it, I felt the weight of the baetyl pressing against me. It didn't want any of us closer, but the pressure didn't physically hurt me.

"Celeste?" I asked.

"I can't go any farther," she said.

"Okay, go back to the surface," I said, not wanting them to wait in pain.

"Drop the boosts now, too," Marcus said.

I nodded. With Marcus and I moving in the opposite direction as the gargoyles, we'd soon be out of range of their magical enhancements. It was better to lose their boosts now than to have their extra magic jerked from us unexpectedly.

"We could wait here," Oliver suggested.

I shook my head, remembering how the baetyl had viewed Oliver and Celeste as deformed gargoyles. "We actually might be better off if the baetyl doesn't sense a connection to you in our magic," I said.

"Oh." Oliver's ruff drooped.

"Hurry," Celeste said. She withdrew her enhancement, and the level of magic in the link diminished. With a sigh, Oliver cut off his boost, too, and followed Celeste out of the tunnel. Marcus had already turned away, drawing magic through me to keep Rourke aloft. The muggy air suctioned around my feet like molasses, as if it was trying to glue my boots to the tunnel. We both leaned forward, our steps exaggerated, and I was reminded of Oliver walking as if bracing against a hurricane-strength wind when he'd returned to the baetyl to help me pull Marcus out. Several yards later, the air element grew slick in Marcus's grip, slipping and twisting under Rourke. After another four labored steps, Marcus lost control of it completely and Rourke smacked to the rock floor. I pulled magic from the link and checked his health. I didn't know if I should have been thankful or worried to find it unchanged.

"We're not close enough," I said, but Marcus already knew that through the link. He gathered air again, but it slipped away before he had enough to lift the gargoyle.

"Maybe we can drag him," I suggested.

"How much farther can you walk?"

Good question. I trudged past Marcus, and the glowball trailing me flickered and extinguished. I made it another dozen steps, each progressively more difficult. We were close, with the baetyl looming around the bend. Tentatively, I reached for it, then jerked back when a malevolent presence swiped at me. I was no longer welcome.

I turned around, steadying myself on the wall, and reached for Rourke, using the combined weight of Marcus's and my linked magic. Air slipped from my grip again and again, and I couldn't budge the gargoyle. Leaving the glowball behind, Marcus waded into the darkness with me, muscling himself two steps closer to the baetyl through brute force. The ominous weight of the baetyl tightened like a cat crouching, readying itself to pounce.

"Stop!" I gathered our magic into a quartz shield, prepared to throw all our strength into defending Marcus. He stopped, giving me an unreadable look in the dim light.

"It's not going to let us any closer, and it doesn't matter if we can't bring the gargoyles with us," I said.

He waded back to my side as if moving through waist-high mud, his exaggerated motions looking absurd in the empty tunnel. The baetyl relaxed but didn't take its awareness from us. Grudgingly, I let Marcus disband my shield and attempt to pull Rourke closer to us. Magic worked no better for him than it had for me. Together, we slogged back up the tunnel. Each step grew lighter and easier, and I fought the urge to run back to the surface, knowing it was at least partially the baetyl's compulsion.

"Now what?" Marcus asked.

"The plan hasn't changed. We need to get the gargoyles as close to the baetyl as possible. Maybe if we get enough of them together, it'll recognize them and let us take them in." It was a slim possibility, but having something to do was better than giving in to the despair ghosting my thoughts. We'd come too far to stop now.

Celeste allowed herself one mournful whine when we told her we hadn't been able to get Rourke into the baetyl; then she insisted on boosting us as far as the baetyl would allow so we didn't fatigue ourselves carrying the gargoyles into the tunnel. Oliver was more than happy to back her up.

With their help, we were able to bring the curled-up fox and the owl-headed rabbit together, but the rest of the gargoyles were too large and had to be carried individually.

"It makes my insides hurt, like it's trying to change me," Oliver said after our fifth trip into the tunnel.

I whirled to face him. "Out. *Now,*" I barked, remembering the baetyl's desire to snuff out his life and breathe its own pattern into him. I hurried Oliver from the tunnel, herding Celeste with him, and refused to let them back in when Marcus and I returned to the surface.

"I need to know you're safe. Besides, there's not much else you can do. We can carry the last gargoyle by ourselves."

Oliver's defeated posture and woeful eyes squeezed my heart, but I didn't back down. He'd risked his life for me twice already today—once by entering the baetyl to begin with and again when he returned to help me pull Marcus out. I wasn't going to let him endanger himself unnecessarily now.

Marcus and I carried each gargoyle as close to the baetyl as we could, physically pushing the lighter ones closer when magic failed us, but every time we were stopped by the baetyl before we reached the entrance. Where we were forced to drop each gargoyle didn't follow a pattern; the baetyl let us carry the heavy wolf farther than the much lighter curled-up fox but not as far as owl-rabbit. The last, the sardonyx tiger, slipped from our grip just in front of Rourke.

Panting, I hobbled a few steps to the tiger's side and draped an arm over her shoulders, resting my head on her motionless side while I caught my breath. I badly wanted to sit, but I wasn't sure I'd be able to get back up.

I wondered if the gargoyles could sense the baetyl. Did they know they were mere feet from the magic they needed to revive them? I reached into the tiger with a probe of the elements—fighting to hold even a tiny bit of fire, air, water, and wood. The gargoyle felt no stronger than she had on the surface. Possibly weaker.

We needed to feed the gargoyles magic.

I straightened, seeing my horror reflected in Marcus's expression as we both came to the same realization.

"How are we going to give them magic here? I can barely hold an element," I said.

"You don't seem to have a problem with quartz-tuned earth."

True. The baetyl had a soft spot for quartz, but I couldn't do much with a singular element, and whatever I did wouldn't be enough. Feeding the gargoyles magic was a stop-gap measure until we could get them into the baetyl. If we couldn't get past the baetyl's barrier, it wouldn't matter how much magic we threw at the gargoyles; they wouldn't wake and they wouldn't get better.

Why hadn't I thought to bring the gargoyles into the baetyl before I'd sealed it? Or earlier, before I'd healed the heart? Why had I sealed the baetyl at all? I should have known it wouldn't let me, a human, back inside after it was sealed, but I'd been too exhausted to think that far ahead. Some guardian I made. I might have doomed these gargoyles in my attempt to save them.

I squelched my self-recriminations. Focusing on the past and things I couldn't change wasn't going to save the gargoyles. I needed to work with the problems as they were now.

As far as I could tell, there was only one solution.

"I need to wake them," I said.

"Can you?"

"I don't know, but I'm going to try," I said. I gave the tiger a nervous pat, wishing Oliver were at my side. The gargoyles were so weak that forcing them from their comatose state could kill them. I wouldn't even consider it if the only other option wasn't watching them fade away on the doorstep of their cynosure baetyl. I considered what I had to work with. A simple infusion of quartz magic wouldn't be enough to wake the gargoyles. I would have to attempt something far more drastic—and dangerous.

Tugging my hair behind my ear, I moved to the warthog-headed bear, the strongest of all the gargoyles. If any were going to survive waking, it'd be her.

She should have glistened like snow in the golden light of Marcus's glowball, but her white quartz body was marred with grit etched into her pockmarked sides. Sickly green prasiolite striations wrapped her wide belly and coated her folded wings.

"What's the plan?"

"First, we drop our link," I said.

Marcus didn't comply. "Why? We're stronger together."

Because being linked mucks up my individuality. Only I couldn't tell him that, or he'd guess what I planned and stop me.

"Waking the gargoyle might attract the baetyl's attention. I need one of us to be on guard," I said instead. The weight of the baetyl pressed against my thoughts, and my fear was genuine. What if it lashed out, seeing me as an enemy to its gargoyle?

"All the more reason for me to be inside the link, helping you fight off the baetyl's lure."

I shook my head. "It's not like that now. The baetyl doesn't like me anymore."

"How do you know?" The shadows cast by the flickering glow-balls made his scowl more impressive, but I was immune.

"I tried to connect with it to see if it'd let me through."

"You did *what*?"

"And it slapped me aside. It's done with me."

His thick jaw muscle bounced as he ground his teeth. "That was stupid."

"Yep." No more stupid than what I was about to try, but these gargoyles deserved a chance to live, and I wouldn't stop until I'd exhausted my options—short of killing myself in the process. "So I don't need you in the link. I need you to protect us while I do my healer work and try to wake a comatose gargoyle."

My healer work, such a nice euphemistic phrase. So much better than telling him I was going to try to imprint part of my spirit into the warthog's and use my energy to wake her.

I hid my trembling hands against the gargoyle's round side. I'd shifted pieces of my spirit from my body before at Focal Park when Elsa's invention had latched on to Oliver and his siblings. It'd been the only way to simultaneously break the connection between the deadly magic and the gargoyles, and it'd been an act of desperation I hadn't realized until later could have killed me.

By comparison, using a piece of my spirit to stimulate a single gargoyle wasn't half as dangerous. For starters, it wouldn't kill me. But if I could think of any other means of compelling the gargoyles from their comas, I wouldn't have considered using my spirit. If this went wrong, a part of myself could be forever trapped inside the gargoyle, and having my spirit split would leave me mentally unbalanced or physically diminished, or both—for life.

I concentrated to keep my breathing even and not give away the frantic beat of my heart.

"We're wasting time," I said, my words clipped with tension.

Marcus stared down the tunnel, the end outlined by the faint glow of the baetyl around the corner. I knew he was weighing our options. When the link dissolved, I closed my throat around a belated protest. The magic available to me shrank, and for a second I was the small, ugly creature inside the baetyl again, letting go of all its fathomless power.

Marcus shifted closer and I purposely didn't look at him. If he read the fear in my expression, he'd try to interfere again. Closing my eyes, I grounded myself inside my body. *I am Mika Stillwater, gargoyle guardian.*

The familiar moist, earthy notes of the tunnel and the dry, smooth odor of quartz reassured me, as did Marcus's warm scent. He'd stood close enough to be accused of hovering, but having his solid presence at my back helped quiet the jangle of doubts bombarding me. The tangy odor of kachina greenthread and lamb's ear leaves wafted from us both, an unnecessary reminder of the dangers.

Fingers crossed, I gathered the familiar blend of gargoyle-tuned elements and eased my magic into the warthog without opening my eyes. Holding the magic steady, I simultaneously sank into my own body, searching for the central core of my individuality—my spirit.

I wouldn't have known what to feel for if I hadn't learned the trick of separating my spirit and body in Focal Park. Then, the act had been a blind, last-ditch effort flowing from a string of elemental maneuvers that had already tugged me a half dozen different directions. Separating my spirit and dividing it among the gargoyles had been a natural extension of the magic I'd already been doing. Here, my actions were deliberate, my mind quiet, and loosening even a small sliver of my spirit from my body made me tremble with trepidation.

Afraid to pause and give Marcus a chance to stop me, I peeled a piece from the pulsing nebula of my spirit as easily as plucking a petal from a rose—it came free with only a mild tug. Or almost free. A slender thread spun from my body to connect with the petal, lengthening as I coaxed the petal from my body and into the warthog's. With almost magnetic attraction, the petal merged with my magic.

My breath released in a shaky hiss as the warthog's pain became my own. During the magic storms, her stubby tail and the tips of her tusks had been chipped and her folded wings were abraded. The pulsing pain of the new injuries settled into the dull aches of her body, which suffered from malnutrition and erosion. The puncture in my thigh pulsed in response, but I distanced myself from my body and did my best to ignore the gargoyle's pain, too. Once I got her into the baetyl, she'd be better.

I dove through her, searching for the spark of her life. It was nothing I could see with my eyes, but I could feel it with my magic. The essence of the warthog lay nestled among layers of elements deep in her heart. I altered my magic to match her prasiolite-striped white quartz body, then subtly tweaked the quartz to resonate more closely with the baetyl's energy.

What would have been easier than inhaling when I'd been linked with the baetyl took my full concentration now. Since I couldn't remember the bulk of the baetyl's pattern, I had to rely on the glimpses I caught to spark my memory, then alter the delicate blend of elements to match.

I knew the moment I got it just right. The tiny remnant of the warthog hiding in her core turned, and in my mind's eye, her spirit took the form of pure golden light in the shape of her body. She stood cocooned in a sphere of white quartz crisscrossed with mint and forest-green prasiolite striations, and her liquid gold eyes regarded my spirit with profound sorrow. Loneliness from decades of isolation crashed through me, and the shock of feeling her emotion as if it were my own jarred me. Healing gargoyles gave me access to their physical sensations, not their emotional ones. The elements trembled in my grasp and I struggled to hold myself in place. Any change in my magic might push me out of her, or worse, injure her.

I'm here to help. All you have to do is wake up. I pictured the baetyl and tried to give it a joyous sensation. Hoping she could feel my emotions as clearly as I could hers, I fed her my affection, my hope for her to wake, and my eagerness for her to be whole and healthy—and with it, I twined my piece of spirit around her spark of life. The crush of loneliness cracked, allowing in such a fragile emotion I didn't recognize it at first: hope.

That's it. Wake up. Walk into the baetyl.

She turned from me, and her head lifted as if she could see the baetyl now. Her thick wings unfurled and she took a step—

Her spark blurred; then she was back in her frozen form, wings trapped against her back. Despair drowned me, and I fought to stay in place.

You can do it, I encouraged. I siphoned more of my spirit into her, cocooning her in petals of energy. *Try again. You've only got a few feet...*

She looked at me, and her eyes had no room for lies. She couldn't do it. She didn't have the strength.

Together, then. We'll do it together.

Thrusting aside my fear, I abandoned my careful half-measures and yanked my spirit free of my body and into the warthog, encasing her fragile spark in the entirety of my spirit's energy. The final nuances of her body clarified in my mind's eye, and I tweaked my magic, melding with her. I turned my—our—head toward the baetyl and poured my will into the gargoyle.

15

Walk. *Take a step. Move.*

My back foot shifted, little more than a twitch, but the sensation opened a forgotten door. Awareness of my body spread upward. I lifted my head on a neck gone stiff as stone. My wings—

Fear jumbled my thoughts. The last time...

The baetyl...

I am a gargoyle guardian!

The magic slipped and shuddered in my control, threatening to fracture. I could feel my wings, glorious green prasiolite, but...but...

I do not have wings!

I yanked my magic to free it, but it snagged and held. Pain slashed me, hot and sharp. I needed to get out, to escape—

"Easy, Mika. Don't rip it. You're okay. Just take it slow."

The rumble of Marcus's voice cut through my panic and I stilled. My body shuddered with an echo of someone else's pain. The warthog. Not my body—hers. Except there was no distinction. I had wings because she had wings.

I'd hoped to use my spirit to restore the gargoyle's ability to walk; instead, I'd imprinted my spirit onto hers and it'd given *me* control over her body. Fear tingled through a confusion of arms and legs, heads and spines. I took a deep breath through two sets of lungs and oriented on the warthog's spirit again. She trembled inside my control, but with hope, not fear.

"That's better. Now ease back out," Marcus said.

I tilted my head to look at him, disoriented by the low angle. He hunched over something in his arms, talking to it, not me. With a jolt, I realized that was *me* cradled against his chest. My body lay in a loose sprawl, eyes closed, mouth open, green ointment dotting my pale face. The fiery light of the glowballs shimmered in the fan of my strawberry-blond hair and emphasized the dark purple circles under my eyes. Had I always looked so fragile?

The longer I looked at my body, the more foreign the gargoyle's felt. When vertigo skewed my sight, I turned away.

Something kissed my spirit, the feeling so sweet and pure that my heart felt like it'd sing from my chest. I stared at the glow at the end of the tunnel. *Home.* My cynosure baetyl reached for me, pulling me to it, and I welcomed the assistance.

I jerked into motion, clumsily navigating on four stiff legs. My wings flexed with each step, the unfamiliar muscles twitching in my limited control.

"Mika, no. It's too dangerous."

Everything ached, and the pain grew with each step as my body woke. My skin was chapped from tusk to tail, my feet were bruised from holding the same position for decades, and my chipped tusks stung. The baetyl vowed to soothe it all away. I gathered its siren song of promises into my heart and pushed through the pain and sluggishness of my stiff body. When I rounded the corner, the baetyl filled my vision and I ran the last stumbling steps.

A film of the baetyl's protective ward coated the opening, and when I burst through it, magic poured into me. I drank it down, savoring the cascade of relief as the baetyl massaged my body back into harmony and soothed away the aches and pains of decades.

I stretched my wings wide, body humming with pleasure. I was whole.

The elements swirled through me, and I folded them, amplifying—

That's how a boost works!

My shocked delight separated me from the gargoyle. For a moment, I was an amazed observer. I'd never understood how a gargoyle could create more magic out of the existing elements, but from my new perspective, it seemed obvious. Then my access to the world through her eyes slipped from my control. The space between our spirits grew, and I had the impression of the warthog regarding me with the wise eyes of her spirit before she shoved me from her body.

I tried to hang on, clinging to elemental fibers inside her until I saw the damage I created. I wasn't supposed to hurt gargoyles. I was a healer.

With that thought, I lost my anchor and my detached spirit shot fast as an arrow back to my body, slamming home.

I gasped for air like I'd been underwater, back arching, eyes flying open to stare up at the shadowy ceiling of the tunnel. My heart hammered in my chest and I panted, trying to remember who I was, where I was, *what* I was.

I am Mika Stillwater. I am a gargoyle healer. I am a gargoyle guardian.

My spirit settled into my body, binding with the minute piece I'd left behind. I couldn't see it in myself as I could in the gargoyle, but I didn't need to. I could feel the rightness. I wriggled my fingers and toes, stifling a groan as my body's pains awoke. The blissful sensation of the baetyl healing the warthog's wounds faded to a wistful memory.

I sat up, and Marcus's hand settled at my back to support me. I braced a hand on the floor to balance against a wave of dizziness while I looked around. It hadn't been a dream. The warthog was gone.

"I did it." I grinned at Marcus. "I got a gargoyle into the baetyl." I'd walked her body in as if it were my own. The thought made me queasy and giddy at the same time. "If I can do it once, I can do it seven times. I'm saving all these gargoyles' lives!"

"I thought you were done with shoving your life in front of every problem."

"I am."

"Then what do you call that stunt?"

"A calculated risk that—"

"Risk?! This is exactly what you did at Focal Park."

"No, it's not. I've thought this through—"

"You shoved your spirit into a gargoyle just like last ti—"

"I didn't divide myself up."

"Oh, so that makes it better?" Marcus rose to his feet in a smooth motion and paced away from me, fists clenched.

"Listen to me. I'm giving the gargoyles the strength they need. I can't get them into the baetyl by physical or magical strength, but I can by—"

"By sticking the essence that makes you, you into another living creature. That's not *right*. It's not natural or safe or a reasonable risk."

"It is for me."

I'd come here with the impossible mission of battling my way through deadly magic storms, finding a secretive baetyl hidden inside the mountain, fixing it without even knowing exactly what a baetyl was, and then getting the sick gargoyles inside. I had doubted the success of this mission a thousand times. Yet, despite all the hardships, I'd done it. I couldn't—*wouldn't*—stop this close to the finish line.

"I'm not attempting this with just any troubled creature. I'm a—"

"Don't say it."

"Gargoyle guardian," I finished.

"Damn it."

"Whatever it is that made me capable of healing the baetyl is the same part of me that makes it okay for me to transplant my spirit into a gargoyle. *Temporarily.* My magic is somehow close to theirs. It means they're safe with me and I'm safe with them. This isn't a martyr mission."

Veins stood out on Marcus's neck as he loomed over me, his forearms corded with tension. "You didn't know who you were."

"I was disoriented for a moment."

"You were unresponsive for fifteen minutes."

"That long?" I rolled to my knees— Wait, hadn't I been standing in front of the warthog? I recalled a shadowy memory of looking at myself through the warthog's eyes. Marcus had been holding me in his arms. "Ah, thank you for catching me?"

Marcus gave me an exasperated look. "Someone had to protect the tunnel from the impact of your thick skull."

"Good point. I'll make sure to be sitting next time." Fifteen minutes? I assessed the flickers of life inside the remaining gargoyles. I'd have to leave the strongest for last and work faster. None of the gargoyles looked like they would survive another hour.

"Are you sure there's no other way?" Marcus asked.

I stood but relaxed my defiant posture when I saw his concern.

"I can't think of one. Can you?"

He shook his head.

Rourke's will to live was fading fast, and I surged to his side, sat, and shoved a braid of magic and spirit into him. Marcus cursed, then his warmth settled beside me.

"Damn it, be careful," he growled.

I was faster this time, dropping through the layers of Rourke's pain and tweaking my magic to resonate with his unique signature. The baetyl's pattern drifted in and out of my awareness, and I altered my magic to harmonize with it when I could but didn't let myself be distracted by chasing it.

When my magic clicked in perfect synchronization with Rourke, I saw him in my mind's eye. He didn't react, his inner self as frozen as his physical body. Gently, I wrapped him in love and admiration and thick layers of my spirit. We merged, and the weight of his body became my own.

I knew what to expect this time, but it made it no less disorienting. Or easier. I gathered my will and funneled it through my spirit and out to our limbs. Forcing our body to fold so we could walk on all fours took herculean effort. Our wings hung heavy and useless at our sides, trailing on the rock ground for four torturous steps before the baetyl's song infiltrated my body. After that, each step grew easier. I still had to shove and strain to carry my unwieldy bulk, but the song urged me on.

Crossing into the baetyl felt like walking through a cleansing shower. I closed my eyes in bliss as magic bathed me from the inside out and the outside in. After decades of fighting, I relaxed and reveled in being alive. When I opened my eyes, I saw the warthog take flight, flapping lazily to a higher perch, folding and twisting the baetyl's magic for the sheer joy of it.

I rolled onto my back and spread my wings on the tiny crystals, their sharp points a delightful massage against muscles and feathers long unused. My antlers scraped the crystals, making the quartz sing.

Something nudged me, a gentle but persistent prod, and I spiraled down into my—our—body. Blinking, I looked up into the bright eyes of Rourke's spirit. His gratitude wrapped me like a soft blanket even as he used an antler to push me again. With a smile, I let go, and my spirit winged back to my human body.

"Mika?"

Who?

I squinted, the bright light hurting my eyes. Someone crouched over me. *Marcus.*

"I am Mika Stillwater," I said, and the words felt right even if I wasn't completely sure what they meant.

"You are a gargoyle healer and guardian."

Right. My spirit and mind clicked into sync. I was in Marcus's lap, cradled against his chest and arm. *Safe,* my heart whispered.

Seeing the empty tunnel where Rourke had stood minutes before made my heart swell with elation. I couldn't wait to deliver the good news to Celeste. We'd done it: We'd saved her mate.

"How long?" I asked.

Marcus shook his head. "I don't know. A little longer, I think."

Longer? I'd tried to be faster, but it had been hard to remember my purpose over the call of the baetyl. If Rourke hadn't nudged me from his body, I'd still be there.

Marcus studied my face, worry lines etching his forehead. He held me close enough that I could count the flecks of navy in his lapis lazuli eyes, but I looked away, not wanting him to see how much I didn't want to move.

Pushing out of his arms took willpower I didn't have to spare, and I selected the next weakest gargoyle—the rabbit-owl. Like Celeste, whose head and front legs were those of an eagle, his front legs and chest were all owl, and though his body was far more compact than the two previous gargoyles I'd inhabited, once I wrapped him in my spirit, it took more effort not less to hop him into the baetyl. Despite my best intentions, I forgot about everything but the baetyl's song and the glorious sensation of being home until the gargoyle raked his talons against my spirit and forced me back to my body.

Marcus was holding me when I opened my eyes to the bleak brown walls of the tunnel, and he assured me I was Mika Stillwater, gargoyle healer and guardian. I watched his lips move, heard the words vibrate against my eardrums, but he had to repeat himself several times before the sounds connected with my brain and made sense.

The citrine and smoky quartz badger with a seahorse head was next, then the onyx wolf. Following my magic into the gargoyles to find their weak spirits was easier when I started with my body right next to theirs, and if Marcus hadn't been watching, I would have crawled to the gargoyles. Instead, I forced myself to stand and walk, though Marcus had to wrap an arm around my waist to keep me from falling. He didn't comment on my fatigue or argue for me to slow down. The gargoyles were fading too fast for me to take a break. Or a nap.

I dearly wanted a nap—at least when I inhabited my own body. When I was in the baetyl, in those timeless moments before the gargoyles kicked me out of their bodies, I lived in their sublime bliss. There, I was rejuvenated. The baetyl, which had been a deadly, alluring source of power to me when I'd climbed into the heart and healed it, was sweet and comforting when I forgot I wasn't a gargoyle. It made snapping back to my own body worse each time, the euphoric moments in the baetyl emphasizing my body's growing misery. Sweat and time counteracted the greenthread's numbing properties, and a multitude of injuries clamored with increasing fervor each time I settled back into my own skin.

Worse was the loss of the baetyl—its beauty, its soothing song, its promise of rejuvenation.

I lingered in the badger and longer still in the wolf, forgetting myself in their all-consuming relief to be home and healing. With each gargoyle, I gained more understanding of how they interacted with magic, and it was amazing. As a human, I could use the elements, channeling them into different shapes and patterns to create an outcome. As a gargoyle, I didn't have to reach for the elements; they saturated me. Amplifying magic was a simple matter of folding it to make the elements denser. Focusing the effect, I could direct it where I wanted . . .

Each time I came back to my body, what had been so clear as a gargoyle didn't make sense as a human. How could the elements be folded? How could you direct magic without using it? I tried to cling to the memory, but the drone of a voice would cut through my puzzled thoughts, and I'd lose it.

"You are Mika Stillwater, gargoyle guardian and healer."

I focused on the intense stare of the man above me and the words he delivered with a vehemence that said they were important. "Your parents are water elementals. You live in Terra Haven."

I frowned at the unfamiliar syllables.

"Say it with me. Say, 'I am Mika Stillwater.'"

My hip throbbed, my arms stung. My head wanted to fall off my shoulders. Nothing was proportioned right. Where were my wings?

The man jabbed my breastbone with a stiff finger. I winced and frowned at him. A glowball hovered close beside us, casting stark shadows that pooled in the crease between his eyebrows and the hollows around his eyes.

"You. Open your mouth and say it," he ordered.

"I am Mika Still . . ."

"Mika Stillwater. Say it."

"Mika Stillwater." I repeated the words twice, their shape familiar in my mouth.

"You are the foolish and stubborn gargoyle guardian, Mika Stillwater."

I stiffened, recognizing my name. Alarm skittered down my spine as I reconnected with my body. I hadn't recognized myself. At all.

Marcus must have read the fear in my eyes and known I'd returned, because he stopped talking. He shifted, pulling me tighter against him.

"You're okay. You're back. Everything's okay."

Everything was not okay. My hands didn't lift when I reach for Marcus. The baetyl sang just below my hearing range, a hum that made my jaw ache and sparkles dance through my vision. I didn't want to be able to hear it—it was calling to gargoyles, and I *shouldn't* be able to hear it—but I couldn't stop myself from straining to make out the notes. The harder I concentrated, the more my head pounded. But that wasn't the worst of it. Without looking, without moving, I could feel the remaining tiger and fox gargoyles.

My awareness of the gargoyles wasn't natural. It wasn't human. It was something the baetyl could do. I should have needed magic, but I'd blurred the lines. I'd reshaped myself too many times and too quickly, first in the baetyl and now with the gargoyles. I was losing myself.

When I shifted, the tunnel darkened and spun. I righted it with a blink. "How long?"

"Too long."

"Okay. Tiger next." Just as I could sense the location of both gargoyles, I didn't need magic to tell she was the weaker of the two.

"Mika . . ."

"She's fading too fast."

"So are you."

I tilted my face up to look at Marcus, my head resting on his shoulder, my body cradled by his. I fought the desire to close my eyes and relax against him. "I'll recover."

"Take a break," he urged.

I tried to stand, but my body didn't even sit up. I couldn't feel my feet. Dropping my lashes to hide my panic, I focused on wriggling my toes. When they responded, I let out a slow breath. *Tired. I'm just tired.* If I stopped now, I wouldn't be able to start again, not for hours. By then, both gargoyles would be dead and I would never be able to live with myself.

The tiger stood frozen at the bend in the tunnel behind us, farther from the baetyl entrance than the fox. She was only five feet from us, but it might as well have been five miles if I had to walk it alone.

"Please don't try to stop me."

Marcus scowled, but he surprised me when he stood with me in his arms and walked to the tiger.

"Thank you."

I fell into the tiger and didn't stop falling until I stood in front of her inner self. Her body's shape ghosted at the edges, as if the golden light of her spirit were evaporating.

Or dying.

I saw the truth of my realization in her eyes and felt her acceptance of her death pulse between us.

No. I'm here to save you. The baetyl is right here. All we have to do is walk a few dozen feet.

I pushed my spirit closer, but she flared bright. The impression of a roaring tiger, sharp teeth, and rending claws flashed almost too fast to follow. I retreated, and the gargoyle's fuzzy shape returned.

You can't give up, I commanded, not sure how much she could hear. I willed her to live, to fight. She smiled, her cat mouth curling up around her thick muzzle, and sent me a feeling of serenity.

Don't you dare. I shoved my spirit toward her again, enveloping her, holding the effervescent pieces of her together by sheer will. She didn't struggle this time; she purred. The soundless vibrations resonated with love and gratitude . . . and forgiveness.

I clung to her, desperate to save her. We were so close. If she would hang on just a bit longer, I could save her.

I poured more of my will into hers, capturing her, holding her. I could do this. I could walk her into the baetyl.

My awareness expanded to her limbs—

Sharp pains tore through me. It wasn't the gargoyle fighting; she'd relaxed in my grasp. It was the strain of anchoring the gargoyle to her body eating through me, pulling my spirit apart. It shredded my strength, shredded me. If I held on much longer, she would pull me apart.

If I let go, she'd die.

I hung suspended in that moment of love and guilt, forgiveness and torture. I couldn't save her. I couldn't abandon her.

I couldn't abandon the fox, either. If I clung tight enough, fought hard enough, I could overpower the tiger's fading will and walk her into the baetyl, but doing so would leave nothing of me to help the fox.

It'd leave nothing of *me*. If I saved her, it would be the last thing I'd do, and I'd promised myself I would be more than a martyr. I'd be a true guardian.

Letting go hurt far worse than holding on. I released the tiger, and in the agony of my decision, her gratitude caressed like a soothing balm across my spirit. She turned her golden tiger's head to me, and her eyes held nothing but love.

Then her form shifted and stretched, growing less and less substantial. I waited beside her, sending her my love, until a wash of profound relief exploded from her spirit, bowling me over. When I reoriented, she'd ceased to exist.

My eyes opened on a blurry world. Tears ran down my temples into my hair, and the sounds escaping my throat and echoing in the tunnel frightened me.

"Mika?"

"She didn't make it," I sobbed. I couldn't find my paw—hand—to wipe away the tears.

The baetyl's song filtered through my tears, new mournful notes quieting my sniffles. I cocked my head, listening. I was really hearing it, the melody unfurling inside me.

"I'm so sorry, Mika."

Power swelled behind that song, urging me back to my task. I had one more gargoyle to save, and the fox's life guttered on the cusp of being extinguished.

"I need to help the fox," I mumbled through numb lips.

"No. You need to rest. You can't—"

I glanced up into his eyes, and I knew the weight of the baetyl looked out at him through mine.

"Mika . . . don't—"

"I'm coming back," I whispered, and I didn't know if I was talking to Marcus or the baetyl.

"Mika!"

I dropped out of my body into the fox's, and it felt like going home.

16

I uncurled my tail, surged to my feet with an assisting flap of my long wings, and stretched. My awareness of my body puzzled me. Of course my legs were all proportional and used for walking. Of course I had wings. Of course my body was beautiful tigereye and citrine.

Every square inch of me hurt, my body cramped from decades of paralysis and my skin gouged and chapped. The itch in my tail was new. I twisted to examine the patch of clear quartz sealing a fresh wound and caught sight of the humans. The man knelt over a sleeping woman, his face close to her ear, his lips moving. His voice buzzed against my mind, and I shook my head to dispel a wave of dizziness. I focused on my tail again, puzzling over the anomalous patch. It looked like the work of a healer, but I didn't remember a healer. I didn't remember being hurt. I didn't remember . . .

My baetyl's song whispered in my ears, chasing every other thought from my head. I stretched the stiffness from my paws again, then trotted down the tunnel. Home. I was going home after far too long.

I burst into the baetyl and leapt into flight. Magic breathed through me, and I hungrily folded it into myself. My wings beat, tenderly at first, then with greater ease. I soared through the baetyl, letting the air carry my pain away. I was whole.

My wings banked, the muscles acting as if they had a mind of their own, and I stumbled to a landing on a high grotto filled with rose quartz. Shaking my head, I turned around and prepared to leap, but my back legs refused to budge.

I growled, the sound ragged in my unused throat. I wouldn't be frozen again. I was safe. I was home. Nothing could stop me.

I pushed from the ledge and my heart lodged in my throat when my wings didn't open. Clawing at the air, I caught the edge of a thick amethyst crystal, nails scraping the slick surface before my wings finally flared open and I shoved into the air. I'd barely gained altitude when my body dove out of control, pulling up just before I crashed into the jagged floor.

Whining, I tried to look at my wings, now folded on my back, but I couldn't move my head. Panic thundered in my heart. I fought the hidden bonds as the baetyl darkened until I couldn't see.

The fox split her spirit from mine. The shock of separation sliced through me like a blade. Distressed, I rushed the fox.

Don't do this. I need you, I thought. She could remain in the baetyl, in our home. With her, I was safe. She was alive. She wouldn't die. I'd never have to leave.

The fox nipped me, and her spirit's sharp teeth pinched. I didn't care, too filled with the terror of being abandoned. I swelled, wrapping around the fox again, trying to join with her, but she wasn't compliant this time. She fought back, and her nips became agonizing bites and unheard growls. Flinching, I gave ground and she chased me until I had nowhere left to go.

I popped free of the fox's body and floundered in an abyss. All sense of direction and purpose drifted away from me. I hung there, suspended in nothing, lost and confused.

"Go home, Guardian," someone growled.

Home? I spun the word in my thoughts, then released it into the void. It divided and multiplied, taking a thousand different shapes until . . .

Home. This was home. It was in the shape of every layer of quartz and in the interaction of every element. And the elements . . . They floated with me, crisper than I'd ever seen them, five pieces of the same magic. Enraptured, I drifted among them, glorifying in their perfection. The pattern of the baetyl filled me with rapture; the patterns of life moving in it elicited pride and awe. I belonged here, a part of this world and the elements. I couldn't see myself, but I could feel *me*. I was beautiful and perfect, in harmony with everything around me.

Fire lit through me, the scorching pain spinning the world around me. A buzzing enveloped me, and I pushed it away, only to be singed again. I screamed and tried to fight off the flames, but they'd disappeared. Unbalanced and hurting, I sought out my previous bliss, but it eluded me. The clarity of the elements had blurred, disguising the gorgeous patterns hidden among them. Something had stolen my perfection, and without it, I didn't belong here.

Irate, I chased the fire the next time it attacked. When I found the source, I pounced, wrapping around it to extinguish it. Flames licked through me. Snarled inside the agonizing blast were the other four elements in a pattern I didn't recognize and that didn't matter. It wasn't a true pattern. It wasn't beautiful. It was a trap.

I fought, entangling myself further. The buzzing had become a drone that encased me, constricting the binding elements.

"Damn it, Mika, I won't let you die."

Agony seared through me and my eyes burst open. A claustrophobic world greeted me, filled with dreary shades of brown and black. I closed my eyes. I wanted to go back to floating with the elements.

Fresh pain forced my eyes open again.

"You are Mika Stillwater. You are a gargoyle healer and guardian. You . . ."

The sounds washed over me. My eyes roved over the tiny, drab world, stopping when they encountered blue. It wasn't gargoyle blue but it had its own beauty, flecked with navy . . .

The baetyl's sweet promise sang at the edge of my perception, and

I closed my eyes again and stretched for it. I started to drift free of the trap, but sparks rained pain through me, tightening me in place. When the world jostled, I looked around with fresh hope, but I hadn't escaped. Above me, the rocky brown ceiling shifted and the baetyl grew farther away, its song fading. Tears leaked from my eyes.

"Your parents are water elementals. You have a younger sister. You once seared your eyebrows off in an Elemental's Apprentice duel. You make miniature figurines with quartz that look like they could come alive."

Golden warmth hit my face and I squinted against the bright light. A vast indigo sky arched overhead and spun toward a lighter blue horizon and the sun's fiery orb cresting the green tree-covered hills. Wind picked at my loose hair, carrying the crisp scent of dew and pine and damp soil. The man was still speaking, his voice a pleasant rumble. I relaxed and let myself go.

The trap holding me loosened and I was floating. All remnants of pain faded, taking with it my exhaustion. I didn't have to fight anymore. I could just let go.

White light swept over the hills, erasing them. It grew brighter until it consumed the sky, my body, and everything in between. I looked into the face of every possibility, every truth, and love infused me. Everything was okay. All I had to do was . . .

Let . . .

Go.

17

"Mika!"

The trilling voice speared through me. The bright light trembled.

"Mika, wake up."

Oliver.

I fell, sinking into a body. *My body?* Air rushed into my lungs, drawing pain in its wake. Groaning, I opened my eyes.

A carnelian gargoyle stood over me, the sunlight on his flared wings making them look like fans of flame. He thrust his worried square face into mine. "Mika?"

Oliver. I knew him, knew he was important to me, but everything felt fuzzy. The gargoyles—

I had to get the gargoyles into the baetyl!

Tentatively, I gathered elements to reach for Oliver. He couldn't move himself, so I had to get him inside before he died. Except, he *was* moving. I let the elements unravel, confused.

"Come on, Mika. Come back to us, you stubborn woman."

I shifted to look for the source of the rough, masculine voice, surprised to find the man's face inches from mine. I was in his arms, and the feeling was as familiar as his voice. *Marcus.* His fierce scowl should have been intimidating, but it infused me with warmth.

"You are Mika Stillwater. You live in Terra Haven in a tiny apartment in Ms. Zuberrie's house. Your best friend is Kylie Grayson. Oliver is your gargoyle companion."

A zing of recognition sparked. He was telling me about myself. I tried to concentrate but the words couldn't compete with my emotions. I liked being held by Marcus. I liked the concern so evident in his tone.

Oliver rested his muzzle on my stomach, and a rush of love for the gargoyle drowned out all other sensations. When I turned back to Marcus, an echo of that love, softer, less sure, darted through me. Lifting a hand to grip the back of his neck, I pulled Marcus to me.

The soft heat of his surprised exhale fanned across my mouth, followed by the delicious, shocking contact of his lips. Tingles raced through my body and my spirit snicked home.

Marcus hesitated; then he kissed me back, his arms tightening around me.

"I am Mika Stillwater," I said when he pulled back a few inches.

His luminous blue eyes searched my face and a decade of worry lifted from his expression.

"Thank you for saving me," I said.

"I thought you were going to die," he whispered, the words a confession.

"I think I did." With every passing second in my body, my memory of my spirit being adrift faded, but the emotional resonance remained. I'd experienced an unearthly bliss born of an indescribable harmony, and the sensation remained imprinted on my spirit.

"But you brought me back. You and Oliver."

Oliver whined and Marcus helped me sit up so I could hug the young gargoyle. He cradled me gently in his stone wings, his silent enhancement a balm to my battered spirit. The knowledge of how to fold the elements like a gargoyle lurked on the edge of my memory but refused to surface. Snippets of the baetyl's pattern and the pattern of all life taunted my memory, too, but I didn't chase them. That wisdom wasn't meant for me, not now. Not in this life.

I rolled the elements, savoring their textures while I petted Oliver's smooth scales. I could feel him in the boost almost like a magic signature. My awareness of Oliver wasn't new; I'd been able to distinguish his enhancement from other gargoyles' for a while now.

The same couldn't be said for my newfound ability to pinpoint the location of him, Celeste, and, much fainter, the gargoyles in the baetyl, without looking. I didn't know what to make of it, but I'd have plenty of time to think about it. Later.

When Oliver released me to snuggle against my side, I sought out Celeste with my eyes. She perched above the cave opening, giving us space.

"Rourke is safe," I said. The last word caught in an unexpectedly thick throat as I remembered the tiger fading in front of me. Despite my best efforts, she'd died on the doorstep of her baetyl. Her profound relief at the end didn't assuage my guilt completely, but I thought I understood it. I still wished I could have saved her.

"Your bravery will never be forgotten, Guardian Mika," Celeste said.

I blinked away my tears and acknowledged my success. I'd done it. I'd saved the dormant gargoyles and healed a baetyl. I'd earned the title the gargoyles had bestowed upon me.

"My name is Mika Stillwater. I am a gargoyle guardian," I whispered, feeling the truth of my words resonate through my spirit. Joy sang in my veins when I turned to Marcus. "And I want to get busy living."

I leaned toward him and he met me halfway, a smile on his lips when we kissed.

EPILOGUE

The baetyl chased us off Reaper's Ridge. By the time Marcus had repaired the sled, its malevolent, squeezing pressure had inflicted us both with splitting headaches. Jittery with a need to leave, I stumbled to collect our gear and shooed Oliver into the air to meet us down the mountain where it was safer. Celeste stayed only because she had to pull the sled, and she huddled in a tight knot, pain pinching her face. Marcus settled the loop of rope around Celeste's chest as I was crawling into the back of the hovering sled, and she set off, shoulders hunched, the moment he joined me.

In terse silence, Marcus twined his fingers through mine, and we clutched the sides of the sled for balance with our free hands as Celeste galloped down the jagged slope, following the path of least resistance. I twisted to watch the tunnel entrance disappear, jaw clenched against the escalating pain hammering against the inside of my skull.

When a fold in the hillside hid the opening from view, my breath hitched with unexpected grief. I would never see the baetyl again—never again be a part of its awesome, terrifying power. Tears blurred my vision as I glanced down to my hand intertwined with Marcus's. I wasn't the same woman who had climbed Reaper's Ridge. The sparkling amethyst scars in my pale flesh and the twin carnelian hexagons on my shoulder blades were my only visible souvenirs, but the baetyl had wrought changes in me that went far deeper. For a few brief moments, I'd been so much more than a singular person in a tiny, fragile body. I'd been linked with a truly ancient entity, privy to spectacular secrets beyond the scope of human understanding.

I mourned the loss of that connection far more than the loss of the baetyl's power.

Marcus squeezed my hand. "Are you okay?" he shouted, the wind whipping his words away.

I nodded because it was easier than trying to explain, especially while being jounced around the back of the sled during our break-neck descent.

The faster Celeste ran, the tighter my fear ratcheted. I checked over my shoulder repeatedly, every time expecting to spot a ravenous monster barreling down on us. It was only the irrationality of my growing panic that helped me see it for what it really was: another of the baetyl's natural defenses awakening. Knowing my escalating terror was generated by the baetyl did nothing to calm me. I'd been a part of its immense power—playing off my unconscious fears was the least of what it could do.

Marcus released my hand to pull his crossbow from his bag and lay it across his lap. He scanned our surroundings for the enemy his brain insisted lurked just out of sight.

"It's not real. It's the baetyl."

"I know, but this helps," he said, and I realized he hadn't notched an arrow.

Gradually, the agony in my temples subsided, along with the hunted feeling that had lodged between my shoulder blades. Celeste slowed to a less hazardous speed, but she didn't stop to rest. Lulled by her steady footsteps and the cessation of pain, I closed my eyes, jolting awake when my body tilted.

"Why don't you lie down?" Marcus suggested.

He scooted to the front of the sled to sit sideways behind the driver's box, one arm draped over the seat so he could lean against it.

Until a healer could mend the lacerations on his back, resting against his side was probably the most comfortable position he could attain. I stretched out with my head pillowed on Marcus's pack and closed my eyes.

Without distractions, my new ability to sense the location of gargoyles pushed to the forefront of my awareness. They registered in my mind as unique bundles of energy, Celeste larger, based on her proximity, and Oliver smaller and distant as he circled in the sky. More faintly still were the six gargoyles inside the mountain behind me.

I could locate the baetyl with my eyes closed.

The thought pulled me from the edge of sleep. With this new power, I could detect *any* baetyl if I was close enough. I might not be able to get through its defenses, but I would be able to point right to it. It was the kind of knowledge people like Walter would kill for.

But no one would ever know. It would be my secret.

I woke at the abandoned Hidden Cache train station. The solid weight of Oliver pressed against my left side from my head to my feet, and his sunrise-orange eyes glowing less than a foot from my face were the first things I saw. I smiled and reached for him, groaning when the movement set off my body's litany of complaints. Oliver pressed his face into my palm and closed his eyes in contentment. The sun had passed its zenith, and Celeste didn't slow as she crossed the tracks, trotting across the quiet meadow on a narrow trail cut through the weeds by giant cerberi feet.

"Where are we going?" I asked, sitting up.

Marcus hadn't moved from his seat at the front of the sled, and the dark hollows under his eyes told me he hadn't gotten any rest, either.

"To see a man about a sled," he said.

The thought of seeing Gus's face when we showed up on his doorstep made me grin. "He's going to be outraged that we're not dead."

Marcus scoffed with feigned indignation. "As if something as feeble as Reaper's Ridge could kill us."

He couldn't hide his pained grimace when he shifted, but that didn't stop him from closing the distance between us and brushing a kiss across my lips. My heart sped in my chest, and I leaned into him, savoring the contact.

"Um, I'm going to fly around a bit," Oliver said, launching from the back of the sled. He dipped toward the earth, caught himself, and flapped upward into a long, lazy circle around us.

"We really should be headed toward a healer," I said.

"We are. Gus lives in a town with a small FPD base. It's how I was able to hire him on such short notice. Anyway, bases always have a healer on staff."

"Okay, healer, then Gus."

"Gus first. I'm not giving the scrawny bastard a chance to slip away."

"Good point. How much farther?"

"If Celeste can keep this pace up, another three or four hours."

I winced in sympathy. It would be faster than returning to Terra Haven, even if we had a train waiting to pick us up at the abandoned station, but it was still a long time for him to suffer.

"Do we have any greenthread left?" I asked.

I took Marcus's grunt as a yes and rummaged through his pack, retrieving a depressingly small roll of lamb's ear leaves and a mostly empty bottle of greenthread.

"Turn around so I can lift your shirt," I ordered.

He obliged and bunched his shirt into his armpits. The strips of previously gray cloth holding the lamb's ear bandages to his back were now blackened with dried blood and caked with a crusty green substance that alarmed me until I realized it was greenthread, not infection. I had to soak the bandages before I could remove them; then I dabbed on the last of the greenthread and layered the lamb's ear leaves over his flayed back.

While I worked, Celeste loped across mile after mile. Oliver returned to the sled every time he saw something he deemed amazing—a field of bright orange poppies, a dairy farm, a flock of caladrii—and I vowed to take him on a vacation so he could see more of the world than Terra Haven. I envisioned trips that included Marcus, our combined magic keeping Oliver healthy even in the most remote locations. Plus, the thought of having Marcus all to myself, without either of us in crisis or injured, sounded divine.

I wasn't surprised when Marcus nodded off, his head pillowed on the driver's seat, greenthread numbing what had to be the excruciating pain of his wounds. I stayed next to him, ready to catch him if he tipped toward his back in his sleep, and I watched the rounded foothills flow past and the weed-clogged trail grow into a slender dirt road, content to turn my brain off for a while.

My gaze returned frequently to Reaper's Ridge, its white peak prominent despite the increasing distance between us. I couldn't decide which amazed me more: its quiet, storm-free expanse or the fact that I had not only climbed the ridge and survived, but I also could claim half the credit for disbanding all the deadly storms. The presence of the hidden baetyl ensured the ridge still wasn't safe for humans, but with its protective measures functioning correctly again, now people would be turned aside instead of killed.

Marcus jerked awake at sunset, making a quick assessment of the sled, the hills, me, and everything in between before relaxing again. Then he kissed me long and hard so I "wouldn't forget."

"Forget what?" I asked breathlessly.

"Me. You forgot me after Focal Park—"

"I did not!"

"And I don't want that to happen again, so . . ."

His second kiss lasted longer than the first, and I was almost disappointed when we reached the outskirts of a town a few minutes later. Nestled in a narrow valley and flanked by a patchwork of vineyards, it appeared far too picturesque to house Gus in its midst, though Marcus assured me we were in the right place.

Oliver returned to the sled, landing gracefully on the driver's seat. He bunched his body to fit on the narrow bench, and coils of his tail spilled to the floor, the red-orange carnelian gleaming in the final rays of the setting sun. By the time Celeste marched us through downtown, twilight had settled over the sleepy streets, but the sight of a gargoyle pulling a sled that appeared to be driven by another gargoyle drew people out to the walkways and windows to gawk as we passed. Marcus and I got as many curious stares, most likely because we looked like avalanche victims, recently freed from the rubble.

Marcus pointed out the Federal Pentagon Defense base tucked behind the main street. Its high adobe walls and towers peppered with arrow slits loomed over the graceful architecture of the rest of the town, hearkening to a more dangerous era. So long as it included a healer and a working shower, I didn't care how militant it looked.

"Are you sure—" I started to ask, attuned to Marcus's growing stiffness as the last of the greenthread's numbness wore off.

"Gus first," he growled.

"Gus first," Oliver echoed, but his attempt at sounding menacing came out musical.

Marcus directed Celeste to a tiny, secluded cottage, where climbing roses coated the whitewashed siding, and pink and white blooms cascaded from the shingle roof to the diamond-pane windows. It even had a white picket fence wrapping the flower-filled front yard. I'd pictured Gus living in a rotting lean-to, most likely next to a stream that served as his drinking water, lavatory, and once-a-month bathwater. Or better yet, in a cave, where he slept piled atop his cerberi.

"Are you sure this is it?" I asked.

As if in response to my question, a chorus of howls emanated from behind the cottage, the harmony of three throats unmistakably a cerberus's. More howls joined the first only to be cut off abruptly at a sharp whistle.

"This is the place," Marcus said. He jumped down, and the tightening of his jaw was the only indication he gave that the movement hurt his back.

I wasn't half as graceful or prideful. My body had stiffened at every joint, and I groaned my way to the ground, clutching the side of the sled as I worked blood back into my feet and convinced my thighs to support me. Beneath my shirt, dried greenthread and lamb's ear leaves crunched, and brown and green dust sifted from my cuffs and untucked hem. I ran a hand through my hair, futilely attempting to comb out the snarls, and settled for tucking dirt-coated strawberry-blond chunks behind my ears. I started to pat the dust off my pants but froze when I heard Gus's voice.

"Damn idiot woman had that FPD fella twisted around her pinkie finger. Not that I blame him; she was a looker, but no piece of tail is worth risking your hide on Reaper's Ridge." His voice floated around the side of the house, and I straightened, expecting to see him saunter into sight. His next words were inaudible, but his cackle set my teeth on edge. When a few other men joined him, I realized Gus must be entertaining out back.

"I disagree," Marcus whispered. "You're exactly the kind of piece of tail that's worth risking Reaper's Ridge for."

I snorted and rolled my eyes.

Oliver hopped from the seat, using his wings to glide to a silent landing. Even full grown, he wouldn't reach half Celeste's height, but his short stature didn't preclude him from looking fierce when he bristled his orange ruff and stiffened every spike along his spine. Gus's house should have gone up in flames from the heat of his glare alone.

Celeste's indignation had nothing to do with Gus's insulting conversation and everything to do with having been witnessed in her debasing role as a pack animal by half the town. The moment we stopped, she yanked free of the rope and stalked away from the sled, tail lashing. I followed her on hobbling steps.

"Thank you, Celeste. It would have taken us days to reach here without your help," I said.

She trained her hard amethyst eyes on me, nodding fractionally. Twelve hours of almost nonstop running against the loose rope had chafed a raw line into the onyx and amethyst feathers across her chest, and I healed the wounds with her consent. Despite her stiff posture, exhaustion weighted her body. After I assured her we would be fine without her assistance, she flapped heavily toward the FPD base, her black and purple body disappearing against the darkening sky.

We left the sled and circled the house, guided by the ambient light of the rising moon and the flicker of flames around the corner. Oliver loped at my side, wings tight to his body but his expression baleful enough to remind me of the apparitional gargoyles inside the baetyl.

"So here's this city twit with a fool notion of taming the ridge with a bunch of dud gargoyles," Gus continued, oblivious to our approach. "All of them were frozen stiff, and you couldn't lift a pitcher of water with the boost they gave off, but that wasn't going to stop her."

"No one ever accused anyone out of Terra Haven of having two thoughts to rub together to keep warm," a different male voice chimed in.

"They ain't got any money sense, either, praise the gods," Gus said with a chuckle. "Between delivering them to the ridge and what I'll earn when I pick up their corpses, I'll be building a new kennel before winter. Bless those poor, dead idiots."

The rumble of masculine laughter swelled. I almost felt like joining in when we rounded the corner and Gus caught sight of us. He choked on an inhalation and clutched his chest through a wracking coughing fit, never taking his round eyes off us. Or rather, never taking his eyes off *me*.

Oliver glowed in the firelight like liquid flame reshaped into an enraged dragon, and he hissed at Gus with undisguised animosity. On my other side, Marcus loomed, looking every inch the FPD warrior and equally as irate as Oliver. Without taking another step, he filled the empty space of the tiny patio and seemed to crowd the three men sitting around a small terra-cotta fire pit. Next to him, I should have been invisible, but Gus stared at me with the fixated disbelief of a man seeing a ghost.

The two other men jerked straight in their chairs. Both rivaled Gus in age, though the years had been kinder to them. Unlike Gus, they sized up my companions first, and the larger fellow's hand fell away from the heavy dagger at his waist when he met Marcus's hard eyes.

"Friends of yours, Gus?" the skinnier man asked. He clamped a cigar between his teeth and leaned back in contrived nonchalance, his eyes flicking back and forth between Oliver and Marcus.

"We're just three corpses come back to collect our due," Marcus said. He spoke softly, which only tightened the tension in the other men.

Gus finally looked at Marcus, and his breathing calmed to a wheeze. Shaking his head, he grabbed a glass bottle near his foot and took a swig of its amber contents. "You've got nothing to collect here."

"We had a deal."

Gus's companions flinched at the ice in Marcus's tone, but Gus waved his words aside. "You said you'd return the sled *after* you went up Reaper's Ridge. Yet here you are—"

"Yes, here we are," I said, stepping forward to draw Gus's attention back to me. My movement played the firelight across the shimmery amethyst scars on the backs of my hands, and the skinny man's mouth dropped open, freeing his cigar to roll down his chest to his lap. He stared, unaware, for several seconds before leaping to his feet with a curse and patting down the smoldering front of his pants.

Gus's face had lost some color, but he continued gamely. "So you have some sense after all, girl. How far up Reaper's did you get before you turned tail?"

"To the top. I really don't know what all the fuss was about. After we dispersed the storms, it was a pleasant hike and a great view."

"Dispersed the storms," he scoffed, but his gaze shifted to look over my shoulder toward Reaper's Ridge.

Up until yesterday, even from this distance, the wild flares of firestorms and sporadic lightning would have been visible on a clear night like this. Tonight, only the faint outlines of the dark hills against the starry sky defined the mountains, Reaper's Ridge just one among many shadowy peaks.

"Well, I'll be . . ." said the heavyset man, standing and squinting in disbelief.

"That's impossible," Gus said.

"Maybe for people around here, but not for a girl from Terra Haven." I couldn't resist the taunt. "Now, I believe you owe us some money."

Gus glowered at me, and I could practically see the gears turning behind his cagey eyes. He stood, spat to the side, and clapped his stained brown cowboy hat to his head. "I'll need to inspect that sled. If it's damaged…"

Marcus arched a brow and escorted Gus to the sled. I remained near the fire, enjoying the warmth almost as much as the discomfort of the two men who couldn't decide if they should stare at my face or my scars.

"How?" the skinny one worked himself up to ask.

"Gargoyles. Never underestimate them."

They both turned disbelieving eyes on Oliver. He yawned, displaying sharp incisors, and flared his wings so the light danced across them. If the men weren't impressed, they were fools.

"Fine," Gus said as he returned with Marcus. "I'll give you your money back."

"You'll pay us the full amount you promised," Marcus said.

"Do I look like I have that kind of money lying around?" Gus gestured to his threadbare clothing.

"You'll find it. Otherwise, I'll have a word with the captain of the base, and you can kiss any future contracts with the FPD good-bye."

Gus sucked on his teeth and glared at Marcus. "Fine. Wait here." He spun and headed away from the house up a shallow rise toward a long, low barn.

"You have a tendency of running away," I said. "Why don't I keep you company so you don't lose your way?"

Gus shot me a nasty glance over his shoulder, but his eyes were a little too wide and ruined his glare. When Marcus gestured for Oliver to accompany me, the young gargoyle leapt to the edge of the fire pit and launched over the heads of the two men in a spectacular display of agility and intimidation. The men cursed and ducked, and the skinny one fell out of his chair. Smothering my laughter, I strode after

Gus, stretching my legs to catch up without running. For whatever reason, I made Gus nervous now, and I didn't want to ruin it by giggling.

The riot of barks set off by Oliver's landing confirmed the barn was actually a large-scale kennel, the kind where the individual cages were as large as horse stalls to fit the pony-size cerberi. The concussive *woofs* and higher-pitched baying rattled my brain in my skull once we were inside the enclosed confines of the barn, and I hunched against the deafening assault. Gus marched up the central aisle, mouthing inaudible curses but doing nothing to quiet the racket. Seeing my discomfort, Oliver loosed a sharp whistle and every cerberus in the building quieted between one breath and the next.

Gus spun and stared at me. I pretended not to notice.

"Thank you, Oliver."

"You're welcome," he said, oblivious to Gus's reaction as he loped along the cage fronts, touching noses with the cerberi as he passed.

Gus clicked his mouth shut and stuffed his hat tighter to his head. Heavy breathing sounds replaced the silence as dozens of panting muzzles pressed to the slatted fronts of the cages, all sniffing and straining to get closer to us. Fumes of dog breath did nothing for the already musty air, and I took shallow breaths, hoping Gus would be quick.

The wiry man stomped to the largest cage at the end of the barn, waiting until I was almost at his side before throwing open the door. Three enormous heads burst out of the enclosure, growling in unison, teeth chattering a soft warning. With a height that dwarfed the other cerberi, this one wouldn't have to stretch to crush my throat in any one of its immense jaws.

Gus checked my reaction, clearly expecting me to cower in fear. I crossed my arms and affected a bored expression, though if Oliver hadn't been beside me, his magical enhancement at the ready, I would have been shaking in my boots. Pretending I wasn't mentally preparing a dense quartz shield to protect Oliver and myself if the cerberus attacked, I raised an eyebrow at Gus in a fair imitation of exasperation.

"Your oversized dog isn't going to scare me, Gus. I survived Reaper's Ridge."

"So you say," he muttered. He barked a one-word command, and the enormous cerberus sat. Two heads continued to glower at me, but the third turned to lick a slimy trail from Gus's collarbone to his hat. Gus shoved past the head with a grunt, crossing the kennel to unearth a small box from a niche in the floor. The cerberus tracked him with one head, the other two locked on me.

"You don't believe me?" I asked, studying the back of my hands. In the soft overhead lights, the amethyst scars appeared to shift of their own accord. I flexed my fingers, remembering how right it had felt to use the baetyl's power to grow crystal from my thin bones. I hadn't admitted it to Marcus, or even to myself until that moment, but I found the scars beautiful.

The cerberus leaned a head close to sniff me, and I extended my hand, forgetting to be afraid. Moist nostrils pressed to the scars, and a soft *woof* escaped a different throat. When I met the cerberus's gaze, he whined and lay down, resting all three heads on the floor in front of him. Eyes unfocused, I stared at the cerberus and stretched my shoulders, missing my wings . . .

Gus turned around with a glare, but his steps faltered at whatever he saw in my expression. I blinked, coming fully back to the moment. The memory of the baetyl faded, and I stifled a yawn. This time my lack of trepidation was unfeigned when I reached over the subdued cerberus for Gus's wad of cash. Gus hesitated, then smacked the bundle into my palm. He started toward the door of the kennel, but I didn't move out of his way as I counted the bills.

"This is only as much as Marcus paid you. The deal was half again as much for returning the sled."

"It was in full working order when I gave it to you—"

"Which is exactly how we're returning it, but you're right; I didn't factor in how much Marcus should charge you for repairing it. He's an FPD fire elemental, and everyone knows they get a good salary, so if we estimate his hourly rate . . ."

"Now hang on, there, girl. That's not what I meant."

"But you have a point. So why don't you hand over the *full* sum you said you'd pay to get the sled back, plus half of the fee you charged me to take us to Reaper's Ridge—seeing as how you got us only halfway there—and we'll call it even."

Gus's jaw muscle worked as his gaze flicked between my bland expression and the scars on my hands; then he spun on a heel to dig through his stash of money again. Oliver undulated up to the cerberus and scratched him behind one of his ears. I stepped back when the three-headed dog tried to get his back foot up to help Oliver out.

When Gus caught sight of his formerly intimidating cerberus practically rolling belly up for my gargoyle, his mouth pinched so tight I thought he'd crack a tooth. He slapped another stack of bills into my hand, and I took my time counting them, watching Oliver out of the corner of my eye and trying not to smile.

When I was satisfied Gus hadn't stiffed us, I stuffed the bills into my back pocket, wincing when I hit bruised flesh, and signaled Oliver that it was time to leave. He reluctantly loped toward the exit.

"Useless mutt," Gus growled. The cerberus stood and licked Gus's face affectionately before he could close the kennel door. A chorus of whines and pants followed us out of the barn.

Marcus's gaze sought mine the moment we emerged from the barn, his thunderous scowl softening marginally at the sight of us. Gus's friends didn't seem to notice the change in him, and they fidgeted nervously as we approached.

"I might have to go check out the ridge—see if you're telling the truth about the storms being gone," Gus mused as we stepped back into the firelight.

"Go ahead. But to shut down those storms, the gargoyles and I had to set powerful protection wards. You won't get close to the top— or to those mine shafts, if that's what you're thinking."

Gus had the grace to look embarrassed that I'd seen through him so easily. "If *you* got up there, I don't think I'll have a problem," he grumbled.

"Knock yourself out trying," I said. Memory of the pulsing

migraine and menacing presence of the baetyl pursuing us stole the flippancy from my tone, making the words come out hard. I thought I'd ruined my exit, but Gus's troubled expression said otherwise.

We paused at the sled to collect our packs, and I handed the cash over to Marcus, expecting him to pocket it. Instead, he counted out what he'd paid Gus for the sled, then gave the rest of the money back to me. "You earned it."

I stuffed it into my bag with a soft sigh of relief. I would be able to pay rent and have some left over, maybe enough to replace the clothes I'd ruined on this trip.

I shouldered my bag and Marcus picked his up with one hand, letting it dangle rather than slinging it across his injured back. He reached his free hand out to me, and we twined our fingers together. Oliver squeezed between us, bumping our hands with his head. His jaw cracked in a tongue-lolling yawn, and he tilted against me. Marcus caught us both when I staggered under the gargoyle's weight.

"Do you mind if I fly ahead? I'm tired."

"Go for it. We'll be right behind you," I said.

He trundled a few steps forward, then flapped heavily into the air.

Marcus and I followed, walking hand in hand down the moonlit street, and I couldn't help thinking it would have been a lot more romantic if we both weren't injured and covered in dried sweat, pungent ointment, and half a mountain of dirt. I lifted my shirt and sniffed, grimacing. A bath couldn't come soon enough.

"Hang on." Marcus jerked to a halt, his expression comically troubled. "Did this trip count as a first date?"

I cocked my head, ruminating out loud. "We did stay overnight in a very exotic location. You even made me dinner. Yeah, I think that counts as a date."

"Well, crap. How can I possible top *that*?"

"You'll think of something." I stood on my tiptoes and kissed him, rejoicing in the realization that our adventures together were only just beginning.

LURED

A BONUS GARGOYLE GUARDIAN
CHRONICLES NOVELLA—IN PRINT FOR
THE FIRST TIME

ABOUT LURED

If something threatens a gargoyle's life, Mika's confident she can handle it. But can she save the day when it's Marcus who needs to be rescued?

AUTHOR'S NOTE

I hope you enjoyed the first three books of the Gargoyle Guardian Chronicles! As my way of saying thank you to all the fans who supported the series early on (and who requested more books in the world), I wrote Lured. *Like you, I wanted more time with Mika and Oliver.*

And I couldn't resist making Mika's life a little more difficult . . .

LURED

The cerberi took a sharp corner of the forested lane at a lope, whipping our cramped floating carriage around the bend behind them, and the centrifugal force wedged me against Marcus on the bench seat. I wriggled to straighten, but Marcus draped an arm around my shoulders and anchored me in place.

"I'm beginning to see the advantages of this tiny contraption," he said, a smile in his voice.

"Oh?" I shoved a clump of my strawberry-blond hair out of my eyes, only to have it whip back across my mouth.

Marcus shifted, his knees knocking against the driver's seat. His blue eyes skimmed down my face to rest on my lips. "It makes it easy to do this."

I read the heat in his gaze and arched my neck to meet him for a kiss, bracing one hand on his muscular thigh, the other against the red velvet armrest for balance. He snuggled me closer, and I melted against his broad chest.

A kaleidoscope of sunlight and shadows flickered across my closed eyelids, and I smiled against Marcus's firm lips, enchanted by the perfection of the moment.

In the driver's seat, Gus cleared his throat with a hoarse, phlegmy sound and spit over the side of the carriage, jolting me back to reality. Marcus deflected the splatter with a well-timed brush of air, but the moment was ruined. Sighing, I leaned back, not missing the laughter in Marcus's eyes. At least one of us found Gus's perpetual rudeness amusing.

After our triumphant return from Reaper's Ridge last night, I thought I'd seen the last of the grouchy cerberi sled runner, only to learn this morning when we prepared to leave that the stage coach wasn't due for another week and the nearest train station was a two-day hike. Resigned, we'd returned to Gus's kennels.

Gus and I shared one thing in common: our mutual dislike. He'd earned my scorn when he exploited my desperation to save the lives of seven sick gargoyles to make a profit. In return, I'd garnered his animosity by surviving the perils of Reaper's Ridge and returning to force him to repay me. In fact, I'd made a tidy profit off the old man.

In a blatant ploy to overcharge us and recoup some of his forfeited riches, Gus had pulled out his most expensive passenger carriage. Or maybe he'd been trying to discourage us with the fussy little box designed to carry two average-size people. If not for the lack of legroom, Marcus might have been comfortable alone on the plush velvet seat. With me beside him and our two bags stuffed on the floorboard beneath my feet, the elegant carriage turned into a mild torture device.

There hadn't been room left for the gargoyles. Fortunately, Celeste had decided to head back to Terra Haven earlier that morning. The enormous gryphon gargoyle had gotten us to safety, but she'd chafed at being away from her home. Flying, she could reach the city before nightfall, her route far more direct than ours. Oliver, my self-proclaimed companion, went wherever I did, but he'd been more than happy to fly above the carriage. Most of his young life had been spent in the city, and an aerial exploration of the countryside appealed to his adventurer's spirit.

I'd lost sight of his carnelian Chinese dragon body behind the thick canopy of pine and oaks, but I could still pinpoint his location with eerie accuracy. I had Reaper's Ridge—or more accurately, the baetyl—to thank for my newfound ability. I still wasn't sure if it would last or what to make of it, but for now it was comforting to be able to keep tabs on my adolescent companion when he was out of sight.

Another turn mashed me against Marcus, and my knees knocked together as I shifted to get pressure off my tailbone. With my feet propped on our bags, my heels almost as high as the bench seat, finding a stable position had proved futile. I probably would have been more comfortable sitting on Marcus's lap—and I might have been bold enough to suggest it if Gus hadn't been present.

"Quit yer jostling back there. It's giving me heartburn," Gus groused.

"Try being downwind of you," I shot back. Between the breath of four panting cerberi—all twelve of their muzzles open wide with strings of drool trailing from their lolling tongues—and Gus's own signature scent of cerberi kennel and stale cigar smoke, it was little wonder my nostrils had given up hours ago. I'd welcomed the reprieve.

Gus tugged the reins, weaving the cerberi down a straight stretch of the dirt road, driving obnoxiously wide around a few leafy weeds and snapping my head back and forth on my neck. I wedged my feet tighter against the bags, making sure I gave the back of the driver's seat a good kick.

Pretending to speak to Marcus, I said, "I never realized how hard it is to steer a sled in a straight line. All the drivers in Terra Haven make it look easy."

"Mika . . ." Marcus murmured in a halfhearted rebuke.

Gus's spine stiffened. "City carriages are cheap pieces of crap. This here is a Cadence 156. Only three hundred of them were ever made. I'm not scratching her up just to smooth out the ride for your pampered backside." He stroked a gnarled hand down the carriage's glossy black side.

I rolled my eyes. "Right. You wouldn't want to make your passengers comfortable."

"Not unless my passengers want to pay to have the Cadence

refinished."

"Nice try, Gus."

I crossed my arms over my chest and glared at the old man's knobby spine beneath his threadbare shirt. He peeked over his shoulder at me, then swerved around a grassy weed too short to touch the bottom of our elevated carriage. I jerked my arms apart to brace myself, not missing Gus's satisfied smile.

Marcus's chest vibrated against my left shoulder, and when I realized he was silently laughing at me, I transferred my glower to him. I couldn't hold on to my irritation, though. The wind tousled his thick dark hair and flattened his shirt against his sculpted chest, and when he flashed me The Smile—the one that made my stomach flip and heartbeat accelerate—my lips curled up involuntarily. Marcus and I had shared plenty of serious life-and-death experiences, but I was only just beginning to discover his affectionate, teasing side, and I really liked it. When he leaned in for another kiss, I met him halfway, anchored in his arms as the carriage canted through another sharp turn. A tiny hum of pleasure slid up my throat before I could suppress it.

"Do you hear that?" Gus asked.

Resolutely ignoring him, I deepened the kiss, sliding my tongue along Marcus's bottom lip. His hand drifted up the back of my neck into my hair, pulling me closer. I attempted to oblige, hampered by the cramped seat.

"It sounds . . . sweet," Gus said. "Do you hear it, Fed Man?" He reached back and thumped Marcus on the shoulder.

Marcus jerked back to scowl at Gus, and I hid my smug smile. Finally it wasn't just me the old man was irritating.

"This has got to sto—" Marcus cut himself off, cocking his head to listen. He shifted, releasing me to scrutinize our surroundings.

I straightened, drawing on the five elements and holding them ready, unsure what I was preparing for. Raw earth, air, water, fire, and wood hummed inside me, but I chafed at the limited amount. I peered through the leaves in Oliver's direction, trying to make him out through the foliage. I'd feel a lot safer with his enhancement.

Gus whistled a soft command and the cerberi slowed to a trot. Both men tensed, straining to hear. I held my breath, trying to pick up on any out-of-place sounds. Wind whispered through the oak leaves high above us and a few birds sang to each other. Beneath my feet, the bags shifted, and the seed crystals in my pack clacked together.

Marcus jabbed his hand over Gus's left shoulder. "There. I think it's coming from that direction."

"What is it?" I caught the faint garbled notes of a tone-deaf bird, but that hardly seemed cause for alarm.

"Shush," Marcus said. He leaned forward, his wide shoulders pushing me against the armrest.

"Is it dangerous?" I whispered. "Should we call Oliver—"

"Quit yappin', woman," Gus barked. "I lost it."

I spared a glare for the obnoxious man, then turned to Marcus, waiting for his response. He scanned the dense forest to the left of the road, ignoring me.

"There," Marcus said, pointing again in the direction of the bizarre bird noises.

Gus yanked the reins, and the cerberi pivoted to the left, crashing through the manzanita beside the road. The bush's spiny branches scratched against the underside of Gus's precious carriage, rattling the whole box, and I grabbed the door panel for balance.

"What's going on?" I demanded, searching Marcus's profile. A thick bramble slashed across my knuckles, and I jerked my hand inside the carriage with a yelp, ducking a second later to avoid a branch to the face. The warbling song grew louder, but if it was something dangerous, Marcus would have been reaching for the elements and his crossbow on the floorboard. Instead, he looked eager, almost excited.

I shook Marcus's arm, and he slapped my hand aside without looking at me.

"Hey, that hurt," I said, shocked.

"Quiet," he growled.

I cradled my stinging fingers to my chest. What had gotten into him?

"Faster," he ordered.

Gus nodded and whistled a new command. As one, the four cerberi surged into a gallop. Heedless of the damage inflicted on the Cadence, Gus steered the three-headed hounds straight for the bird sounds, avoiding trees but scraping the sides and bottom of the carriage as the cerberi plowed through small bushes.

Dumbfounded, I crouched in a tight ball and clung to the seat. Marcus held himself rigid in the jouncing carriage, head canted to listen for the strange song over the cerberi's racket, and I did my best not to touch him.

Without slowing her mad dash, the lead cerberus leapt a thick oak log and disappeared down a leaf-strewn slope. The next followed a step later, the towline between the cerberi arching into the air.

Oh no. I wedged the toes of my shoes into our bags and clutched the back of the driver's seat with both hands just as the last cerberus cleared the fallen tree. The carriage catapulted into the air. Helplessly, I launched free of the seat, then slammed back into place as we plunged down the hill. The cerberi surged up the opposite side of the shallow ravine, bounding over the rim so fast that the bottom of the carriage smacked the hill before the flotation spell bucked us back into the air, tossing me around like a doll.

Zigzagging around thick trunks, the racing cerberi turned the towline into a whip, with the carriage flicking back and forth at the end, out of control. For the first time, I was grateful for the slender width of the Cadence: Narrower than the three-headed dogs, the carriage fit anywhere the cerberi did—though not half as gracefully at these breakneck speeds. We ricocheted off a broad oak trunk, slammed into an outcrop of granite hard enough to crack the carriage's wood paneling, and scraped through a gauntlet of pines, leaving behind a waist-high strip of black paint. Marcus crowded me, preventing me from getting a solid seat, and every bounce levitated me. I clung to the driver's seat, heart hammering against my rib cage, fearing each collision would pitch me from the carriage.

"Slow down. You're going to get us killed!" I yelled, eyes watering when the next bounce snapped my teeth together and I bit the edge of my tongue.

Gus urged the cerberi even faster; he and Marcus were as oblivious to me as they were to the imminent destruction of the carriage. Both men stared with unnerving intensity in the direction of the strange song.

"Marcus, you're scaring me. What *is* it?"

Finally he looked at me, and the fury contorting his face stole my breath.

"Shut up," he snarled.

I fell back in the seat, then clawed for purchase when the carriage tipped to the right and Marcus's hip smacked into me, pushing me half out of the tiny box. Pine branches slashed my face, threatening to dislodge me, and I formed a hasty shield of woven strands of air. Without a boost from Oliver, I could barely hold enough air element to buffer my face, but it gave me the reprieve I needed to scramble back into the seat. When the carriage righted, Marcus crouched, hands braced on the driver's seat as if he were planning to spring off the front of the speeding carriage. He never once glanced my way, not to check if I was okay or to help me right myself inside the carriage.

The cerberi burst through the trees onto a gravelly beach at the edge of a tranquil lake, the serene setting as jarring to my panicked brain as the blinding sunlight glinting off the placid surface. With the cerberi's thunderous footsteps muffled by mud, the tone-deaf bird song swelled to fill the quiet.

I thought Gus would drive us straight into the water, but he tugged the reins, whistled a command, and the cerberi swerved to follow the curve of the lake. They didn't slow, not even as we approached a reed-choked tributary. I cowered behind Gus as the tall stalks whipped through the carriage, burying my face in the crook of an elbow to avoid the stinging lashes. My head cracked against Gus's elbow moments later when we slammed to a stop.

Scrambling free of the Cadence, I fell through a flurry of exploded cattail seeds, landing on my hands and knees on the rocky beach before sprinting up the hill. Spinning around, I grabbed as much magic as I could hold and prepared to defend myself. Against what, I wasn't sure. Something was wrong with Marcus. Something was probably wrong with Gus, too, but I didn't care about him.

Neither man looked in my direction. They both stared out at the lake with vapid expressions of adoration.

A siren undulated in the water less than fifteen feet from the shoreline, her gilled neck fluttering in a nonstop, deadly melody. The notes of her song slurred against my eardrums, harsh and garbled, like a flute played out of tune underwater, but whatever the men heard held them entranced.

Marcus tumbled from the carriage, landing on all fours more clumsily than I had. In disjointed increments, he straightened to his full height, never once removing his eyes from the siren. Gus collapsed to his knees when he landed, falling again before managing a stiff, wide-legged stance. In eerie synchronization, Marcus and Gus took a step, arms rigid at their sides, feet landing flat and clumsy.

I'd seen Marcus move with a dancer's grace after a day of battle, much less after a few hours in a cramped carriage. Yet now, every stride looked forced, his movements stiff and awkward, as if he'd never used his legs before.

Goose bumps rushed over my skin when I realized the truth: It wasn't Marcus and Gus forgetting how to walk; it was the siren controlling them.

Shambling like animated corpses, they lurched three steps toward the lake before I shook myself out of my horrified trance. An honest-to-goodness siren floated less than ten feet offshore. If we were still back in the forest, I might have stood a chance of breaking her spell on the men; now that she was in their sights, it would be impossible.

But I wouldn't let that stop me from trying.

Heart in my throat, I sprinted around the cerberi, wishing I knew a few of Gus's whistle commands. The three-headed dogs had collapsed onto their bellies, tongues lolling from their mouths, sides heaving. A few heads watched the siren and a few watched Gus, but none looked ready to jump to Gus's aid—or mine.

I planted myself in Marcus's path, careful not to turn my back to the siren. A couple dozen feet separated me from the deadly enchantress, half of them water, putting me far too close to her for my comfort. She tracked me with flat gray-black fish eyes set too wide on her humanoid face. Fleshy lips parted beneath two slit holes that served as her nose, revealing a mouthful of needlelike teeth. She hissed at me, projecting the sound from her mouth without interrupting the garbled song emitting from her gills. Other than the grayish green tint of her rubbery skin and the webbing between her fingers, the portion of her visible above the water vaguely resembled a petite woman, with a trim waist, tiny breasts, severely sloped shoulders, and yellow-brown slimy hair. Water churned around her waist as she used her tail to hold herself upright, and from the glimpses I caught in the frothy water, there was nothing small about her eel-like bottom half.

"Wake up, Velasquez," I barked, hoping that by using Marcus's last name, I'd sound like a captain of a Federal Pentagon Defense squad. As an FPD warrior, Marcus was used to taking orders, but it still surprised me when he jerked to a halt. His dark blue eyes remained locked on the siren, his vapid smile out of place on the hard planes of his face. Gus froze beside him, proving Marcus hadn't heard me; the siren had stopped him. I waved a hand in front of his face, careful to stay out of his reach. As much as I wanted to shake him, I was leery of even touching him, flashing back to his furious expression in the carriage. As long as he was under the siren's spell, especially now that his body was in her control, I couldn't trust him not to use his considerable size against me.

"Human female, take the furry hydras and go." The voice burbled from the siren's mouth a few decibels louder than her song and far more melodious to my ears.

I shifted, keeping Marcus in my periphery and backing farther out of his reach. *Furry hydras?* Ah, the cerberi.

"Release the men first," I said.

"They are not yours. A man in true love cannot be spelled. You have no claim here."

I sized her up, acutely aware that I'd never be able to best her in a direct elemental confrontation. It was a safe assumption that her command of water element outstripped mine, and even though my elemental strength lay in earth, a natural dam to water, the levels I could wield wouldn't be much defense if she attacked. However, she hadn't pulled Marcus and Gus into the water yet. Maybe I had a chance of talking her out of this before it escalated to violence.

"These *are* my men. Marcus belongs to me." I tried to project more confidence than I felt. Marcus and I had survived a few harrowing situations together and shared a few kisses. *Love* wasn't a word that had been mentioned yet, but the potential existed.

I squinted at Gus. Adoration softened the leathery wrinkles of his face, and a bit of drool glistened in the corner of his upturned mouth. He'd lost his cowboy hat somewhere during our wild rush through the forest, and his greasy gray hair matted to his scalp. Standing unnaturally straight, he looked scrawnier than ever. If our positions were reversed, I doubted Gus would have wasted time before driving off and leaving me to die. Gritting my teeth, I forced myself to add, "That one belongs to me, too."

"You lie. They are *mine!*"

"Mika!" Oliver plummeted out of the sky, the gargoyle's orange-red carnelian body as bright in the midday sun as a falling comet. He landed at the water's edge, and the siren shied back, her song faltering.

Marcus blinked, his foolish smile flattening to a familiar line and the muscles of his wide jaw tightening.

"That's it. Fight her magic, Marcus," I urged.

Oliver's enhancement opened a well of elemental magic inside me, and I grabbed for every ounce I could hold. Alone, I hadn't been a match for the siren, but maybe paired with Oliver I stood a chance.

"Is that a siren?" Oliver asked. His glowing orange eyes were as wide as saucers as he stared across the water. "A lightning siren?"

"A *what*?" I whirled to face the siren.

A crackle of electricity slithered up her body and balled in her hand.

I stared at the refined form of fire, blood draining from my head. Facing off against a merwoman able to sing men to their deaths wasn't enough; now she had to be a powerful fire elemental, too?

"This would be a really great time to snap out of it, Marcus," I said, using a sheet of air to smack him in the face since I couldn't risk stepping close enough to slap him. He blinked and his fingers twitched; then the siren's discordant song swelled, and his eyes glazed over again. I backed up when Marcus and Gus lurched forward in unison. In a few more steps, they'd be in the water. Everything I'd ever heard about sirens claimed they took great delight in drowning men, and they needed only an inch or two of water to accomplish their goal. I had to act fast, but what was I supposed to do?

A second ribbon of blue-white power rippled up the siren's body, joining the crackling magic already in her palm.

"Mika . . ." Oliver said.

"I see it."

The siren flattened her hand on the surface of the water, loosing the writhing ball of electricity. It speared across the lake straight for me.

"Get back!" I shouted, stumbling backward. Oliver levitated on a hasty downdraft, clearing the damp soil seconds before the electricity crackled beneath him. With no time to dodge, I shoved earth element into the ground and yanked up a dense knee-high barrier of bedrock.

The lightning never reached me; it died at the rim of the damp shoreline a half dozen feet from my pathetic wall.

Oliver's truncated launch forced him to touch down moments later, but he sprang back into the air, not setting down again until he'd flapped to my side. I unfolded from where I crouched behind my barrier, disbelieving my luck. Her reach didn't extend beyond the water. Oliver and I were safe—but Marcus wasn't.

The siren turned her flat eyes on the men, gills fluttering with her eerie song. I watched helplessly as Marcus approached the water, one disjointed step after the next.

"What wrong with them?" Oliver asked.

"They're under the siren's spell, and they're going to die if we don't break it."

"Can you do that?"

"I might not need to," I said, an idea forming. "If they can't hear the song, it can't control them."

Straining for every particle of air element I could hold, I braided dense bands into half spheres and dropped them over the men's heads, tying the soundproof helmets in place under their chins with knotted air. Short of burying their heads in the sandy bank, it was the best I could do.

Marcus and Gus halted stiffly a few feet from the water line. Neither man turned, and with their backs to me, I couldn't see their expressions, but a flutter of hope stirred in my chest when Marcus clenched his fists.

The siren smiled, fleshy lips stretching toward her flat ears. The notes of her song turned sharp, drilling into my eardrums. I clapped my hands over my ears, adding muffling air magic and burrowing it into my ear canals to dampen the racket. Nothing helped. The cerberi sat back on their haunches, lifted their numerous heads, and howled warbling accompaniment at full volume. Their deep voices should have drowned out the siren's song, but her song penetrated through their deafening cacophony as easily as through my magic.

Sharp spears of earth burst from Gus, shredding the soundproof barrier around his head, then Marcus's. The backlash of my broken magic slapped against my brain, and I reeled in place, vision blackening. Oliver braced me with a wing, supporting me until I regained my balance.

The siren's song deepened again, no longer piercing my eardrums. Behind us, the cerberi's howls subsided into growls. They were all on their feet now, heads swiveling to assess for danger, hackles raised. The three-headed dogs were the least of my concerns, though. I stared at Marcus's back, fresh dread curdling in my stomach.

"Why did Gus do that?" Oliver asked.

"The siren made him." My fingers shook as I pushed my hair out of my face. If she could control the men's magic, she could use Marcus to kill us both. Even aided by Oliver, I didn't have the strength or skills to defend against an FPD fire elemental's attack—especially not if he was backed by Gus, a strong air elemental in his own right.

I needed to even the odds. If I couldn't break both men free from the spell at the same time, maybe I could free just one of them. With either man on my side, we'd stand a much better chance of all of us leaving here alive. I didn't hesitate in my choice, either. Bitterly acknowledging that my decision had less to do with my affection for Marcus and more to do with my fear of what he could do to me under the siren's control, I focused on saving him first.

"You are too weak, human female," the siren hissed. "Give up and leave already."

As I gathered elements for another attempt to free Marcus, Gus rocked around to face me. I changed tactics, reaching earth element into the ground, prepared to mound another dirt wall to hide behind, but the old man continued to turn. He took a few pitched steps toward the cerberi before stumbling to a halt. Using quick snaps of air, he flicked open the buckles holding the cerberi to the towline. Freed, they approached Gus on tentative feet, heads swinging between the siren and their master.

"Gus! How did you free yourself?" Oliver loped toward the cerberi handler.

"Oliver, wait! I don't think he's—"

Oliver jerked short when Gus pursed his lips and released a series of whistles. The cerberi milled in confusion, bunching closer to Gus. A furrow appeared between his brows and he whistled again, lifting a hand to point at me.

Twelve canine heads swiveled in my direction. Twelve thick throats growled, teeth chattering like bone castanets. The hairs on my arms stood on end and a spurt of terror weakened my knees as they surged toward me, malice glistening in their intelligent eyes.

Oliver leapt into their path, wings flared wide, as if his sinuous body and delicate stone feathers could derail four charging horse-size cerberi.

"Oliver! *Move!*" I threw a wall of fire between my gargoyle and the cerberi. The huge three-headed dogs shied back from the heat, pivoting to circle around the edges of the flames. They bayed in frustration when I spread the fire into a long V, pinning them in, but it was a temporary solution, and one that strained the limits of my magic.

Heedless to my orders, Oliver held his position, clearly determined to protect me.

I flung myself into motion, racing toward him. It'd be easier to ring *us* in fire than the cerberi, and once we were safe, I could figure out what to do to help Marcus.

Oliver pursed his lips and whistled short, quick notes. The milling cerberi stilled, heads cocked as they listened. At another distinctive whistle, all four lay down, heads flopping onto the ground in front of them, eyes locked on Oliver through the flickering flames.

"You can drop the fire," Oliver said when I reached his side.

Warily, I dissipated the burning wall from the outside edges inward, leaving us behind its protection as I monitored the cerberi's reactions. The cerberus closest to us huffed three harmonious sighs and relaxed.

"I'd forgotten you could do that," I said.

Oliver grinned. "I wasn't sure I could."

I expected the siren to try to retake control of the cerberi through Gus, but his lips remained slack, and he stared vacantly toward the lake. Oddly, his eyebrows were furrowed. Was he upset the cerberi hadn't mauled me, or was he trying to fight the siren's spell?

Knowing Gus, he probably had indigestion.

The sounds of splashing water momentarily drowned out the siren's perpetual song, and the reprieve heightened my awareness of a throbbing in my temples. Keeping a suspicious eye on the docile cerberi, I checked the lake. Frothy water churned around the siren's waist and electricity crackled up her body.

"Why won't you leave, puny human?" Her face contorted with rage as she slapped her palms onto the surface of the lake, shooting rapid-fire bursts of blue-white lightning to the shore, where they died at the water's edge. If they'd continued their trajectory across dry land, Oliver and I would have been incinerated.

"Is she throwing a fit?" Oliver asked, speaking from the side of his mouth.

"It looks that way." It might have been comical, if not for her deadly potential. Marcus stood less than two feet from the waterline, and with the siren's thrashing, each wave lapped closer to his boots. I needed to get him out of there.

Before I could take a step, the siren calmed, her song sharpened, and Marcus moved. His upper body twisted toward me first, and then his legs followed. I swallowed hard. No one seemed to be behind his eyes; no recognition crossed his face.

"Marcus wouldn't . . ." Oliver began, trailing off when Marcus lifted an arm, fingers cupped. A yellow flame danced in his palm, growing to a white-hot ball of fire twice the size of his fist.

"Marcus wouldn't, but she would," I said.

In a chilling echo of the siren, Marcus pointed his arm at the cerberi, fingers splayed flat against an unseen surface, and the fireball exploded from his fingertips. Lacking the time to raise a wall of earth, I tossed a cloud of topsoil into the air and formed a clumsy ward of water magic around it. The molten ball ate through my hasty barrier, exiting the other side as an intense blast of hot air that rocked me back on my heels. Charred dust sifted like ash to the ground. When I reached for more magic, it fed along blistered mental pathways.

Ow.

The cerberi leapt to their feet, growling in agitation. Staring into Marcus's empty eyes, I felt like joining them.

"Wake up, Marcus. Come on, fight back."

His extended arm swung to point at me, fire kindling in his palm. This theatrical buildup of magic wasn't something Marcus would have ever done or needed to do; he could have created a fireball twice my height in the amount of time it took for the spinning orange flame to grow as large as my head. But it was exactly what the siren had done with electricity. Maybe she didn't have as much power or grasp of the elements as I thought.

This time when Marcus released the fireball, I was ready. Rather than trying to stop the powerful blast of magic, I deflected it with a solid quartz-tuned earth shield. The flames bounced off my elemental barricade and shot skyward, dispersing harmlessly into the atmosphere, but the effort staggered me.

Marcus—no, the *siren*—didn't wait for me to recover. She had raised Marcus's other arm, kindling another fireball while I'd been distracted with the first. A smaller but no less deadly orange ball speared toward the cerberi and Oliver. I formed a hasty shield in its path, and the flames caromed off it into the ground, scorching the earth inches in front of the closest cerberus. The cerberi started barking in earnest. Just as their deafening howls hadn't drowned out the siren's song, neither did their clamorous furor.

"Oliver, get the cerberi out of here. That way," I ordered, pointing. Bunched together, we made an easy target for the siren, so I sprinted in the opposite direction.

Oliver launched into the air with a trill and a complicated whistle. Baying, the cerberi spun in circles beneath him, then tore up the shore after the flying gargoyle.

I dove behind the carriage, using precious seconds to deactivate the flotation spell. The battered carriage crashed to the ground, and I dropped down with it, deflecting the next fiery attack from relative safety. Peeking over the rim of the carriage, I checked the siren. She was focused on the cerberi, and Marcus blasted another ball of flames in their direction. Oliver banked, blocking the fire with his stone wing, then floundered back into the air.

I sprang to my feet, waving my arms to get the siren's attention.

"Stop it!" I yelled. "They're leaving. Isn't that what you wanted? Now give me my men back!"

The siren hissed, and Marcus's next fireball barreled toward me, this one aimed for my head. I flattened against the ground, shielding my face from the heat of the fire as it passed over me. It burrowed into the dry shore farther up the sloped bank. Staring at the long scorch mark, I squelched a whimper. The siren was learning Marcus's strength. I wouldn't be able to defend against his attacks much longer.

"Marcus, this isn't you!" I shouted, wriggling onto the balls of my feet and peering over the edge of the carriage. "You're a Federal Pentagon Defense warrior. You protect people. You protect *me*. I wouldn't have survived Reaper's Ridge without you."

From the corner of my eye, I saw the cerberi and Oliver plunge into the forest and disappear into the dense shadows, but I didn't look away from Marcus.

His eyes shifted and my breath caught when he looked right at me. Holding my breath, I straightened, hoping that seeing me standing vulnerable before him would help him fight the siren's control. His deep blue eyes locked on my face, but his arms remained outstretched, and fresh fire kindled beneath his palms. Remembering the siren's claim that men who were in love couldn't be spelled, I used my last weapon.

"Marcus Velasquez, I love you." Blood thundered against my eardrums. I didn't know if it was strictly true, but I wasn't going to mince words when our lives were on the line. Just as boldly, I declared, "And you love me. I know you can fight through this. You won't hurt me."

Marcus released another fireball, this one moving so slowly I reached out with water and earth and extinguished it in flight. His arms flexed, dipping toward the ground, and a heavy scowl darkened his features—Marcus was fighting the siren's compulsion.

His next fireball fell well short of the carriage, but my grin faded when the siren undulated toward the shore. Fists clenched and gills fluttering, her song swelled in volume to be heard over the thrashing of her tail. Sweat beaded on Marcus's forehead and his fingers twitched; then his eyes glazed over and two fireballs formed instantaneously in his palms. Rapid-fire, he flung them at me.

Cursing, I dropped behind my shelter and wove a thick elemental shield around the carriage. It withstood the impact of five fireballs before it shattered and the carriage burst into flames.

"Crap!" I shoved earth element into the soil and pulled a wall of dirt over the flames, extinguishing them and half burying the carriage. Our bags slammed into the damaged door beside me and snapped it in half, spilling the packs onto my lap with a shovelful of dirt. The ground shook as I yanked even more soil against the far side of the carriage to create a makeshift bunker. Marcus's attack never let up, and each strike against the dirt-enshrouded carriage rattled my eyes in their sockets and made my collection of seed crystals clatter together.

"Incoming!" Oliver shouted. He burst from the trees and careened across the beach, diving and ducking through a volley of fire. Swinging wide and low, he angled toward my hideout, banking briefly before tucking his wings and dropping the last few inches to the ground. His feet furrowed deep into the soil as he hurtled toward me, and I ducked behind my arm to shield my eyes from flying debris. Oliver slammed into the carriage, splintering the side panel and raining dirt down on us both.

Coughing, I tugged the neck of my shirt over my nose as the billowing dust settled in a fine grit over us both.

"Now what?" he panted.

We ducked as a flurry of fireballs rattled the blockade.

"We can't keep hiding here," I said, yanking my shirt back into place.

As if to emphasize the point, a sizzle of fire arched inches above our heads before exploding against the ground behind us, blasting a small crater into the rocky beach. Oliver flared his wings protectively over our heads, tenting us in carnelian. I curled into a tight ball, chin tucked to my knees, nose to nose with Oliver, and he cocooned his wings around us.

"Thank you," I said. Sealed inside his protective embrace, I took my first full breath since Gus had launched us into the forest.

Marcus's assault against the barricade continued, muted but no less deadly. For now, my defenses were holding, but any minute the siren would think of something worse she could make Marcus throw at me. In the meantime, we were stuck and getting no closer to helping either of the men escape.

"We need to break the siren's spell," I said.

"How?" Oliver's breath fanned across my face, its familiar quartz scent grounding me.

"I don't know."

I couldn't talk Marcus out of her spell, not when she could simply sing louder and drown me out. The elements couldn't be made dense enough to block her magical song, so I couldn't deafen the men. Thanks to the cerberi, I knew that creating an even louder noise wouldn't work either. Nor could I drag the men away against their will, especially not with the siren turning them against me.

I'd already ruled out attacking the siren directly. My strengths lay in healing gargoyles and working with quartz. I didn't have the magic skills necessary to scare the siren away, and even if I did, with her controlling Gus and Marcus, I wouldn't survive a three-against-one attack.

I toyed with the idea of asking Oliver to command the cerberi to attack the siren while I distracted her, but I closed my mouth before the first word escaped. Sending the cerberi into the lake would only get them electrocuted.

What I really needed was Marcus fighting alongside me.

I rubbed my temples. The dome of Oliver's wings muted the strident notes of the siren's song and distorted the warble until it was unrecognizable. If only the men could—

I jerked straight, banging my head on Oliver's wings. Wincing, I scrunched back around my knees and gave the gargoyle an awkward hug.

"Oliver! You're brilliant!"

"I am?"

"Listen. If the men heard the siren muffled like this, they wouldn't be enthralled. Her magic is in her song, but if we can distort it, we'll disrupt her power."

Oliver grinned, prancing in place. "I'm brilliant! All I have to do is wrap my wings around Marcus and . . ." Smile fading, his chin drooped to rest on my knees. "How am I going to do that?"

"You're not. We're going to use seed crystals."

"You're going to put quartz domes over their heads?"

I wormed my hand into my bag, which was pressed against me, and measured the volume of seed crystals by touch. "I don't think that would work." I didn't have enough; besides, if the siren used the men against each other, domes would make fragile targets. "It'll have to be smaller and sturdier, something that fits just over their ears."

Heat radiated through Oliver's wings as another fireball blasted far too close overhead, and dirt sprayed against our ankles from the impact of the projectile against the nearby ground. Sweat plastered my shirt to my back. Each fireball was landing closer, and the still air inside Oliver's wings was heating like an oven. We were running out of time.

I tipped my bag over, and Oliver and I pawed aside my clothes, revealing a pile of marble-size flawless clear crystals. Wrapping three crystals in air to lift them off the ground, I tuned earth element to quartz and fed the elemental magic through the seeds. With speed born from years of practice, I fused the crystals together, then flattened them into a sheet before curving the edges to form a small bowl. Typically I created fluid shapes out of quartz—elegant, lifelike figurines of gargoyles and smooth jewelry designed to feel as soft as liquid. Forcing crimps and kinks into the quartz went against my instincts, but to make the greatest distortions, I needed hard angles and sharp edges. When I finished, the quartz resembled crumpled paper more than stone.

"Lower a wing. I want to test this." I cupped the quartz around one ear and plugged the other with a finger.

Oliver opened his wings and the siren's song hit the thick, crimped quartz, distorting to a dissonant racket against my eardrum.

"That's it," I said.

Oliver tightened his wings around us again and I created another earpiece, working fast in the hot confines. If they hadn't been so cumbersome, I would have crafted all four while in the shelter of Oliver's wings, but I needed to maximize my maneuverability if I planned to survive facing off against Marcus without the bunker between us. It'd be a lot harder to react while juggling four earpieces, so I settled for filling my pockets with extra seed crystals.

"We'll rescue Marcus first," I said. Before he burned us both to cinders.

"How? He's not going to let us get close."

"He was fighting the siren earlier. If we can distract her, he should be able to resist her long enough for me to attach these to his ears."

"I could throw things at her."

I opened my mouth to dismiss the idea, then changed my mind. "That might work. As long as you don't get too close. And don't touch the water." Oliver looked like solid stone, but he was so much more, and I feared the siren's jolts of electricity would be just as deadly for a gargoyle as a human.

"I'll be careful. Good luck."

The acid in my stomach sloshed. "You too."

Wishing I had better options—or *any* other option—I cradled the crumpled quartz to my stomach with one arm, fisted loose pebbles in the other, and gave Oliver a nod. He dug all four feet into the dirt for fistfuls of ammunition, then launched straight up. I rolled to the right, avoiding a face full of dirt that rained from his claws. When I sprang to my feet, I held a shield of water and earth between me and Marcus.

He stood in the same stiff, imposing stance as before, arms raised and muscles tense as if he were holding back an invisible force. Fire kindled and shot from his palms almost nonstop, making his hands look perpetually wreathed in flames—and proving the siren was getting a better grasp of his skills and how to utilize them. His left hand shifted, tracking my movement independent of his eyes, and fireballs shot from his palm straight for my chest. The first slammed into my shield before I got my feet beneath me, blasting it apart. The backlash of my shattered magic lanced agony through my skull, and I barely formed a second shield before the next fireball destroyed it. Half blind with pain, I sprinted in an erratic zigzag to evade his attacks.

Oliver swept overhead, raining fist-size rocks upon the siren. She shrieked, her song faltering. With a deft twist of her tail, she jetti-soned a spout of electricity-sparking water in Oliver's direction, and his wings blurred as he dodged backward, narrowly avoiding being shocked.

Marcus's next fireball went wide; the one after fell to the ground near his feet. A heavy scowl erased his vapid expression and he strained to lower his arms. I darted forward, but the siren saw me and ratcheted up the volume of her song. Marcus locked his eyes on me, and his jaw bunched with his internal struggle, but fresh flames danced on his fingers.

Suddenly he froze and Gus shifted in my periphery. Massive curls of air element spun from the cerberus handler, pushing waves of air across the shore and knocking Oliver sideways as he skimmed the ground for more ammunition. The gargoyle tumbled feet over wings along the rocky shoreline, trilling in alarm.

With an angry cry, I sprinted around Marcus and flung my fistful of pebbles at the siren. Most fell well short, but a few hit her torso. The tenor of her warbling song turned sharp, Gus's body went limp, and from three feet away, I watched Marcus's eyes go vacant.

"Marcus! It's me!"

A huge, fully formed fireball burst from his palm, and I dove to the side, rolling to keep my momentum. Pain blossomed along my spine as the fire licked across my back. I sprang to my feet with too little space between us and threw one quartz cup at Marcus's head, catching it with a weave of air as I flattened to the ground to avoid another blast.

I jumped back to my feet close enough to see flecks of black in Marcus's empty blue eyes, almost close enough for him to touch. He jerked his hand in my direction, and I wrapped his arm in a thick shield of water element, drawing on every remaining drop of my gargoyle-enhanced magic. When the next fiery missile launched from his palm, it extinguished in the sparse inches between us.

"Come on, Marcus. Fight her." Using the weave of air, I slammed the quartz cup over his ear with more precision than gentleness.

Marcus stilled and his eyes shifted again to find me. His fingers fisted and his elbow bent, then straightened. The siren shrieked, her song burrowing into my brain, and Marcus shook his head, grabbing for the distortion cup. With a pinch of quartz-tuned earth, I crimped the crystal against his ear tight enough to draw blood.

Oliver darted overhead, pelting the siren with rocks, flying far too low. I wanted to watch him, to help him, but I couldn't afford to waste the opportunity. Quelling my trepidation, I slid under Marcus's stiff arms and clapped the second quartz cup to his left ear, pinching it in place so firmly that I feared I'd pierced his upper lobe.

I backed up, removing the shield from Marcus's arm and reshaping it to hold between us.

He blinked, dark blue eyes assessing his surroundings with habitual vigilance, and my knees weakened in relief. Frowning, he shook his head, hands tentatively rising to touch my makeshift crystal muffs.

Oliver blasted toward the tree line with an exultant shout, chased by an arc of electrically charged water that splashed down close enough to raise all the hairs on my body. Marcus spun, not quite facing the lake and the siren. However, the complicated five-element shield he formed sat solidly between us and the shrieking merwoman.

"We need to get back," I said, grabbing Marcus's hand.

He shook me off, his shield unraveling. "Get to safety, Mika. Run," he growled through gritted teeth. His feet twisted toward the lake, then his torso, the motions unnatural and out of his control. He fought to keep his eyes off the siren.

"I'm not leaving without you."

The earpieces were working, at least partially. Using pincers of earth element, I reshaped the crumpled quartz cups over his ears to even more extreme angles, pinching the bottom of both into his earlobes until they drew blood. With exquisite care, I pushed a tunnel of quartz into each ear canal.

Marcus jerked backward so fast he clipped my chin with his elbow, then caught me as I started to fall, tipping me over his shoulder as if I were weightless. I clawed handholds into his shirt, torn between clinging to him in case he tried to throw me into the water and fighting to escape in case he walked in while still holding me.

"Marcus! Are you okay?" I braced my knees on his chest, ready to kick and claw my way free, knowing that doing so would leave us both injured.

"What?" he asked.

My heart lifted on a surge of hope.

"Put me down," I yelled, twisting to direct my voice up his back toward his ears.

He tightened his hold on me, spun around, and ran. His shoulder punched into my rib cage, each stride a bruising jab, but when I caught sight of the siren, I forgot all about the pain.

Her long gray-green tail smacked against the surface of the lake again and again, propelling a series of building waves toward the shore, each crest dancing with the siren's blue-white power. The first crashed into the dirt inches behind Marcus's heels, and the crackle of electricity popped against the soil, arching to pierce Marcus's boot. He jumped, and I lost my handholds, flopping helplessly against him as he sprinted up the beach.

Abruptly he planted his feet, lifting me from his shoulder and dropping me to my hands and knees so fast my teeth clicked together.

"Stay down!" he barked.

Gus stood a few feet in front of us in the same rigid pose Marcus had exhibited, arms splayed in front of him, massive bands of air generating a focused, hurricane-strength windstorm. Marcus enveloped us in a shield of earth just as Gus released his magic. A gigantic dirt storm spun from the old man and engulfed us. If not for Marcus, I would have been tossed down the beach the same way Oliver had been; instead, the dust and wind parted around us, leaving us in a calm bubble.

"Link?" I shouted, hoping Marcus could hear me through the quartz distortion cups. If we combined our magic, Marcus would be able to use all the power I held, too.

"Oliver, boost me!" he roared.

The gargoyle swooped behind Gus, clutching egg-size rocks in his four feet. He didn't look our way, but he must have complied because Marcus's earth shield began to advance on Gus, pressing forward until it smothered the old man's magic.

Breathless, I tracked Oliver as he pelted the siren with stones while dodging spouts of electrically charged water, his sinuous body twisting and spinning, narrowly avoiding her attacks.

"Do you have more?" Marcus shouted, grabbing my bicep with one hand and pointing to his ear with the other.

I tore my gaze from Oliver and shoved my free hand into my pocket, coming out with seed crystals.

"Let's go." He hoisted me to my feet, never letting go of my bicep as we ran through the settling dust to Gus.

Damn, it was good to have him back on my side.

Marcus trapped Gus in thick bands of air, pinning the scrawny man's arms to his sides. Eerily, Gus's arms struggled and he pitted his magic against Marcus's in a violent, silent fight, but his face remained vacuously serene. I made quick work of another quartz distortion cup and slapped it to Gus's ear, pinched it in place with more care than I'd been able to use on Marcus, and delicately tunneled a piece of the quartz into Gus's ear canal.

He blinked faded brown eyes, focusing on Marcus before his gaze slid to the lake and the siren who writhed near the shore, lightning crackling around her fingertips. His struggles slackened but didn't let up.

I yanked more seed crystals from my pockets and spun quartz-tuned earth through them, my alterations practiced and efficient. When I pinched the crumpled cup onto Gus's other ear, his whole body jerked in Marcus's bonds. His panicked gaze darted around the beach even as he released an ear-piercing whistle.

Cerberi bounded out of the forest and swarmed us, knocking me into Gus in their enthusiasm to get closer to him. I clutched the old man when he would have fallen, bruising myself on his pointy elbows, and released him as soon as Marcus dropped the bands of air keeping him immobile.

Ducking out of slobbering range, I turned warily to face the siren. She snarled and slapped her hands to the water, sending jolts of electricity out into the lake. Her song soared to deafening heights, and I squeezed my hands to my ears.

Oliver landed nearby, sides heaving, tongue lolling from his mouth.

"What now?" he shouted.

I glanced to Marcus. If it were up to me, we'd chase her back beneath the water with a few extra-hot fireballs.

Marcus didn't respond, his gaze on the lake. Alarmed that he might be falling back under the siren's spell, I pinched his arm. He closed his hand softly over mine.

"Look," he said.

I followed his line of sight, heart sinking when I spotted the ripples of something large moving beneath the surface, headed straight for the siren. Either she'd called for backup or all her tantrum antics had caught the attention of a larger predator. Either way, I didn't want to stick around to find out.

"We need to go. Now!" I shouted.

"Gather up," Marcus bellowed over me. He propelled me sideways, reaching around me to yank on Gus's sleeve to get his attention. Gus jerked his hands from the crystals around his ears and looked out to the lake, then whistled three different notes. The cerberi went on point, shoving in front of us, all twelve heads focused on the water. Oliver loped to Marcus's left side, rearing up on his hind legs to peer over the cerberi.

A new siren burst from the water, dwarfing our attacker. She dwarfed Marcus, too, and that was only the human portion we could see above the water. Streams of water cascaded from her slimy yellow-brown hair and electricity crackled in her gray-green webbed hands. Beneath the water, an eel tail as thick as a tree trunk seethed, massive coils twisting above the surface to wrap protectively around the smaller siren.

She sang a song of fury and vengeance, and it hit my eardrums like liquid sunshine, sliding into my body and sapping the energy from my limbs. I leaned forward, straining toward the music, and bumped against the hindquarters of a cerberus. One of its three heads whipped around to growl at me, the sound sweeping a chill down my body and breaking the siren's trance. On the other side of Marcus, Oliver shook his head and dropped to all fours.

"She almost enchanted me." I shared a frightened look with Oliver.

"Me too," he said.

I checked Marcus and Gus, but both men studied the enormous siren warily, clearly not under her thrall. Unwillingly, my gaze drifted back toward the water, and I slapped my cheeks to distract myself.

"Oliver, I need you." My voice trembled. Sirens were supposedly able to spell only men, but her song beckoned me, urging me to look at her again, pulling me toward the water.

"Should I throw more rocks?" Oliver asked, his voice small.

I shook my head and shuffled around Marcus to touch the gargoyle, refusing to lift my eyes to the lake. "No. I need you to keep me focused. Fluctuate your boost in me, on and off, but keep it strong in Marcus and Gus. Can you do that?"

He nodded.

"Will it keep you too distracted for the siren to control you?" I asked.

"I . . . I think so."

The volume of magic available to me dipped to my limited personal levels, reducing me to an average talent in earth, fire, and wood and leaving me even weaker with water and air. A breath later, Oliver's boost filled me, opening twice as much magic to me so I felt as strong as a full-spectrum elemental. Then it fell away. My stomach churned at the sickening flip-flop of magic, and I chanced a glance at the siren.

A ball of lightning bounced between her palms, arching gracefully through the air. Dry land wasn't going to keep us safe from her.

Standing on tiptoe to get close to Marcus's ear and hoping he could understand my words, I shouted, "Shouldn't we be running?"

"Stay calm," he barked. He fanned a complicated shield of water and earth element around our mismatched group.

"Did you think to find my daughter without protection, humans?" the siren demanded, the sibilant sound of the last word sharp and cutting.

Daughter? This kept getting better and better.

The mother eyed the shield, then shifted her attention to the men, altering her song. Whatever compulsion had tugged at me fell away, but Marcus and Gus didn't react either. Her daughter gestured to Marcus, then to her ears, and I didn't need to be close enough to hear the conversation to know she'd just told her mom about my quartz distortion cups.

The mother shrieked, the shrill cry stabbing through my eardrums. I pressed my palms to my ears, expecting to feel blood trickling from my ear canals. As one, the cerberi rolled their heads back and howled at the sky.

Marcus grabbed my elbow, his lips mouthing words I couldn't hear. Eyes widening with growing horror, I stared at his chest. Quartz shards glistened against the fabric of his shirt. The crystals over his ears had been shattered.

The siren had destroyed our only defense.

I stepped back, out of Marcus's hold, and his expression shuttered when he saw my fear. This time, I had no trouble reading his lips.

"Run."

The siren's song died, arresting me in place. The cerberi panted loud enough to drown out the splash of the sirens' lashing tails, but the rest of us held our breath, bodies tense. Oliver steadied his enhancement within me, filling me with power, but my body still reeled, this time with the knowledge that Marcus was right: I couldn't magic our way to safety this time. Fleeing was my only option, and even then it'd be all but impossible. If she could pull me and a gargoyle under her spell, the large siren definitely had the skill to manipulate Marcus and Gus at the same time—not that she needed to bother with them. She appeared to have plenty of power in her own right.

The mother looked down at the small siren. "Are you hurt?"

The daughter shook her head.

"Which one attacked you?"

"She did." She jabbed a finger at me. "And her gargoyle."

I fought against the urge to cower behind the cerberi.

"The female?" The mother swung toward me, lake water churning around her waist. I kept a close eye on her gills, prepared to sprint for the forest if she so much as fluttered out a note. "Explain yourself, human."

I swallowed to work moisture into my mouth, thoughts scrambling for a way to reason with the powerful siren. "I was protecting my men."

"They are not hers. They came willingly," the young siren said, her chin lifting defiantly.

"They came *willingly*?" her mother echoed in a chilling tone. "You sang them here?" Electricity danced through her wet hair and lit her face with its harsh blue light. If I were her daughter, I would have backed up.

"I wanted to see if I could." The smaller siren dropped her eyes.

"I did not raise a heathen, and you're no tadpole," the mother thundered. Electric sparks rained from the mother's hair into the water, and her daughter flinched as if pinched. "Humans are fragile, and only the weak play with them."

The mother lifted her gaze to mine, addressing me as if I stood alone on the beach.

"Human woman, I apologize for my daughter's rash actions and for any harm she inflicted on your men. You have my word it will *never* happen again."

"Ah . . ." I said, not sure if I'd heard her right. Did this mean we weren't going to die?

The siren dismissed me with a nod, a milky-white film covering her eyes in a quick blink. Wrapping an arm around her daughter, she propelled her away from the shore, but her voice carried back to us.

"Your rebellious behavior has gone too far this time. No. Don't talk. I don't want to hear your excuses. If you're going to act like a tadpole, I'm going to treat you like one . . ." Still lecturing, she dragged her daughter under the water's surface. Their long tails slithered through the air; then the sirens disappeared.

No one moved as we watched the ripples fade, but my relief was so profound I might have temporarily floated.

"Did we just get rescued by the siren's *mother*?" Gus asked, spitting to the side. At the sound of his voice, the cerberi relaxed, dropping their heads to sniff the beach.

"We got rescued by Mika," Marcus said, turning to me. He tugged the remaining bloody shards from his ears without so much as a flinch. "If you hadn't saved us from the first siren, we wouldn't have been alive when the mom came along. These crystal earpieces were ingenious."

"Thanks. I wouldn't have thought of them without Oliver."

The gargoyle preened, especially when Marcus heaped on praise at his quick handling of the cerberi. Gus, busy checking over the three-headed hounds, muttered to himself about needing to retrain the cerberi to respond to signals only he knew.

"I can't believe how easily the siren lured me in. Once I heard her song, I had to find her." Marcus brushed dirt from my cheek with a gentle touch, then pulled me into his arms. "Are you hurt?"

I shook my head. A few bruises and scrapes weren't worth mentioning.

"I could have killed you with those fireballs."

"It wasn't you."

I used a featherlight brush of earth to collect the shattered quartz from his clothes, then dusted pulverized quartz glitter from his ears, careful to avoid his wounds. "I'm sorry about cutting you," I said.

"Remember, I'm a tough FPD guy. I've hurt myself worse shaving. Of course, I'm beginning to think the FPD doesn't have anything on gargoyle guardians. You've taken on Reaper's Ridge, and now you faced off against a siren."

"Mika is an extraordinary guardian," Oliver said, grinning with pride.

"Mmm, you're definitely one of a kind, Mika." Marcus tightened his embrace, dipping his knees in a silent invitation for me to wrap my arms around his neck.

I happily obliged, savoring both the thrill of his body pressed against mine and my restored sense of safety in his arms. Brushing my fingers through the short hair at the nape of his neck, I smiled to see his pupils dilate. Then he leaned down the last few inches, and my eyelids drifted shut in anticipation of a kiss.

"I haven't forgotten what you said," Marcus breathed against my lips.

"Hmm?" I tried pulling him the last half inch to me, but it was like attempting to move a mountain.

"That you love me."

My eyes popped open in shock. "Um . . . I—"

"You also said that I love you. That was a bit presumptuous, don't you think?"

"Hey! I was defending you—" I saw the mirth crinkling the corners of Marcus's eyes at the same time that I realized the absurdity of my argument. I changed tactics, teasing back. "After all I've done for you, you *should* love me."

"Who says I don't?"

My heart somersaulted in my chest, stealing my breath. I searched Marcus's serious lapis lazuli eyes, the teasing of a moment ago absent.

Gus harrumphed and spat. "You two are making me sick. Just kiss already."

Marcus quirked an eyebrow at my poleaxed expression; then, grinning, he brushed his lips across mine.

A zing of pleasure jolted through my body, snapping me back into action. I tugged Marcus closer, kissing him soundly, and not even Gus's curses when he spied the broken carriage could ruin the perfection of the moment.

I'd just realized I was in love.

ABOUT THE AUTHOR

REBECCA CHASTAIN is a feminist, animal advocate, and nature devotee. She believes empathy is a hero's trait and love is a motive, an inside job, and a transformative energy that shapes each person's world. She is the *USA Today* bestselling author of the Gargoyle Guardian Chronicles series, the Terra Haven Chronicles series that begins with DEADLINES & DRYADS, and the Madison Fox urban fantasy series.

If given the opportunity, Rebecca will befriend your cat.

Visit RebeccaChastain.com
for free stories, bonus materials, updates, and so much more!

FROM *USA TODAY*
BESTSELLING AUTHOR

REBECCA CHASTAIN

Madison's new job would be perfect,
if not for all the creatures trying to
eat her soul...

A FISTFUL OF EVIL
A FISTFUL OF FIRE
A FISTFUL OF FROST

PRAISE FOR THE MADISON FOX NOVELS

RebeccaChastain.com

www.ingramcontent.com/pod-product-compliance
Lightning Source LLC
Chambersburg PA
CBHW030645120726
47905CB00001B/59